QTP

DOMINANT CORD TRIO

BOOKS 1-3

SADIE HALLER

QTP

~ Books by Sadie Haller ~
Dominant Cord
One Gold Heart
One Gold Knot
One Gold Triquetra

Tainted Pearl
Tainted Pearl
Tainted Shadow

Frisky Beavers
Prime Minister
Dr. Bad Boy
Full Mountie
Mr. Hat Trick (coming 2017)

ONE GOLD HEART

ABOUT THE BOOK

Mac Wallis agrees to join the wind quintet, Dominant Cord, for the Christmas concert season as a favour to an old friend. It's her first step towards recovery after a vicious attack more than a decade before. However, sparks fly when Dominant Cord's unofficial leader, flutist, Finn Taylor takes issue with Mac's reliance on medication in order to perform.

Mac can't understand why the jerk who so completely humiliated her at their first rehearsal keeps showing up in her late-night fantasies as the Dom of her dreams. It's not even like he's the good kind of bad boy.

After his marriage ended in disaster, Finn tries to steer clear of damaged women, but as a Dom, he feels compelled put aside his own hang-up to help Mac reclaim her independence and her former life.

For my amazing Grandma.
I miss you every day, but especially at Christmas.

ONE

MAC CHECKED the caller ID and grinned as she answered, "Hi, Sully."

"I need a huge favour."

"I'm quite certain it's customary to at least say hello, maybe even engage in a little small talk before making requests," Mac scolded.

"Look Mac, I'm desperate and I don't have time to suck up. I was stupid and went on a date yesterday to the outdoor skating rink, and—"

Mac interrupted. "But you can't skate."

"Yeah, back to the 'I was stupid' part. Anyway, I broke two ribs when I crashed into the side railing and I'm out of commission for the next six weeks."

"I'd have more sympathy if you'd stop thinking with your dick, you know."

"I don't need sympathy, just a favour. Dominant

Cord has gigs booked for most of December, starting Friday, and I need you to sub for me."

Mac cringed. "Tell me you don't mean Friday, as in day after tomorrow Friday."

"Yes, that's exactly the Friday I mean."

"Bugger. You, of all people, know I hate performing. There must be someone else you can call on."

"'Fraid not. Everybody's booked solid. C'mon Mac, you know I wouldn't ask this of you if I had any other option."

"You are such a weasel."

"I knew I could count on you."

Mac was suspicious. "Hang on, what are we playing?"

"Bach's Christmas Oratorio," Sully mumbled.

"For that, you miserable lump of knob cheese you are paying for the beta-blockers and you owe me a favour to be named later."

"Done."

"Shit, that was too easy. I have a couple of errands to run this morning. I'll swing by to pick up the music and get the details from you on my way home."

"Fabulous. I'll see you soon."

"Yeah, just feckin' fabulous," Mac muttered as she hung up the phone.

Mac rang the bell, nervously clenching her fists as

she waited. Minutes later, she took another anxious look at her watch and rechecked the house number against the address Sully had given her. Yup, apparently, this was the place. She rang the bell again and waited. Irritated and out of patience, she decided to make one last effort before giving up. As she prepared to knock, the door was replaced by a broad chest and impressive biceps accentuated by a muscle-hugging, black t-shirt. She stomped on her lust. She was here to work, and didn't need to complicate her life any further.

"What?"

Mac took an involuntary step back and looked way up. She briefly regarded his handsome face, but his Guiness-brown eyes had her wet and tingly before she could regain her composure. She extended her hand and said, "Um, hi. I'm Mac Wallis, Sully's sub."

The man gave her the once over and blew out an exasperated breath. "You've got the date wrong, pet. The play party isn't until Sunday night."

His deep voice resonated within Mac's chest, sending another trickle of moisture into her panties. "Sunday? Sully told me we were scheduled to play on Friday night."

"I don't think so, pet. We're otherwise engaged on Friday. Where is Sully, anyway? He should have been here ten minutes ago."

"He's at home, where else would he be?"

"Here. He is supposed to be here for a rehearsal, dammit"

Realisation dawned and Mac held up her index finger. "Hang on a mo." She suspected this man wasn't often interrupted by a finger waving woman, and his surprised look amused her. She reached into her bag, pulled out her phone, and punched in Sully's number.

She didn't wait for his greeting before laying into him. "That favour to be named later just doubled, pal. I'm standing in front of a very grumpy man who wants to know why you're not here and I am. I'll be generous and assume you are loopy on pain meds and forgot. I'm going to give the phone to Mr. Peevy-pants, and you will rectify the situation immediately."

Mac handed the phone over and stomped off the porch, needing the space to cool off. She was already so stressed about having to play for strangers on crappy reeds, she didn't need to colour it with anger and arousal. Bugger that feckin' weasel, Sully, anyway. She kept her back to the house as she inhaled deeply through her nose, letting each breath trickle from her mouth.

She was almost calm when Mr. Sexy-voice invaded her happy place. "Mac, he wants a quick word."

She turned slowly and took one more deep breath before heading back up the stairs to reclaim her phone. "This had better be fixed, because if there is even the slightest problem, I'm done. Are we clear?"

"I am SO sorry, Mac. Really, I meant to call and—"

"I don't want excuses, Sully. Just tell me it's sorted."

"It's sorted."

Mac disconnected, and returned the phone to her bag.

"That was rude. You didn't even say goodbye."

Mac's eyes flashed as she wagged her finger again. "Stop right there. I am doing him a huge favour. Far bigger than I think you could ever understand. His fuck-up increased the value of that favour and we've been friends long enough that we don't always have to observe telephone etiquette. I am here as Sully's substitute because he is unable to play. Can I assume we are both on the same page, now? "

"Yes, we're on the same page, and if it makes you feel any better, I did give him shit for not giving me a heads-up. I'm sorry for the misunderstanding. Perhaps we can start again?"

Mac nodded and extended her hand. "Hi, I'm Mac Wallis, and I'm here to substitute for Sully while he is incapacitated."

The man took it and said, "Nice to meet you Mac. I'm Finn Taylor, and I play flute. I appreciate you agreeing to step in for Sully and help us out. Come on inside and meet the rest of the group."

Mac followed Finn into the house. She removed her shoes and set her bags on the floor before shrugging out of her coat. Finn took it from her as she slid her arms free, and hung it on the coat tree in the corner.

"The music room is at the back of the house. We'll swing through the kitchen and get you some water on the way."

"Thanks."

"So, where and when did you and Sully meet?"

Mac had to cut him off right there. Her attraction to Finn was already problematic, fostering any kind of personal connection would be a disaster. "Look, Finn, I'm here to do a job, nothing more."

Finn grabbed a glass from the cupboard and set it on the counter before fetching the jug of filtered water from the fridge. "Okay, no personal stuff. How about professional? I trust Sully to send us someone capable, but what are your credentials?" He asked, as he filled her glass.

"I got my Bachelor of Music in performance from McGill," Mac stated in a tone that declared the subject closed.

Apparently, Finn had other ideas. "And...?"

"And, that's it."

"That takes care of educational, what about professional?"

"I don't play professionally. I hate performing. Like I said, this is a huge favour for Sully."

Finn returned the jug to the fridge and paused a moment before turning to face her. "What on earth was Sully thinking? How are you going to manage our concert schedule if you hate performing?"

Mac lifted her chin and looked him dead in the

eye. "Sully was thinking he was down to his very last, desperate hope. And I will manage with the help of beta-blockers."

"Sweet, sweaty Jesus, what a cluster-fuck," Finn muttered as he stalked to the music room.

"Brace yourselves," Finn shouted just before he and Mac entered. "Sully's gone and busted a couple of ribs, his replacement doesn't play professionally, and the icing on the cake? She requires drugs to perform."

He took a brief look at the trio of shocked faces before he continued. "This is Mac Wallis." He shifted his attention back to Mac, mildly curious at her wary, sideways glance at the piano. He pointed to an empty chair. "You can sit there." He introduced the rest of the quintet, pointing to each in turn. "That's Jack Riley on bassoon, Wilson Kennedy on clarinet, and Griff Edwards on horn." Not giving anyone an opportunity to do more than nod in greeting, Finn carried on. "Now let's get started. We're already running late. Mac, how long until your reeds will be ready to play?"

Mac settled into her chair. She immediately opened her instrument case and tucked the top-joint of her oboe into her armpit while she continued with her preparations. "I soaked them before I left, so they should be good to go as soon as I have my top-joint warmed up. Give me two or three minutes to get myself organised?"

"Like I have a fucking choice."

Mac stopped what she was doing and glared at Finn, her eyes bright with hurt and indignation. Then she unloaded. "Look, I've had just about enough of the snide, snarky bullshit. You don't want me here. I get it. I don't want me here either, but the way I see it, you've got three options. You find someone else to replace Sully, you cancel all your gigs until he's better, or you deal with me. I'll give you until the end of this rehearsal to make your decision, but I will not put up with any more of your unprofessional behaviour. Just because I don't sing for my supper, don't get the idea that you can treat me with any less respect than you would Sully."

Ignoring the audience, Finn replied, "Fair point. Are you just about ready to start?"

"Absofeckinglutely."

"Okay, let's do a full run-through without stopping, then we'll see what we have to work with."

Finn kept an eye on Mac throughout the rehearsal, ready to cue her the moment she got lost. To his relief, the opportunity never came. She played perfectly. Instruments were laid to rest with the death of the final note, and applause quickly replaced the stunned silence.

Jack gave Mac a quick wink. "Well, Finn, I know which option I'm voting for."

Finn was surprised by the unfamiliar feeling of jealousy. Where had that come from?

Wilson piped up. "Well done, Mac. I have to know, was that straight sight reading, or have you played this before?"

"I played it years ago at university, but not since. I had hoped to have time to go over it before coming to rehearsal, but with a concert on Friday, making reeds was my priority."

Finn finally found his voice. "You played it well here in rehearsal conditions, but I'm concerned about how you'll do in performance, especially when you're drugged up."

"Knock it off, Finn," Griff snapped. "If Sully trusts Mac and her abilities enough to send her to us as his replacement, I think we need to accept she'll be fine."

"I'm just uncomfortable about people relying on performance enhancing drugs."

"I guess Viagra's not an option for you then," Mac snapped.

The others sniggered as Finn's eyes flashed, but Mac didn't back down. "This may have been just a rehearsal for you, but for me, it was worse than a performance. In a performance, I'm playing for strangers who are there to enjoy the music. Here, I was playing for strangers who were looking to pick apart every little thing. Now, I'm tired, grumpy, and ready to go home. So, what's your decision, Finn?"

"I still don't like that you use drugs, but we have no choice. You're in."

"You make it sound like I'm a crack-head. If you can come up with a drug-free way for me to cope with my performance anxiety, I'm all ears. Not that it's any of your business, Mr. Just-Say-No, but the beta-blockers were the absolute last resort for me. Without them, I wouldn't have graduated from university. Now, if we're done here, I'm going home."

"Yeah, we're done. Same time tomorrow night. I'll need your contact information. Phone numbers and email, please. Here's mine." Finn handed over a business card.

Mac grabbed her wallet from her purse and slipped his card into one of the compartments, before pulling out one of her own. "Here." She slapped the card down on the seat next to her and proceeded to stow her gear.

As they packed up, the rest of the quintet watched the sparks fly between Finn and Mac. They said their farewells, and Finn didn't miss the look of panic in Mac's eyes as the others left en-mass.

He crouched next to her, bothered by her obvious distress. "I'm sorry, I'm not making a very good impression. I'm angry at the situation, and I've been taking it out on you. I'm not usually this much of an asshole. You were great tonight, and I look forward to playing with you." He left out the part about his wish for an alternative because her need for medication completely freaked him out.

"You're forgiven. I'm sorry too. It's not like I've been all sweetness and light. And before you blame it on the beta-blockers, I've been every shade of pissed off since I got that call from Sully this morning. The beta-blockers didn't make their appearance until just before I headed over here. Now, I really do need to get going."

Finn stood to give her space while he watched her gather her belongings and scurry out the door. Sully would be getting a call as soon as she was gone. Fucker.

"WHAT THE FUCK, MAN," Finn bellowed, "You sent us a drug addicted amateur."

"Bullshit. I sent you one of the best oboists I know. The only reason she's not on my sub-list, let alone at the top of it, is her crippling performance anxiety. Trust me, if I'd had any other options, I wouldn't have done this to her."

"Seriously? Done this to her? What about what you've done to us? We're going to crash and burn out there."

"You can't tell me that she wasn't perfection itself, so what's really got your boxers in a braid?"

"I admit it, she played beautifully. Pitch perfect, and not a note out of place. But she needs drugs to play. I can't deal with that."

"No, she doesn't need drugs to play. She needs prescription medication to perform. She was fine when we first started university, but as the music became more difficult, and the performance requirements more demanding, she developed anxiety so unmanageable, we couldn't get her on stage. She could get to the wings, but then she'd just sink to the floor and shake. She hates performing because she hates taking beta-blockers. I doubt you're going to believe me, but I'll say it anyway, Mac does not require medication for anxiety outside of performance situations. So, do me a favour, try to put aside your own issues, and accept that she's willing to put aside hers to help us out. Oh, and for the record, the only way she's going to make you crash and burn, is if she changes her mind about playing. It seems to me, you are the only one who is likely to make that happen."

"Way to make me feel like even more of an asshole."

"Oh shit, what did you do?"

"I was angry. I'm still angry, but I was angry and I took it out on her."

"Way to go, Finn."

"Well, a heads up before she showed at my door declaring herself as your submissive might have been helpful."

"Back up. What do you mean, declaring herself as my submissive?"

"I opened the door, and she said, 'I'm Mac, I'm Sully's sub.' Fuck, man, I thought she was yet another in your impressive collection of ditzy subs and she'd got the day of the play party wrong."

"Ow, ow, fucking ow. Fuck, don't make me laugh, please don't tell me any more. At least not until I am under the full effects of really good pain meds. Seriously, you thought I would have a sub of mine show up to a play party alone?"

"It didn't seem like you, but with such a restricted guest-list, I wasn't sure.

"Now you can be sure. There is no way I would let a sub show up anywhere to play without me."

"A little late, but good to know. I guess I really have some sucking up to do."

"Yup. And because I like you, I'm going to give you some helpful tips."

MAC CALLED SULLY AS SOON as she got home. "I'm so feckin' mad at you, I could break every single reed you have and leave you with nothing but commercial student reeds to perform on."

"I'm sorry, Mac. I fucked up. I get it. Now stop busting my balls and tell me how it went."

"Great. Between your buddy mistaking me for one of your bondage-bunnies and accusing me of being a drug addict, my evening was complete."

"Okay, you've made your point, things aren't

exactly smooth between you and Finn, but personal friction aside, how did rehearsal go?"

"It went fine. Fortunately, they're doing something I've played before, even if it was forever ago. Thank fuck I didn't have to sight-read."

"I knew it'd work out. There's another rehearsal tomorrow night, right?"

"Yeah. I'm struggling on whether to take blockers this time. Tonight was a no-brainer, but I hate taking them unless I absolutely have to."

"Why don't you hold off, but have them with you so you can take one if you find you need it. Maybe just knowing they're there will be enough for you to manage without."

"Yeah, I guess I could do that, but if I do end up needing them, I don't want to waste everyone else's time while I wait for them to take effect."

"I wouldn't worry. They are concert-ready, and they'll be happy enough with a little extra gossip time while your meds kick in. Are you okay, now?"

"Yeah, I'm calmer, and a little less angry with you, but that doesn't let you off the hook. You are into me for two, count 'em, two favours to be named later."

"Yeah, yeah, I know, and I'm sure you'll take every opportunity to remind me."

"Of course I will. Right, I'm going to bed now. I'm wiped. Good night. I hope your ribs start to feel better really soon."

"Thanks. G'night, Mac."

MAC STARED into the dark as she stroked her cat, Gounod. He was settled in his usual spot, full length between her legs with his head and front paw resting on her upper thigh. She'd tried every technique for falling asleep she could think of, but her mind would not shut off. She kept thinking back to Finn, and wondered how she could possibly be attracted to such an asshole?

It's not like he comes across as the sexy bad-boy type, either. He may believe otherwise, but he's just an asshole, plain and simple. He accused her of being a drug addict and treated her like she was some skid-row junkie. That alone should have killed all feeling in her girly-bits. Nothing turned her off faster than humiliation, but damn, if this guy didn't seem to work some kind of hoo-hoo voodoo.

And with that thought, her pussy was swollen and needy, and she wasted no time giving in to its demand. Gounod growled his outrage as she shifted him out of her way. Mac rolled her eyes and laughed. "Suck it up you big baby, you can come back later when I'm done taking care of the other pussy in my life." She reached into the drawer of her bedside table for her Rabbit. She slid it into her eager cunt and flipped the switch to nirvana. Three orgasms later, she drifted into a fitful sleep.

FINN STOOD in the shower and let the spray envelop him like a warm blanket as he thought back through his evening. Damn she was cute. Even standing at full height, her mop of dark, curly hair would barely skim the bottom of his chin. He first noticed her soulful eyes, but it was that sassy mouth of hers that was going to get him into trouble.

The little head sure didn't care if she was a druggie. From the moment he'd opened the door, his cock was fully present and accounted for. Thank fuck he'd gone for the tighty-whities and loose fitting trousers. The last thing he needed was the rest of the guys riding him over a tent-pole in his pants.

Finn fisted his erection and stroked it from root to tip as he imagined Mac's luscious pink lips wrapped around him. Taking him deep, swallowing him whole. His breathing increased, his heart pounded. After sporting an erection for hours, the image of Mac on her knees and his cock down her throat had him exploding with a speed he hadn't experienced since he'd watched his first porn film as a teenager.

Once he'd finally made it to bed, Finn carefully considered each of Sully's suggestions for fixing things with Mac.

TWO

Mac checked the caller ID and groaned before answering. "Hello?"

"Mac, hi, it's Finn."

Mac tried to keep the wariness from her voice as she responded. "Yes?"

"I was wondering if you could come over a little early tonight?"

"Why?"

"You said if I had any ideas on how to keep you from needing beta-blockers, you were all ears."

"I am all ears, and you have one of them right now, so, how about you tell me what you have in mind."

"I'd rather talk in person. You'll be coming over anyway, so, unless you have other plans you can't reschedule, what can it hurt? I was thinking you could join me for dinner. It would be refreshing to cook for more than just myself."

Mac didn't bother to hide her irritation. "Look Finn, you don't approve of me, and I don't like you. I'm doing a favour for a friend, and that's as far as it goes. I appreciate that you've been giving thought to an alternative way to deal with my performance anxiety, but as far as I know, I've tried it all, and the reality is, I don't trust you. You have a hang-up. That's not my problem."

"Mac, I'm sorry I've given you reason not to trust that I'm working in your best interests, but maybe you could try trusting that I'm working in mine, and my hang-up could provide you with an alternative to medication."

"No. I'll be there and ready to play by seven. That is the extent of my obligation to Sully, and by extension, to you. I have a busy day ahead, so if there is nothing else?"

"No, I don't think so."

"Fine, then I'll see you this evening, goodbye"

"Bye."

<hr>

Mac opened the text without checking who sent it.

'Open your front door.'

A quick look at her inbox confirmed it was from Sully. What was he up to? She opened the door to a small basket of goodies from her favourite chocolate shop and smiled. She picked up the basket and brought it inside, feeling no urgency to read the card. Experience told her Sully was sorry, and chocolate consumption always took priority.

She ripped the cellophane from the basket and sorted the chocolates in order of preference. As usual, she started with her least favourites, and finished with the ones she liked best. She popped the first chocolate into her mouth before grabbing the envelope and removing the card it contained. As she read, the confection turned to mud in her mouth and she promptly spit it into the discarded wrapping. She grabbed her phone and punched in Sully's number.

"You rat-bastard. You feckin', sneaky, wasted sper—"

"Hold on, Mac. Just hear me out, okay? Please?" Sully took advantage of the brief silence and continued. "Finn fucked up. He knows he fucked up, and he's just looking for a chance to make it as right as possible. I feel partially responsible for this mess, so I need to do what I can to help fix it."

"Deceiving me is not how you fix things, Sully. You sent that text. You deliberately led me to believe those chocolates were from you. How am I supposed to trust you when you'd do something like this?"

"Yeah, I sent the text to ensure you would open the door. I should have known you would assume the package was from me, but I didn't deliberately mislead you. I'm sorry, sweetie. I hate the effect my lack of caution is having on you. Who'd have thought an afternoon skating date would have such crazy consequences."

"Fucker."

"Here's the thing, I think both you and Finn overreacted, and we need to get some kind of truce in place before tonight's rehearsal. I know you turned down supper at Finn's, but how about I order in and you two meet here, in somewhat neutral territory?"

"You'll be there, too?"

"Of course."

Mac considered everything Sully'd said, and after being friends for so many years, she knew he would never do anything deliberately to jeopardise their relationship. Besides, with the demanding concert schedule ahead of her, the last thing she needed was tension between herself and a fellow musician. "Fine." Mac huffed. "I'll be there at five and there had better be Indian."

"Great. I'll give Finn a call and I'll see you at five."

Mac stabbed the end button and threw her phone on the sofa as she thought about what to do with the chocolates. The peevish part of her wanted to package them back up and return them to Finn, but the rest of her wanted to cue up a DVD and gorge herself on them while she worked on reeds. With a concert the following night, it would be a struggle to have performance-worthy reeds ready in time. Her love of chocolate won out, and she settled in for a reed-making marathon with her buddies, chocolate, and The Doctor.

It was Finn who opened the door when Mac arrived at Sully's house. "Oh, hi. Um, thanks for the chocolates, I enjoyed them." Mac stepped inside, kicked off her shoes and hung her coat on a hook behind the door. "They're my favourites, but you already knew that."

"Hi, yourself, and you're welcome." There was a twinkle in Finn's eyes as he asked, "Did you enjoy them all?"

"Of course I did. I have virtually no self-control when it comes to good chocolate. No, to be perfectly honest, I have absolutely no self-control when it comes to chocolate of any kind."

"Tell me that's not all you ate today."

"Do you really want me to tell you that, or do you want me to tell you the truth."

Finn flipped his gaze skyward and shook his head in disbelief. "Well, at least you'll be having a somewhat healthy supper before rehearsal. It arrived just a few minutes ago. How about you join Sully in the dining room and I'll bring the food through?"

"Okay, but I don't mind giving you a hand."

"No, no, you go ahead and get yourself settled at the table, I'll be in with the food in no time."

Mac stepped into the dining room and greeted her friend. "Hey, how are you feeling?"

"Well, I've certainly been better. How about you?"

She leaned down and laid a gentle kiss on the top of Sully's head before settling herself in the chair to his right. "I've been better too, but at least all my ribs are intact."

"Well, that's something, isn't it?"

"Here we go." Finn set two dishes on the table. "Start serving yourselves and I'll be back with the rest."

Mac picked up Sully's plate and started loading it. Noting his raised eyebrows, she admonished, "Don't you get any funny ideas, bucko. You know I'll never sub to you."

"Yeah, but you'll sub for me." Sully shot her that lop-sided grin that other subs found irresistible.

"Shut up, Sully. I have no idea why you keep trying with the grin. After more than a decade, you should acknowledge I'm immune, and give up."

"True, but the optimist in me says that as long as we're both breathing, there's a chance."

Finn placed the last of the food on the table and sat in the seat to Sully's left before dishing up his own meal.

"I wouldn't call that optimism, Sully," Mac retorted, "I would call it not knowing when to quit."

"Cheeky wench. You'd miss it if I didn't shoot you the Sully grin every once in a while."

Mac's voice oozed sarcasm as she raised an eyebrow. "Okay, I admit it, my life would be devoid of meaning if I were to never again be the recipient of your knicker-dropping grin." She turned to Finn and asked, "Can you please pass the Naan?"

THREE

Mac enjoyed the good-natured banter she shared with Sully while they ate, but once supper was done, Sully's voice turned serious.

"All right you two. It's time to work out the issues and figure a way for you to get along. We all know my part in this mess, and the toll it's taken. The way I see it we only have one issue to address. Mac needing medication to control performance anxiety, and Finn's fanatical repugnance to any kind of drug dependency."

"Hold on, Sully, I believe there are situations where medication is appropriate," Finn objected.

Mac's voice dripped with disdain. "Oh, you mean like when a guy wants to fuck, and can't get it up?"

"Mac, that's enough," Sully snapped. "Both of you, not one more word before I'm done."

With nods from both Finn and Mac, Sully continued, "Considering the situation, I am not going to maintain any confidences for either of you if I think they will help us come to an understanding. Agreed?" Sully looked at Mac and waited for her nod before turning to Finn for his.

"Mac, Finn's wife died from a heroin overdose. She suffered from panic attacks. Her doctor prescribed medication, but it wasn't long before she started self-medicating and heroin became her drug of choice."

Finn nodded at Sully and took over. "She was looking to numb out. The medication she was prescribed didn't do it for her, so she sought out drugs that would. By the time I'd clued in, she'd already worked her way up to heroin. I was so caught up in my career, I didn't notice things were so bad until it was too late. I thought I had convinced her to go to rehab, but before I could make arrangements, she'd overdosed. She was in her car when they found her body."

"Holy shit. That's awful." Mac met Finn's gaze with tears in her eyes. "I'm so sorry."

Knowing what Sully was about to reveal about herself, Mac gave him a quick glance and said, "I've got this." She turned back to Finn and, after a big shaky breath, she began.

"I didn't always suffer from performance anxiety. Well, I was always a little nervous before playing, but it was the kind of nervous that I think helped me give a little something extra that wasn't there at rehearsal."

Sully stroked Mac's forearm and encouraged her to continue. "Deep breath, sweetie. You're doing fine.

Better it comes from you. The more you talk about it, the smaller it gets. I promise."

She didn't want to do this. Saying it out loud would bring it back and make it real. She much preferred to keep it safely in her back pocket where she could sit on it and squish it into something tiny and inconsequential.

Mac sucked in another big breath and let it trickle through her clenched teeth. "I had just finished my final recital and my first gruelling year of university was over. I was in a practice room putting my gear away...I didn't hear the door open, I was so far in my head. After a performance, it takes hours before I mellow out. Anyway, I had just finished zipping up my case, when I was grabbed by the hair and my face was slammed into the wall. The next thing I knew, my mouth was taped shut, and I was strapped naked to the piano bench and being told with each agonising thrust that I had no business playing a flawless recital. That it should have been his. The next thing I remember was freaking out in the ambulance. I'll let Sully tell the rest. I only know his version, anyway."

Sully continued to stroke Mac's arm. "Understanding Mac's need to decompress after a concert, I didn't go with her to pack up, but I was so pumped by her fabulous performance, I got impatient and went to look for her."

Mac listened to Sully recount the part she was missing. She both loved and hated that she couldn't remember. She loved not having more horrible memories to live with, but hated having even the smallest part of her mind stolen by the actions of another.

"I knew something was wrong when I saw the blind was down on the window of the practice room. Mac never, ever closed the blinds. I unlocked the door, and well, you know what I saw when I opened it.

"The guy was another oboist in our studio. Mac's perfect performance took him out of contention for a scholarship that provided the winner with a new instrument, tuition and living expenses for the remaining three years. Attacking Mac was how he managed his disappointment."

Mac stole a look at Finn to gauge his reaction. The tears in his eyes were her first indication that maybe he wasn't quite as big an asshole as she'd first thought.

"Anyway, I pulled him off and kneed him in the balls with everything I had and called 911. I freed Mac and covered her with her coat. She wouldn't let me hold her or comfort her. All I could do was watch her rock in the corner. Fucking broke my heart. Every time that fucker lifted his head, I gave him another shot to the nads until the cops arrived."

Finn's voice cracked with emotion. "Christ. Mac, I just don't have words. I'm sorry doesn't even come close."

Mac sat still and stared at her empty plate as she packed up her emotional baggage and jammed it back into her pocket. She was relieved when Sully changed the subject. It was nice that he knew her so well.

"Right, how about you make Mac a nice cup of tea. She likes it a bit on the strong side with a good amount of milk."

Finn rose from his seat and started gathering dishes. "Tea, I can do. How about you, Sully?"

"What I'd really like is a good stiff drink, but I'll settle for a Coke."

"Right then, I'll be back in a jiffy," Finn said.

"Mac, sweetie?"

Mac looked up at Sully. "Yeah?"

"Oh honey, I'm so sorry. That's the last thing in the world I wanted to do, but I knew in the end it would be the kindest. I'm sure you don't think so now..."

"No, it's fine, Sully. It was a long time ago, and I should be over it."

"Yes, it was a long time ago, but no, you'll never be over it, and nobody who loves you would ever expect you to be. All we want for you is to find a way to live, really live, in spite of it. In the meantime, you have to go out there and save my ass. I love you, Mac."

"I love you too, you wanker. Now did somebody mention tea?"

Finn put the kettle on and started loading the dishwasher. Sully's sanitised version had him believing she was medicating over a few butterflies in her belly, but this was a game changer. Rape was not the land mine he thought he'd be dodging. The longer he sat through the sordid tale, the more his stomach felt like returning his supper, along with everything else he'd consumed in the last week.

He sure had a lot of shitty behaviour to make up for. Luckily, he had Sully's handy dandy list of helpful tips and suggestions. That should provide a safe starting point.

He was staring out the window into the darkness when he heard dishes being set on the counter. He turned to see Mac, looking fairly well composed, considering. "Thanks. I was just about to come and get them, but got lost in the void."

"You're welcome. Can I help with anything?"

"No, I'm almost done." Finn gestured to the table. "Mac, can we sit and talk for a minute?"

"I suppose," she said, as she sat in the chair closest to her.

Finn took the chair across from her. "I know I've been an insufferable prick at best. I'm sorry. From Sully's explanation, I pegged you as the sort of person who'd turn to chemicals over a broken nail. That's the sort of person my wife was. If she couldn't get a manicure the moment the urge struck her, she popped a pill. If she couldn't find exactly the right colour shoes to match her new dress, she popped a pill."

Mac's mouth dropped open. "You're kidding, right?"

"I wish I were. You and I have good reasons for our issues. I think I get that you and my wife are nothing alike and I'm done using her behaviour to judge you. Whether you take meds or not is none of my business, and I'll consider the matter closed. How about you?"

Mac winked. "What matter?"

Finn smiled back at her. "I'll finish cleaning up here and I'll bring your tea in when I'm done. Can you grab a Coke for Sully? "

"Sure, no problem. Thanks for making tea. And thanks for not getting weird or treating me like a freak after hearing my tale of woe."

Having no idea how best to respond, he simply said, "You're welcome."

Finn watched Mac take a Coke from the fridge and leave to sit with Sully. He packed away the leftovers and finished dealing with the kitchen. By the time the kettle had boiled, he had the beginnings of an action plan. He prepared Mac's tea then grabbed himself a Coke from the fridge on his way to the dining room.

Finn placed the steaming mug in front of Mac. "Here you go. I hope it's how you like it. Sully, why don't we go sit in the living room where I'm sure you'd be more comfortable."

"Great idea. You guys go on in, it'll take me a minute to get mobile, and while I'm already up, I may as well hit the head. I'll try not to be long, but I'm not exactly a speed demon these days."

Mac and Finn waited until Sully got to his feet before grabbing their drinks and making their way to the living room. Finn invited Mac to sit on the sofa before settling himself on the floor next to her legs. At her confused look, he said, "Sully said you love a good foot rub, and given you won't be getting any from him for a while, and you're bailing us out of a jam, and I've been such an asshole, and feel free to stop me any time..."

Mac giggled, "No, no, you're doing fine, carry on."

"Imp." He shot her a cheeky grin. "Well?"

"While I love a good foot rub, my hands are in greater need. I haven't done this much reed work in such a short time since university."

"I can do hands." Finn shifted from the floor and sat next to Mac, careful to leave what he hoped was enough space for her to be comfortable.

Sully arrived and parked himself in the chair with the best view of the action.

Finn started with Mac's left hand, working deep into the muscle at the base of her thumb before moving outward and gently rubbing each finger from palm to tip.

By the time Finn had moved on to her right hand, Mac's eyes were closed and her head settled against the back of the sofa. Every so often, she gave a small moan, each sending another shot of blood to Finn's already over-inflated penis.

"Mac, I'd quit with the moaning if I were you. I think you're restricting Finn's blood flow to his brain," Sully teased.

She lifted a foot and wiggled her toes at Sully. "Careful, or I'll let him rub my feet just to spite you. Finn, please tell me you don't have a foot fetish too."

Finn laughed. "No, your feet only need be wary of Sully the foot fondler. I just like making a woman feel good, so I'm happy to rub whatever she wants me to."

Mac blushed and Finn took pity on her. "Five more minutes, and then we have to get going."

Mac glanced at her watch. "You may need to get going, but I don't need to leave for another twenty minutes."

"Leave when I do, and you can have another hand rub before the rest of the guys arrive."

"That's okay. I'm perfectly happy with the one I got."

Finn looked to Sully for support, but only got the universal code for quit while you are behind — an index finger slicing across his throat. He nodded and gave the back of Mac's hand a gentle pat. "Right then, I have to get moving. I will see you soon, and drive carefully."

Finn rose and gave Sully's shoulder a farewell squeeze and with a pointed look said, "I'll talk to you later."

"You bet."

Mac glowered at Sully

"Oh, don't look at me like that, Mac. He wasn't to know I'm the only man you'll be alone with. That is going to have to change, you know. There are men who are good, and kind, and trustworthy. Men who would treat you like you deserve to be treated. There are men out there who you can be alone with and be safe. Men you can even have sex with. Honey, it's time to push your boundaries, and I think Finn might be the guy to do it with."

"I want my quiet life back, Sully. It was quiet up until yesterday." Mac knew he was right, but that didn't change how she felt.

"Sometimes, we can't go back. Come on, Mac, you know he gets your motor going. I thought you were going to come right there in that chair just from that hand massage."

"I will concede that I may have felt a wee tingle in parts that have been tingle-less for a number of years."

"I knew it."

"Oh, don't go getting all smug on me. I have a perfectly good Rabbit to take care of that annoying little tingle."

"It'll do for now, sweetie."

"I've got to get moving too. What can I do for you before I go?"

"I think I'll be fine, kiddo. Once you're on your way, I'll just settle myself in bed with a nice pain pill, a can of Coke, and my remote control."

"Okay, if you're sure."

"I'm good. You don't want to be late."

"I won't be. You head off to bed. I'll just set some reeds to soak and lock up when I leave."

"Alright. G'night, sweetheart."

"G'night, Sully."

FINN FLOPPED into his favourite armchair as he held the phone to his ear. "Hi, it's about time you called."

"Sorry. Mac only just left. I know she was holding off until the last possible minute."

"And why is that exactly, Sully?" Finn asked.

"Yeah, I knew this is why you wanted me to call. I wish we'd got it all out of the way tonight, but you have to agree, she'd had more than enough, especially this close to a performance."

Finn thought back to the determined look on Mac's face when Sully was done telling the story, and realised she'd been at her limit. "Good grief, just get on with it before she gets here."

"She can't be alone with a man. I'm the only one she feels safe with."

"Well that explains the look in her eyes when the guys all left last night."

"We're going to have to work on it. I've let it go far too long. In the meantime, make sure she's never left alone, okay?"

"Got it. That fucker really did a number on her. Please tell me he got all that was coming to him."

Sully gave a heavy sigh. "He got fourteen years, but only has to serve just over nine. That means he gets out next year. It took almost two years from laying charges to sentencing. He was denied bail for all that time, and at sentencing, the judge refused to give him any credit for time served. Otherwise, he'd have been out already"

The ball of anger in Finn's stomach grew with each new detail about Mac's attack and its repercussions. "Not enough, but at least he got jail-time. I guess getting caught in the act would go a long way to a conviction."

"Yeah. You'd think the dumb fuck would have pleaded guilty, but he fought to the bitter end. I don't think that won him any points with the judge."

"Okay, so is there anything else I should know?"

"I think that's it, except maybe just let the beta-blocker issue go. At least until she's done subbing for me."

"I already did. Mac and I had that conversation in the kitchen when she brought in the dishes. I would like to find a way to help her so she doesn't need them to perform, but after tonight's horrifying revelations, I will hold off. Now about the play party on Sunday. I know you won't be playing, but do you think there's any chance you could get Mac to come?"

"I'll see what I can do. I've been known to play the guilt card on occasion. This might be an appropriate time."

"Didn't you use it to get her to play for you?"

"Nope. That was an act of love, pure and simple. The guilt card is only required if I ask something truly decadent of her."

"Gotta go, that's the door. I'll catch you later."

"G'night."

MAC STROKED Gounod on her lap as she waited for Sully to answer his phone.

"Hey, how did it go tonight, sweetie?"

"Really well. I didn't even need to take a beta blocker."

"That's awesome. I knew you'd be fine."

"I know that won't be the case tomorrow night, though."

"That's okay, do what you can. Finn gets it. He won't be on your case about it any more, but that doesn't mean he won't work at finding another way to deal."

"Yeah, I know. We talked about it earlier. It was hard to believe he was the same person I met last night.

He went from total asshole to sweet and thoughtful. It almost gave me whiplash."

"I told you he really wasn't an asshole. What happened with his wife warped his view of anxiety and medication."

"Yeah, I get it. At least we're able to have a functional working relationship."

"That's a start. So, Finn's got a play party coming up on Sunday. I won't be able to play, but I'm going to attend anyway. How about you join me."

Mac's answer was instant. "No."

"Aw, come on, Mac. It'll be fun. You don't have to play. Just keep me company."

"Fuck you, Sully. You aren't being fair. I know when you're inching towards a guilt trip. It's not going to work this time."

"It's not some random party, Mac. It's restricted to the quintet members and their subs. There's no pressure. It's just a social occasion where we get to let off steam. You aren't the only one who needs to decompress after performing. When we have a crazy concert schedule, like we do every December, Finn throws end of week play parties."

"No. I am not part of the quintet, and I am not anyone's sub."

"Right now you are part of the quintet, and while you may not belong to anyone, you are a sub."

"Fuck. Why are you pushing this? I agreed to perform a bunch of concerts in your place. That was all we'd agreed to. You never said anything about play parties, or any other social activities."

"True, I didn't include socialising in my request, but I'm asking now. I want to go to the party, and if I don't get to play, I'd like to have someone to keep me company."

Mac was torn. She'd spent years avoiding social situations. She felt safer and more in control that way, but sometimes she missed letting loose and having some fun with a group of people.

"I wouldn't be expected to play?"

"Not if you don't want to. You know the way it works. Nothing's changed. Safe, Sane, and Consensual. You know I'd cut off my lips and rip my own lungs out before I'd ever put you at risk."

"Yeah, but would you play a concert on a commercial reed?"

"In a heartbeat. So, will ya, will ya?"

Mac could feel herself being swayed. Sully had protected her for years. Her head knew he would never put her safety at risk, but that didn't stop her from being afraid.

"I don't know. It's been so long since I've been to any party, let alone a kinky one."

I know, sweetheart. Just give it a try. If it's too much for you, we'll leave. Who knows, you might just have a little fun for a change.

"I hate you, Sully. I really, really hate you."

"No you don't. You love me to pieces. You can pick me up at seven."

"Fine. G'night."

"Good night, sweetheart."

Miserable fucker. Yet another thing he'd talked her into. How much more upheaval would he wreak upon her before his ribs healed. Oh well, she'd had a pretty good rehearsal, and getting through without needing a blocker made it that much better. That hand rub sure helped mitigate the earlier unpleasantness of the evening, and now she and Finn were no longer at odds with each other, she hoped things would go smoothly until her obligation to Sully and his quintet was over.

FOUR

Mac was bombarded by the other members of the quintet the moment they left the stage.

"Great concert, Mac," Griff said, as he gave her a pat on the shoulder.

"Yeah, I thought I'd seen your A game, but, wow." Jack added.

"Thanks, guys. I think we all kicked-ass tonight and I'm glad I didn't let you down."

"You were completely fab. Wanna join us at the pub for a drink to wind down?" Wilson asked.

"I appreciate the offer, but I need to head home. I decompress better there."

"Okay, but we'll be at the Squeaky Wheel if you change your mind."

Mac donned her coat and grabbed her gear as she headed for her car. "Good night. I'll see you all tomorrow night."

The men waved to Mac as she left. Finn opened the door for her, watching until he she'd made it safely to her vehicle and was driving away. He appreciated that she checked the inside of her car carefully before opening the door and getting in. He would have preferred to walk her to her car, but based on what Sully'd told him, he figured she wouldn't be good with that, and he didn't want to put her on the spot by asking.

Baby steps. She rehearsed the night before without meds. That was huge to him. She'd agreed to come to the play party with Sully. That was huge in a whole other way. Well, off to the pub to drink with the boys. He'd have to give them some background on Mac so they could be aware of possible triggers. Why did he always have to fall for the damaged ones? At least with Mac, her anxiety was strictly limited to performance situations. As long as it stayed that way, he would deal.

MAC'S PHONE started ringing just as she settled into bed with a steaming cup of tea. She knew who it would be, even before looking at the caller ID.

"Hi, Sully."

"Hey gorgeous, great gig tonight. I don't think I've ever heard you sound better."

"You were there?"

"Of course I was there. Your first performance in

years? I'd have to be crossing the threshold of death's door to miss that."

"Thanks for being there. You should have told me you were coming."

"Nope, you had enough on your mind. I didn't want to risk being any kind of distraction for you. Anyway, I know you have a post-performance ritual, so I will let you get back to it. I just wanted to let you know how awesome you were and how proud of you I am."

"Thanks. Sometimes, I think you know me way too well, but I'm really glad you do."

"Goodnight, sweetheart."

"Goodnight."

Mac sipped her tea as she considered her best friend. He would make someone very lucky one day. Too bad he didn't have a nice, regular woman to be taking care of him while he's out of commission. On second thought, it's probably just as well. His rampant libido and non-existent self control would likely hold back his recovery. Hell, that's what got his ribs broken in the first place. At least he wouldn't get a chance to over-do it at the play party. That was probably the only good thing she could come up with about letting Sully talk her into going.

Bugger. It had been so long since she'd been around any of that kind of activity in real life. She had been just getting involved when her world imploded. While her interest remained, she limited her indulgence to online lurking. She and Sully talked about it, but mostly in the context of his exploits.

While she often masturbated to Sully's anecdotes, it was only the sub's experience that turned her on. Because theirs was a sibling-like relationship, she consciously replaced Sully with the Dom of her dreams. Somehow over the last few days, the Dom of her dreams had morphed into Finn.

Finn. How on earth was she going to handle watching him play with someone else? True, the only playing she'd done in years happened in her head, and the prospect of a physical experience was too terrifying to contemplate. Of course, she didn't have to watch Finn. The rest of the quintet would be there. She could watch them. Besides, she was only going to keep Sully from feeling like a wallflower. Maybe just being there, watching the action live, would help her shift from fantasy-land to reality.

FIVE

Mac fidgeted as she and Sully waited at Finn's front door. "It'll be fine. I'll be there the whole time, but if I do have to leave you for any reason, you know, like taking a piss, I'll make sure you are safe and not left alone. Trust me."

"I do trust you. You know I do. That doesn't make this any less scary, though."

"It's okay to be scared as long as it doesn't hold you back. You've been letting it hold you back for too long."

Their conversation stopped as they heard the lock being released, and they both turned to face the door.

Finn appeared and smiled. "Great, you both made it. Come on in, we're just getting organised. Now that you're here, we can get started."

Mac and Sully entered and stowed their outer-wear. Finn continued as he locked the door behind them, "I've set up seating for you in the after-care area, which should afford you both a good view of most, if not all the action. There is a refreshment table there as well, so please, do help yourselves."

They made their way through to the kitchen, where an open door revealed a staircase to the basement.

"Hold onto the banister and watch your step. It's a little steep. We can't afford another injured oboist."

At the bottom of the stairs, Mac got her first glimpse of the playroom. It was post and beam and seemed to span almost the entire footprint of the house. Her first instinct was to turn tail and run, but curiosity and her commitment to Sully won out. That, and Sully prodding her along from behind.

She spotted the after-care area in the far corner and they skirted the perimeter of the room to get there without disturbing those who were already playing.

"You're a real joker. A fainting couch? Fuck, Finn, why don't you just lop off my balls right now," Sully complained.

"Oh, suck it up, buttercup. It was the most comfortable option I could think of. I could go get you a ladder-back chair from the kitchen if you would prefer, because that nice comfy chair next to the couch is for Mac."

Mac smirked at the exchange and felt her shoulders relax a bit.

"Have a seat while our diva decides whether he requires an uncomfortable chair to prove his manliness." Finn indicated a recliner to Mac that would have suited Sully's needs perfectly, and feeling a touch mischievous, she accepted.

Sully huffed. "Fuck you, Finn. And you too, Mac."

Mac rolled her eyes at Finn and giggled. He responded with a wink, sparking that increasingly familiar tingle between her legs.

"Oh, settle yourself down before you disturb a scene." Finn reached for a Coke and waited for Sully to get himself comfortable before handing it over. "Can I get you something, Mac?"

"I'm fine for now, thanks."

Mac gave a little jump when she felt Finn settle on the floor and take her right foot in his hands. "What on earth are you doing? You should be attending to your sub, not fulfilling Sully's foot fantasies."

"And if I had a sub here, I would be attending to her needs. Since I don't, I am free to attend to yours. Now just sit back, watch whatever scenes interest you, and enjoy."

Finn kept a close eye on which scenes grabbed Mac's attention and filed them away for future reference. The activities she watched openly would be good rewards for her trying the ones she was uncomfortable about, yet found irresistible. He continued to rub her feet, but occasionally worked his way up to her calves, careful not to overstay his welcome.

The way Mac's eyes kept wandering to the corner of the room where Jackson sat in a chair, spanking the sub draped over his lap, gave Finn his first clue to what Mac found appealing. If it hadn't been for her slight shiver and the small, sharp intake of breath, he would have missed her quick glance at Wilson working his rope magic. Interesting. Something to keep in mind for the very distant future, if ever. He knew what seemed arousing in fantasy, could be disastrous in reality, and with Mac's experience, he didn't feel particularly optimistic on that front. While he liked to work with rope occasionally, it didn't get him all fired up like it did Wilson.

Mac interrupted his thoughts. "Finn, you can stop any time."

"I told you I would be attending your needs today, and unless there is something you need more than your feet rubbed, I'm happy to keep doing what I'm doing. Is there something more pressing you need?"

"Um, no. It's just that you've been at it for an awfully long time, and while it feels great, I don't want to monopolise you."

"We'll just carry on then, shall we?"

"Yeah, I guess."

EVEN THOUGH EVERYONE else was leaving, Mac didn't want to go. She was completely relaxed, and one look at Sully told her he was perfectly happy to stay put. To hell with it. She wanted to spend more time with Finn and with Sully here, she was safe.

She looked up and smiled as Finn returned to the playroom after seeing the last of his guests out the door.

"Mmm, there's nothing I like better than a contented smile, especially if I helped produce it."

"Stop fishing. Yes, you're the main cause, but don't let it go to your head."

"I'll try not to. It's getting late, and Sully is looking rather comfortable. How about you both spend the night?"

Mac sucked in a breath and let it out slowly as she tried to control her panic. "Absolutely not. Sully can stay. I'll pick him up in the morning and take him home."

Sully piped up. "Oh, Mac, come on, it's just a sleep-over. You can even bring me breakfast in bed. It'll be fun. You may not think so right now because it's outside of your comfort-zone, but honey, you've gotta start pushing the boundaries, and with me here, and Finn knowing the whole score, it's probably the safest opportunity you could ask for."

"I can't believe you think the prospect of me bringing you breakfast in bed qualifies as incentive. I already moved out of my comfort-zone by attending this party. Don't you think that's enough for one day?"

"I know how hard it was for you to come tonight. But you are so strong, and so capable of pushing harder than this, and I think you should. You know about safewords. Stay a little longer, and see how you feel. If you're uncomfortable, just say yellow, and we'll do whatever is necessary to get you back to green, and if you really need to bail, just call red. Okay?"

"I don't know, Sully. I'm scared."

"I know, sweetheart. We talked about this. I want you to think very carefully, will giving in to your fear be holding you back?"

Mac waffled back and forth, but in her heart, she knew Sully was right. She was letting fear hold her back. She hated when Sully was right. It made him rather insufferable as he rubbed it in. Fuck it. Every time she let her fear rule her, that monster won. Maybe it was time to start taking back her life. "If I were to stay, where would I sleep?"

Finn spoke up. "I have a couple of spare rooms. I promise, absolutely nothing will happen you don't want to happen. Okay? Like Sully said, you have safewords, and they work for every situation, no matter what."

Mac hugged her knees, and rested her chin on top of them. She closed her eyes, took in a long, deep breath, held it, and waited for her heart to stop hammering before she let it escape. "Okay, I'll try."

"Good," Sully said, "now can we move this party

upstairs? As comfy as this damned fainting couch is, I don't want to end up sleeping on it."

So far, so good, Finn thought as he followed Sully and Mac up the stairs. He and Sully figured they'd be doing well if they got Mac to stay until everyone else had left the play party. That she had agreed to spend the night, was beyond a bonus. Of course agreeing to spend the night, and actually doing it, were two completely different things. "Sully, how about you come with me to show Mac to her room before you head on to yours."

"We're going to bed now?" Mac asked.

Finn couldn't help but feel a little triumphant at the disappointment he saw on Mac's face. So far, the night had been a total success, and he was not going to do anything to jeopardise it. "Yes, we're going to bed now. One look, and I can tell you're both shattered. A good night's sleep is what we all need, so let's get a move on."

SIX

THE SCREAM that jolted him from sleep had already stopped, but the muffled moans had him out of bed and through the door before his brain had really kicked in. "What the fuck?" It was fortunate he'd chosen to wear pyjama bottoms to bed, because he was already in Mac's room before his choice of sleepwear became a consideration. He raced to the bed and crouched next to it as he flipped on the lamp. He remained perfectly still and spoke softly. "Mac, wake up, love. It's just a bad dream. I'm not going to touch you, but you need to wake up, baby."

Mac continued to moan, and Finn let out a sigh of relief as he heard Sully come shuffling through the door. "Thank fuck. Get in here and do something. I don't want to touch her and freak her out more, but she's not responding to my words."

"Dammit, I thought she was over this. I'll talk to

her, but you're going to have to hold her, because she might struggle, even with me. Just try and hold her so she'll see me when she opens her eyes."

Finn eased onto the bed beside Mac. As he slipped his arms around her and gently pulled her into his side, she went limp and stopped moaning. He rocked her gently as he stroked her hand and rubbed his cheek against the top of her head.

"Mac, wake up, sweetie. Finn's got you." Sully stroked her cheek and tried again. "Come on, Mac. You need to wake up. Finn's got you, but you're safe. I promise, you're safe."

Finn knew the instant she woke up. Her body stiffened for a moment before the struggling began.

"Enough," Finn ordered. Mac obeyed and Finn continued, "Mac, you're fine love. You were having a nightmare, and just talking to you wasn't helping. Give me a colour."

After a brief pause, Mac replied, "Yellow."

"Yellow we can work with. Does something need to change, or do you just need a minute."

Mac took a little longer, then relaxed back into Finn's side as she said, "I just need a minute."

Sully stroked Mac's cheek once more and asked, "Do you need me to stay, or are you okay with me heading back to my own bed?"

Mac turned her head and looked into Finn's eyes before answering. "I think I'll be okay, you go back to bed."

"Brave girl. I'll see you in the morning."

Finn shifted their bodies so he was sitting against the headboard with Mac's body snuggled tight to his side, her legs draped over his lap.

They sat like that for a long time before Mac finally spoke. "Finn?"

"Yeah?"

"Thank you."

"What for?"

"Not being the asshole I first thought you were for starters, I think."

Finn chuckled. "Thank you for not being the junkie I first took you for."

"What a pair we are."

"Well, now that we know what we aren't, how about we get a better idea of what we are?"

"Okay, you go first."

"Remember, you can still use your safewords at any time."

"I'll remember."

Finn thought hard. Talk about walking a fine line. What to ask that pushes the envelope without tearing it? He needed to make this question count because he didn't want to make her shut down. "Right then, let's go for an easy one. What's your favourite part of a man's body. Where do your eyes go first when you meet a man you find interesting?"

"I check out the upper arms. I like them to be muscular, but not in a body-builder way. If a guy needs to flex his biceps in the mirror, his arms are too muscular. I want to feel like those arms are for holding me and keeping me safe, not for his own personal eye-candy."

Finn chuckled. "I can assure you that I never flex any of my muscles in a mirror. I'm going to cheat a bit, and ask a follow up question. How would you rate my arms?"

He resisted the groan that threatened when Mac reached up and gave his left biceps a bit of a squeeze.

"I'd say you're well within acceptable muscular parameters."

"That's a relief. Your turn to ask me something."

"Same question."

"My favourite part on a man's body is..."

Mac giggled. "Smart-ass. You know what I meant."

Finn toyed with giving a less provocative answer, but he refused to be anything less than completely honest. "Okay, I'd have to say lips. They're so very versatile."

"I buy that."

Finn watched with interest as Mac caught her lower lip in her teeth and screwed her eyes shut. He waited patiently for her to resolve her inner conflict.

With her eyes still squeezed shut, she said, "You got a follow up, so it's only fair that I do too. How would you rate my lips?" She'd no sooner got the words out and her face was buried into his shoulder.

Finn just about stopped breathing. It was the

logical follow up, but that she'd asked it had him scrambling for a satisfactory answer that wouldn't scare the shit out of her. Finally, he went with his instincts.

He took her chin between his thumb and forefinger, then gently guided her face to meet his. He paused for a moment and looked into her eyes before touching his lips to hers. "Kissable, most definitely kissable," he declared. He gave her another, slightly longer kiss before releasing her chin. Finn was worried he'd pushed too far, but it was too to late change it.

Mac sighed. "That's a relief."

Finn hugged Mac a little closer to him and kissed the top of her head. "Are you up for another question, or are you ready to go back to sleep?"

"I'm feeling pretty sleepy."

"Alright. Let's get you all tucked in before I head back to bed, then."

Mac stiffened, then asked, "Can you stay with me? At least until I fall asleep?"

"Whatever you need."

Finn extricated himself from Mac and waited for her to settle back into bed. Sensing she needed him to do more than sit on the edge of the bed and hold her hand until she fell asleep, he eased in, then tucked her into his side with her head resting on his chest. "This okay?"

Finn felt her nod. He waited a few extra minutes after her body went slack to be sure she was asleep before trying to disengage himself from their tangled bodies. He wanted to stay, but didn't want to do anything that might snuff out that tiny glimmer of trust she was developing in him.

SOMETHING WAS WRONG. Mac clawed her way from sleep as she realised Finn was getting out of bed. She'd felt safe and content in his arms. Panic gripped her, and she said the first thing that came to mind. "Yellow."

"What?"

"Yellow."

"Okay. Does something need to change, or do you just need a minute?"

"That depends."

"You're going to have to give me more than that, baby."

"It depends on whether you're leaving or just shifting position."

Please don't leave me. She was surprised by her silent plea. Sully had slept with her and kept her safe for months after it happened, but never once, did she feel content.

Finn stroked her cheek. "I promised to stay until you fell asleep. I thought you had, so I was heading back to my own bed. Now, what do you need, so we can fix it?

Mac paused, squeezing her hands in and out of

fists before she gathered the courage to respond. "I need you to stay."

"Brave girl. That was a pretty scary thing to say, wasn't it?"

"Yeah."

"Here's the deal, Mac. The last thing I want to do right now is leave. So I need to be absolutely clear about what you are asking. There can be no room for interpretation. Are you asking me to sleep in this bed, snuggled up with you for the rest of the night?"

Mac's heart was beating nineteen to the dozen, but she wanted him to stay more than she was scared. "Yes, I want you to sleep with me cuddled safe in your arms for the rest of the night."

"I can do that, my sweet, brave girl."

As Finn settled in next to Mac, she instantly burrowed into his side and relaxed. Moments later, as she was drifting back to sleep, she wished Finn had kissed her good night.

SEVEN

THE FIRST RAYS of morning were trickling through the blinds and Finn lay on his side watching Mac as she slept. He recalled the two kisses they'd shared the previous night along with her murmured wish, and cursed the thought as he inched his pelvis away to keep his inconvenient erection from scaring her. He was already concerned about how she'd react to waking up with him in her bed.

Would it be best to sneak out of bed and let her wake up alone or not? He teetered back and forth a number of times before not won. Selfish bastard that he was, he couldn't bear to leave her before he absolutely had to.

He knew he should let her sleep until she was ready to wake up on her own, but his usual intractable self-control was distinctly absent. That happened a lot when it came to Mac.

He wet his index finger and traced it around Mac's lips. Her eyelids flickered and then opened. There was a moment of confusion in her eyes before she smiled wide and said, "You stayed."

"I told you I would. I'm sorry to wake you, but I wanted to give you the goodnight kiss you asked for last night, and I couldn't wait any longer."

"I remember thinking it, but I don't remember saying it out loud. And if you did hear me ask, why didn't you do it last night?

"You were mumbling and not fully awake. I would have loved to kiss you goodnight then, but I wanted you to be awake enough to enjoy it with me."

"You didn't want to freak me out when I was half a sleep."

"That too. So, can I kiss you goodnight now?"

Mac nodded, and Finn said, "I need to hear the words, Mac. I know it's hard, but I'm not willing to risk fucking up whatever we might have, on miscommunication."

"Fair enough. May I have my goodnight kiss now?"

Finn answered with his lips barely touching hers. A whisper that increased in volume as Mac's lips parted to allow his teasing tongue entry.

Finn eased back and gazed into Mac's eyes. "Goodnight, Mac." After a short pause, he said, "May I kiss you good morning?"

Mac responded with an enthusiastic, "Yes, please."

Finn demanded more with this kiss, and Mac

opened to him without hesitation. He wanted to lose himself in her mouth and kiss her for days. He shifted gears, and gentled the kiss before he reluctantly pulled away. He returned his gaze to hers and grinned. "Wow, that was some kiss good morning."

"A girl could get used to spending the night with a man if the morning promises kisses like that."

Finn knew he was falling harder with each passing day, and it scared him more than he wanted to admit. Especially to himself. "Alright, greedy-lips. It's time to get moving. We have an invalid in the next room who's probably wide awake and wondering why he's still waiting for his breakfast in bed."

"Hell, I think you just may know Sully almost as well as I do."

"Quite possibly. I'm going to go check on him and put some clothes on. I'll meet you in the kitchen."

"You do know I can't cook, right?"

"I'm sure you can manage to throw some slices of bread in a toaster and slather them in coronary-inducing quantities of butter."

"Yeah, I can just about manage that."

Finn poked his head through the doorway and wasn't surprised to find Sully awake and full of questions.

"It was mighty quiet after I returned to my very

lonely bed last night. No screaming from nightmares or mind-blowing orgasms. And where's my breakfast?"

"Good morning to you too, you cheeky fuck."

"Tell me what happened after I left. You know how I hate being left out of the know."

"We asked each other a getting to know you question. She gave my biceps a squeeze, I gave her lips a smooch, I spent the night snuggled up with her, and now it's morning."

"I suspect you've omitted a few details, but that's okay, I'll press Mac for them later." Sully cocked his head. "Seriously, she was okay last night and this morning?"

"Yeah. Actually, she was way better than I had any right to hope she'd be. I really like her, and I don't want to fuck up."

"You're doing fine. I should have started urging her to break free of her self-imposed exile years ago, but it was too easy to let her hide from the world, and lean on me. It broke my heart to watch her world shrink to nothing but her cat and me, but I was too scared to give her some tough love in case she shut me out too.

"At least now, it looks like she's finally ready to take back her life, and I think you're the guy to help her do it. If it weren't for my damn foot fetish, I'm sure she'd be all over me. But, c'est la vie."

"Sorry, pal, I think your foot-fetish is just her excuse to let you down gently. I was thinking about Christmas. Does she spend it with family?"

"No. Every year I try to get her to come and spend it with me at my parents' house, and every year she turns me down flat. She spends it by herself and she insists that's how she likes it. Maybe this year will be different."

"Maybe. I'd best get downstairs and get your breakfast started. I lit a fire under Mac's ass to meet me in the kitchen, and I doubt she'll thrilled if I make her wait. She insists she can't cook."

"And, she'd be right. I'm not kidding when I say, no matter what, do not let her cook."

"I've put her on toast duty. Please tell me that's safe."

"That's about the only thing that is safe, provided you have the toaster settings to barely tanned."

"Good to know. I'll see you in a bit with breakfast and coffee."

FINN WATCHED Mac struggle with the coffee maker for a few minutes before taking pity on her. "I'll do that, you go sit down."

"What took you so long? I told you I can't cook."

"Sully was being nosy. I didn't realise your inability to cook extended to use of a coffee maker.

"I drink tea, so I only needed to master a kettle. I assume, given how long you were with him, his Lordship had the blow by blow of last night. I can't believe men accuse women of being gossip-mongers."

Finn let out a rumbling laugh. "While he has been provided with a brief overview, he plans to grill you for the details. As for blow by blow, I'm quite certain I would have noticed, and remembered had blowing been involved." He gave Mac an exaggerated wink and said, "I can only hope there will be some in my future."

"You never know what the future holds, do you? If, when I woke up yesterday, someone had said I would spend the night in bed with any man, let alone you, I would have laughed myself sick."

Mac's unguarded response was delightful. So much for the erection he'd wrangled into submission not ten minutes earlier. "I think we need to change the subject."

"Okay, I can blow it off if you can."

"You did that on purpose, imp."

"Didn't you have some bread you wanted me to toast and butter?"

Finn gathered the bread and butter and set it on the counter in front of the toaster. "There you go. I figure four slices for me, another four for Sully, and however many you'll eat should do it."

"On it."

"How do you like your bacon and eggs?"

"I like my bacon completely crispy and my eggs over-easy."

Finn leaned down and gave her a peck on the nose. "A woman after my own heart. There's nothing like the full cholesterol meal deal to get a good start on the day."

The smile she gave him melted him to his toes. Oh boy, was he in trouble.

***

"I COME BEARING BREAKFAST, you lazy-ass pecker-head." Mac sauntered into Sully's room and waited for him to raise himself up before setting the bed-tray over his legs.

"Well good morning to you, my little ray of sunshine. Did you sleep well?"

"You can stop right now. Whatever Finn told you when you pumped him for information is all you're going to get, you nosy git."

"I'll take that as a yes." He grinned at her and she stuck her tongue out at him.

"You're awfully lucky I love you, you know."

"I do know. You like him, don't you?"

Sometimes she wondered if Sully could read minds because he had an eerie way of knowing what was going on in her head. "So many parts of me don't want to for so many different reasons, but yeah, I like him. It's like driving downhill in the snow. Unless I want to crash, I can only go forward, moving ever faster, and there's no way to reverse out of it."

"Then stop trying to put it in reverse. As long as

there are no sharp bends in the road ahead, just sit back and enjoy the ride."

"I hate you."

"I know. Where's your breakfast?"

"Finn's bringing ours up as soon as it's ready. We figured with you being the big baby you are, we should get yours done and served first."

"I'm not a baby. I'm a finely tuned instrument that's been banged up and is in for repair."

"Whatever you need to believe, Sully."

"You are such a cheeky wench. I don't know why I put up with you."

"I let you rub my feet."

"Yeah, there is that."

FINN LOOKED up as Mac brought Sully's breakfast tray into the kitchen. "Thanks Mac, if you leave it on the counter, I'll take care of it."

She put the tray down. "I don't mind loading the dishwasher, unless you're obsessive compulsive and will reload it to your exacting specifications the moment my back's turned."

"No, I'm not that bad. If you really want to load the dishes, I'd be a fool to say no."

Finn stopped wiping down the stove for a moment and enjoyed the view of her ass as she bent to put the plates on the bottom rack. Perfect position for a nice spanking. He turned away and returned to his task. Plenty of time to fantasise later.

When he'd finished wiping all the surfaces, Finn crossed the floor and stood next to Mac. "Thanks for your help, love."

"You're welcome. Thank you for cooking breakfast. It was really good."

"Anytime." Finn's eyes focused on Mac's lips, and he had to ask. "Can I kiss you?"

Mac nodded and tilted her head up. Finn leaned down, cupping her cheek as he placed a firm kiss on her lips. He chose not to deepen it. His lips had already written cheques his dick wouldn't be cashing anytime soon.

He eased away. The sound of a voice clearing in the doorway changed his mind about dipping in for another.

"I do hope I'm not interrupting."

Finn glowered at Sully. "Fuck you. What are you doing up?"

Sully's cheeky smile lit the room. "I've had my breakfast in bed, and now I'm ready to start my day. If I let this wee wench sub for me too long, you guys'll toss my ass aside and give her my chair."

"You know damn well your chair is perfectly safe," Mac retorted.

"My chair may be, but sweetie, you are still the most amazing oboist I know, and I can't think of a bigger, badder, in your face, fuck you and the horse you rode in on to that mother-fucking piece of shit, than to go pro.

Mac collapsed onto the nearest chair. "We've talked this to death. Not going to happen. I'm perfectly happy playing just for me."

"We'll revisit this when I have working ribs and you've finished an entire Christmas concert schedule."

"Let's not and say we did."

"I'm going to let this drop for now, but it will come up again. Count on it. Now, I'm going to gather my bits and pieces and call a cab."

"I already told you I would drive you home, and besides, poor Gounod's been home alone all night."

"He's a fucking cat. As long as he has food, water, and a place to bury his shit, he's good."

"You can't hold a grudge just because he peed in your shoes once when he was a kitten."

"I can, and do."

Fine, but I'm still driving you home. Go get your shit together and I'll meet you in the living room."

Sully shuffled off, and Finn spoke up. "I'm going to ask you something, and I want you to think about it very carefully before you answer."

"Okay?"

"Do you think you could ever feel comfortable being alone with me?"

"I don't have to think about that. I was alone with you all night."

"Not really, Sully was in the next room."

"He may have been in the next room, but you know as well as I do, he'd have been the next best thing to useless if I'd really needed him."

"Fair enough. In that case, would you like to come over for dinner and a movie tonight? Remember, you always have your safewords, and they work for everything."

"Oh, what the hell. Go big, or go home, right? A few kisses after more than a decade without makes a girl feel a little reckless. What time shall I be here?"

"How about six?"

"Sounds good to me."

MAC HADN'T EVEN GOT her seatbelt on before Sully began his inquisition. "So, what did you two talk about in the kitchen before we left?"

Mac growled as she started the car. "None of your business, you nosy bugger."

"True, but humour me."

Before driving off, Mac turned to face Sully. "Alright, given you're my safe-call, but God help me if I need you. I'm going back tonight for dinner and a film."

"Go you." Sully patted her on the leg. "I mean that, Mac. I'm not being funny. I am so, so happy you've finally found someone you feel safe to be alone with. You deserve that. He's a good man. I've known him a long time and I've seen how he plays. And before you say a word, I know damn well he won't even think about playing with you until he knows, not sure, not confident, but knows it's what you want. I trust him to take good care of you. You have to promise me two things. One, before making any rash decisions you will come to me if you are even the tiniest bit unsure about anything. And two, you will communicate clearly with Finn. Can you promise me those two things?"

Mac considered for a moment. "I promise. You're the only man in the world, for now anyway, who I trust absolutely. If you tell me he has your trust, then I will give him the opportunity to earn mine."

"Good enough. Jeezus, woman, are you purposely picking the bumpiest route home and aiming for every single pothole along the way?"

"Sorry, bud. Road bumpiness increases exponentially to the degree of pain you're experiencing. We'll be home soon, then you can have some pain meds and go to bed with a Coke and your remote control."

"I expect you to call tomorrow with a full report on the evening's shenanigans."

"Of course you do. I'll call, and I may take pity on your poor sorry ass and provide you with a vignette of the evening, but don't count on it. Part of my decision may depend on how much more complaining you do between now and when I get you tucked into bed."

EIGHT

FINN SMILED WIDE as he opened the door to Mac. Welcome back. It's been a pretty lonely day. How was Gounod when you got home?"

"Oh My God! You'd think I'd taken the vacuum to him followed by a thorough dunking in ice-water. He yelled at me for hours. Hours. I shit you not. Even after I gave in and opened a tin of tuna, he continued to tell me off. Who knew a cat could yell with his mouth full?"

"Poor kitty."

"Poor kitty? I'm surprised my ears aren't bleeding."

"Would a kiss help."

"It couldn't hurt."

Finn wrapped his arms around Mac and lifted her from the floor before he caressed her lips with his own. "Better?"

"Not sure. Maybe you should do that again."

He did, and her moan was all the encouragement he needed. He deepened the kiss and in one smooth motion, he had her in his arms, bridal fashion. He carried her to the sofa and sat with her in his lap. He slowly broke the kiss and looked into Mac's eyes. "Better now?"

Mac sighed. "Definitely."

"Good. Are you hungry?"

"I could eat."

"Sully said you like lasagne. I made it myself. No oven-ready abominations from the supermarket for me."

"I love lasagne. And home-made? That's a real treat."

"What I want to do, is sit here and kiss you silly, but it might be better to do that without the risk of being interrupted by growling bellies. Up you get." Finn released his grip, and Mac slid off his lap and started towards the kitchen.

"Oh no you don't. Dining room, you."

"You don't want any help?"

"Not this time. For now, just let me dote on you."

"I'm not comfortable with being doted on. I've been taking care of myself for a long time."

"We'll work on that. Off with you. I'll be through in a minute."

Mac laid her knife and fork on her empty plate and groaned. "That was fabulous. I really shouldn't have eaten that much, but I can't remember the last time I had truly home-made lasagne. And no, restaurant lasagne doesn't qualify, no matter how authentic the claim."

"Thank you. I'm glad you enjoyed it. I do love a woman that eats."

"I like food too much to be one of those women who orders a salad and only eats half a cherry tomato and a lettuce leaf for fear she'll get fat and no man will want her. Fuck that for a lark. Either you like me for who I am, or move on."

"I like you very much for who you are."

Mac blushed. "Aw crap, I wasn't fishing, you know."

"I know. Just putting it out there so you don't need to wonder."

"Well, so you don't need to wonder either, I like you for who you are too."

Finn smiled wide. "Ready for our movie?"

"Nope, we have a table to clear and a kitchen to clean first."

"What if I told you I'd take care of it later?"

"I'd tell you we should both deal with it now. It will take less time, be easier to clean, and it won't be lurking, waiting to pounce when you'd rather be doing something else."

"You're right, but I told you I would be doting on you."

"You can resume your dotage after."

"Alright, let's get this done, so we can snuggle and watch a film."

"What if we were to skip the film and just snuggle?"

"I'd be good with that. I'm curious about why, though."

"I need this to be real, and if we watch a film, it's too easy for me to check out."

"Are you sure this is what you want?"

"Not really, but I want to try. It wouldn't really be any different than last night, except we'd both be awake."

"Let's get a move on."

***

"How're you doing, Mac?"

They'd been cuddling in silence on the sofa for a good half hour before Finn spoke up.

"Okay, I think. It's scary, but not. The idea of it is scary, but it feels way more good than it does scary." Mac wasn't ready to admit out loud that the good was feeling safe and content in Finn's arms. Out loud made it real, and this was all way too new for her to let it be real yet.

"That's what I like to hear. Are you up for a little exploring?"

"Depends. What kind of exploring?"

"Mostly talking, but there'll be a little touching. Your safewords are still in play and work for everything. Okay?"

Butterflies attacked her stomach with a vengeance and she had to concentrate on not letting them take over. "I think so. What kind of talking, and what kind of touching?"

"I want to talk to you about boundaries, limits, wants, and needs. As for touching, I can't touch you anywhere or in any way that is sexual, but you can touch me anywhere and any way you want, and I'll keep my hands at my sides."

"I don't know..."

"About what? The talking, the touching, or both?"

"The touching part mostly, but I'm kind of nervous about the talking part too."

"Like I said, safewords apply. You've used them and they've worked so far, but it's up to you."

"I think I might be okay with the talking part."

"What are your safewords?"

"Yellow for I need something to change, or I need a minute, and red to bail."

"Good. It's no secret that you are submissive and I know there was a time when you physically participated in BDSM activities. If you felt safe, and had the opportunity, do you think you would like to dip your toe back in the BDSM pond?"

Mac took her time gathering her thoughts. This had to be one of the last questions she expected to be asked, but strangely, one that had been at the front of her mind for quite some time. "Yeah, I think so."

"Brave girl. The next question is a follow up on the last. What do you think would make you feel safe enough to try?"

In theory, this was easy. In practice, Mac wasn't so sure. "Sully would have to be there, no nudity, and no restraints."

Finn gave a slight chuckle. "You've given this a little thought."

"Yeah. Truth is, I still want it, but it scares me, so I've been living vicariously through Sully and the internet."

"Not very rewarding, is it?"

Mac shook her head. "No. Sully's been telling me for years that I've been letting the bastard win by letting his actions impose limits on my life. I know he's right, but it's only recently I've felt ready to try."

"Bonus question. Do you think you'd feel safe enough to try with me?"

"Maybe. When do I get to ask a question?"

"Okay, it's your turn to ask questions."

Mac's head was full of them, and almost every one pertained to her fear of not being enough, in some capacity or another. "Would you walk away from me if it turns out I can't play?"

"Remember earlier, we were talking about accepting people for who they are? Well, this is part of it. I want to exchange check-lists later, and when we do, I'm sure there will be things that are a hard limit for you that I enjoy. I'm also sure, there are going to be lots of things on that check-list that we both enjoy. I'm not willing to throw away an otherwise great relationship because of a few incompatibilities. I wouldn't worry about not being able to play. You may never be able to play in the way you used to, but there are plenty of ways to play."

"What if I can never have sex again?"

"Honey, let's not borrow trouble. Yes, you've got some issues that are complicating to a relationship. But I'm willing to put in whatever work is necessary to give you and me a real shot. It won't be easy, but I need to know you aren't going to run away when things get tough too."

"It's scary."

"I know, but sometimes the worthwhile things are. So, wanna go steady?"

Mac shot him a cheeky grin. "Do I get to wear your class ring?"

"Something like that."

There was something in the way he said it that made Mac suspect he was talking about a collar, so she decided to press. "Care to elaborate?"

"You'll get it when your ready for it."

Mac felt almost certain Finn meant a collar, and the idea excited her. "Okay, I'll go steady with you."

"You know that means kissing."

"I should hope so."

"I want to try something. This is a great position for snuggling, but for kissing? Not so much. Could you try lying on top of me?"

"Okay."

They shifted so Finn was lying on his back on the sofa with Mac on top, enfolded in Finn's arms. Before she'd even realised she was hyper-ventilating, Finn had shifted them to their sides with him positioned against the back of the sofa, leaving Mac an unobstructed escape route.

"Fuck, fuck, fuck." Mac buried her head beneath her arm as mortification branded her cheeks. She couldn't even lay on top of a guy without losing it. What kind of future could they possibly have?

"Hey, it's okay." Finn stroked up and down her arm. "You gave it a try. That's the worst part, you know. That first time you try something that scares you witless. You're dealing with some big shit. I know it's going to get in the way more often than not, and we'll deal with it all as it comes. Can you look at me?"

"No."

"Why not?"

"Because I'm too embarrassed."

"I don't know what you've got to be embarrassed

about. I asked you to try something, and you did exactly what I asked. That's nothing to be embarrassed about. When a sub safewords after trying something, but it's too much, do you think that sub should feel embarrassed?"

"Of course not."

"Okay, let's look at what just happened as if it were a scene. We tried something you were unsure of, and as your Dom, I noticed you had a problem and called the scene before you had a chance to safeword. Do you think that you, as the sub, should feel embarrassed?"

Mac latched onto the words, your Dom, and felt a warm glow deep in her belly. Then she remembered he'd asked a question. "No."

"Remember when you asked me about what if you can't play, and I said there were all kinds of ways to play. While I didn't mean it to be, for all intents and purposes, that was a scene. And it was successful. Your Dom asked you to try something, and you did. Can you please look at me now?"

Mac rubbed her face on her sleeve, erasing the tears before she shifted and caught Finn's gaze.

He trailed a finger down her face. "Thank you for trying. That was a big, scary step and I'm proud of you."

Mac gave him an uncertain smile, unprepared for the comfort his words provided.

"So, is lying on top of me a soft or hard limit?"

She closed her eyes and let herself relive the

feeling for a moment. Scary, but not crippling. "Soft limit."

"Good. When you fill in your check-list, you will add lying on top of me to your soft limits."

Mac nodded, and feeling bold, asked, "Can I sleep here tonight? Like we did last night?"

"Of course you can. We're going steady. But are you sure?"

"I want to try. I was fine last night and I want to see if I'll be fine again."

"Alright, but sweetie, you need to know that just being near you makes me hard, and while I try to keep my erection from touching you, I can't guarantee it while we're sleeping."

"I understand, and I did notice. Please don't any more. I'm not saying rub yourself on me every chance you get, for now anyway, but don't censor yourself. Not with actions, or words. I don't want you to tiptoe around my issues. I would rather deal with a bad reaction than miss out on any more life."

"You got it. Wanna go to bed now?" Finn waggled his eyebrows, making Mac giggle.

"Yeah, but I had better call Sully first and let him know. He'll worry, otherwise."

"You do that, and I'll go find you a t-shirt to sleep in and meet you upstairs.

Finn was already in bed reading by the time Mac arrived. He looked up from his book when she tapped on the door frame. "Silly girl, we're going steady. That means you don't have to knock. There's a t-shirt there on the end of the bed for you. Before you go change, What did Mr. Worry-wart have to say?"

"He called me a dirty stop-out."

"Mmm, lucky me. I'm rather partial to oboe playing dirty stop-outs. What else did he say?"

"Nothing of note beyond calling me names."

"You still okay?"

"A little nervous, but I think so."

"Good. Go get changed and come to bed. I grabbed your toothbrush from the guest bathroom and left it for you beside the sink"

"Thanks." Mac picked up the t-shirt and trundled off to the bathroom.

Finn gave up on his book. There was no way he could get his mind off the prospect of spending the night alone with her. It could end up anywhere between idyllic and disaster. He'd be thrilled if they ended up at any point on the idyllic side of that spectrum.

Finn beamed at Mac as she inched her way back into the bedroom. "Welcome back." He flipped the covers down in invitation. Mac perched on the edge of the bed for a moment before laying on her back, so tense, she seemed ready to levitate. "Sweetie, you need to let your muscles go a little, or you're going to be awfully sore tomorrow. Can I massage your shoulders a bit?"

"I don't know if this was such a good idea after all."

"Whatever you need, baby. You have safewords. Give me a colour."

"Yellow."

"Okay, yellow. What do you need?"

"I don't know."

"Yes, you do. Take a breath and think about it for a minute. What is the problem, and what needs to happen?"

"I'm scared."

"Do you need a minute for the scared feeling to go away, or do we need to change something?"

"Dammit. I'm such a mess. I'm sorry, Finn. I should go home. I don't even know why I asked for this."

"Yeah, you are a mess, but we can work with mess. You asked for this because it's what you want. I agreed because it's what I want and what you need. If you really need to go home, then call red. We agreed on safewords, and you've been very good with yellow. Going home because this is too much is exactly when you should use red. Are you still yellow, or are you red?"

"I'm still yellow."

"Good. Back to what we need to do to get you back to green."

"I need a hug."

"That's an easy fix." Finn gently gathered Mac into his side and wrapped his arms around her. You are so brave, do you know that?"

"I don't feel brave. I feel like a flake."

"Being brave is doing something when it's scary. You've done so many things that scare you in the last week. I bet more than you've done in the last five years. Am I right?"

"Probably."

"Do you want to fall asleep like this, or should we try spooning?"

"That's a hard one."

Finn groaned. "You're killing me. If you were any other sub, you'd be getting punished for teasing me with sexual innuendo, but in your case, I think it's a positive step forward. For now."

Mac looked up at Finn's face and flashed him a cheeky grin. He smiled back and said, "Kiss me goodnight."

She stretched up and gave him a firm kiss on the mouth and held it for a second before burrowing herself into his side.

He caressed her cheek and said, "Thank you, love. I'll expect a good morning kiss upon waking. Sweet dreams, baby."

"Goodnight, Finn. Thank you for being patient with me."

"My pleasure. Now, sleep."

NINE

"Hi Mac, I just called to wish you luck for tonight."

"Thanks, Sully. How are you feeling?"

"Still fucking ouchy, but they keep insisting I will live. Some days, I'm not convinced."

"Don't over-do it. Our deal has an expiry date. I only agreed to the Christmas schedule, not one concert more, and you are already into me for two, count 'em, two very large favours to be named later."

"See, I knew you'd be reminding me at every opportunity. I'm almost sorry I called. So, enough with the small talk, how are things going with Finn? You've slept over every night this week."

Mac smiled. "Things are going fine. He's so tolerant and patient. If I were him, I'd have dumped my ass before I'd even picked it up."

"Stop getting down on yourself. I am so proud of you and how far you've come. You deserve good things, and I think Finn is one of them. Truth be told, I think he deserves you too. You're good people."

"While I have you on the phone, can I ask a favour?"

"Sure. Is this one of those to be named later favours I owe you?"

"Nope, because I think you're going to like this one."

"Lay it on me."

"A few nights ago, Finn asked me if I'd be willing to try a scene if I felt safe and had the opportunity. I told him I would, but no nudity, no restraints, and you had to be there. I want to try before the play party on Sunday. Will you help?"

"What does Finn say?"

"I haven't talked to him about it. I wanted to talk to you first because I want it to be a surprise, but I don't know if that's really feasible."

"You know I'll do whatever you need. I'll be honoured to help, but this isn't the kind of surprise you can spring on him. The three of us are going to have to have a long, detailed discussion about this. How about tomorrow over lunch. That should give you both time to be rested after tonight's concert, but provide plenty of time for us to figure it all out before you need to prepare for tomorrow night's gig."

"Thanks, Sully."

"You're welcome. Do you want to talk to Finn about this, or would you like me to do it."

"I'll do it."

"Good girl."

"I'll let that slide."

"Cheeky wench."

"Sully?"

"Yes, my sweet?"

"Thank you for always being there. I don't think I would have survived without you."

"You're welcome. Whatever you need, Mac. Always."

"Okay, enough. I'm getting all soppy. I've gotta go, it's almost show time."

"I'll see you at lunch tomorrow. I'll take a cab, so you don't need to worry about me when deciding where you'll be laying your head tonight."

"Alright. I'll see you tomorrow."

Mac turned around to see Finn and she gave him her biggest smile.

"What are you up to? That's not the usual smile you have for me."

"I wanted to wait until later, but I guess now is as good a time as any." Mac closed her eyes and let the words spill out as fast as she could. "I just got off the phone with Sully. I want a scene before Sunday's play party, and Sully has agreed to help. I wanted it to be a surprise, but Sully said it wasn't the kind of surprise one springs on you."

"Sully was right. I appreciate the sentiment, Mac, but, do you think you're ready for this?"

"I'm going to have to be ready some day, and Sunday is as good a day as any. Besides, it's not like you've haven't taken every opportunity to slip in a little D/s dynamic when you thought I wasn't looking."

"Guilty as charged. Okay, we can give it a go, but first we'll have to discuss our check-lists. We can go over them tonight when we get home. Also, we'll have to get together to talk it through with Sully."

"Already sorted. He's coming to lunch tomorrow. Oh shit. I really shouldn't have made plans for you and your house without checking. I'm sorry. Do you want me to call him back and reschedule?

"Stop and take a breath. It's fine. Yes, you should probably check with me before booking me or my house, but if I had something planned for tomorrow, you'd have known it, so no harm done."

TEN

Finn woke Mac by peppering her face with tiny kisses. Once her eyes were open, he settled in for a long, deep kiss. "Good morning, baby. You had a quiet night last night."

Mac's eyes lit up as she smiled. "I did. I'm a little surprised, considering I'm nervous about this afternoon."

"We'll take it all really slow. You'll know exactly how the scene is going to go. No surprises and no pressure. I've got your hard limits branded in my brain, but we'll go over them again with Sully before we start.

It occurred to me last night, we've never discussed your orgasms. You've slept here every night for a week. So, I know you haven't had any then, but have you been giving yourself orgasms when you are at your place?"

"I've been responsible for my own orgasm pretty

much my whole life, so, yes, I've been taking care of business when I get home."

"That stops now. Regardless of whether or not we have sex, the only orgasms you get are the ones I let you have. Are we clear?"

Mac scowled."What's the big deal? God only knows when, or even if I'm ever going to have sex again, so..."

"Enough. Beyond the fact that I told you no, I do have a reason for denying you. How many orgasms do you give yourself a week, on average?"

"I dunno, between three and five a day, so twenty-one to thirty-five a week?"

"Do you ever go a day or more without?"

"Rarely. Orgasms make me happy, so I may as well be happy every day."

"I'm afraid you won't be getting that kind of happy for a while, sweetheart."

"You can't be with me all day every day, so what's to stop me from giving myself orgasms when you aren't around?"

"You know the answer to that, Mac. Do you trust me?"

"Yeah, actually I do."

"Do you trust me to make decisions that may not result in your immediate gratification?"

"I think so."

"Not good enough, Mac. If I'm your Dom, and let's face it, you said it yourself the other night, we've got some semblance of a D/s relationship, then your job as my sub is to obey me, or use your safeword."

"You have a fair point. And yes, I do trust you. I'm just not happy that you're taking my orgasms away."

"I'm not taking them away, I'm just deferring them. Don't worry, you'll get them back, and I think you will be much happier with them when you do."

"I'm going to trust you on this, but if what you claim doesn't come to pass, you may want to be very cautious in everything you do, and you may need to sleep with one eye open."

Finn chuckled. "I won't let you down, love. I promise."

"So, um, how long will I be orgasmless, anyway?"

"As long as I say you will. End of discussion."

"I could be certifiably insane by the end of the week, you know."

"I doubt it, but it's a chance I'm willing to take."

"I don't think I like you very much right now."

"Are you feeling deprived and needy already? When was your last orgasm?"

"Friday. I didn't have time yesterday. What little time I had at home was spent placating a very angry kitty."

"About Gounod. I think you should bring him to stay here. He's more than welcome. You sleep here every night, and while I could stay with you sometimes, except for poor Gounod being lonely, our current sleeping arrangements seem to be working. So, what do you say?"

"He might pee or poop somewhere inappropriate to make his displeasure known."

"That's okay, we'll steal a pair of Sully's shoes for him."

Mac struggled not to laugh, "Okay, we can try it for a week, but I reserve the right to safeword out and you'll have to be the one to steal Sully's shoes."

"Deal. I'm hungry. How about some breakfast?"

"A most excellent idea. Shall I make toast?"

"Absolutely. You're getting quite good at it."

"Make sure my bacon is extra crispy."

"As you wish. Now up with you, wench."

MAC ABSORBED the warmth of Finn's embrace as she tried to decide whether she was completely crazy, or just a little nuts. What was she thinking, asking for a scene? Red. One little word and it all goes away. Then what? The prospect of never knowing was becoming worse than taking a chance.

"You're thinking too hard, sweetie. Colour, please."

"I needed a minute with myself, but I'm green"

"Alright, love, just like we talked about. A nice simple over the knee spanking. You've got a bra and underwear on and Sully's here. I won't use restraints, but if you move your hands or legs, even an inch from where I put them, I will have to hold you down for your own safety. You can do this. Five smacks and we're done. Ready?"

"What if I said no?"

"Then we'd wait until you are ready or safeword out. Are you saying no?"

"I'm saying yes, I'm ready."

"Good girl.

"I'm going to go sit on that chair now. Sully is going to be sitting next to me so you can see his face. When I call you, come to me and lay over my lap. I'll use my hands to help you get into the right position, but as long as you stay still, I'll only rest my left hand on the small of your back. If you move, I'll need to use my leg to keep your legs still, and my hand will hold your hands at the small of your back. Understood?"

"Got it."

"Good girl."

Mac couldn't help feeling abandoned when Finn left for his chair. She was thankful he didn't make her wait too long before calling her because she was worried she'd wimp out.

Finn beckoned. "I'm ready for you, love." Mac took a couple of shaky breaths before walking across the room and laying herself over his lap. "Good girl. You're doing fine. I need you to shift forward so your hips are snug against my thigh and then extend your legs back with your knees straight. Bend your toes like you're wearing high heels and use them to support your legs."

"I don't know if I can do this. I feel like I'm going to topple over."

"You've got it exactly right. Don't worry love, you'll feel a lot more stable in just a minute. Now, I want you to stretch your hands to the floor until you can touch it with your palms... Perfect." Mac felt like she was playing some perverted version of Twister. Once Finn placed his hand on the small of her back, her universe righted itself. "Mac, safewords please?"

"Yellow for a minute or to change something, red to bail."

"Good, here we go." Mac waited for the first strike, but when it didn't come, she started to lift her head. "Don't move. I'll get to it on my time, not yours."

A pause, and then a hand rubbing circles over her ass-cheeks. The rubbing morphed into kneading, and back to rubbing. When the first blow finally came, it nearly took her breath away. She had been so wrapped up in the massage, she wasn't prepared for the smack itself, let alone the force of it.

"FUCK!"

"Give me a colour."

Mac paused for a minute and caught her breath. "Green. I'm green."

"Good girl. You'll learn to expect the unexpected."

The pain continued to bloom and her bottom warmed. Finn resumed her ass massage and just as she relaxed into it, he struck her other buttock.

"FUCK, that hurts." Mac sucked in a big breath and groaned.

"Colour, love."

"Green."

"Such a good girl. Only three more."

"Can we pretend we're done?"

"Not if you want to graduate from fantasy-land to the real world."

Mac was relieved when Finn went back to that nice rubbing massage, and almost reared up when he launched two more smacks in quick succession. One on each cheek. The only thing that stopped her was the tiny voice of self-preservation reminding her, moving meant restraint.

"FECKING GODDAM SON OF A FECKING BITCH!"

"Colour, Mac?"

"I'm fecking green, but that was mean."

"Think about where you are and what you've taken so far. Not just for me, but for yourself. Sweetheart, you are so amazing. You've had four really big swats and you didn't move. You came pretty close with those last two, but you didn't. We're down to the last one, okay? I won't make you wait this time."

Before she could answer, her ass was on fire. It was harder than the rest and right on her sit-spot.

"I don't like you very much right now."

"That's okay. You will again later, and I can wait. Up you get." Finn wrapped a blanket around her and led her to the after-care area. He sat down and pulled her into his lap, mindful of her tender bottom. Mac snuggled in and automatically opened her lips to the water-bottle Finn held there. She drank greedily, not realising how thirsty she was. When she'd had enough, she pulled her head away, and accepted the small piece of chocolate Finn slipped into her mouth. She sucked on it as she let her mind hover into nothingness.

FINN CAUGHT Sully's eye and motioned his head as an invitation to join them on the sofa. "What do you think, Sully?"

"Almost perfect. So much better than I dared hope for. She was focused entirely on you. While I'd like to think that was because she trusts you completely, I suspect it was more because subconsciously, she knew I was here and it was safe to let go."

"Yeah, that's pretty much what I thought too, and I'm good with that. Whatever it takes, right?"

Sully tapped his finger on his chin. "Yeah. You'll do."

"Cheeky fuck."

"I'm going to go rest on the fainting couch for a while. I want to be wide awake for the evening's entertainment. If I can't play, I intend to collect plenty of wank-fodder."

Finn hugged Mac a little tighter and buried his

nose in her hair as he murmured, "How are you doing, baby? Are you awake yet?"

"I did good?"

"You were perfect, sweetheart. How do you feel?"

"Relaxed."

Finn chuckled. "Yes, you are." He gently tapped her temple with his index finger. "But what about in here?"

"Quiet."

"Excellent."

"I don't think I want to play at the party."

"It's all up to you. Do you want to sit and watch like last time, or do you need to be completely away from it?"

"I want to watch. I'm not up for others seeing me vulnerable."

"Whatever you need. Now rest for a bit."

<hr>

With such a successful afternoon in the playroom, that night Finn decided to push a little harder. "Mac, it's time for you to get used to us being naked and touching. I know you don't feel safe playing naked, so we won't. But from now on, unless you safeword, we sleep naked and shower together. That means washing each other."

"You don't mean right now, do you?"

"Yes, I mean right now."

"Can't we wait until tomorrow so I can have some time to get used to the idea?"

"No. You're more likely to work yourself up and talk yourself out of it. You'll undress me, but I'll let you remove your own clothes." Finn placed his hand at the small of Mac's back and urged her towards the bathroom. "Come on, love, time to go." Mac shuffled in front of him, but stopped in the bathroom doorway. "Colour, Mac?"

"Yellow."

"Okay. What do you need?"

Mac clenched and unclenched her fists a few times before responding. "I need a minute."

"Okay, take all the time you need." Finn traced lazy circles up and down her back until she resumed her trek to the shower. "So brave, sweetheart. Here's your only choice. Do you want to undress me first, or yourself. You don't need to speak. Your choice will be reflected in your actions."

Finn watched as Mac's face contorted with indecision. Relief washed over him when she didn't safeword, but instead reached forward, grasped the bottom of his t-shirt and lifted it. He beamed at her as he bent down so she could get it over his head and free of his arms. "You're doing great, love."

Mac dropped the shirt on the floor, and after a few false starts, she managed to fumble the button of Finn's jeans open. Her fingers trembled as she slid the zipper down, and she took a sharp intake of breath when she discovered he wasn't wearing underwear. She finally slipped his jeans to his ankles and off each foot. He stood naked before her, humbled by her triumphant grin. "Nicely done, sweetness. I'll get the shower warmed up and you can join me once you're undressed."

Finn monitored Mac's progress through the frosted glass of the shower stall, ready to deal with any sign of hesitance or indecision. He was pleased that, while slow, her progress was steady. He opened the door for her just as she reached it. "In you come, baby. The water is nice and warm." Finn shifted and Mac stepped into the spray.

"Let's get your hair wet so I can wash it first. Then I'll wash your body while we let the conditioner work its magic." Finn massaged Mac's scalp as he shampooed her hair. Her moans of pleasure were almost enough to send him over the edge.

"Let's rinse, then we'll condition." Mac tipped her head back, eyes closed and held still until the water ran clear down her back.

Finn caressed her cheek. "Time for conditioner, love." He worked the conditioner into her hair with the same care as he had the shampoo. When he was sure her hair was completely slathered, he guided her out of the spray. "Stand there. I want your feet shoulder width apart and then I want you to stay perfectly still. I'll move you as needed.

Mac nodded and Finn grabbed a wash-cloth and

loaded it with shower gel. He started at her neck and lathered his way across her left shoulder, down her arm to her fingertips. He returned to her neck and did the same for her right side. "I'm going to do your back now, okay?"

"Okay."

"Good girl." Finn moved behind her and rubbed the cloth side to side from her neck to the top of her buttocks. "It's time to do your bum now, love. Deep breath, and let it out slowly."

Mac did as she was told. She flinched a little as Finn rubbed her tender cheeks, but held her ground. Finn wasn't surprised when she tensed as he began to ease her buttocks apart. "Another deep breath, Mac. You're doing great. Washing your body is all that's going to happen to you. I promise." Mac took another deep breath, and her muscles relaxed a little as she let it out. "Good girl. I'm going to do your front now."

Finn moved to face her and started at her neck again, this time, working down her chest. She seemed relatively calm, so he lingered over her breasts for a moment, purposely avoiding her nipples. He felt a jolt of satisfaction as her nipples puckered and she let out a frustrated groan. He continued his journey south, stopping just shy of her pubis.

"Okay, gorgeous, we're in the home stretch. I'm going to do your legs now, but I'm going to start at your toes and work my way up. You can place a hand on the wall if you feel unsteady."

Finn crouched at Mac's feet. He lifted her left and washed it thoroughly before moving up her leg until he was nearly at the top. He did the same to the other and then rose to face her. "Remember, sweetheart, I'm just washing you. Nothing more. Okay?"

"Yeah."

Finn kept his eyes on Mac's as he slipped his hands between her legs. Her mouth opened slightly and she closed her eyes as he gently spread her pussy lips between his thumb and forefinger, letting them brush against her clit. He held them open while he used the cloth in his other hand to wash her. When she tried to tilt her pelvis towards the cloth, he pulled it away. "There, all done. Time to get you all rinsed off now, love."

Finn guided her back under the spray. "Well done, Mac. You may do whatever you need to get rid of all the soap, but don't spend too long on your pussy. You don't have my permission to do anything more than rinse it. Clear?"

"Clear."

"Good. Once you're done, it's your turn to wash my body. You may do it any way you want, but you must wash my entire body."

Mac's lip quivered. "Everything?"

"Everything. You'll be fine. You have safewords. Use them if you need them." He was glad that Mac didn't dawdle over rinsing. He was anxious to get her to bed and move on to the next part of his plan.

While she clearly struggled with a lot of the things they did together, her determination to conquer her fears was inspiring. It was this tenacity that convinced him she could, and would, heal enough for them to enjoy a normal, healthy sex life together. He wasn't a fool, he knew it was going to take a lot more time and patience, but the deeper she burrowed into his heart, the more confident he felt she was worth it.

Mac's hands on his chest brought Finn back from his thoughts. "Done?"

"Yeah. I'm ready to wash you now."

"First, this." Finn took Mac's face in his hands and kissed her gently. "I am proud of you, sweetness. We're almost done."

"Finn, can you close your eyes while I do this? I've never done this, not even before...I think I might find it easier if you aren't watching me."

"Whatever you need, as long as you do it, or safeword."

"Thanks. Can you bend down a bit so I can reach your head?"

Finn settled himself on the floor of the shower, eyes closed, kneeling up in front of Mac so she could easily reach his head to wash his hair. She was quick, but thorough, and his scalp felt tingly when she was done. She took the same cloth Finn used, and added more shower gel. She washed as much of his upper-body as she could comfortably reach before asking him to rise.

Mac's hands over his body sent Finn's cock into

over-drive. She came to an abrupt halt just above his navel, and concerned, he opened his eyes and looked down at her. "Honey, it's just a body part. No different than my foot, or my toe, or my hand, or my nose."

"It can hurt me."

"It can, but if you don't want it to, I won't let it. I promise. My hand hurt you today, but only because you said it could. Same thing with my penis. In case you haven't noticed, it's been like this pretty much since I opened the door the night we met. And while it's generally in charge of whether it's up or down, I'm in charge of everything else. Do you trust me to do everything I can to keep you safe?"

"Yeah. It's just sometimes I get freaked out."

"I know, and that's okay. We're going to have a lot of ups and downs, both good and bad. As long as somewhere deep inside, you trust that I'll do everything in my power to keep you as safe as Sully does, then everything is going to be fine. I promise."

"You make a lot of promises."

"Only those I can keep. Are you ready to continue?"

"Yes. Close your eyes again, please."

Finn closed his eyes and it took everything he had to keep from coming when she lathered his balls and stroked the sudsy cloth up and down his shaft. Finn reached down and touched her hand. "Mac, fair warning, if you keep that up, I'm going to come, and I don't think you're ready for that. I'm clean enough.

"What if I want to make you come?"

"That's very generous of you, but I think we'll leave that for another time. Now, let's get finished. I'm tired and would like to get to bed soon."

Mac finished up fairly quickly. Finn wasn't surprised that once she'd got past the part of his body she was most scared of, the rest was easy. "Well done, love. You can enjoy the shower while I dry off. Then, when you come out, I'll towel you off and blow your hair dry."

ELEVEN

A WHOLE FECKIN' week without an orgasm. Mac was feeling needy, and Finn, the bastard, seemed to always know when she was on the verge of taking the edge off. Every time she thought she'd sneak away, he diverted her attention to something else. She was sure she really would go crazy if she didn't get some relief soon. She finally stopped complaining about it when he warned her he'd make her wait an extra day for every time she brought the subject up. That wasn't a chance she was willing to take.

To make matters worse, he touched her everywhere except where she really wanted. He would always get so close she thought it would happen, then poof, gone. It was like he had sexual attention deficit disorder.

She'd hoped giving him an orgasm in the shower every night might encourage him to reciprocate, but every time she tried, he stopped her. Then he'd wait until she was finished washing him, before giving himself an orgasm and making her rewash his lower body. Fucker.

Mac was greeted by a far too cheerful Finn as she entered the kitchen.

"Good morning. How come you're scowling, love?"

Mac pasted an insincere smile to her face. "I'm not scowling. I'm a happy, happy girl." His chuckle brought her scowl back before she could to stop it.

Finn held out a mug. "Come and get some tea, grumpy-girl." Mac grudgingly accepted the tea and sat at the table.

Finn sat in the chair beside her and took a long sip of his coffee. "Mac, it's time to talk about some things. I need to know if you can put the grumpy on hold for a few minutes or so." Mac shrugged, then nodded. "That wasn't very convincing, love. Wanna try again?"

"Yes. What do you want to talk about?"

"Let's start with Christmas. Sully says you spend it alone every year."

"Not quite, I have Gounod. That's how I like it, and that's how it's going to stay."

"I host an afternoon gathering and pot-luck supper for friends who would otherwise spend it alone. I cook a turkey and everyone else brings the fixings. You're on dessert. Please, for the love of everything that's holy, don't make it yourself. Store-bought will be fine.

"Maybe you didn't hear me. I spend my Christmas

with Gounod, so you'll have to assign store-bought dessert to someone else."

"I did hear you, sweetness. Christmas is three days away, we have a concert tomorrow night, and Gounod is here. You're both settled. Is spending a lonely Christmas in your house with only Gounod for company worth uprooting the two of you for a single night?"

"Who says it would be only one night? My obligation to Dominant Cord is over when the last note has been played tomorrow night."

"Sweetheart, you sleep here because we're going steady, which is not limited to your time with Dominant Cord. We like each other, we trust each other, and we agreed to do whatever is necessary to give whatever this is we have, a real shot. I know it's scary. But it's just the next scary thing in the long line of scary things you've faced in recent weeks."

"I don't know."

"That's an improvement on no. How about we call this yellow for now. You can take some time with it, and if it's still yellow in the morning, then we'll see if we can come up with changes we can both live with. Okay?"

Mac felt miserable. She was mixed up. She'd spent so many Christmases alone, it was what she was comfortable with, but she couldn't lie to herself. Every one of those lonely Christmases had her wishing she had someone special she could spend it with. Sully was wonderful, but she relied on him too much as it was, she couldn't allow her hangups and problems to taint Christmas with his family. "Okay, let's hold off until the morning."

"Good. Next order of business. Play party tonight."

"I won't be playing."

"Okay. Can we have a small scene this afternoon?"

"What kind of scene?"

"A slight variation on the one from last week. Either you take your spanking naked with Sully here, or you keep your bra and panties, but no Sully." It took Mac a few seconds to absorb what Finn was asking. Naked around Sully, or scene without him? What an impossible choice. "You have safewords, baby. They work anytime, including right now, but I'm going to change this one up a little. Yellow is only for more time, but you will have to choose one of the two options I gave you. Otherwise, you have to call red."

"Yellow."

"Good girl. Give Sully a call and talk it through with him. I'm sure that'll help with your decision. I'm going to go get things organised in the playroom."

MAC ABSENTLY STROKED GOUNOD. "And now, I don't know what to do."

"Sweetie, what does your heart say?" Sully asked.

"lub-dub, you prick."

"Such a funny girl."

"My heart tells me I need to wean myself off of you."

"I knew you'd get there one day."

Macs chest tightened. "I'm sorry I've been such a burden."

"Stop it. You've never, ever been a burden. All I did was hold the back of the bike until you felt safe enough for me to let go. That's what love is, sweetheart. You'd do exactly the same for me."

"No question."

"So, will you tell me how the rest of my day is going, so I can plan accordingly."

Mac knew it was time to let Sully release the back of her bike. "You're off the hook. I'll see you tonight. I love you."

"I love you too."

AT THE SOUND of Mac on the stairs, Finn put down the chair he was carrying and sat in it while he waited for her to appear.

"There you are love. Did you talk to Sully?"

"Yeah. Thanks for the suggestion, it helped."

"And? Have you picked an option?"

"No Sully."

Finn decided not to give her a chance to over-think

it. "In that case, there's no time like the present. Strip to your bra and panties or safeword."

Mac started with her shirt and made slow steady progress as Finn looked on in anticipation. As the last piece of clothing fell to the floor, he said, "You can leave them there, but in future, you will fold your clothes and set them down neatly when I tell you to strip."

"Sorry."

"No need to apologise. It's not something we've discussed, so it's not something I would reasonably expect. Come here and position yourself exactly the way you were last time."

Mac crossed the floor and laid herself over Finn's lap without hesitation. Finn felt she wiggled a little too much as she settled into position. She was becoming quite a tease, but he didn't feel the need to correct her like he would any other sub. He found he really didn't care whether it was her past, or her personality that allowed him to tolerate behaviour bordering on bratty. There would still be consequences, but they would be the sort to limit the behaviour, not obliterate it.

"Are you quite settled, Mac?" She wiggled again, and Finn knew it was deliberate. He almost felt guilty at the pleasure he'd get from giving Mac her first real punishment. Putting his sadistic tendencies aside hadn't been much of a hardship, but the chance to explore Mac's pain threshold as a result of her own behaviour was too good to pass up. "Mac, I think you're wiggling around more you need to. Am I right?"

"Maaaaybe."

"I need a straight answer, love."

"Yes, but it was too tempting."

"There are many things about you I find too tempting, but I control myself. I think you purposely wiggled more than necessary when you first got yourself settled. I'll give you that one for free, but what came after, you'll have to pay for at the end of the scene. I'm feeling generous, so I will give you two options. You may either have two extra smacks with my hand on your bare bum, or five strokes with a tawse over your panties. Pick one."

"Bare bum."

Finn was relieved. While his intention was to give Mac options designed to help her work through issues stemming from the attack, he knew there was every possibility it could backfire. He never offered her a choice he wasn't prepared to follow through on, but so far, he'd been lucky. "Just like last time, I won't hold you down as long as you stay still. Clear?"

"Clear."

"Safewords?"

"Yellow to pause, red to bail."

"Here we go, then."

Finn rubbed, squeezed and kneaded Mac's ass, and the moment her glutes went slack, he brought his hand down once on each cheek and resumed his massage.

"OWWWWW! YOU HURT ME!"

"Breathe through it, love. You've got a ways to go yet and I'm just getting warmed up."

"I don't like you any more. That nice massaginess doesn't feel so nice any more. You're mean."

"I know." Finn continued massaging. He waited until her ass-cheeks relaxed, before giving her another two hard smacks and more massage.

"FUCK!"

"Breathe, baby. Just breathe. One more of these, then we'll get your punishment out of the way. After that, we can go have a snuggle, and you can have some chocolate from your favourite shop."

"I don't care. I hate you and I hate chocolate."

"I know, sweetheart."

"Don't feckin' patronise me"

"Enough, Mac. I'll tolerate some rudeness because you are taking pain for me, and if that's what it takes to get you through it, then I'll go with it for now. But you took it too far. Now you know where the line is, cross it, and there will be consequences. Clear?"

"Clear."

Finn rubbed Mac's ass gently, but he only gave her a few seconds before he nailed her in her sit-spot.

"THAT FECKING HURTS!"

"I know, honey, but now you've got two more and these ones are punishment."

"I'm really sorry I wiggled to tease you."

"I believe you. That doesn't get you out of it,

though. I'll always give you any punishment you earn. There might be times when I will defer it, but I promise I'll always give it to you."

"That's one promise I would be perfectly happy if you didn't keep."

"Enough stalling. Let's get this over with, I want to snuggle with you."

"Fine."

"Good girl. Now stay still, I'm going to slip your panties down just enough so they don't block where I'll be spanking. Colour?"

"I'm green."

"Good girl." Finn shifted and caught hold of the sides of Mac's panties. He wiggled and pulled until they were completely clear of her ass. The crotch was soaked. This counted for multiple points in favour of going ahead with his after party plans.

Normally, he would let some tension mount, but Mac was at green and with this being her first punishment, he wanted to keep things as positive as he could. He hauled his arm back and smacked her full-force on the sit-spot of her left side, and before she had a chance to register the pain, he did the same to her right, then pulled up her panties. Her deep intake of breath told him, it was going to be one long, loud scream.

He waited patiently until her lungs were empty before speaking. "All done, baby, but you need to breathe through the pain. Now up we get. I've got a nice cosy blanket just for you. We'll go have a snuggle on the sofa and you can have some water and chocolate."

Finn wrapped Mac in her blanket, and carried her across to the sofa, careful of her sore ass as he settled her on his lap. He reached for a bottle of water and lifted it to her lips. It was then, he finally got a good look at her face. Tears streamed, but her eyes twinkled and relief washed over him. He hadn't totally fucked up.

He let Mac suck back water until she pulled away from the bottle on her own. He smirked a little when she looked at him, her eyes expectant and her mouth open. "Oh honey, right now, looking at your mouth open like that makes me want to feed my cock to you one inch at a time."

"Chocolate. You promised chocolate, and you said you always keep your promises."

"Cock? Yes, I would happily give you cock."

"Finn, please don't tease me. You promised me good chocolate."

"Yes, I did, and you told me you hate chocolate. I should deprive you and feed you cock instead for uttering such a blatant untruth, but I'll accept that it falls within acceptable boundaries when you're taking pain for me." Finn slid a square of chocolate into his mouth, and slipped it into Mac's with his tongue as he kissed her.

"Mmmm, best chocolate delivery method ever."

"I'm looking forward to showing you all of my

chocolate delivery methods. When your ready for more, just wiggle your bum."

———

Mac was startled out of her reverie by Sully's voice. "You're looking a little dreamy, Mac"

"Hey, you're kind of early, aren't you?"

"Yeah, I may have let go of the back of your bike, but that doesn't mean I didn't need to check up on you in case you fell off."

"Thanks. You are a sweet man. If only we could find you a nice subby-type who likes having her feet played with."

"Let's keep that on hold until my ribs are better."

"I'm just poking. I would beat you myself if you tried to play while you're messed up."

"Enough about me and not playing. I want to know all about how it went with you today?"

"Actually, it was good. I didn't freak out and I didn't safeword. Not even yellow. Not only that, I earned a punishment and I took it."

"Oh Mac, I'm so proud of you. Hang on, punishment? What punishment?"

"I teased Finn by being wigglier than I should when I was settling in for our scene and he called me on it. I had the choice between two with his hand on my bare ass, or five with a tawse over my panties. I went with the bare ass."

Sully chuckled. "Very, very wise choice, sweetheart. Your panties wouldn't have provided any protection from a tawse, and trust me, whatever you got from Finn's hand wasn't anything close to the pain you'd have felt from the tawse. And, you'd have felt that pain five times, not two."

"I kind of figured."

"Are you really okay, though?"

"Yeah, I am. I know you're going to shower me with smuggery and 'I told you so,' but you were right. The more scary things I do, the less scary the next one seems."

"Sweetie, my pride in you is boundless. You are amazing, and you deserve to break free of the box you built around yourself. Now, enough sap. It's suppertime, and I brought your favourite."

TWELVE

Finn never got tired of seeing Mac in his bed, waiting for him to join her. He smiled and slipped in beside her. "How would you like an orgasm tonight?"

"I would kill for an orgasm tonight."

"No need to go that far, although, you may come to regret your decision."

"No, I really want an orgasm, and I'll do pretty much anything to get one."

"I noticed when I pulled your panties down for your last two spanks this afternoon, they were very, very wet. What do you think caused that?"

"I don't know."

"Don't know, or don't want to say?"

"Don't want to say."

"Fair enough. How about I make a little guess and you nod if I get it right?"

"I can do that."

"I think your panties were soaking wet because that spanking made you horny. Is that true?" Mac nodded and Finn continued. "What I didn't get an opportunity to assess, was whether those last two smacks killed your horniness, increased your horniness, or had no effect. So, just nod when I get to the right answer. More horny?" Mac gave another nod. "This makes things interesting. Here's the plan. I will let you have an orgasm and you will even get to choose the method — the catch is, you may only choose from the options I give you. Still want an orgasm?"

"Like you wouldn't believe."

"Safewords?"

"yellow to pause, red to bail."

"Good. Here are your options, you may have one orgasm from my mouth while I inflict all manner of pain, or you may have three orgasms from a vibrator while I have my cock buried deep inside you."

Mac groaned. "You're enjoying this way too much."

Finn grinned. "Of course. I'm a sadist. I'm waiting."

"Jeez. I don't know. One orgasm if I take pain, or three orgasms if I let you fuck me."

"I never said anything about fucking you. I said you'd have them with my cock inside you."

"You would just leave it there without moving?"

"That's exactly what I'd do. I'm betting your

vibrator sees more action than I'm proposing for my cock."

"That doesn't make it any less terrifying."

"I know, love. Either way, you'll get at least one orgasm, but you have to work for it."

"What if I can't do it?"

"You have safewords."

"But if I call red, I won't get my orgasm."

"Correct. However, you can call yellow and try your other option first."

"So, if I try one option, but end up not being able to deal, I still have a chance to get my orgasm if I call yellow and switch options?"

"That's precisely what I'm saying. If, however, you can't deal with the other option either, you will have to wait until I offer you another opportunity to earn an orgasm."

"You are diabolical."

"And your point is?"

There was a long silence before Mac finally spoke, her voice, shaky. "I'm sorry, Finn. I can't do it. Red."

Finn wasn't surprised, more relieved. He'd been pushing her so hard, he had concerns over whether he could trust her to know when to call red. He smiled and stroked her hair."Good for you."

Mac's eyes went wide in confusion. "You aren't mad?"

He kissed the tip of her nose. "Of course not. You have the power, love. It's yours to give, and yours to take back. Right now it's all yours. It's been a pretty heavy day for you, sweetheart. Are you ready to get some sleep?"

"You are mad."

"No, I'm not mad at all. I'm adjusting tonight's plans, nothing more. Is there something else you want to do before we go to sleep?"

"Can we cuddle?"

Finn pulled Mac into his side and held her close as he gently stroked her face. "Always."

IT WAS STILL DARK when Finn woke to a hand snaking its way down his torso. He grabbed it before it reached his navel. He reached over and switched on the light. "It's the middle of the night. What's going on, love?"

"I was thinking about earlier, when I called red."

"Okay, what about it?"

"I let that bastard win tonight. He made me scared of sex, and that fear deprived me of an orgasm or three. I don't want him to have that kind of power over me any more."

"What do you want to do about it?"

"Aw, fuck. I want three orgasms, no pain, and I want to be able to have a normal sex life."

Finn was conflicted. He so desperately wanted to agree, but he didn't want this to end up making things worse for her. Caution won out. "I don't know about this, love. I think we should hold off for a bit to give you more time to get used to the idea."

"No. I've been thinking about it for hours. You said all you'll ever ask me to do is try, and I want to try."

"Okay. If you're sure, we can try, but you have to promise to call red if you are even a little bit uncomfortable."

"I promise."

"Good. Just like a scene, I'm going to give you the details up front. No surprises, I promise."

"Okay."

"I am going to lay here on my back with my hands at my side, and you are going to sit on my cock. You may go as slowly as you need, but you may only travel downward unless you safeword. Once I am completely inside you, I'm going to need to use my hands for the vibrator, okay?"

"As okay as it's going to get."

"Fair enough. One more choice before we begin. Do you want to put the condom on, or shall I?"

"I want to do it."

Finn turned and opened the drawer of his bedside table. From it, he extracted a condom, a Rabbit and a bullet. He turned back to Mac and handed her the condom. He grinned as he held up the Rabbit. "A birdie told me this is your vibrator of choice, but I think the bullet will better serve our purpose tonight. "

"I don't know whether to thank that birdie, or give all his shoes to Gounod."

Finn chuckled. "Okay, love, one last thing before you put my condom on. Are you wet, or do we need lube?"

"Believe it or not, I'm totally wet."

"Show me." Mac flushed, but dipped a finger inside and held it in front of him. He opened his mouth and she slipped her wet finger in. Finn moaned as he sucked her finger clean before releasing it. She was killing him. "Honey, I sure like the taste of things to come. Condom, please."

Mac opened the packet and removed the condom before kneeling beside Finn. She rolled it onto his cock and winked, looking pleased with herself when she was done. "There."

"Good girl. Whenever you're ready." She shifted so she had one knee either side of Finn's body. It took all his concentration to stay perfectly still while he watched Mac struggle with her task "Colour, Mac?"

"Greenish Yellow?"

"Okay. Not a standard response, but we'll go with it. We're on your time, baby. No hurry."

"Oh, we're in a hurry, pal. I want my feckin' orgasms, dammit."

"Alrighty, then." Finn watched Mac briefly close her eyes before reaching down and grasping the base of his cock. She held it steady as she positioned herself so the tip was touching her entrance. "Colour?"

"I'm surprisingly green."

Finn watched Mac's pussy swallow his cock one

agonising inch at a time. He fought his need for control, his arms rigidly at his sides, bullet clenched in his fist. The minute she bottomed out, he had the vibrator on and positioned over her clit.

"I'M GOING TO COME, I'm going to come…" The bullet buzzed against her clit and Mac let out a low moan as her world exploded in a kaleidoscope of colour.

"Two more, baby."

Mac leaned forward, placing her hands on Finn's chest for support as she undulated her hips to increase the pressure of the vibrator on her clit. The pleasure built again and she whined as her pelvis jerked uncontrollably.

"There you go, sweetheart. Last one."

Mac wasn't sure she had another in her. She didn't think she'd come so hard in her life. Maybe there was something to this whole orgasm deferral thing.

Finn's eyes twinkled. "Honey, if you can think, I'm not doing my job properly."

The speed of the vibrator increased and she was completely overwhelmed by the sensation. "Stop, stop, stop, please stop. I can't take any more."

FINN IMMEDIATELY KILLED the vibrator and replaced

his hands at his sides. His first instinct was to pull Mac off him, but he was terrified that touching her would be worse than leaving her be, so he remained perfectly still. "Colour, love?"

"Yellow."

"Good. What do you need?"

"I need a hug"

"Okay. Do you want to climb off me first?"

"No. I'm okay. Actually, I like how you feel inside me. I just couldn't take another orgasm."

"In that case, how about you lay yourself down on my chest and I'll give you that hug. You can have the last orgasm another time."

Mac lay down with her right cheek resting on Finn's chest. He wrapped his arms around her back and tilted his head forward to kiss the top of her head.

"What about you?" Mac asked.

"What about me?"

"You must be going nuts, being inside me and not coming."

"I'm fine. I am so proud of you right now, I could burst."

"I'm proud of me too."

"Good girl. Are you ready for sleep now?"

"Almost. I want you to come inside me first."

"That's thoughtful of you, sweetness, but—"

"Please, Finn. I want to try more. I'm feeling really brave right now, even without feeling insanely needy. Like you keep saying, I've got safewords."

Finn let Mac go and set his hands back at his sides. "You're in charge."

"In that case, please put your hands on my hips and take control."

"Honey, I don't want to take any chances with you."

"I'm asking you to. I'm being clear in what I want. Please?"

Finn knew he wouldn't last long, and he was grateful. Maybe this wasn't a bad idea. After all, he and Sully had been after her to push her boundaries. "Alright. You have your safewords, but I want you to keep your hands on mine and pull on them if you need me to let go of you."

"Okay."

Finn started with his hands on Mac's knees and slid them up her legs until they rested on her hips. Mac put her hands over them and squeezed. "You can hold them harder than that."

"You told me I was in control. This is how it's going to be. This time. Eyes on me." Finn fixed his eyes on Mac's as he held her hips still and gently pumped himself in and out of her body. With a wicked smile, she began clenching her inner muscles and it was all over. His hands tightened on her hips and he thrust wildly, finally holding her hard to him as his orgasm subsided.

As sanity returned, Finn realised what he'd done and tried to pull his hands from Mac's hips. "Baby, I'm so sorry."

Mac grinned and held his hands in place for a moment before letting go and laying back down on his chest. "There's nothing to be sorry for. It was wonderful and amazing."

"Honey, you didn't come."

"No, not this time. But after those first two orgasms, I don't feel deprived. I think it might even be better that I didn't. The last time a man was inside me I didn't come either. For obvious reasons. Apparently, not only can I have sex, it doesn't have to be wrapped in an orgasm for me to enjoy it."

"Did you really enjoy it?"

"Yeah. I did. I think I might want to do that again, really soon."

"I may need a little recovery time. You blew more than my mind, love."

"Good."

Finn knew sex wasn't always going to go so smoothly, but this first time being such a success had him cautiously optimistic about their future. There was still a plethora of sexual land mines to navigate, and for the short-term, they would have a detailed plan for each sexual encounter, even though it would not be part of a scene. That fucker did a good job of tainting sex and bondage for Mac. Perhaps one day, they'd get her to a point where she could handle being restrained and maybe even during sex, he mused. Slow down and deal with sex first.

Mac's voice brought him out of his head. "You're thinking awfully hard. What's the matter?"

"Just thinking about the future."

"Anything you'd care to share with me?"

"Sure. I was thinking about sex."

"Mmmm. What about it?"

"That we're going to have lots more of it, but we need to be prepared for issues to come up, and accept them as part of the process. We'll have to explore and experiment in order to establish your limits. While what we just shared was incredible, neither of us will be satisfied with what we did tonight being the only dish on the menu."

"I know, and I trust you."

"That means everything to me, baby. I need to get rid of this condom before we have a problem. Can you please lift off slowly?" Finn slipped his hand between their bodies and held the condom in place as Mac raised herself up and over to Finn's side. "I'll be back in just a minute, sweetheart. You stay put. I'll bring a nice warm cloth to clean you up.

Mac had barely started her second cup of tea before Finn resurrected their discussion of Christmas plans.

"We agreed that you'd give me an answer this morning."

"You don't let anything go, do you?"

"Nope. A deferral is the best you can hope for. So?"

After so much upheaval in her life lately, Mac was tempted to escape it by continuing her solo Christmas routine. However, deep down she knew it would be a disaster. She felt safe and alive when she was with Finn. Being home alone, at best made her feel numb. "I guess I'll be hunting and gathering dessert."

"Excellent. Last concert tonight. I'll miss having you play with Dominant Cord, but lucky for me, I can play with you any time I like, day or night. Finn waggled his eyebrows and stole a kiss.

THIRTEEN

Mac slipped out of Finn's bed. She had to get away and think. She grabbed her robe and slipped it on as she tip-toed from the room. Tea. She'd ruminate over a quiet cup of tea.

Gounod wove between her feet as she put the kettle on. She absently bent and picked him up, as she scratched beneath his chin. "What do you think, little brat?"

"I don't know what he thinks, but I'm thinking, why aren't you in bed where you belong?"

Mac nearly dropped the cat as she spun to face Finn. "I couldn't sleep."

"Apparently. What's wrong, love?"

"Probably final concert adrenalin pumping through my veins."

"Sit down." Mac did as she was told and Finn took a seat next to her. "Let's try again. What's wrong?"

"I don't know. I feel all mixed up. One minute I'm happy and life's great, the next, I feel like I'm making a huge mistake and my world is going to explode. We're done with the Christmas concerts and I don't know why I'm still here."

"Sweetheart, you're here because that's what we both want. This is between you and me on a personal level. The only way this connects professionally is how we met. I know you're scared. You've got all kinds of good reasons to be, but we're working on them. Together."

"I don't know. I keep feeling like I should go home."

Finn laid a hand over Mac's. "What do you have waiting for you there?"

"My life."

"Tell me what that life has that you can't have here?"

"Control. I have no control here."

"You have all the control, love. Nothing happens you don't want. You may give me your power, but you can take it away with a single word. You've proven that."

"No, I mean, at home, my life was ordered exactly how I like it."

"Really? You still haven't answered me. What does that life have that you can't have here?"

"Fuck, I don't know. I just want to run away to where I feel safe."

"What makes that life more safe than this one?"

Mac was irritated. He was worse than a bloody shrink with all this probing. "I don't know. Stop asking me these questions. I just want to run away."

"Honey, you've been on your own for a really long time. You've only ever had Sully to rely on, and I suspect you didn't lean on him nearly enough. Being alone is what you're used to, so that's what makes you feel comfortable and safe. I get that.

"This is pretty scary for me too. It's been a long time since I've committed to more than a scene or two and some sex. You're the first person I've been serious about since I lost my wife. When we first got together, you were worried about me running from you. Look at me. I'm right here, Mac, and I'm not leaving. Give us a chance and stay. Please?"

Mac looked at Finn, a tear trickling down her cheek. "You're right, I'm terrified. What if this doesn't work out? What if you come to hate me?"

Finn wiped the tear away. "Then we deal. No more borrowing trouble."

"I don't know if I can do this, Finn."

"I'm not asking you to do this. I'm only asking you to try."

Mac nodded and Finn pulled her into his lap, wrapping his arms around her. "Let me take you back to bed. We're both exhausted. Things will look better in the morning."

FOURTEEN

Finn trailed a finger down Mac's back. "Santa comes tonight."

"I just bet he does."

After her emotional upheaval the previous night, Finn was glad to see she'd regained some spunk. "Careful, or he might not let you come with him."

"Sorry Santa."

"You just might be." Finn cupped Mac's face in his hand. "Remember when I asked you to go steady and you asked if you get to wear my class ring?"

"Yeah, you said, 'Something like that,' as I recall."

He released her face and took her hand. In it, he placed the small box he'd been holding behind his back. "Mac. Will you wear my something like a class ring?"

She looked down at the box in her hand and opened it to reveal a gold chain with a heart-shaped padlock and keys. She looked at Finn, her eyes filled with tears. "This is a lot more serious than a class ring."

"Yes, it is. I love you, Mac." Finn leaned in and kissed her. "Will you wear it? Please?"

"I can't believe you love me."

"Of course I love you. What's not to believe. You're sweet, and beautiful, and sexy and you keep my dick hard just by being in the general vicinity, you are a talented musician, and you make me so very, very happy."

"But—"

"Enough with the self-doubt. Will you wear it?"

"Of course I'll wear it."

Finn took the chain from the box and placed it around Mac's neck. He kissed her as he clicked the lock in place. "I think you may be paying for making me wait like that when you already knew your answer."

"In what currency?"

"Oh, you are awfully feisty this Christmas Eve."

"I'm excited. It's time for Santa to open a gift from his sub."

Mac ran out of the room and returned moments later sporting a Santa hat and carrying an exquisitely wrapped box. "Here."

Finn took the box and untied the ribbon.

"Hurry up."

"Patience, elf. It's my present and I will open it in my own time." He picked at the tape and carefully removed the paper. It was too lovely to tear, especially since it came from his first gift from Mac. He already planned to use it next time he gave her a present. He wasn't embarrassed to be sentimental about such things.

He opened the lid. Inside lay a set of black leather wrist and ankle cuffs inlaid with little red hearts. He looked up at Mac and cocked an eyebrow.

"Okay, so it's kind of a twist on how a guy buys a woman lingerie, but it's really a present for him."

"You need to be absolutely clear with me about what these mean, love, because there is no room for error."

"I want you to restrain me while we have every kind of sex."

"Honey, we've only just started having sex of any kind. Yes, it's been going fabulously, and I'm all for you pushing your boundaries, but don't you think it's a little soon to be adding bondage and exotic flavours to the menu?"

"I need to try. If I can do this, then everything else should be a walk in the park, don't you think?"

"No. I don't think. I'm not saying no to trying this, but you need to understand that conquering something near the top of your scary list doesn't mean that everything below it will no longer be scary or a potential issue."

"Yeah, I get that. I suppose, I'm a little high from all my successes and maybe letting them go to my head."

"I want you to celebrate every success you have in whatever way works for you. Just know that I'll be here when I think you need a voice of reason."

"Does this mean we can try?"

"Yes, but in addition to your safewords, you're going to hold a ball in each hand. If either ball drops, its the same as saying red. Everything stops and I get you free. Clear?"

"Clear."

"Safewords?"

Yellow for a minute or to make a change, red to bail."

"Good. And the added safety feature?"

"If I drop either ball, it's the same as saying red."

"Good girl. When I get upstairs, I want to see you laying on your back, and naked on the bed. I want your arms above your head and your legs spread wide. You've got five minutes. Go."

He wondered if she realised her real Christmas gift to him was her trust. Now he had to go upstairs and not fuck it up. No pressure.

MAC MOSTLY OBEYED Finn's order. She lay naked and splayed on his bed, but she kept bringing a hand to her neck so she could fondle her collar. She knew that's what it was, and she intended to get him to call it that before the night was out. What a crazy month it'd been. She felt almost like Jack in the box. Each revolution of the handle conquered another fear. She wondered if this would be the revolution where the top popped open and she sprung out. Free.

"While you aren't lying exactly as I told you, it is Christmas, and you are only disobeying to fondle your—"

Mac didn't wait for him to use that silly euphemism again. "Collar. It's a collar and you can call it what it is. I won't suffer an attack of the vapours."

"Yes, it's a collar. You like it?"

"Very much."

"Good. You may continue to fondle it until I am ready to cuff that wrist. In the meantime, here's how it's going to go. You'll stay on your back the whole time. I'm going to cuff you and clip you to the corners of the bed. I've decided I'm a bit peckish, so I'll be having a little Mac-snack. If all goes well, then I'll feed you some cock. When I've decided you've had enough, I'm going to slide my cock into your cunt for a while. The finale will be my cock in your ass while your pussy is full of Rabbit. You get to have an 'all you can come' night as your reward. Do you still want to try?"

Mac didn't know how she could be so terrified and excited at the same time. She wanted to try, but even though she'd said all kinds of sex, she didn't think that Finn would plan an all inclusive buffet. And anal? She hadn't considered that one. Maybe Finn was right and she was being a little ambitious. "Yellow."

"Okay, what do you need?"

"I don't know about anal."

"What don't you know?"

"I'm scared. I know we do stuff that hurts, but it's a good hurt. Anal was a bad hurt."

"Okay. Think back. Was it only anal that was a bad hurt, or did he hurt your pussy too?"

"Both."

"You trusted me not to hurt your pussy, and how's that working out for you?"

Mac cocked her head slightly and shrugged. "Pretty good."

"I'll take that. You have safewords and ball dropping as an added safety feature, right?"

"Yeah."

"So, do you think you can trust me enough to try? There's no wrong answer, love. I know you trust me. We're talking about one thing that scares you, and not trusting me with that right now is okay. You've already come such a long way in such a short time. Whatever you decide is perfect."

"You won't do anything from behind?"

"Not a thing. You'll be able to see me the whole time."

"Then I want to try."

"Brave girl. I'm going to start with your legs." Finn reached into the box and extracted the larger pair of cuffs. He was slow and deliberate as he attached them, planting a kiss on each ankle before clipping it to a corner of the foot-board. "Colour?"

"Green."

"Good." Finn reached to the floor and pulled a ball from the toy bag he'd set there when he came in, and placed it in Mac's left hand. He fastened a cuff to her wrist and kissed it before clipping it to the left corner of the headboard. He reached into his bag for another ball. He gently disengaged Mac's right hand from her collar and placed the ball in her palm. "Colour?"

"Green."

"Excellent." He fastened the remaining cuff and kissed her wrist before he clipped it to the headboard. He rested his forehead on hers for a moment. "Colour, love?"

"Green."

"Safewords?"

"Yellow for a minute or change, red to bail. If I drop a ball, it means red."

"You've been such a good girl this year, Santa has a nice treat for his sub." Finn kissed his way down Mac's body, stopping to suck on a nipple, giving it a sharp nip before doing the same to the other.

Mac arched her back and clenched the muscles in her pussy in answer to the zing that travelled straight from her nipple to her cunt. "Oh shit, Finn."

"Are you saying you'd like more?"

"Please."

"Not this time, love. Santa still has a treat to deliver." Finn kissed his way down to Mac's belly button, then shifted himself between her legs and licked from the bottom of her weeping slit to her clit, where he lingered, tickling random patterns over it with the tip of his tongue.

Mac moaned and lifted her hips upward, seeking more. Finn adjusted, allowing only feather-light contact between tongue and clit. He circled her entrance with a finger a few times before sliding in and playing with her G-spot.

The man was infuriating. "Pleeeease," Mac whimpered, frantically bucking her hips.

Finn reached up with his free hand and gave her nipple a rough pinch. "Be a good girl and hold still. You'll get what you need."

Finn continued teasing her until her pussy was dribbling down to her asshole. He lubricated his pinky with her fluid before pressing the very tip of it against her rosette. He took her clit into his mouth, and sucked in time with his finger-strokes to her G-spot until she was on the verge of coming. As she went over, he steadily eased his pinky in her ass up to his third knuckle and held it perfectly still, slipping it out again as her orgasm subsided. "Colour, love?"

"Christmas tree green."

"Good to know. I don't usually like to deviate from the originally scheduled programme, but I think I'll make an exception. While you're sucking my cock, you may have the Rabbit, provided you also have your ass plugged."

"If it means more orgasms, I can be flexible."

"Good girl." Finn grabbed the Rabbit and lube from the bedside table before reaching into the toy-bag for a small butt plug. He slid the Rabbit into her sodden pussy and set it on low. "How are you doing, love?"

"I'd like an orgasm now."

He snapped the lid of lube open and squirted a dollop on his fingers. "Patience, sweetheart." He spread it around her anus and easily sneaked his pinky in and out. He squeezed more into his palm and slathered it all over the plug before placing it at her back entrance. He increased the speed on the Rabbit and applied steady pressure to the plug until it was fully seated. "Colour, love?"

With the Rabbit driving Mac towards a nice big orgasm, she barely noticed the plug as it slid inside her. "Still really green."

"I'm so proud of you." Finn withdrew from between Mac's legs and kissed his way back up her body, taking extra time and care with her nipples. "I want to clamp these, but tonight is only about pleasure. We'll leave pain for another time."

He straddled her chest, wedging his thighs beneath her up-stretched arms so his cock was directly in front of her face. He placed a hand behind Mac's skull and tilted her head forward while he grasped the base of his cock with the other. "Open." Mac's lips parted and Finn slowly fed his cock into her eager mouth.

"Mmm, that feels good, baby." He slid most of the way out. "Now suck hard." He gave a few quick, shallow pumps before he eased his way in, almost to her tonsils, then he held still. "Swallow, and don't stop until I tell you, love."

With each swallow, he barely nudged the tip of his cock against the back of her throat before retreating again, careful to avoid making her gag. When she started moaning, he knew it was time to move on and he gradually pulled his shaft free of her mouth. "So good, love, but I don't want to come yet. I've a couple more places I need to be. Colour?"

"I'm still green."

"Excellent. I can see you're a little tied up, so I guess I'll have to dress myself for the occasion." He lifted his leg over to get off Mac's chest, snagged a condom, and rolled it on.

He checked the circulation in Mac's hands and feet then knelt between her legs. "Right love, the plug stays, but I'll be filling in for the Rabbit. Colour?"

"Nice and green."

He turned the Rabbit off and set it to the side. "Wonderful. Would you like to come?"

"Boy would I ever."

"Good." She moaned and clenched her teeth as he slid inside. He latched onto her right thigh for leverage as he thrust deep. He snatched the bullet and set it buzzing against her clit. He was tempted to let her come now, but he really wanted her good and needy before he tried to fuck her ass. He considered for a moment, then decided not to stretch this session out much longer. She'd been such a trouper and he wanted the night to end on a high note. He removed the bullet and withdrew his cock. "It's time, baby. Colour?"

"Not so green."

"Are you yellow, love?"

"Not quite."

"Let's talk for a minute then. What are you scared of?"

"Bad hurt."

"Have I given you any bad hurt tonight?"

"Yes."

Finn raised a single eyebrow at her. "What was bad hurt and why didn't you say anything?"

"You pinched my nipple, but I knew I deserved it."

Finn chuckled. Okay. Was that really bad hurt, or are you just stalling?"

"Stalling," she confessed. "You didn't really give me any bad hurt."

"And how are you feeling with the plug?"

"Weird, but it doesn't hurt."

"I'm bigger than the plug, but I will do everything I can to keep you from feeling bad hurt, okay?"

"I know. You promised me tonight was all I can come, and I'm sure I can come more than this."

"I'll make sure you get to come as much as you

want. I bet I'll even make you come while I'm fucking your ass."

"I bet you won't."

"You're on. What do you want if you win?"

"If I don't come while you're fucking my ass, you don't ever get to fuck it again."

"Alright, but if I do make you come while fucking your ass, you have to wear the butt plug of my choice all day tomorrow, and I get to fuck your ass any time I want."

"I don't know, you sound way too confident."

"Do we have a deal, or not? The longer you stall, the longer you have to wait for your orgasms."

"Deal."

"Brave girl. Too bad you're going to lose. I have just the plug in mind for you tomorrow."

"I'll take my chances. My luck's been holding out pretty well so far."

"We'll see. Colour?"

"Green."

"Here we go then." Finn replaced the Rabbit in Mac's pussy and turned it on the lowest setting. He squeezed a large puddle of lube into his palm and coated his cock thoroughly. Then he carefully removed the plug and positioned the lube at her anus and squeezed some into her rectum before inserting a finger to spread it around. He positioned the tip of his cock and paused. "Colour, love?"

"Green," she squeaked.

"Good girl. Push out as I push in. It'll make things go much smoother." Finn flipped the switch and increased the Rabbit's speed and leaned in, using the weight of his body to provide steady pressure. "Breathe, baby, you need to breathe. Slow, steady breaths, in and out. Almost there, love." As he felt her slight push, he leaned a little harder, and there it was, that pop of cock breaching ass. "Colour love?"

"Yellow."

"Okay, we're going to rest for a minute and let you get used to it. The hardest part is over, you know. The head is inside you. Any pain?"

She paused before answering. "No. A little burn, but no bad pain."

"Perfect. It'll feel nothing but good, really soon, I promise."

"You and your damn promises."

"Colour?"

"I'm closing in on green."

"Excellent." Finn resumed his steady pressure and kept going until his body was flush with hers. "There we go, baby. All in. Still green?"

"Yes."

"Then, it's orgasm time." He increased the speed on the vibrator and pulled out leaving just the head inside. He drizzled more lube over his cock and pushed back in to the hilt and held for a moment as he studied Mac's face. She had an almost serene smile on her face and she still held the balls in her hands. He braced his hands on her hips and withdrew to the head one more time before he was certain she was ready for him to fuck her. He pumped in and out, his momentum increasing with each thrust.

Mac threw her head back and let out a high-pitched whine as her hips gyrated and her legs shook.

With Mac in the throes of her orgasm, Finn picked up the pace, hammering at her furiously. When she came again, he let go and erupted with such intensity, he was a little concerned for the integrity of the condom. "Colour, love?"

"Holly jolly green."

"Perfect. I'm going to pull out and get you loose. Then I'll be back to clean you up." He bit back a sigh of relief as he pulled out and saw the condom had survived the encounter. He unclipped Mac's restraints and gave her a quick kiss on the lips before retreating to the bathroom to dispose of the condom and grab a warm, damp cloth. He was surprised to feel a hand on his back, and turned to see Mac sporting a huge grin. "You were supposed to stay put and I was going to come and take care of you."

"I thought a shower together would be better."

"I love the way you think, baby."

"I love you, Finn."

Finn stared at Mac for a moment, a little stunned. Somewhere inside, he was sure she loved him, but he didn't think she was ready to say it out loud. He swung her off her feet as he grabbed her in a tight hug and said, "I love you too, Mac," before he kissed her silly.

MAC CHECKED THE CALLER ID, and grinned as she answered, "Merry Christmas, Sully." She shifted, trying to find a comfortable position. She almost yelped when the plug in her ass started vibrating, and she silently vowed never to bet against Finn again.

"Merry Christmas, gorgeous. Was Santa good to you?"

"Santa was very good to me. And so were you. I don't know how to thank you for always giving me exactly what I needed at precisely the right time."

"It's a Dom thing. As for thanking me, how about letting me off the hook for those two favours to be named later?"

"No way, there is not a sub on the planet who would give up unspecified favours from a Dom. Best Christmas ever."

ACKNOWLEDGMENTS

Madelynne Ellis for her endless support. Elise Logan for being the first to beta-read and showing me the errors of my way. The wonderful gang of Divas who are generous in so many ways. And of course, my wonderful, supportive husband, who says yes to almost everything...except another dog.

ONE GOLD KNOT

She didn't do relationships. She didn't even do all night.

After years of avoiding her teenage crush, Hildy Klein is shocked to come face to face with Wilson Kennedy.

Her uncle's wake isn't the place to unravel all the ways that Wilson could leave her emotionally vulnerable and exposed, yet his gentle persistence is impossible to ignore.

But Wilson is no longer that boy in her fantasies, and now Hildy must decide if she will give up control and commit to the protective, kinky Dom he's become.

For my sweet, wonderful sister, J.
You are everything I aspire to be.

ONE

Wilson did a double take at the sign on the back of the Smart Car parked in front of The Squeaky Wheel, not sure he'd read it right. He turned to Sully and raised a brow. "Newly Dead?"

Sully chuckled. "Erich's instructions for his wake were frustratingly detailed."

They stomped the snow from their feet and entered the pub. Wilson immediately spotted the other members of their wind quintet, Dominant Cord, at the bar. He snagged Sully's sleeve and gently pulled him along as he went to join the group.

"Hey guys, we finally made it."

"Hi Wil, I was getting a little concerned," Finn said.

"Blame Sully. I had to drive like my grandmother because our delicate flower bitched and complained about his sore ribs."

Mac snorted and rolled her eyes. "Good grief, Sully. I don't know how you're supposed to be ready to play the upcoming concerts if you can't even handle a car-ride without whining."

"Geez, what does it take for a guy to get a little sympathy?"

"You could stop letting your cock make your dating decisions."

"Well, I'd never been ice-skating before, and it sounded like fun—"

Shaking her head in obvious disbelief, Mac interrupted. "Bullshit, Sully. You just wanted to touch her feet. Too bad you broke your ribs before you had the chance to be the perfect gentleman and help remove her skates."

Wilson lost interest in the conversation. While banter between Mac and Sully was generally entertaining, he was fed up with hearing about Sully's injury. He let his eyes wander, and the lone woman in the back corner of the room caught his attention. Hildy. He'd only met her that one time, years ago, but she snuck into his dreams with disturbing regularity. Her demeanour screamed stay away, but her haunted look made him want to scoop her into his arms and comfort her. "I'll be back later."

Griff followed his gaze and said, "Yeah, good luck with that."

Wilson crossed the floor, never once taking his eyes off his quarry.

The moment Wilson turned from the bar and caught her eye, Hildy was positive the universe was a sadistic asshole.

When he'd walked in with Sully earlier, her stomach hit the floor and her heart raced so fast she thought she might black out. She couldn't believe her good fortune when he'd headed straight to the bar without so much as a side-ways glance.

Deep down, she knew he'd come, no matter how hard she tried to convince herself otherwise. It was bad enough she had to be here and say goodbye to the one person in her family who loved her — she didn't need her teenage crush bearing witness to her all-consuming grief, too.

Her only option now was to gain the upper-hand and get rid of him. She looked him in the eye. "Hello Wilson. Is there something I can help you with?"

"Hey, Hildy," he smiled and offered his hand, "it's been a long time, I didn't think you'd remember me."

Remember? How could she forget? That day was branded on her soul. Every night since then, she imagined she was swaddled in his arms instead of her blanket. And she always fucked with her eyes closed so she could pretend Wil was the one she was with.

Her mind drifted back to her fifteen year old self. Back then, she practised on her uncle's piano because her parents had sold hers when she stopped being their performing monkey. They'd been livid when she'd stood before that capacity crowd and made her apologies as she announced her immediate retirement.

She stamped down her outrage and forced her thoughts back to the day she met Wilson. Normally, she was long gone before students arrived for their lessons, but she'd been learning a new piece and was oblivious to her surroundings until her uncle placed a gentle hand on her shoulder.

Hildy nodded. "Yeah, I remember. My uncle cajoled me into accompanying you, and afterwards, you walked me to the library." That wasn't all he'd done that afternoon. He'd touched her, held her, oh, and he'd kissed her. She'd been emotionally ill-equipped to handle the unfamiliar feelings, and she'd successfully avoided further contact with him. Until now.

"That's right." Wilson's smile morphed into that irresistible lop-sided grin. He paused, his eyes swept across the empty table top and then back to her face. "How about I grab us a drink and we can catch up?"

Hildy silently cursed temptation and lied. "If you don't mind, I'd prefer to be on my own."

Wilson lifted an eyebrow. "Are you positive?"

From the corner of her eye Hildy saw the elderly couple walk in. Fuck. Georg and Martha. The universe was definitely not on her side today. They headed straight for her and she needed Wilson gone. Now. She'd survived a lot over the years, but she couldn't handle being humiliated by them in front of the only guy she'd ever met who could matter. "Absolutely. Now, if you don't mind...?"

To her horror, he pulled out the chair next her and sat. Then it was too late. They stood before her, and she couldn't do anything but ride out the oncoming shit-storm.

"Brunehilde." She could hear the sneer in his voice, and she tried not to cringe at the use of her full name. "I should have known you'd show up where you're not welcome. But then, you never were a smart girl, so I'll spell it out for you in short, simple words. Get the fuck out, you selfish cunt." Hildy stared blankly at the wall and mentally assumed the fetal position, prepared for the rest of Georg's tirade.

"That's enough. Nobody speaks to Hildy like that. Go find somewhere else to spew your toxic feculence." It was Wilson's dangerously quiet voice that yanked Hildy from her safe place. She looked over to see her uninvited guest had risen to his feet, towering over the couple as he upbraided them.

"How dare you," Martha sputtered, "is that how you were taught to speak to your elders?"

"No, this is how I was taught to stick up for someone who is being bullied. Age, gender, and relationship are irrelevant."

Hildy could barely keep her jaw off the floor. The only person who ever effectively stood up to them in her defence was dead.

"Well, I never. I don't need to stand here and be insulted like this. Come on Georg, let's go find somewhere to sit." Martha dragged Georg with her as she stalked off towards an empty table.

Sully arrived moments later. "I'm sorry, sweetie, I got side-tracked. Are you okay? They weren't invited, but I should have known they'd show up anyway."

"I'm fine." Hildy angled her head towards Wilson. "Besides, your buddy here delivered a most righteous smack-down."

Sully grinned. "Damn, and I missed it."

"Yes, you did. I might fill you in on the all the juicy details over dinner one night this week, if you're buying." Hildy batted her eyelashes and shot Sully a cheeky smile.

"Deal. Now, I've got to get this show on the road." Sully leaned in to give Hildy a kiss on the cheek and whispered, "I know you need some space, but let him stay, sweets. Trust me."

"I'll consider it."

"Good enough. You're up first. I figured you'd prefer to get it all done and out of the way."

After all these years, she shouldn't be surprised at his ability to anticipate her needs. Her uncle taught him well. She choked back her tears. "Thank you."

As he was leaving, Sully pointed to Wilson and said, "Trust. Me."

Wilson's gentle touch on her shoulder felt nice in a way that still scared her. "Hildy, what can I do?"

Dammit, she needed him to go away. "Look, I appreciate you sticking up for me, but I can take care of myself. Now, if you don't mind, I really do want to be left alone"

"Hildy, whether you realise it or not, what you want is not necessarily what you need. I'll sit here quietly and you can pretend to be alone if you like, but you need a buffer."

"Why do men always think they know what's best for me?"

"Honey, I just watched you disappear inside yourself. I wouldn't leave anyone open to more of that kind of abuse. It's clear you're hurting, and I only want to give you a safe environment in which to cope. Can you let me do that?"

She was torn, but her intense urge to run home and bundle up in her blanket was eclipsed by love and respect for her uncle. She had come emotionally prepared to deal with Georg and Martha, but this handsome, kind, annoying man had thrown her off, and now she felt vulnerable. Wilson's voice interrupted her inner turmoil.

"Stop, you're going to give yourself an aneurysm. Just breathe. I'm going to get you some water, but before I leave, I'm going to give you a quick kiss on the lips because I think an implied relationship might help keep those ass-hats at bay."

Hildy didn't have time to respond before his lips grazed her own. All those lonely nights she lay awake remembering the feel of his kisses did nothing to prepare her for the riot this one incited between her thighs. It was the first good feeling she'd had in days. She stole glance at Martha and Georg, and took some perverse pleasure at their indignant scowls. Maybe company wasn't a bad idea. Besides, he was still awfully pretty to look at, and maybe she'd score another kiss or two. She wished she could take him home for a good fuck, but he was her long-time crush and she didn't do relationships. Hell, she didn't even do all night, and she was willing to bet he did both.

"Here you go."

Hildy snapped out of her daydream and managed a small smile for Wilson as he set the water in front of her. "Thank you."

He trailed a finger down her cheek. "You're welcome."

His small gesture created a big wet spot in her panties and an even bigger lump in her belly. She didn't know how to process touching like this. Too scary. A kiss would have been better. She could handle kissing. Fuck, company was such a bad idea. "You haven't asked me who they are."

"No, I haven't. Like everything else, you'll tell me when you're ready. Now, hush. I promised to just sit here and let you be."

Ready? She was never ready, but she'd opened the door, and it was time to shove Wilson through it. "Not your typical meet the parents, was it?"

"Your parents? Are you fucking shitting me?"

Hildy cringed slightly before straightening and lifting her chin. "I wish I were, but there it is. I didn't even rate a booby prize in the parent lottery."

"I guess not, and I'm sorry for that." Wilson cupped her cheek and leaned in for another kiss. "It looks like things are going to get started soon. Is there anything you need before it gets crazy?"

What the fuck? People couldn't dump her fast enough after meeting her parents. This was one man Hildy did not know how to handle. He said and did all the right things. How could he possibly know what she needed when she didn't even know herself?

"No, thank you. My uncle asked me to come out of retirement and perform tonight, just for him. It's been a long time since I've had an audience, so, I'm going to need a few minutes to myself to get my head screwed on straight."

"Whatever you need."

Hildy took some deep breaths in an effort to calm down. Damn Uncle Erich anyway for making her promise to do this. Why did he have to get sick and die? Life was so fucking unfair. She didn't realise she was crying until she felt the tears being wiped from her face. She looked at Wilson and tried to smile.

"It's okay, sweetie, you go ahead and let it out."

"Later. I'll let it out later. I really do need to get my shit together. The worst thing I can do is fuck this up with my parents right there."

Wilson stroked her cheek as he gazed into her eyes. "What's your favourite colour?"

"What?"

He winked and shot her that sexy lopsided grin of his. "Work with me here."

Against her better judgement, Hildy gave in and played along. "Dark purple, what's yours?"

"That pretty shade of hazel I see when I look into your eyes."

"Feeding me lines of bullshit is not helpful."

"Sweetheart, I don't bullshit. Ever. Favourite thing to have for supper?"

"Hmmm," Hildy tapped her chin as she considered, "chicken sandwiches with mayonnaise and cranberry sauce."

Wilson laughed. "That's lunch."

"It's whatever I want it to be. So there." Hildy grinned and stuck her tongue out.

"You're awfully cheeky. If you were mine, there might be consequences for display like that."

"Well, I'm not yours." Hildy paused, then curiosity got the better of her. "But if I were, what kind of consequences?"

"Oh honey, this is not the kind of conversation I had in mind. Not yet, anyway."

Hildy had known Sully her whole life; she knew precisely what sorts of shenanigans his quintet got up to in Finn's basement, and she had a pretty good idea what Wilson meant by consequences. Surprisingly, she found the prospect arousing, but Wil was right about this not being where her head should be right now. She squeezed her legs together and tried not to squirm, but that wet spot in her panties kept growing.

Her focus shifted as Sully's voice drifted through the sound system. "May I have your attention, everyone." Once the room was silent, he continued, "We're here to celebrate the life of Erich Klein. I know most of you were unaware of his illness, and his death came as a shock. That's how he wanted it. Shortly before he died, Erich sat me down and gave me a long list of orders to be executed upon his death and threatened to haunt me silly if I didn't. Needless to say, the miserable bugger has kept me hopping from the moment he kicked the bucket.

"As you can see," Sully pointed at the glass box on the bar, "I've burnt the body, but only because I couldn't convince the undertaker to embalm him with good single malt scotch. Make sure you have a drink with him and tell him a funny story.

"Erich had three absolute loves in his life. Ted, music, and Hildy. He lost Ted in their third year of university, back when gay-bashing wasn't a hate-crime. With Ted gone, he buried himself in the deepest part of the closet, music his only joy. Then Hildy came along and filled the hole in his heart.

"At Erich's request, Hildy has agreed perform *Gounod's Funeral March of a Marionette*. For the non-music geeks here today, you may recognise it as the theme music from the TV show, *Alfred Hitchcock Presents.*"

Hildy had known this moment was coming for days, but she still felt woefully unprepared. As she stood, Wilson took her hand and kissed her knuckles. "You'll be fine sweetheart. I'll be right here when you're done."

Hildy forced herself towards the piano. Her heart was broken, but her uncle didn't want her to be sad. She thought back to all his other seemingly impossible edicts, and almost smiled. As she reached the performance area, Sully gave her a gentle hug and whispered, "It'll be fine. He loved you. Now give him everything you've got."

Before settling at the piano, Hildy looked up into Sully's watery eyes. "Thanks."

As soon as she played the first notes, the people and the room no longer existed for her. There was only the piano, and the music. The tightness in her chest eased, and she felt just a little less sad. Her uncle had an uncanny ability to give her what she needed. Even in death.

Wilson watched as Hildy poured herself into the music. He thought back to the unforgivable way her parents treated her. He stole a glance at the couple in question and wasn't surprised to see them sporting identical scowls. Fuck 'em.

He was glad he'd made that split-second decision to shield Hildy from that noxious pair of wank-stains, and he didn't consider it a hardship to continue. That glint in her eye when she asked him about consequences was promising. He wasn't opposed to a little funishment. Damn. Her long legs and luscious lips had him more than interested, but the way she caressed that piano made him wish his cock were the ivory beneath her fingers. No doubt every other man in the room had similar thoughts.

With the decay of the final note, Wilson hurried to meet Hildy and escort her back to their table. His drive to protect her was strong, but the broken look on her face during the incident with her parents had him almost feral.

Sully thanked Hildy, and Wilson gathered her close, planting a kiss the top of her head. "That was beautiful, love." He kept his arm around her as he guided her along. Before she could take her seat, he parked himself on his own and pulled her onto his lap. He was quick to wrap his arms around her and tuck her head beneath his chin. He breathed easy once he felt her body relax. "There you go, sweetheart, just rest." With a nod of reassurance to Sully, Wilson hugged Hildy a little tighter and rocked her back and forth as she sobbed. "Let it out, love, I've got you, and I'll keep you safe."

Sully headed towards Wilson and Hildy as soon as he finished introducing the next performance. "Is she okay, Wil?"

"She will be. Right now she needs a cuddle and good cry."

"Agreed. Should I make other arrangements for getting home?"

"Nope, I'm a firm believer in leave with the one ya brung. That said, I think we'll be in charge of making sure Hildy gets home safely."

Hildy pulled her head back from Wilson's body. "I am perfectly capable of getting myself home safely, thank you very much."

Sully reached out and stroked her hair. "Nobody is saying otherwise, sweetheart, but it's been a difficult, emotional day, and unfortunately, it's likely to get worse before it gets better. I need you to trust me when I tell you it will get much, much better, but for now, let us support you, okay?"

With a long sigh, Hildy gave in. "Okay. I'm too wrung out to argue."

"Promise?"

"I promise."

"Good girl. Wil, I have to go up there and do more official stuff..."

"No worries, I've got her back. One thing, though. Can you give Mac a heads-up on the situation? I don't want Hildy to be alone anywhere, and I can't be with her if she needs the facilities."

"No need, she caught that little encounter with the cum infested pus bubbles and was all set to kick some ass. Your way was likely more elegant, but hers is always worth the price of admission."

"I'll die a happy man if I get through the rest of my life without feeling the sharp-side of her tongue."

"Good luck with that. Oops, that's my cue. Gotta go. Hildy, remember, Wilson is here to lean on, and you promised."

Hildy nodded and buried herself in Wilson's arms. He kissed the top of her head before resting his cheek there.

WILSON OPENED the front passenger door of his car. "In you get, Hildy. Sully can sit in the back."

"I don't mind taking the back seat. Sully's injured, so he should get the front."

"Not a chance, I had to put up with him in the front the whole way here. He's notorious for back-seat driving, so he may as well be appropriately located."

"I thought you liked me, Wilson," Sully complained.

"I do like you, but given the choice between a hot woman and you sitting next me, you're going to lose every single time."

Hildy's face flushed and she dropped her gaze to the ground.

"Now look what you did," Sully accused.

"It's fine, Sully, really. Stop fussing. One minute you act like Wilson is the best thing that could possibly happen to me, and the next you're behaving like he's an axe-murderer."

"You know me, I'm not happy unless I'm fussing."

"Well, yeah, but stop it." Hildy demanded.

"Get in the car. I hurt, and I want to go home."

"Oh god." Wilson turned to Hildy. "Do you mind if we drop Sully off first? I'd like to get home before dawn."

Hildy chuckled. "Nope, I'm all for self-preservation, and this will minimise how much complaining we both have to endure."

"Seriously? You too, Hildy?"

"Oh, suck it up, you big baby," Wilson ordered. "It's been almost six weeks since you broke those ribs. If you can't handle a ride in the car, how do you expect to be ready to play in time for all the Valentine's gigs?"

"I'll manage just fine as long as you don't add to the damage now."

"Oh for fuck's sake. Get in the back and be quiet or we'll visit every pot-hole and speed bump in the city before I drop you right back here and you can get a cab home." Wilson lifted his eyebrows. "Still want to bitch about my driving?"

Sully clamped his lips shut and slid into the back of the car.

Hildy sniggered. "Thanks, Wilson. I am SO

making a special note of this. I don't think I've ever seen anyone shut Sully up so effectively without a ball-gag."

"Ball-gag? Tell me it's true and there is photographic evidence." Wilson glanced up at the rear-view mirror for Sully's reaction. Nothing. Damn him and that inscrutable face of his. He turned his head for a quick look at Hildy and not only knew she told the truth, but whip poker with her would be oodles of fun. "Well, is there?"

"No comment," Hildy said as she turned her face towards the passenger side window.

Wilson snuck another quick glance in the rear-view mirror, and was sure he saw a flash of relief in Sully's eyes. Interesting. This would be worth pursuing.

The ride to Sully's place was quiet and uneventful, but once Sully was safely indoors, that changed. Wilson drove a few blocks and parked the car. He turned to Hildy, and with a penetrating stare, he began his interrogation.

"You had to know I wouldn't let this one go, so I suggest you give in gracefully and tell me all there is to know about Sully wearing a ball-gag."

"I have nothing to tell you."

Wilson's eyes flashed. "That's complete bullshit. Let's get one thing straight, right now. You do not lie to me. Ever. Not even little tiny white ones meant to avoid hurt feelings. Are we clear?"

"You're in no position to make demands of me. In addition, Mr. Hypocrite, you sit there and tell me never to lie to you, but your implication of a relationship to keep Martha and Georg off my back sure smells like a lie to me."

"True, it was certainly a lie by implication, but I lied to a pair of bullies with whom I have no obligation of trust so I could protect a woman with whom I am interested in exploring a trusting relationship."

"Look, while I appreciate what you did to protect me, our implied relationship ended the moment we left the Squeaky Wheel. Now, if you don't mind, I'm tired and I'd like to go home."

"Regardless of whether we're romantically involved or not, we now have a relationship of a sort, and I will accept nothing less than the truth from you."

"Our relationship, whatever it may be, ends the moment I get out of this car, which will be here and now if we're not moving in the next ten seconds."

"Hold on..."

"Eight...seven..."

Wilson started the car and eased onto the road. "Can we at least talk whilst I'm driving?"

"No. I just want to get home. It's been a long, tedious day."

"Okay, quiet it is."

Wilson briefly considered taking the long way to Hildy's house in case she might be tempted to engage in some conversation, but if he were to have any chance with her, he needed to play it completely straight. Even in the silence, the ten minutes it took to get Hildy home sped by too quickly and left Wilson wanting more.

"Thanks for the ride."

"You're welcome, sweetheart." Wilson got out of the car along with Hildy.

"What are you doing?"

"Making sure you get home safely. Just go with it and let me be the gentleman my mother thinks she raised."

Hildy rolled her eyes and sped up the path to her house, Wilson keeping pace beside her. Once Hildy had the door open, Wilson placed his hands on her upper arms and gently turned her towards him. "Since our relationship is about to turn into a pumpkin, may I please have one last kiss?"

"Good grief, Wilson, will you give it up already?"

"I'm persistent. It's one of my many redeeming qualities."

"Oh, what the hell. One kiss."

Wilson gathered Hildy into his arms. He touched his lips her forehead, her nose, and finally to her lips before trailing his tongue along the seam of her mouth. She opened to him and he deepened the kiss, tangling his tongue with hers in between teasing sucks and nips. When Wilson finally eased way from Hildy, he studied her face and smiled. She was just as affected. "What time shall I pick you up in the morning to get your car?"

"You don't need to do that. I can manage on my own."

"I won't leave you stranded for tomorrow. So, what time would you like me to pick you up in the morning?"

Hildy huffed. "Can you be here by eight-fifteen? I have a student at nine."

"I'll be here. Goodnight, sweetheart. Now, go inside and lock the door. I'm not moving from this spot until you do."

"You are awfully bossy."

"It comes with the territory. You'll get used to it."

"Cocky much?"

"Go."

"Alright, I'm going, I'm going."

Once he heard the deadbolt snick into place, Wilson returned to his car and headed home. He'd known she'd be at Erich's wake, but he hadn't been prepared for how intensely attracted he still was to her. He thought back to that afternoon when they were teenagers. He was pretty sure he'd been her first kiss. Damn, he'd wanted to be her first everything, but he never saw her again. He didn't need to be her first anymore, but he did want to be her only.

TWO

Hildy opened the door to a far too cheery looking Wilson. "Seriously? It's not even seven-thirty. Nobody has a right to look that happy this early in the morning. I'm sure we agreed you'd pick me up at eight-fifteen."

"While I am a trifle early, I do come bearing coffee and croissants."

She'd had a restless night and she wanted to stay irritated, but couldn't. "Actually, I slept though my alarm. Now I get to start my day with both breakfast and caffeine. Thank you."

"Does this mean I've earned a good morning kiss?"

"You are incorrigible."

"So my mother keeps telling me. I'm still waiting for my answer."

Hildy considered his request. His kisses tested her self-control to the limit, and last night she'd been on the verge of inviting him in. However, giving him quick peck on the lips should be okay. "Only if you let me drink my coffee in peace. I am not a morning person."

Wilson's ability give her the quiet she needed to prepare herself for the day ahead was a relief. The very few men she'd woken up with had been incapable. Oh, they'd be quiet for a minute or two when she asked them, but they couldn't handle the silence. She wondered how long Wilson could hold out. He'd surprised her the previous evening when he'd complied with her request for a quiet journey home, but that was only ten minutes.

Then she realised he wouldn't ask about Sully and the ball-gags as long as he was being quiet. If she could keep this up until she got to her car, she'd be off the hook. No looking for ways to tell the truth without giving anything away. She picked off pieces of the croissant and slipped them into her mouth between sips of coffee. Then it hit her. He knew how she took it. Sully was such a blabbermouth. She finished her breakfast and drained her cup.

"Right, I need to jump in the shower and throw some clothes on, then I'll be ready to go." Hildy leaned in and gave Wilson the kiss he'd earned. Damn, he made her tingle all over. She pulled away quickly, he was far too tempting.

WILSON REMAINED silent for the short journey back

to the Squeaky Wheel. Hildy needed space. He could give her that, and it allowed him time to consider her other needs. His long conversation with Sully the previous night had given him a better idea of who Hildy was, but even Sully, who knew her best, was not privy to all that made her tick.

"Thanks for the ride, I appreciate it."

"You're most welcome. I'm sure I'll see you around."

"Yeah, maybe, but don't count on it."

"Would you like to bet on it?"

"Nope, the only luck I have is generally very bad. Now, I need to go or I'm going to be late."

"Alright, no betting. A kiss and hug goodbye?"

"No hug. Just a quick kiss." Hildy amended.

"A quick kiss, then. "Wilson's eyes never left hers as he took her face in his hands, and when their lips touched, he needed more. His instincts took over and he was lost. He wrapped his arms around her and tried to deepen the kiss, his tongue coaxing her to open for him.

He knew he'd screwed up the moment he'd done it, but by then, it was too late. Hildy yanked back and scrambled out of the car. She poked her head back in. "Silly me, I thought you might be different, but you really are a hypocrite. You agree to one thing and do another, just like most everyone else I've ever met. I don't ever want to see you again." She slammed the door and stalked to her car.

Wilson waited until she'd driven off before restarting his vehicle. He'd meant to return home, but instead, he ended up at Sully's.

———

HE LAUNCHED into his tale of woe the moment the door opened. "I fucked up, and now I need your help."

"You'd best come in, then." Sully stepped aside and allowed Wilson to pass, then followed him into the kitchen. He poured them each a cup of coffee and joined Wil at the table. A long sip later, he asked, "What did you do?" Sully remained silent until Wil finished telling him of his morning encounter with Hildy.

"Fuck, fuck, fuck. Goddammit, Wil. You're the epitome of patience, and never impulsive. I warned you last night to tread very, very carefully. She let you touch and hold her — something I've never seen her let anyone do besides Erich and me. I thought you might actually be someone with whom she could feel safe enough with to involve herself romantically."

"I have no excuse. That rocket clearly exploded before lift-off, so now I need to fix this for both of us."

"I don't know, Wil. Your fuck-up pretty much squandered my credibility. I told her she could trust you and you made a liar out of me." Sully closed his eyes and tapped his chin with his forefinger. "Give me a few days to see what I can do. In the meantime, stay away from her and don't come over here without calling first."

He was so ridiculously desperate, he'd have agreed to perform their next concert wearing nothing but a cock-ring. "Okay."

"Good boy."

"That's hilarious coming from a Dom whose mouth is, apparently, no stranger to a ball-gag."

Sully's expression gave nothing away. "Pure speculation on your part."

"Maybe, but I don't think so."

"Whatever. Now, fuck off, I've got to go slip into my superhero persona. I have relationships to rescue."

Wilson snorted. "Superhero! Dream on, Sully."

"I still owe Mac two favours to be named later. If I pull this off, they become your responsibility."

"Deal. Keep me updated. It's going to kill me sitting at home wondering what's going on."

"Yes, yes. Now, piss off, I have plans to make."

Wilson got up to leave and paused. "I'm sorry I fucked up, Sully. If nothing else, I hope you can salvage your relationship with Hildy."

"She and I have been friends her whole life, I doubt she'll ditch my ass over this. However, she will probably make me suffer for a bit, and that's okay, I'll take it out on you." Wilson nodded and left.

Hildy stared at the ringing phone. She was tempted to let it go to voice-mail, but she knew he'd just keep calling until she answered.

"Hello, Sully, you rat-bastard. You're lucky I bothered to answer." She flopped onto the sofa and put her feet up on the coffee table.

"Well, I'm glad you did. I have some business that requires your attention. Can you swing by tonight?"

"Can't we do it over the phone?"

"No, there's paperwork and signatures involved. Besides, I can start atoning for my sins by providing you with a yummy supper."

"Pizza from Cheeses Crust?"

"Is there anywhere else?"

"Just you and me?"

"If by just you and me, you mean no Wilson, then yes, just us. I made him promise to stay away. Good enough?"

"I can live with that."

"Thank you. Can we talk about what happened today?"

Hildy groaned. "Do we have to?"

"No, but I feel responsible. I shouldn't have trusted anyone else with your safety."

Sometimes, he really was an over-protective dolt. "You buffoon, safety wasn't the issue. Trust was the issue, and while Wilson had managed to earn a little, he pissed it away in the space of a heartbeat."

"And he knew it the very moment he did it. With

most people, I wouldn't bother advocating a second chance, but I've known him a very long time. I have seen him at both his strongest, and his most vulnerable. This is the first time I've known him to be impulsive. That tells me that there's something about you that short-circuited his rigid self-control."

And there he was, back to meddlesome. "Stop right there, Sully. I wasn't interested in him before he proved himself a hypocrite, so why would I open myself up to him now?"

"I'm not suggesting you marry the guy, or even date him. Just give him a chance to show you he's a pretty good guy who sometimes makes mistakes, but will always do everything he can to fix them."

"To be honest, Sully, I wasn't going to ever see him again regardless of whether he fucked-up or not. I'll admit to a bit of an interesting spark. But I'm smart enough to know it is nothing more than an emotional reaction to grief combined with the knight in shining armour routine he pulled when my parents showed up. Sleep took care of that."

"Okay, I won't push for you to socialise with him, but will you let him get his trustworthiness back to zero?"

"He did save my ass this morning. You told him to show up with breakfast and coffee, didn't you?" Hildy wondered why Sully was pushing this so hard.

"Busted. I gave Finn help when it came to Mac, so

it was only fair to give Wil a little guidance on navigating the maze that is Hildy Klein."

"You are nothing but a hopeless romantic. How about you stop trying to make matches for your friends and work a little harder on one for yourself. It's time you stop being a man-slut and settle down with a nice little switch."

"You didn't say anything to Wilson about my occasional side-trips to the ouchy end of the hitty-stick, did you?"

"Of course not. Nobody's business but yours. I'm sorry I let that bit about the ball-gag slip out last night."

"Ah, the truth comes out. You're drowning in guilt for almost outing me. I thought your forgiveness was a little too easily won. A word of warning, sweetie, you'll need to be on your guard with Wil over your little slip. He brought it up with me today, so he's not going to let it go."

"You know, Sully, if you'd just come clean with the group, neither of us would have to watch our mouths. What's the big deal?"

"Dominant Cord. That doesn't exactly scream four Doms and a switch, does it?"

Hildy let out a long, exasperated breath. "You are such an idiot. You said it yourself, occasional trips. That doesn't make you less of a Dom. What's with the identity crisis?"

"I don't know. Maybe it's because I haven't played

in weeks, and these broken ribs make me feel less-than."

"Whiner. Hurry up and get healed so you can pick up a hitty-stick and strike terror in the backsides of subbies everywhere."

"Are you sure you're not kinky?"

"Nope, not a bit. What time's supper?"

"I'll order for about six, but how about you be here for five so we can go through the paperwork first, then relax."

"There really is paperwork? I thought you were making up a reason for me to come over."

"While I did want you to come over, I was not going to fuck up by giving you a bullshit story. You're Erich's sole beneficiary, and there is a whole bunch of paperwork I need to go through with you. I'll see you later."

"See ya." Hildy disconnected the call and set her phone down on the sofa. She thought back to Sully's question about being kinky. Her answer was automatic, but no longer fully honest. Great, she'd flat-out lied to Sully. Another thing to feel guilty over. Sully'd been regularly asking her that same question for so many years, the answer was out before she'd taken last night's conversation with Wilson into account.

Consequences. Before Wil had brought the subject up, she hadn't felt more than mild curiosity about the sorts of activities Sully and his friends engaged in. But as soon as Wil had said mine, and consequences, she was done for.

As much as she wanted to pretend she hadn't developed an interest in the kinky side of life, she knew she'd have to come clean with Sully. He'd been telling her for years she'd change her tune one day. It was just her luck one day happened to be at her uncle's funeral. She glanced at the clock, plenty of time to have a long, hot soak in the tub. Her week had gone to shit in a handbag when Sully told her of her uncle's death, and that handbag had to have the interior proportions of a TARDIS, because the shit just kept on coming.

Hildy twisted the taps on the tub, and after a couple of minutes checked the temperature with her hand. Cold. She turned off the cold, and on discovering there was no hot water, she was ready to give up and go to bed. She was tempted to call Sully and cancel, but if she gave her inability to bathe as an excuse, he'd just tell her to come early and bathe there. Aw hell, she wanted a nice hot bath, and considering the big gift of 'I told you so' she was about to bestow upon him, the least Sully could do was supply her with a tub full of hot water for a couple of hours. She shut off the faucet and went in search of her phone.

<hr>

"ARE YOU EVER COMING OUT? You take the most epic baths of anyone I've ever known."

Hildy groaned, marked her place, and set her book on the closed lid of the toilet. "I'll be down in fifteen minutes, now leave me be."

"Hurry up, I'm tired of having a naked woman in my house and not being able to play with her."

Maybe she was right to wait until after her bath to give him his 'I told you so' moment. While she trusted him completely, she was sure her handbag had room for more shit, and she was not about to hold it open.

She pulled the plug and stood, letting the water slide off her body and into the tub before grabbing one of Sully's thick, fluffy towels. She loved these towels. In most things, Sully was the classic, manly bachelor, but he did have the odd redeeming domestic quirk, and a closet full of plush towels was one of them. She threw on her clothes and headed down to 'fess up to Sully."

"Hey gorgeous. Feel better?"

"A little."

"Aw, sweetie, come sit down. What's wrong?"

There was no holding back; her confession gushed from her lips. "I lied to you. When I said I had no interest in kink, I lied. There's really no excuse for it, but it had been the truth for so long, when you asked the usual question, I gave you my usual answer and once it was out, I didn't know what to do..."

Sully finished for her. "But the guilt was eating you alive, and you just had to own up. Sweetie, thanks for your honesty. Truth is, I ask that question more because I liked to fluster you than out of self-interest. If

I were a proper gentleman, I'd leave it there, but I'm a nosy busy-body. When did it change?"

"Believe it or not, last night."

Sully's eyes twinkled. "Wilson did get to you, then?"

"He did, but what I said about not wanting to see him again was true."

"A one-eighty like that is bound to scare the beejeezus out of you, and the last thing I can imagine you'd want to do is spend time with someone who has such a profound effect on your sexuality."

"Fuck, Sully, sometimes I swear you're psychic, or something."

"Not even close. I'd say it has more to do with knowing you since we were kids. So, what happened last night that changed your mind about kink?"

"Something Wilson said."

"And..." Sully prompted.

"Damn you, Sully. Are you really going to make me tell you everything?"

"Of course I am. So, spill."

Hildy huffed. "Okay, fine. He said something to the effect of 'if you were really mine, there'd be conse-quences.' Can we drop it now?"

"Hell, no. What on earth did you do that had the potential to earn you a visit from Wil's rather inventive side?"

"I was a bit cheeky and stuck my tongue out."

Sully nodded sagely. "A word of caution. Unless

your tongue is doing delicious things to drive Wilson wild, you may want to keep it safely in your mouth. I am not kidding when I say, he has some pretty effective ways of dealing with cheeky subs who stick their tongues out inappropriately."

"Oh, please. It's safe to say it will never be a problem because I'll never be his."

"Sweetie, I don't know what I want more, for you to be right, or to eat your words. Both options have merit."

"Contrary to your self-important belief, it's not about you. Shouldn't our supper be here by now?"

THREE

HILDY GATHERED the mess of envelopes from the floor below the letter-slot and sifted through them. Mostly junk and bills, but one caught her eye. She checked the return address and briefly considered returning it to the sender. Curiosity won out. She set her morning coffee on the table and slipped her finger beneath the flap, sliding it in one smooth motion from one side to the other. She reached in with her thumb and forefinger and extracted the contents, a folded slip of paper and an old photo of her uncle playing his clarinet.

She smiled. His stance and expression were familiar, the photo was not. She spent a few minutes studying the image, making a mental note to get it framed. Finally, she unfolded the paper and read:

Dear Hildy,

I thought you'd like to have this one.

Wilson

She reread the words and smiled. It screamed Sully and his inability to keep his meddling nose out of anyone's business. She had a call to make.

"You meddlesome old fart."

"Ah the dulcet tones of my favourite piano teacher," Sully replied.

"You coached him. You gave him that photograph to send, didn't you?"

"Calm down. What are you talking about? What photograph?"

"The one of Uncle Erich."

"Sorry sweetie, I don't know what you're talking about."

"Damn."

"What's the matter?"

"I was hoping it was another one of your sneaky ploys so I could use it to justify not forgiving him."

"Why would you need to justify it? Either you do, or you don't. It's not a judgement thing."

"Damn you Sully. I hate that you know me so fucking well."

"Yes, I do, and how many times has it been to your advantage?"

"Way more than I care to admit."

"He's really got your emotions tied in knots, hasn't he?"

"Unfortunately, yes."

"I suspect that's not all he'll have tied in knots before too long."

"What's that supposed to mean?" She asked, already knowing the answer.

"One step at a time. You're interested in the kinky side of life, these days. How about you join me at Finn's next play party. I won't be up for playing, so it would give you a good, safe opportunity to see what it's about. You'll be able to watch and ask all the questions you like."

Seriously? He was expecting her to jump in with both feet and go to a fucking kink-fest? "I don't know, Sully. I don't know if I'm ready for that kind of thing."

"The next party isn't for another week, so no need to decide right away. How about I email you links to some websites with good, accurate information so you can do a little research, okay? If left to your own devices, I shudder to think what kind of freakiness you could stumble upon and scare you away before you even get started."

"I'd appreciate that, Sully. I'll admit to giving in to my curiosity a time or two. I've even gone so far as to do a search, but I've never actually had the nerve to click on any links. The little thumbnails that showed up sent me scurrying for the back-button every single time." Boy had they ever. But they stopped her from wondering.

"Wow, I never thought you had even enough curiosity to type in a search. I guess I don't know you quite as well as I like to think I do."

"Score one for me. I never thought I would see the

day where you weren't at least one step ahead of me. Look, I'm going to go. I have some thinking to do."

"I imagine you do. Give me an hour and there'll be an email bursting with kinky-linky goodness in your inbox."

"Thanks, Sully. I'll catch you later."

"So long, Sweets."

———

It had been days since he'd gone to Sully for help, and Wil's patience was wearing thin. He hadn't heard anything from Hildy either, but he hadn't expected to. He'd have sent that photo regardless of whether they were in a committed relationship or sworn enemies. No strings attached. The ringing phone caught his attention. He took a quick look at the incoming number and smiled. Finally. "Sully, you have uncanny timing. I was just thinking of calling you."

"You're an idiot. I told you to stay the hell away from her. It's only dumb fucking luck your stunt didn't backfire."

Wil walked into the kitchen and poured himself a cup of coffee. "It wasn't a stunt, Sully. I was going through some stuff, reminiscing, and as soon as I saw it, I knew she had to have it."

"Luck was with you, that's for sure. That's not why I called."

"Oh, really?"

"I had a very interesting conversation with Hildy and I'm only sharing it with you because you are relevant to it as both subject, and potential ally."

"Sully, I know you look upon yourself as a kind of fixer, but sometimes, you need to let things work out in their own way."

"Not this time." Sully paused. "That conversation you and she had about ownership and consequences piqued her curiosity, and she's interested in exploring life on the kinky side."

"I'm not surprised. Her reaction was pretty obvious, even though she tried hard to hide it."

Sully cleared his throat. "Given you seem to be the one who woke her desire to explore, I think it makes sense for you to be her guide."

"I don't know. I'm not one for taking on neophytes, even under the most clinical of circumstances." Wil took a sip of coffee and set it on the table. "Yes, she intrigues me. So much so, I made a rookie mistake that not only could have been the absolute end for anything between Hildy and me, it could have caused irreparable damage to your relationship with her."

"Give me a little credit, Wil. I wouldn't be asking this of you if I thought there was any chance you could put my relationship with Hildy at risk. I've already laid some ground-work for you and got her started on the theory portion of her education. Once I'm satisfied she's ready, you'll take care of the practical side."

"I don't know about this, Sully."

"What's to know? You are attracted to each other, and I trust you. Either it works out, or it doesn't."

"Damn it, Sully. She could get hurt emotionally."

"Yeah, she could, but I doubt it. She was destroyed emotionally by her own parents and just lost one of only two people in her life to give her unconditional love. My opinion of you would have to be seriously fucked up for you to be capable of hurting her worse than that."

Wil sighed. "I concede to your superior stubbornness. I will give it a try, but I also need to be satisfied she's ready before we venture into any physical activities."

"I can work with that."

"You said you've got her started on the theoretical. Care to enlighten me on what you mean by that?"

"I sent her links to a bunch of really good websites to get her started. I've ordered her a bunch of books for her e-reader as well. Both fiction and non-fiction. The one thing I didn't do, was send her a check-list. I thought that should be entirely between the two of you."

"Sounds like a good start. Have you spoken with her about having me be her physical guide to all things kinky?"

"Not yet. I wanted to give her time with all the written material first. I expect that will whet her appetite enough to be open to the suggestion."

"You are a sneaky bugger, you know that?"

"I'm all about the big picture. Even if things don't work out between the two of you, I know your treatment of her will put her on the road to a functional, loving, lasting relationship. She deserves that."

"Everyone deserves that. Should I not be in contact with her until you think she's ready to move forward?"

"Actually, no. I'm hoping she'll be up for accompanying me to Finn and Mac's party."

Wil exploded. "What? Are you fucking nuts?"

"Quite probably. I have two ideas from which to choose. The first option is for you attend with a sub and play as normal so Hildy can see you in action, which will hopefully allay any concerns. The second option is for you to go stag so you can pay close attention to her reactions to the activities around her."

"You wouldn't be injecting an element of jealousy in the first scenario would you?"

"Well, I don't suppose a few twinges of jealousy on her part could hurt too much."

"You are a manipulative son of a bitch, Dave Sullivan."

"True, but I have good reasons."

"I think they're better reasons when they don't involve me."

"So, option one, or option two for the play party?"

"None of the above. " Wil tried not to laugh as he proceeded to ruin his friend's plans. "I'll be doing some rope work on Mac, so that's the only place my attention will be. Besides, until you know Hildy is going to attend, I expect there are more pressing matters to handle."

"Good point. Check-list comes to mind. I think that will be the best way to introduce your role in this. Once she's finished with all the reading, I'll bring up the need for her to do a check-list and suggest she exchange with you because it would be completely squicky for her to exchange with me. This whole business is bordering on squicky for me as it is."

⁎ ⁎ ⁎

HILDY TAPPED the table with her nail as the phone on the other end continued to ring. Please don't go to voice mail.

"Hello?"

"Oh Mac, thank fuck."

"Um, who is this?"

"Shit, I'm sorry. It's Hildy Klein, Sully's friend? We met at Erich Klein's wake, and you said I could call you if I ever needed to talk."

"Oh yeah, hi Hildy. What's the matter?"

"I'm sorry to bother you, but I need someone to talk to, and Sully isn't an option." And wasn't that an understatement.

"Do you want to talk now, over the phone, or in person?"

"I think over the phone might be easier. At least you won't be able to see me blush."

"Phone it is. What's up?"

Hildy dragged her fingers through her hair. "Fuck, I don't even know where or how to start."

"Does this have anything to do with Wilson?"

"Sully and his big mouth are dead."

"Calm down, Sully never said a word. I was at your uncle's wake, remember." Mac chuckled a little. "I saw the sizzle between the two of you. Are you coming to the play party?"

"Aw bugger. I'm all new at this kinky thing. I mean really new, as in I had only vague ideas until Sully sent me all those links."

"So, you're new. We've all been new at some point."

"But, I don't know how to do any of this stuff, and what if I hate it?"

"That's what check-lists are for. Have you done one yet?"

"They've come up in some of my reading, but no, I haven't done one. It's not like I have someone to share it with."

"You don't need someone to share it with. It's a great exercise for you to gain understanding of your own sexuality. This whole thing is based on trust, and you need to trust yourself first. I'll warn you up front, if you are completely honest with yourself, some of your answers will shock, and even embarrass you. You'll be tempted to adjust your answers to be more in line with what you perceive as societal norms. Don't. You need to accept yourself and your needs. If you don't, you'll never be satisfied, and honey, there is a lot to be said for satisfaction."

Hildy was more curious than ever. "Where do I find one?"

"There are all kinds available, but I'll email you a copy of the one Finn and I used. It's the same one the rest of Dominant Cord uses, so should you get the opportunity to exchange lists with Wilson, you'll be ahead of the game. Fair warning, it's explicit and I don't think it leaves any kink or fetish unexplored."

"Thanks, Mac. I feel a little better now."

"Good. You still haven't told me if you're coming to the next play party."

"God, no. I don't even know if I could do this in private. How could I possibly do it in public?"

"I get that. It took me quite a while before I was willing to play at one of Finn's parties. I only observed at the first on. The next few after that, Finn and I played beforehand and I continued to observe at the party. Of course, Finn being Finn, concessions have a price. He was lenient the first couple of times. But once I'd become more comfortable with the group generally, and playing with him in particular, the deal was, I could keep some clothes on if I played, but none if I watched. By the time I finally participated fully, I didn't need clothes to play because I was already used to being seen without them."

"But that's so mean."

"It is, and it isn't. For me it's not, because Finn has proven to me time and again that he can be trusted to know what I need and provide it using whatever method he deems necessary. In return, I have proven capable of appropriately using my safewords, yellow when I need a minute or to change something, and red to bail completely. In our house, safewords work for everything, not just kinky sex."

Hildy took a deep breath and let it out. "It's all so overwhelming."

"That's true of most things when you're first learning. I bet Sully bombarded you with tonnes of material to read, didn't he?"

"Did he ever. Of course, I've read it all, a lot of it more than once."

Mac laughed. "Of course you did, and I bet those parts you reread are the ones that got you all hot and bothered and thinking about Wilson, weren't they?"

Heat flooded Hildy's cheeks and she was thankful Mac couldn't see her. "No comment."

"That's an excellent start. I need to go run some errands, but before I leave, I'll fire off that check-list to you so you can get started on it. I'll call you later to see how you're doing. Okay?"

"That would be great. Thanks for all your help, Mac. I really appreciate you taking the time."

"It's nothing. I'm so glad you thought of me. I'd hate for you to be trying to figure this all on your own.

Promise you'll call when you need someone to talk to, okay?"

"I promise. I'll let you get to your errands."

"Remember ,trust and accept yourself whilst filling out the check-list. There are no right or wrong answers to those questions for anyone but you."

"Thanks Mac, I'll talk to you soon."

"See ya."

Hildy trekked to the kitchen to make herself a cup of tea and a snack in anticipation of the mysterious check-list. What a relief she'd managed to find a woman she could talk to about this crazy stuff without fear of being judged. She had some idea of Mac's past, and she was sure Mac had knowledge of her own. They couldn't both be such close friends with Sully and not expect some aspects of their lives to bleed through. She wished she'd met Mac sooner, but it was hardly surprising she hadn't, knowing what she did about Mac's many years of isolation.

WIL RECOGNISED the number on the incoming call. More meddling, no doubt.

"Mac, what a surprise. To what do I owe the pleasure?"

"What are your intentions toward Hildy?"

"Excuse me?"

"You heard me."

"I answer to nobody, sub."

"You can fuck that for a lark, Wil. The only person on the planet who can boss me around is Finn, although, I do let Sully believe he has that kind of power. Seriously, Wil, what's the deal?"

"Why do you want to know?"

"I just got off the phone after having a very interesting conversation with her and I need to know how best to proceed."

"Why didn't you call Sully?"

"Because Sully is effectively her family, and one does not ask family for advice on how to advise another family member as regards the realm of all things kinky. Let's face it, there is a very real possibility of you becoming her Dom."

"When did relationship by committee get enacted?"

"Oh for fuck's sake, Wil, stop being ridiculous."

"Hang on just a minute. I've got Sully essentially telling me I have to be her Dom, and then I have you pestering me for advice on how to deal with Hildy because you figure I'm going to be her Dom. While I did agree to a trial on the physical aspects with Hildy, I only agreed to do this after Sully has her fully prepared. How you got mixed up in all this, I can't begin to understand."

"That part is easy. Sully sent Hildy a whole pile of material to read, which she did. It made her so confused and crazy, she didn't know where to turn. Fortunately for you two bozos, she called me, and I set her straight. For the moment, anyway. Now, I called you for some guidance on how best to help your new sub navigate her journey through the land of kink. Are you going to help, or do you want to take your chances on my judgement?"

"To be fair, you have excellent judgement, and I could reasonably trust you to handle this on your own. That said, you did ask for my input, so I am happy to help where I can."

"Good. Hildy is worried about being a newbie. She's freaked about not knowing what to do, how to act, and I think more importantly, that she won't like it. I asked her if she'd filled out a check-list and she hadn't. I can't imagine this was neglected on purpose, so I sent her the standard one used by Dominant Cord members."

"Dammit."

"Please don't tell me it wasn't a simple over-sight on Sully's part."

"It was rather carefully orchestrated on his part, actually."

"Then he's a buffoon, and you aren't much better for agreeing to it."

"What did you tell her?"

"We talked about trust, and how she had to trust herself first. I told her to be honest with herself and accept her answers without considering anyone else because as far as the rest of the world is, there are no right or wrong answers."

"See, this is exactly why trust your judgement. I think you handled that perfectly. Thank you for doing this. I have a feeling our original plan could have back-fired big time. Maybe Sully and I should leave Hildy's education entirely to you."

"Oh no you don't. You're not getting off that easily. I think you will need to get involved long before there is likely to be any physical activities. I asked her if she was going to attend the play party. She declined, but I think I may be able to persuade her to come. That is, if you two dolts don't fuck it up."

"Dammit, I've never felt so useless about dealing with a woman in my life. I keep doing all the wrong things, and the thing that makes me crazy is this time I think getting it right really matters. For both of us."

"The good news is, she seems to want to get it right for both of you too. I told her to fill out the check-list and I'd call her tonight to talk about it. I would humbly suggest you fill out a shiny new check-list of your own."

"Yeah. Thanks, Mac. I'm glad Hildy has you looking out for her."

"No worries. I'll talk to you later."

"See ya." Wilson ended the call and sat for a moment to let the conversation sink in. Hildy was defi-nitely interested, but feeling self-conscious about her inexperience. Fuck. He wasn't just feeding Sully a line when he said he wasn't into playing with newbies. He liked experienced subs he could trust to know their limits. However, he was surprised to find he hated the idea of anyone else touching her, more than he feared fucking it all up for both of them. Mac said to fill out a new check-list, so he'd best get to it. He hadn't known Mac very long, but so far, she'd shown herself to be smart and wise, with a huge heart.

HILDY WASN'T GENERALLY one to procrastinate, but she had been dreading this call from the moment she'd made her decision.

"Hi Sully, how are you?"

"I'm great, Hildy. How about you? I understand you spoke with Mac."

"I'm fine and yes, Mac and I talked."

"Anything you want to ask me?"

"Nope."

"Will you be joining me at Finn and Mac's this evening?"

She forced herself to speak. "Um, yeah."

"Great, Wilson and I'll be there to pick you up at six."

"But the party doesn't start until half-seven."

"Yeah, but Wilson will have to drive slowly, and this way you can have some time with Mac before the others arrive."

"Sully?"

"What's the matter, kiddo?"

"I know it's none of my business, but..."

Hildy was grateful Sully didn't make her finish the question before answering. "No, sweetie, Wil is not bringing a playmate. That doesn't mean he won't play tonight, though."

"If he doesn't bring someone, then who would he play with?"

"Calm down, you've got a way to go before there's any chance of you playing with anyone. Sometimes Doms, particularly those who have specialised skills, will help another Dom with his sub. Wil is particularly skilled at rope bondage, and occasionally he is called upon to demonstrate a technique or even do all the rope-work so a Dom is able to concentrate on doing other things to his sub."

"Oh." That didn't answer her question, but she wasn't going to ask it a second time.

"By the way, bring your check-list with you."

"News flash, Sully, you aren't getting so much as a peek at my check-list, so I think it's just as well it stays here."

"Honey, For your own safety, someone besides your Dom will need to know exactly what's on that list. Even the most experienced Doms can make a mistake, overlook a limit, or get caught up in the moment. At times like that, even the most experienced sub could fail to safeword, but the risk is so much higher with someone who is inexperienced. You've even admitted to feeling self-conscious about your lack of knowledge and experience. It's those kinds of feelings that could stop a sub from safewording when she really should because she doesn't want to be judged as lacking. Who better than someone who has no sexual interest in you to ensure the scene goes as smoothly as possible?"

"I get it," Hildy said, "but I don't want you to know what turns me on."

"Honey, I don't want to know what turns you on, either, but I sure as fuck want to know what turns you off. I understand, I really do. I promise only to look at the soft and hard limits. I want your experiences to be positive so you can assess your feelings fairly. Most importantly, I want you to have fun and feel great."

"Jeez. It'll be like telling my brother my innermost sexual fantasies."

"I'll try hard not to make it like that. Look on it like I'm a referee at a sporting event. My purpose is to know the rules and make sure everybody plays by them. In this case, the rules are your soft and hard limits. Okay?"

"I'm still not comfortable with this."

"I know, but I love you, and I won't trust your absolute safety in this to anyone but myself. So, either I get a copy, or you don't play."

"I could go to a club," Hildy threatened.

"Not unless you want that bottom of yours every colour of the rainbow. Going to Mac with questions is great, but I draw the line at you looking outside the safety of the quintet to explore the world of kink. Most people adhere to Safe, Sane and Consensual, but it's not a risk I'm going to let you take."

"You are such a control-freak, Sully."

"I love you, and want you to have only the good things in life. I consider the right kink with the right person, or people to be one of those good things, and I'll do what I can to make it happen for you."

"Thank you. I know, deep down, you only want my happiness. I still have a hard time accepting there are people who wish me good rather than harm."

"I know, but you'll get there. I'm going to go now, and I'll see you at six."

"Okay, have a great rest of your afternoon." Hildy waited for the click before she put her phone down. When she'd filled out that damn check-list, she hadn't expected Sully would want to see it. She wondered if she had time to change it, but even as the thought entered her head, she heard Mac telling her to be truthful with herself and there were no right or wrong answers. Besides, Sully did say he would only pay attention to the stuff that turned her off. He'd never let her down before, so she'd trust him.

Fuck. She reached for her phone and dialled. She didn't wait for Mac to say hello. "I need help."

"Oh, sweetie, what can I do?"

"I don't have a clue what to wear tonight."

"Wear whatever you feel comfortable in. You're not playing, and I can assure you, everyone will be too occupied with their own situation to pay any attention to you, or what you're wearing. I know that sounds kind of rude, and self-centred, but it's true. It's a private party, not a club, so there is no dress-code beyond a sub wearing whatever her Dom decides."

"Thanks, Mac. I appreciate you being around for me."

"Anytime, honey. You're coming early, right?"

"Yeah, Sully and Wilson are picking me up at six. Sully said being early would give you and me some time together."

"Perfect. I'll see you when you get here and we'll have a nice chat."

"Okay. See ya."

"Bye."

FOUR

HILDY SMILED as Mac greeted them at the door. "Hi there. Hildy, how about you come with me whilst Sully and Wilson head down to help Finn in the dungeon." Wilson and Sully looked at each other and shrugged.

Mac took Hildy by the hand and led her to the bedroom. "I need to finish getting ready. Finn and I have some special plans tonight, and I wanted to talk to you about them."

"Why would you need to talk to me about plans you have with Finn?"

Mac sat on the bed and invited Hildy to join her. "You are very new and I want you to be prepared for the worst possible scenario. I don't know how much you know about my past, but I'll give you a quick run-down of the sordid details to help you understand the situation.

"I was bound to a piano bench and raped at the

end of my first year of university." Mac paused, rubbing her palms up and down her thighs.

"As a result, I suffered from severe performance anxiety and withdrew to the point where Sully was the only person I maintained a relationship with. Long story short, Sully's injury was the cause of Finn and me getting together and with Finn's love and patience, I've been slowly conquering my fears."

She gave Hildy a half smile. "I've got to the point where Finn can restrain me with leather cuffs, but so far, we've not tried using rope.

"Finn and I had a long talk, and we decided that we would ask Wil for help. Something very simple that is quick and easy to remove. Wilson will be completely in charge of the rope while Finn keeps me otherwise occupied.

"We've planned it to the last detail, but it could go very, very wrong, and I could totally freak out. If that happens, I need you to absolutely understand that I am in complete control of the situation. Nothing will happen that I haven't already consented to. I am pretty good about safewording for myself, but even if I don't, it is likely Finn will realise there is a problem and halt the scene before I even come close to losing it." Mac caught Hildy's gaze. "I need you to promise me you'll stay put and stay calm if things go really bad."

Hildy struggled with the discomfort she felt over Mac's decision to put her physical and emotional safety into the hands of others. "Fuck, Mac. Seriously, why would you take a chance like this?"

"Because some miserable little fucker in my past stole so much from me, and I want it back. All of it. You haven't given me your promise."

She was still uncomfortable about the situation, but she could understand Mac's motivation. "I promise."

"Thank you. I was a little conflicted about doing this at your first party, but in the end, I decided it would be a good learning experience for you regardless of the outcome. If it all goes to shit in a handbag, you will see how loving Doms deal with a scene gone wrong. And if it all goes right, you'll see how a Dom can successfully help his sub overcome her fears."

"I don't know, Mac. Maybe I should go home. You don't need me here to complicate the situation."

"I would like you to be here. But, if it gets to be too much for you, all you have to do is say red to Sully, and he'll get you out of there. All I ask is if you do need to leave, do it quickly and quietly so you don't disturb any scenes."

"I'll try."

"Good enough. That's all anyone should ever ask of you, is to try. Now, let me get changed real quick, and we can head down to check on the fellas."

Hildy's eyes went wide as Mac rose and stripped down to a thong and corset. "Oh, before I forget, there will be sex. Lots of sex, and it's highly unlikely any of it will be soft and gentle. More importantly, you need to be prepared for women being hit. Not just with bare hands, but with all manner of paddles and hitty-sticks. I don't know if anything really prepares you for the first time you see a Dom strike his sub. It's quite shocking, and I know for me, horrifying to feel titillated by it. That's normal. The sub is in control. She has a safeword, and unless the couple have a long-standing relationship, scenes are generally carefully scripted."

"I don't know about this, Mac."

"It'll be fine. There's a first time for everything, and it's rarely as bad as we anticipate. Sully will be with you the whole time, and with the exception of our small scene, Wilson will be too. Ready?"

"As I'll ever be, I suppose."

HILDY LAUGHED when she saw Sully languishing on the fainting couch. "Oh my god. Seriously? You are an even bigger diva than I thought."

"Not this time. This was Finn's idea all the way. I gave in gracefully."

Mac nearly choked on the water she was drinking. "More like went down kicking and screaming, as I recall."

Hildy giggled. "That sounds a little more like Sully."

"I knew it would be a huge mistake for you two to ever meet."

Mac glared at Sully. "I'm pissed at you for not doing it sooner."

"Me too. Bad Sully."

"Finn, are you going to let your sub treat me like this?"

"Hell yeah. Better you than me, my friend."

Mac shot a look at Finn and he turned to Hildy. "Can you give me a hand bringing stuff down from the kitchen, Hildy?"

"Sure, lead the way."

As soon as they were out of earshot, Wilson watched Mac turn on Sully, wagging her finger in his face. "You pay close attention to Hildy, particularly during my scene with Finn and Wil. I've told her the details and what could be the worst case scenario. I told her to use red if she needs you to get her out of here. I know you feel responsible for both of us, but in this instance, I need your first priority to be Hildy. I will have both Finn and Wil to take care of me."

"I don't want you to worry, love, I'll take good care of her."

"Thanks, Sully."

"Mac, are you sure you want to go through with this? I'm concerned about you pushing yourself too far, too fast."

"I'm sure Sully. Finn and I had another long talk about it this morning."

Wilson was surprised when Sully's attention was turned on him. "You'd best keep the right head in the right game. I don't want you concerning yourself over how Hildy's doing when you're working on Mac. Clear?"

"Normally, I'd be offended, but considering how my interest in Hildy has already impaired my judgement once, I'll take the warning in the spirit in which it was meant. However, whilst I am working on Mac, I'm trusting you to focus all your attention on Hildy's well-being for me."

"Now you've both flexed your penises, can we move on to more interesting subjects?" Mac asked.

***

Hildy sat next to Sully, fascinated by the activities going on around her, but her attention kept wandering back to Wilson.

"How are you doing, sweetie?"

"Oh, I'm fine. Stop fussing like a maiden aunt." The words had barely spilled from her lips before the first blow of the evening fell on naked flesh and was followed by a long, low moan. She swung her head in the direction of the sounds and her jaw dropped at the sight. There sat Finn with Mac draped over his lap and his hand poised to strike again. She was appalled at her reaction. Part of her was sure she was witnessing abuse and she should step in to put a stop to it, but the larger part of her was aroused and even envious. Mac's words echoed in her head about the sub being in charge. Still, she'd best check with Sully. He'd never sit by and let something bad happen.

As she turned, ready to ask her question, Sully smiled and said, "She's just fine. Finn is going to get her flying a bit before he brings Wilson in with the rope."

"If you're sure."

"I am positive. If Finn and Mac's scene makes you uncomfortable, I can set you up somewhere else to observe other activities, or take you upstairs."

"No, I think I'll be okay. I was just a little surprised."

"You handled it well. If you are going to continue watching this scene, I really need you to keep your head. Mac has safewords and two experienced Doms watching her closely for any signs of a problem. Finn is madly in love with her and would slice off both his hands with a rusty band-saw before risking her physical or emotional safety. No matter what you think is happening, you absolutely must stay quiet and out of the way."

Hildy nodded. "I know. Mac went over it with me earlier."

"In that case, settle yourself down, I think the show is about to really begin."

Hildy returned her attention to Mac and Finn's

scene. She wasn't prepared for the snarl of jealousy and want she felt when Wilson stepped into the scene area, shirtless and ripped. She squirmed subconsciously in her seat as she scrutinised every naked inch of his torso.

Finn had shifted Mac so she was sitting on his lap, her back against his chest and her legs spread outside of his own. He peppered the crook of her neck with tiny kisses as he took hold of one nipple and pulled it away from her body. He attached a clover clamp on it and let it drop. She'd barely let out a moan before he'd done the same to her other nipple.

Finn lifted his lips to Mac's ear. "Colour, love?"

"I'm green."

The exchange was barely audible, but it helped reduce Hildy's concern. She stole a look at Wilson. He was focused on Finn and Mac, apparently oblivious to everything else going on around him. Finn gave a barely perceptible nod, and as Wilson moved toward the couple, she knew this was as it should be, but she still struggled with the twinges of jealousy that kept pinching her heart.

She flinched, then relaxed when she realised the hand touching her arm belonged to Sully. "He's doing a favour. Nothing more. You don't have to stay."

Hildy turned her head slightly, but didn't take her eyes off the threesome. "No, I'll be fine."

"Okay, but I reserve the right to call red for you if I think it's getting too much for you." Hildy nodded.

Finn took one of Mac's hands and moved it so her arm was positioned straight out in front of her. "Don't move until I tell you otherwise."

"Okay."

"Good girl," Finn said. He gave Wilson another quick nod as he settled a vibrator over Mac's clit and flipped the switch. Mac immediately started rolling her hips. Finn pulled the vibrator away then flicked a crop across Mac's clamped nipples. "I said don't move."

Hildy inhaled sharply and Sully's hand tightened on her arm when she tried to rise from her seat. "Trust me, she's fine. She wouldn't be smiling if she wasn't. Now breathe."

Hildy nodded and took a slow, deep breath as she settled back down, focusing her attention back to Mac's scene.

Mac's head was tilted back and resting on Finn's shoulder. Her eyes were closed and there was no mistaking her expression for anything but bliss.

Wilson stood in front of Mac with a length of purple rope in his hand. He doubled it in half and wrapped it around Mac's wrist, slowly bringing the two loose ends through the folded part of the rope. Then he stopped. Mac was quivering. Finn stroked his knuckles down her cheek. "Colour, love?"

"Yellow"

"Okay. Can we leave the rope where it is, or do you need Wil to take it off?"

"I don't know."

"It's a binary question, Mac. On or off?"

Mac chewed on her lip for a minute, then said, "On. I think I'm okay to carry on."

Finn clearly had other ideas. "I think we'll take a minute or two before we continue." Wilson stepped back and Finn reached back to the little table set to his right and a little behind and grabbed a small tube along with what Hildy now knew to be a butt-plug.

Hildy's hand flew to her mouth, but she watched in morbid fascination as Mac's ass swallowed the plug Finn had generously slathered with lube. She flicked a quick glance in Wilson's direction, noting the detachment with which he watched, before returning her attention to the scene.

Finn repositioned Mac and signalled Wilson to come back. Wilson approached, stopping next to Finn. He leaned down and said something too softly for Hildy to catch. Finn nodded, and Wilson crouched in front of Mac. "I need to hear you tell me you want to continue."

"I'm green."

"No, tell me exactly what you want me to do. I need to hear you say the words, Mac. I will not do this without them."

"I want you to use rope on me exactly like we discussed."

"What did we agree on, Mac?"

"Nothing more than simple arm gauntlets."

"Very good. Are you ready?"

"Yes."

Wilson took hold of the abandoned rope dangling from Mac's wrist and tied a series of loops and knots around her forearm, stopping to check in after each. Mac's breathing seemed rather erratic, but considering the careful attention both Doms were paying to her every move and sound, along with the distractions Finn was providing, Hildy suspected Mac was more likely ready to orgasm than panic.

With the first gauntlet finished Finn removed the vibrator from Mac's clit and gently guided her arm down to her side.

"Ready for the next one, love?"

"I'd rather come."

"Soon, baby. One more gauntlet, then you can come, okay?"

"But I want to come now, you've had me on edge forever. Why can't I have an orgasm now and another after the next gauntlet, dammit?"

"Mac," Finn warned.

"Fuck, I hate this. I just want to come."

"Are you safewording?"

"Will it get me an orgasm faster?"

"Do not try to manipulate me, Mac Wallis. You know it won't end well."

"But Finn..."

"Enough."

Mac pursed her lips together, and dropped her head backwards onto Finn's shoulder.

Hildy was shocked by the exchange. She turned towards Sully and whispered, "I don't understand. I thought subs were supposed to be quiet unless they safeword or are given permission to speak."

"As long as it's Safe, Sane, Consensual, and works for all parties involved, it's all good. Sometimes Doms and subs find dynamic preferences change with the company they keep. Finn used to be one of those strict Doms who punished bratty behaviour hard and fast. Then he met Mac. She has to be pretty outrageous before he'll give her a real punishment for it, and he's particularly tolerant when they're doing a scene and she's pushing her limits. As you can see, she is learning when to stop. Are you still okay?"

"Yeah, I think so. It's all so confusing. I see stuff that gets me kind of excited, but I feel guilty."

"Yeah, it can take some getting used to, but the only way for that to happen is to keep exposing yourself to it in a safe and controlled manner."

"I know I threatened to explore this through other avenues, but I'm glad you put your foot down. I don't think I could have handled this around strangers."

Sully patted her hand and motioned back to the scene.

Finn had returned the vibrator to Mac's clit, and Wilson was just tying off the second gauntlet. As soon as Wilson removed his hands, Finn adjusted something on the vibrator and whispered in Mac's ear. Her hips and legs started to shake, and as she began to wail,

Wilson stepped in and removed the clamps from Mac's nipples before slipping away.

Mac's wails subsided and Finn spoke. "You've been such a good, brave girl, Mac. One more, then I have some nice chocolate for you."

Mac barely acknowledged Finn's words before it was obvious to all she'd been consumed by another orgasm. As soon as Finn discarded the vibrator, Wilson returned and handed him a nice soft looking blanket that was different from the others scattered about the dungeon. Hildy mentally smacked herself, of course, Mac would have her own personal blanket, she lived here.

Finn carefully wrapped the blanket around Mac and carried her to the after-care area, where he sat on a sofa and settled her in his lap. When Hildy saw the content look on Mac's face, she felt a little lonely and a lot envious.

Men were for sexual release and nothing more. Use them before they use you. Now, for the first time she could recall, she felt like she wanted a connection that went deeper than the length of a man's cock.

She was jolted from her thoughts when she felt a pair of arms wrap a soft blanket around her. She started to lean in, then she realised those arms didn't belong to Sully. She snapped her head around to see Wilson wearing a sheepish grin. "What do you think you are doing?"

"After-care, love."

Hildy slipped the blanket off and opened her mouth to speak, but Sully interrupted. "Hildy, we agreed that Wilson would be the one to provide you with practical experience. At least temporarily, that makes Wilson your Dom, and you his sub. Now, consider the situation from his point of view. His sub has just pushed her boundaries well outside her comfort zone. As a Dom, he can't, in good conscience, leave you to deal with it alone. So, here he is trying to take care of your needs and ensure your first experiences as a sub are as positive as possible."

"It's all so damn complicated."

"It usually is, if it's worth having. Now, can I leave you with Wilson and trust you'll let him do whatever he deems necessary to care for you?"

"I don't know."

Wilson interjected. "Safewords work for everything, Hildy. Yellow to pause or make a change, and red if you really can't handle it. Can you give me a chance?"

Hildy turned to Sully for help. One look at his cold eyes, and she wasn't surprised by his parting words. "Safeword and we'll go. Otherwise, Wilson is in charge." Hildy dropped her head in defeat.

"Hildy?" Wilson's voice was soft and patient as he tipped her chin up with his index finger. "Look at me, please."

Hildy couldn't bear to see the pity she knew his

eyes would hold, so she kept her own focused on the floor.

"Hildy, please, I want to talk with you, but eye to eye, as equals, not Dom and sub. Not yet."

Hildy was so absorbed in her study of the dungeon floor, she was unprepared for Wilson's smiling face to block her view.

"There you are. If this is how you want to talk, I can go with it."

Hildy shifted her gaze to the side, and Wilson followed. Frustrated, she looked straight into his eyes. "I don't want to talk right now."

"Fair enough, then safeword out and Sully will take you home."

"No, I'm not a wimp."

"Hold it right there. Wimp? Did you think Mac was being a wimp when she called yellow?"

"No, of course not. That's different."

"No, Hildy, it's not. Nobody is ever a wimp for using a safeword. Are there times when someone abuses it? Of course. In the end, it's their loss, but that still doesn't make them a wimp. Understand?"

"Yes."

"Good girl. Now, can we have this conversation in a more comfortable position? Don't get me wrong, I am willing to have it however you need it to be, but I'm not a fan of crouching for long periods of time."

"Yet you lot expect your subs to always be on their knees."

"We'll get to that misconception in a minute. Can you please answer me? More comfortable position?"

"Okay."

"Thank you." Wilson stood and snagged a nearby chair. He set it down facing Hildy and sat. "Now, as for subs on their knees all the time. Some Doms? Sure. Me? No."

"Why not?"

"It's not my thing. Now isn't the time to go into detail about what is and isn't my thing or your thing. If you've brought your check-list with you, we'll exchange them when we leave and go over them at our leisure. Okay?"

"Okay."

"Good. Next. You've denied me one of my favourite parts of being a Dom, and I would like to fix that now."

"What do you want to do?"

"Give you the after-care you need."

Hildy glanced over at Mac, still snuggled up on Finn's lap and surrendered to that stab of envy she'd felt earlier.

"Okay."

"Good girl. I know that was hard for you. I want to wrap you back up in that blanket and carry you over to where Finn and Mac are, where I am going to snuggle you in my lap and feed you chocolate. Tell me you like chocolate."

"I love chocolate."

Wilson rose from his chair and gathered the blanket back around Hildy. He swooped her into his arms and held her close. She closed her eyes and let her head relax against his chest as she tried to make sense of the jittery feeling she had deep in her belly.

HILDY PANICKED until Wilson's soft voice washed over her.

"You're okay, love. You just had a little nap is all."

"What's going on?" Hildy panicked again and as she struggled, her bonds loosened.

"Hildy, calm down. You fell asleep."

Hildy's mind raced back through the events of the evening before she came up with the only explanation she could for falling asleep as she did. "Did you drug me?"

Mac gasped and Finn's head whirled round to glare at Hildy. She stiffened. "Well, did you?"

Wilson inhaled long and deep. "I can understand why you might think that, love, especially when you're still a bit groggy from an unexpected nap, but take a few minutes. Think about Sully — who, and what he is to you. Then think about whether he would ever put you, or anyone for that matter, in a situation where that could possibly happen. I'll still be here, waiting, when you have your answer."

Hildy pulled the blanket over her head and tighter around her body as she curled into a ball.

"You're going to have to come out sometime, love. I'll be here when you do."

The last thing Hildy expected after she exhibited such abominable behaviour, was to feel Wilson pull her tight to him and stroke his hand up and down her back. She squirmed in discomfort. It was getting hot and stuffy under the blanket. She wanted to come out, but she didn't want Wilson to stop what he was doing, and worse, she didn't want to see the people who must be staring at her making such a spectacle of herself.

"Hildy, are you ready to come out?"

"No."

"Nobody's paying any attention to you. Jack's got Sloane bent over the spanking bench and is laying into her ass with the seat strap from his bassoon and Griff is keeping her mouth busy. Sub in a blanket just can't compete with that."

Hildy shifted the blanket enough to see from one eye. Sure enough, Wilson was telling the truth, not one person in the room was looking at her. Except him. She moved the blanket to expose more of her head. The air in the room felt chilly on her sweaty head and caused her whole body to shiver. She looked up into Wilson's face, and his stony expression contradicted his gentle strokes up and down her back.

"Do you have an answer for me?"

"No, Sully would never, ever do that."

"You're damn right he wouldn't. In addition, by accusing me of drugging you, you are accusing everyone in this room of being complicit. You've essentially branded every person here as untrustworthy. You owe them all an apology, Hildy, but I don't think sorry is going to cut it.

"I'm going to have to decide on an appropriate apology, and once I do, you will have two options. Either you apologise exactly as I tell you, or you safeword out and you won't be welcome to play here.

"Fair warning, I won't make this easy on you. Trust is what everything balances on here. I thought you understood that. Questioning someone's integrity, especially in public, without good reason is beyond serious. If you aren't able to treat those around you, especially Sully, with the same respect they've afforded you, then you need to safeword out now."

Hildy couldn't hold back the tears any longer. Her parents were right, she was stupid. She should have stayed home.

WILSON WAS TORN. He knew damn well her accusation wasn't meant. She fell asleep so fast after that chocolate, it was hardly surprising she would think she'd been drugged. However, deep down she knew Sully would never put her at risk like that, and had she controlled her tongue until her brain was fully engaged, she wouldn't be in this fix. He wished he could tell her it was just a mistake and everything is fine. Unfortunately, he couldn't. As a Dom, he could never let his sub get away with something like this. If she wanted to continue to explore her kinky side, she absolutely had to make amends. Word would get around. Jackson and Griff rarely had a regular sub although, if he wasn't mistaken, this one broke the record for most appearances. It was made clear to subs who came to play at Finn's parties, that they were private and what happened at Finn's stayed at Finn's. But everyone also understood it was an unrealistic expectation, and they governed their behaviour accordingly. He had a fairly good idea of what would be a fitting punishment for Hildy, but he needed to ensure the rest of the group understood just how much she would struggle with it.

"Hildy, I need to go have a quick chat with Sully. Will you be okay on your own for a minute?"

He knew she was still crying, so accepted her nod rather than a proper answer. This time. He gently shifted her sideways, off his lap and onto the sofa. "I'll be back as soon as I can and we'll get this sorted." He didn't expect an answer, so he didn't wait.

He headed straight for Sully, who was parked in front of Jack's scene. He positioned himself to Sully's side and whispered, "I need to talk to you. It's urgent."

"Sully's head swivelled towards Wilson as he glared. "What. Did. You. Do?"

"Hush, just come with me now. We need to hurry."

Sully got up and followed Wilson to a quiet corner of the room. "I didn't do anything." Wilson filled Sully in on what happened and what he planned to do about it. "So, I need you to discretely give the heads-up. You and I both know this is going to be really hard for Hildy to do, and I need to be sure everyone else understands. Particularly Sloane. She's the one most likely to blow this into a complete clusterfuck."

"I'll get Mac to help me. You get back to Hildy. Understand though, for Hildy's sake, beyond getting the word out, I have to stay completely out of this."

"I know, and I respect that."

Sully gave Wilson a quick pat on the shoulder before embarking on his mission. Wilson spun on his heel and returned to the sofa. "Okay, love. Here's the deal. The best way to apologise and prove you didn't mean what you implied is to give them a demonstration of your trust."

"How am I supposed to do that?"

"By doing something you're going to find really hard. With the exception of Sully and myself, you are going to say you're sorry to each person here and give them a hug, which has to last at least ten seconds after they've wrapped their arms around you."

Hildy buried her face in her hands. "There is no way I can do that. How could you possibly ask that of me?"

Wilson wanted to take her in his arms and sooth

her, but that would have to wait until either she apologised to the others or safeworded out. "If it's easy for you, it will mean nothing to them. It's easy to say you're sorry. It's a lot harder to prove it. Mending broken trust is harder still. You broke their trust in you, Hildy. You have to earn it back, and the best way to do that is trust them with something you find hard. If this really is too much for you, then safeword out and I'll take you home."

"I guess your trust is broken too?"

"Nothing that can't be fixed if you want it to."

"I don't know, Wil. You know how I am about being touched."

"Exactly. It's something we were going to work on at some point, but, I sure as hell wasn't expecting it to be at your first play party."

"I'm so, so sorry, Wil."

"Enough. You need to have a hard think about what you're going to do because you don't have much time to make your decision. Jack and Griff look to be close to finishing their scene."

Wilson waited patiently as he watched Hildy struggle with her decision. That she didn't immediately bail confirmed his initial impression. She didn't give up easily. Based on what little he knew of her horrendous childhood, she could very easily have stopped fighting.

"I'll try."

Wilson smiled and reached for her hand to help her up from the sofa. "Try is good. We'll go by sub then her Dom, starting with Mac. By the time we've gone through everyone, Jack, Griff, and Sloane should be just about ready for you."

"Wilson?"

"Yes, love?"

"What do I have to do to apologise to you and Sully?"

"We'll get to that later. As far as Griff, Jack, and Sloane are concerned, your apology to us is a private matter to be witnessed by Mac and Finn."

"I don't understand."

"All they need to know is you'll be making appropriate apologies to all involved. They will see you making enough of your apologies in public to be assured you will follow through with the private ones."

"I'm sorry I ruined your night."

"Enough. It's time to go find Mac and Finn."

<hr>

WHAT HAVE I DONE? Hildy worked hard to keep her breathing slow and regular. Her heart was pounding and her palms were sweaty as Wilson led to make her first apology. Mac. This she could do. She knew Mac. She'd been nothing but kind and supportive, and this was the least she could do after fucking up so badly. She looked to Finn as she approached Mac. He gave a nod, and she stepped forward. "I'm so sorry, Mac. I didn't mean to abuse your trust."

Mac pulled her into her embrace. "No harm done, You're forgiven." Then she whispered into Hildy's ear, "Call me later, we'll talk."

After what seemed like forever, Wilson spoke. "Alright, break it up you two."

Once Mac finally let her go, Hildy turned to Finn and repeated her apology. She thought she was going to pass out when he took her into his arms and gave her a firm, but gentle hug. "Brave girl, you make us proud. You're forgiven, pet."

With each apology, the hugs became less difficult. She felt her chest get lighter as she realised she was down to Griff, Jack, and their sub. She was almost done and nothing bad happened.

She approached Sloane and made her apologies. Unlike the rest of the group who were gracious and welcoming, she waited for Hildy to make body contact and even then, she didn't wrap her arms around Hildy until Jack reminded her. She brought her lips close to Hildy's ear and whispered, "You'll never be forgiven, loser." before pulling away with a glib, "Forgiven."

Hildy was crushed and her face fell. She just wanted to run away, and she was so close to doing just that. Then she caught sight of Sully, nodding his head in silent encouragement. Sully. Two more apologies. Two more hugs. She could do it. Make Sully proud, then she could leave with her head held high and never see these people again.

She lifted her head and turned to apologise to Jack.

This time, she couldn't quite meet his eyes. She tried to make this apology sound as sincere as the rest, but her heart wasn't in it. She struggled to get the words out, before creeping her way into Jack's arms for the mandatory hug. It took an eternity and it was all she could do not to tear herself from his arms and flee. Instead, she stiffened her spine and turned to deliver her final apology.

"That's it, she's done." Hildy never thought she would be so glad to hear Wilson's voice. She forced herself to disentangle from Griff's embrace with as much dignity as she could muster before seeking out the closest person she could trust in this room of liars.

It was Wilson who gathered her in his arms and carried her back to the sofa. Once she was settled back on his lap, he kissed her temple and asked, "What just happened?"

She shook her head. "Nothing, I'm fine."

"Don't ever lie to me, Hildy. What's wrong?"

Just then, a very angry Sully arrived and parked himself next the couple. "What the fuck just happened?"

"That's what I want to know. Start talking, Hildy."

"I don't want to talk about it. I just want to home."

"Is that a red?" Wilson asked.

Hildy was done.

"Yes, it's a fucking red, okay. Red. I'm going home." Wil released her instantly and she scrambled from his lap.

"Okay, give us a few minutes to get organised and we'll take you home."

"No, I'll call a taxi. I don't want to see any of you again. I'm done."

Hildy raced across the dungeon and up the stairs, not caring who saw or what they thought.

Wilson started to rise, intending to go after Hildy, when he felt Sully's hand on his leg "Wil, let her go. She needs her space. She may calm down quickly and let us take her home, but she's most likely going to follow through on the cab. Regardless, you need to let her be. For now."

"Did I push her too far? She was doing so well right up until she got to Sloane."

"No, something happened between Sloane and Hildy. Go get Finn and Mac, and while you're at it, tell Jack and Griff to hang on for a few minutes."

Wilson decided to swing by Jack and Griff first before fetching Mac and Finn. He was surprised to see their sub on her knees and tears streaming down her face. He missed what Jack had to say, but he did see Sloane shaking her head emphatically. Griff looked over as Wil approached and cocked an eyebrow. A silent question.

"Can you two wait a few minutes before going?

Sully and I want to have a quick word. We just need to speak with Finn and Mac first."

"Sure, no problem. In the meantime, I'll get our stuff together."

"Thanks." On his way to get Finn and Mac, Wilson briefly wondered if Jack and Griff had picked up on the sudden change in Hildy after her apology to his sub. He hoped so. It would make sorting this out much easier.

"Finn, Mac, Sully and I would like a word."

Mac shook her head. "I was just going to check on Hildy. She flew out of here like her ass was on fire."

"Sully said it's best to give her some space."

"Sully isn't always the sharpest cookie in the shed, now, is he?"

"Please, Mac? This concerns Hildy."

"Fine, but she'd better still be upstairs by the time we're done or you're in it deep, bucko."

And with that, there was no question Mac had switched from sub to protective mama-bear.

Sully started talking the moment the other three took their seats. "I assume we all saw the same thing. Hildy was doing great until she got to that sub Jack and Griff brought?" The group nodded and he carried on. "Mac, what do you think?"

"It's pretty simple, that bitch had to have said something mean to our Hildy. I was behind her and didn't actually see or hear her say anything, but I did see Hildy's face transform from nervous to devastated in the space of a second."

"Finn?"

I didn't see or hear anything either, but there was a definite and immediate change in Hildy's demeanour." Finn turned to Wilson. "What did she say?"

"Red."

"Wilson asked Jack and Griff to hang back for few minutes. I think we should call them over now, but that sub should stay put until we've talked this through."

The group agreed, and Sully caught Jack's attention and motioned for him to join them. He spoke before anyone else had a chance. "I can only assume this little pow-wow has something to do with what happened between Hildy and Sloane?"

Wilson's eyes blazed. "What did happen?"

"Damned if I know. I asked Sloane, and she said she had no idea what the problem could be. She'd accepted Hildy's apology and that was that."

"Do you believe her?" Finn asked.

"No, I don't. I was just about to get into that with her. What did Hildy say about it?"

"First she denied there was an issue, then she refused to talk about it and called red."

"Fuck! We were really hoping things would work out with this one. I'll deal with her. Then she's done. Is Hildy still here?"

Mac jumped up from her seat. "I'll go check. If she is, what should I do?"

Wilson spoke up. "Keep her here. Do whatever you need to keep her from leaving. I know she called red over whatever went on with Sloane, but I want to make sure everything is okay between us and make sure she gets home safely."

Mac nodded and headed for the stairs.

"What do you have in mind, Jack?"

"I think Sloane needs to learn about telling the truth, and once she's confessed, I think she'll be begging Hildy for forgiveness."

"Absolutely not," Wilson objected.

"What? Why not?"

"She's fragile, Jack. Really, really fragile. If I could have found a way to keep her from having to apologise to everyone, I would have done it in a heartbeat. I wanted to say fuck it and brush it all under the rug anyway. I think the best thing we can do for her right now is keep Sloane well away from her. I'm not saying don't get the truth and mete out punishment. I'm just saying keep Hildy out if it. And Jack?" He shot the other man a pointed look. "I want Hildy kept right out of it."

"Got it. I'll get Sloane to admit the truth, then punish her for the lying. That work for you?"

"Good enough."

"Alright." Jack turned to Sully. "Could you please come and bear witness?"

"My pleasure."

Wilson felt a bit torn. Part of him wanted to watch

Jack and Griff deal with their sub on Hildy's behalf, but a larger part of him wanted to be with Hildy and get things back on track. His need to be with Hildy won and he quietly made his way out of the dungeon, sparing only a passing glance and a twinge of pity for the sub who'd earned punishment at Jack's hand. He'd call Sully later for the details.

His heart broke when he walked into the living room to see Hildy sobbing in Mac's arms. He caught Mac's eye and put a finger to his lips as he made his way towards the sofa. Once he'd crouched in front of Hildy, he gave Mac a quick nod.

"Hildy, Wilson is here, and he wants to talk to you."

As Hildy lifted her head, Wilson took her hand in his and gently rubbed his thumb along her fingers.

"Hildy?"

She slowly met his gaze, but didn't speak.

"Aw, honey, I'm so sorry. Can I please hold you?"

Hildy remained silent, but nodded.

Mac eased away so Wilson could take her place.

"Oh, sweet Hildy, I'm sorry I pushed. I know you don't want to talk about it, so you don't have to. I'm just going to tell you what we know and what's going on. Okay?"

Hildy nodded again, and Wilson continued. "We know Sloane said something to upset you. We all knew it the moment it happened. None of us know what she said, but it was obvious to all, it wasn't even remotely charitable. Jack noticed too, honey. He asked her. She lied to him, and he knew it. After chatting with us, he decided to get the truth out of her and then he'll punish her for lying. While I would like her to get all the punishment she deserves for her actions, Jack is making sure you are in no way connected to why she is being punished. She's not welcome here, and there is no reason why you should ever encounter her again. Okay?"

Hildy shook her head violently and croaked, "No."

"What's the problem, love?"

"I don't want to be the reason for anyone's punishment."

"You aren't. She was asked a question and she lied. We've talked about trust. You had a punishment of your own for breaking it. Lying is not tolerated and is always, always severely punished. It's not your fault."

"Yes it is. If I hadn't screwed up, she wouldn't have lied."

"Maybe not tonight, but I can assure you, she would at some point. She was willing to lie thinking it would keep her out of trouble. That kind of thinking doesn't have a sell-by date, love. She got herself into trouble tonight, just like you did. The difference is you took responsibility for your actions and accepted the consequences. We are all very, very proud of you."

"But I screwed up."

"Yes, you did. You also accepted your punishment gracefully and have been forgiven. The slate is clean."

"Until it gets thrown in my face, you mean."

"Mac, can you please explain?"

Mac returned to the sofa and settled on the floor in front of Hildy. "He's telling you the truth, Hildy. A good Dom doesn't bring up past transgressions once they've been punished and forgiven. Neither does a good sub."

"This is all so crazy making."

Mac patted Hildy's leg as she rose. "Stay there and rest with Wilson. You don't have to figure it all out tonight. Just know you're safe and with people who care."

Wilson rested his cheek on top of Hildy's head and quietly hummed bits of the adagio from Beethoven's *Sonata Pathetique* as he stroked his fingers up and down her arm. When her breathing evened out, he relaxed a bit and set about figuring out how to make this work, and more puzzling, why he wanted to.

HILDY STRUGGLED to stay asleep despite the tickle on her cheek and being told it was time to wake up. She finally gave in and opened her eyes to glare at the fool who dared interrupt the most peaceful sleep she'd had in recent memory. She didn't even try to hide her irritation. "What?"

"It's time to go, love. Sully is spending the night here, and while Finn and Mac have made it clear they have plenty of space and we are both welcome, I thought you'd prefer to sleep in your own bed."

Hildy shook off the sleep induced fog clouding her brain. "Yeah, I would."

"I'll get our stuff together while you get your coat and boots on, okay?"

Hildy nodded and rose from Wilson's lap, surprised at the sudden loneliness she felt. She stole a glance at him as he got to his feet, and the heat she saw in his expression shot straight to her pussy. Her boobs ached for his touch and she recklessly considered taking him home to fuck. She didn't doubt he'd be great in the sack, but she wasn't too sure about this whole kinky thing, and she couldn't imagine he did vanilla. Even if they could find sexual compatibility, the comfort and safety she felt when in his embrace was disconcerting and would make it virtually impossible to maintain a strictly fuck-buddy relationship.

She found her way to the door and pulled on her boots, preferring to wait until they were on their way out before donning her coat. It wasn't long before Wilson returned with Finn and Mac. "Sully's already headed to bed, but he sends his love," Mac said.

"Thanks Mac. Can you tell him I'll pick him up on my way to work and drop him home?"

"No, we'll get him home tomorrow. Don't you worry about a thing. Would you like me to get him to call you?"

"Maybe just tell him I'll give him a shout after work?"

"Sure thing." Mac moved in and gathered Hildy in her arms. "You call me, day or night if you need anything, or just want to talk. Okay?" Hildy nodded and Mac continued. "Fair enough. You did so well, tonight. We're all really proud of you."

Hildy nodded again, knowing her voice would betray her emotions. Mac loosened her grip and passed her into Finn's arms. "Sweet dreams, pet. We'll see you soon."

By the time Finn let Hildy go, Wilson was ready and waiting to help her into her coat. "Come on, sleepy-head. The sooner we go, the sooner you can be snoring on your own pillow."

She shot him a murderous glare. "I don't snore." The twinkle in his eye should have irritated her more, but instead, it fed the nagging ache she felt in her heart.

Hildy waved to Mac and Finn as Wilson slipped his arm through hers and guided her through the front door. "Careful, love. The steps look a bit slippery."

It was on the tip of her tongue to be ornery, but she was tired, and he was right. "I will."

"Good girl."

"The party's over, I think you can quit with the Dom-speak now."

"Hildy, as far as I'm concerned, until I get you safely home, I'm responsible and the dynamic remains in effect."

"And if I safeword out?"

Wilson didn't respond until both he and Hildy were settled in the car. "Then we can drop the dynamic, but I have to ask you to consider carefully whether safewording in this situation would be from feeling overwhelmed and unable to deal, or just a quick and easy out?"

"It was just a question."

"And that was the answer. Are you safewording?"

"Of course not."

"Then the dynamic stays in place until I get you home."

Hildy folded her arms on her chest and snapped, "Fine."

"I can't imagine you are looking for more consequences when we haven't finished with what you've already earned tonight."

"What do you mean?"

"If you recall, you still have to apologise to Sully and me."

"I kind of hoped I was going to get let off the hook."

"Not a chance. Unless you safeword out, we'll be returning to Mac and Finn's tomorrow night to put this unpleasantness behind us."

Hildy sunk lower in her seat and sulked. She was horny, and with this punishment hanging over her head, nailing Wilson was out of the question.

"What are you thinking so hard about, love?"

"Me being stupid."

"You are not stupid."

"Yeah, I am."

"No, love, you aren't. And whenever you say it, I'll make be sure your ass will remind you every time you sit for many days to follow."

"You wouldn't."

"I know Sully doesn't let you get away with talking down about yourself like this, and you can bet that luscious ass of yours, I won't either."

The nearer they drew to Hildy's, the closer they were to separating, and the lonelier she felt. Casual sex was one of the few human interactions she was comfortable initiating. She was rarely rejected, and she had a pretty good instinct for choosing men who stayed just long enough to be polite, but never until morning. Wilson did not fit in that category. If she invited him in for a fuck, she had no doubt he would still be there when her alarm went off.

"When we get to my place, do you want to come in and fuck?" Not what she'd meant to say. Not even close.

"I have to say, love, that's probably the very last thing I expected to hear you say tonight."

"Can we pretend that didn't happen?"

"No, we can't. I do want to come in, and I do want to fuck, but only one of those things is going to happen tonight. You may want to use the time you have left before we arrive to get your head on straight. We've got some talking to do."

Hildy pressed her lips together and squeezed her eyes shut as she silently berated herself for continually being so fucking stupid.

"Saying it in your head is no different to saying it out loud, love. You are not stupid. A little impulsive, perhaps, but not stupid. You've been warned."

Hildy worked at keeping her mind blank for the remainder of the ride home. She was almost calm by the time Wil pulled his key from the ignition.

WILSON SAT at the kitchen table in silence and watched Hildy fidgeting in the seat opposite as he considered the situation. He was in way over his head, and he had no idea what to do about it. What on earth possessed her to proposition him like that? Did she have any idea how fast her words made his cock stand up and take notice? Every single cock-deflation method he tried failed miserably. A swollen, angry penis was the worst possible distraction.

"Here's the deal, Hildy. We're both tired, so I would like to table most of the issues until morning. However, there are some that require immediate attention. Firstly, we need to talk about your proposition in the car."

"Please, Wil, can't we just forget it? I made a mistake. I'm tired and I wasn't thinking."

"That's exactly why we need to talk about this. Why are you so tired?"

"Maybe because I don't sleep very well. It takes me a long time to get to sleep, and even once I get there, I wake up a lot. I don't do medication and I've been like this my whole life, so I'm used to it."

"What about when you sleep with someone? Do you sleep better or worse?"

"The few times anyone has stayed the night meant no sleep at all, so now, I only go to bed with men who fuck and go."

"I see. Are you willing to try an experiment?"

"What kind of experiment?"

"You and I go to bed. We don't fuck, and I stay the night."

"Are you nuts? The only reason for me to let a man in my bed is so I can get my rocks off. Your proposal is the worst of both worlds."

"I'd be lying if I let you think I didn't want you with every inch of my cock. I want to ram it into your pussy over and over until we both explode. I want you on all fours while I bury it in your ass, and I really want you on your knees while you take it deep in your mouth.

"But that's not all I want. I want to work your pussy over with my mouth until you scream. I want to lick, suck, and bite your nipples until you squirm and beg me to let you come, and damn it, I want to kiss you all night long.

"I want to do all those things and more, but I won't. I won't because what you think you want, and what you need are not always the same. Tonight, you won't get what you want, but you will get what you need."

"You walk in here, get me all hot and bothered, then tell me you aren't going to do anything about it because it's not what I need?"

"Pretty much. To be fair, you are not the only one who is all hot and bothered, but you do appear to be the only one who has consistently poor impulse control. I would like to point out, the other reason I won't is because we have not had the all-important check-list talk, which I will not have whilst sporting a raging hard-on. No talk, definitely no sex.

"Fucking men who leave isn't really working for you, is it? From what you've said, it doesn't sound like it improves your sleep quality any. What's the worst that can happen if I stay the night without sexual contact?"

"I could die."

"Now you're being silly. I'll make you a deal. If you don't sleep better, we can have the check-list talk over breakfast, and I'll come back tomorrow night, fuck you six ways from Sunday, wait the appropriate amount of time, and leave. However, if you do sleep better, we have the check-list talk in the morning and then tomorrow night, I get to do anything I want within the limits of your check-list."

"Anything?"

"Anything. Unless you safeword. Deal?"

"It doesn't matter, because I know you'll lose."

"We'll see. It's getting late, so we may as well get this experiment started."

———

HILDY COULDN'T BELIEVE what she'd agreed to. Wilson sleep in her bed? All night, without even an orgasm? How fucking stupid was she? She finished rinsing her toothbrush and popped it in the holder on the side of the vanity.

Wilson spat out the toothpaste in his mouth and caught her eye in the mirror. "Hildy? Don't think it. Your ass won't appreciate it, I promise you."

"How do you always know?"

"As tempting as it is to tell you it's a Dom thing, I won't. Your face doesn't hide much, love. There's this look you get when that thought pops into your head."

"Damn it. I guess I need to work on that."

"By work on that, you had better mean work on not having that thought. Because working on hiding it is no different from lying as far as I'm concerned, and the punishment for lying is probably the most severe I am ever likely to give you. Do you want to risk it?"

Hildy shook her head, but she couldn't ignore how the prospect of severe punishment made her pussy throb and leak.

"Interesting."

"What?"

"Like I said, love. Your face is like a jumbotron transmitting your thoughts to your audience. Don't worry, Hildy. It's a good thing. Come on, let's get to bed."

Hildy led the way to her bedroom and slid beneath the quilt. She lay there, trying not to let her panic show.

"Hildy, love? What is it?" She shook her head. "Please stop trying to hide it, and tell me what the problem is."

She assumed the fetal position and wrapped her arms tightly around herself, too ashamed and embarrassed to answer.

"Come on, love. No judgement. I can't help if you don't tell me how." Wilson gathered her into his arms and held her tight to his body. She was surprised at how much better this felt than being the filling in a quilt burrito.

"This. I need this."

WILSON WOKE with his body still wrapped around Hildy and his unrelenting erection crushed between them. According to the clock, he still had ten minutes before her alarm would go off. He thought back to Hildy's last words before she fell asleep and could make no better sense of them now than he could the night before. What the fuck was 'this'? God, his cock needed some space before the urge to engage in a little frottage became unbearable. He started to loosen his hold on Hildy, but stopped when she began to moan. He pulled her back in tight, and she immediately settled. He repeated his actions and when he got the same result, he knew what 'this' was. He peppered her neck with tiny kisses. Yeah, he should let her sleep until the alarm went off, but a gentle wake up would be much better for both of them.

"It's time to wake up, sleepy-girl."

Half-asleep, Hildy moaned and complained in gibberish.

"Come on love, it's almost time for the alarm."

"No, want more sleep."

"You can have that later. I want you awake before I get up and make you coffee."

"No. More sleep now."

"Oh, sweetheart, I wish I could grant you that, but I know you have to teach today and the alarm is going off in less than a minute."

"Not fair. I get a nice sleep and poof, gone." Hildy pushed slightly against Wilson's arms and he loosened them, letting her shift around unimpeded.

The alarm blared obnoxiously for a few seconds before Hildy struck it dumb with a vicious slap. Wilson got out of bed and started dressing. "Time to get moving. You get yourself sorted, I'll get the coffee going and meet you in the kitchen."

Hildy let out a long-suffering sigh. "Okay."

"Good girl. And don't forget your check-list." Wilson just grinned at her sour look, then left.

Wilson had a big mug of coffee waiting on the table for Hildy by the time she entered the kitchen. "What would you like for breakfast?"

"I can get it."

"That wasn't the question. What would you like?" He loved watching her struggle with the urge to refuse him when it was something she really wanted. Ah, the joys of being a Dom.

"Toast, dammit."

"I understand yours isn't the most sunshiny disposition in the morning, but I would appreciate it if you could be polite."

"Toast, please."

"With pleasure." He slipped two slices of bread in the toaster. What would you like on your toast?"

"Butter and honey, please."

"That wasn't so hard, was it? Now, drink your coffee, your toast will be ready in a few minutes."

Wilson left Hildy to a few minutes of quiet reflection. He'd be disrupting it soon enough.

HILDY SAT, quietly sipping her coffee, her mind busy trying to untangle the deluge of overwhelming feelings. Wilson set the plates of toast on the table, then pulled a sheaf of papers from his pocket and set them in front of her as he sat. "Here's mine. May I have yours?"

Hildy set her cup down and grabbed her own bundle of papers from the chair next to her and slapped them down in the middle of the table. "Here."

Wilson smiled. "Thank you, love. Let me know when you're done."

Hildy grunted and shifted her chair sideways in an attempt to ignore the man who had completely upset her reality. The chuckle she received for her efforts did nothing to improve her mood. She picked up the papers Wilson gave her and started reading.

By the time she reached the second page, her panties were soaked and she knew she was in trouble. So far none the stuff in his 'I could do this all day every day because it's my favourite thing ever' column turned up on her 'not even if it meant death if I don't' column. She chanced a peek at Wilson. The quirk of his lips and the gleam in his eye was unsettling. Shit, she was in seriously deep trouble. She tried to ignore the uneasy feeling in her belly and the wetness between her legs as she read through to the end. She set her shaking hands in her lap and tried to steady her breathing.

"Done, love?"

Denying it wasn't an option. "Yes."

"Good. Do you have any questions or concerns?"

"Only a shed-load."

Wilson rose and came around to her side the table

and took her hands in his as he crouched. "I should hope so. If it makes you feel any better, so do I."

"It doesn't."

"Would you feel more comfortable if we asked and answered each other in writing?"

"Oh hell, yes."

"Okay. Do you have time before we go to Finn and Macs tonight if we do it by email?"

"I guess."

"Good girl. Now go put on fresh panties and finish getting ready for work. I'll clean up."

How the hell did he know? Hildy tried to ignore her burning face. "I don't understand at all. I thought Doms kept subs to do all the domestic stuff."

"Some do. But, it's not my kink. I'm more of an equitable division of labour kind of guy."

His wink had Hildy's pussy leaking with renewed purpose and she couldn't get away fast enough.

            SIX

Wilson waited for Hildy to walk through the door
before he followed her in. Finn was hanging her coat
and Hildy was kicking off her second boot.

"Everything set, Finn?" Wil asked.

"Yup. Sully and Mac are already downstairs. I'm
glad you two finally arrived. She's been baiting him
all day."

"I thought he was supposed to go home this
morning."

"Since when does Sully do what he's supposed to?"

"Point taken."

By the time they reached the stairs to the playroom,
they could hear Mac giving Sully the gears.

"You selfish, miserable fuck. If you aren't capable
of playing by the next concert you had better have
another oboist handy because I am done. Do you hear
me? Done. We had a deal."

"Calm down, Mac."

"Don't you fucking calm down, Mac, me. I kept my end of the deal and more. I don't want to do this any more."

As soon as he reached the bottom of the stairs, Finn spoke up. "Mac. Enough."

"But Finn..."

"Unless you want my tawse on your bare ass right now, enough."

Mac was immediately silent, but anger glowed bright in her eyes.

Wilson took Hildy's hand as they moved to join Sully and Mac in the after-care area. He pulled her down with him as he sat, and arranged her on his lap with her back to his chest so his erection nestled in the seam of her ass. She tried to shift away, but he was ready. He clamped his hands on her hips, and so there was no misunderstanding, he hissed in her ear, "Stay exactly where I put you." She went loose. "Good girl."

Wilson watched as Finn lifted Mac from the sofa and positioned her in much the same way as he had Hildy. The difference was, Mac was naked and Finn had his hands all over her.

With a nod from Wilson, Sully turned to Hildy. "Honey, you did really well last night and we are all so very proud of you. However, you aren't done. You still have two apologies to make and Finn and Mac are here to bear witness. Are you ready?"

Hildy slowly nodded her head, and Wilson took

over. "Okay, honey. You will let Sully rub your feet for ten minutes, then you will apologise. Can you do that?"

Having her feet touched was on her check-list as a soft-limit. Not an issue as feet weren't his kink either, but it was the ideal apology to Sully, whose foot fetish was legendary. He'd had a different idea of how her punishment would play out, but after discovering her soft-limits and their earlier email exchanges addressing questions and concerns, he came up with a much better plan.

"I'll try."

"Good girl. Off you go." He placed his hands on her hips and gave a gentle boost to help her on her way. She stood in front of Sully and waited.

"Lay on the sofa and put your feet in my lap. Whatever you do, don't move. Mac will be your worst nightmare if you do anything to delay my return to active duty."

"I'll be good," Hildy replied, as she settled herself as Sully instructed.

Wilson sat for what seemed like the longest ten minutes of his life alternating his gaze between Sully's happy grin and Hildy's angry grimace. The instant the ten minutes were over, he called, "Time."

Sully shifted Hildy's feet off his lap and released them. She sat up and looked him dead in the eye. "Sully, I'm so sorry for not trusting you."

He pulled her close and kissed the top of her head. "You are forgiven, my love. I know deep down you didn't mean it. But I hope you understand that it wasn't something that could be ignored."

"I do."

He kissed her cheek then released her. "Good enough. It's time to go back to Wilson."

Wilson stood, and as Hildy returned, he pulled her in for a tight hug. "Well done, love. You're down to your last apology. Then we can go. Okay?" He felt her nod, but that wasn't enough this time. "I need to hear it, sweetheart."

"Okay."

He sat her on the sofa and settled next to her. "Hildy, I thought long and hard about this, but I've decided to give you five strokes with my leather belt. You'll be over the spanking bench. No trousers, but you may keep your panties on. As long as you can keep still, you may remain unrestrained. After you've taken your five, you may make your apology. Then it's all done and forgotten. If it becomes too much, you still have your safeword. Also, you need to understand, anyone in the room can safeword for you if they think it in your best interest."

"Everyone keeps telling me the sub is on control, but obviously that's not the case if someone else can safeword."

"Honey, sometimes a sub can't safeword. It may be because she's too deep in sub-space. It could be she can't remember what it is, or she can't get the word out. Unfortunately, there are also times where the situation becomes abusive and someone has to step in. There are some subs who refuse to safeword because they don't want to be a wimp. Sound like anybody you know?"

"But if I safeword, I'm done and can't come back." Hildy was near tears.

"If someone else calls red, then we'll talk about it. Remember, you always have yellow. If you need a break, or something needs to change, you can call yellow. And Hildy, safewording is never, ever wimpy. Are we clear?"

"Yes."

"Good. Shall we get started?"

"Okay."

Wilson took Hildy's hand and stood, bringing her to her feet as he rose. "Mac, can you please take Hildy to the spanking bench and get her set up?"

"Sure thing. Come on, Hildy, the sooner we get ready, the sooner this is all done and over with."

Wilson watched Mac lead Hildy away before he turned to Finn and Sully. "I am in over my head with her. She's so fragile and I'm terrified I'm going to do some real damage."

"Oh suck it up, Wil. I already told you, the damage was done years ago. She's comfortable with you. She lets you touch her and hold her without trying to run away like a scalded cat."

"Yeah, about that holding thing. She slept fine when I had my body wrapped around her, but if I tried to let her go, she fussed. Any idea what that's about?"

Wilson glanced at the women. They were still getting sorted. He still had a couple of minutes.

"She didn't roll herself up in her quilt?"

"No. When we got into bed, something was bugging her, but she wouldn't tell me what. As soon as I hugged her to me, she fell asleep."

"Yeah, it's a coping thing. Her parents never touched or hugged her. Wrapping herself up in her bedding is how she got through."

"Fuck. And now I have to go beat her ass with my belt."

"Bet she enjoys it."

"I guess we're about to find out."

The men wandered across the room where Mac had Hildy carefully arranged on the spanking bench. She turned as they approached and smiled at Wilson. "She's ready."

"Thanks Mac. Would you mind sitting by her head and giving her some moral support?"

"No problem."

Wilson walked up to the bench and smoothed his hand down Hildy's back. "Hildy, I'm going to take my belt off and double it over. I want you to understand, at no time will anything but the leather of the strap touch your body. The buckle will be in my hand and I will not do anything to cause you harm. Okay?"

"Okay."

"Alright then. Can you give me a colour? Green if

we're good to go, yellow if you need a minute. Red if you're done."

"I'm green."

"Good girl."

Wilson unbuckled his belt making it jingle as loudly as possible before drawing the leather through the loops. He flicked his wrist, snapping the tail as it slipped through the final loop. He wanted Hildy to associate these sounds with anticipation of what would follow.

HILDY BUCKED her hips and kicked wildly as her hands shot back to protect her ass. The blinding pain paralysed her lungs and made her light headed. "Breathe through it honey. It'll pass, I promise." Mac's soothing voice slipped through the foggy chaos in her brain. "Breathe with me. In....and out...in...and out." Hildy slowly regained control and finally started breathing in concert with Mac's steady rhythm.

"Hildy?" Wilson. Between Mac's gentle voice and the deep breathing, she was calm, and she'd almost forgotten. "Hildy, I need you to answer me, love."

She kept her eyes shut. "What?"

"Hildy, look at me."

"I don't want to."

"Now."

Hildy lifted her lids part way and saw nothing but concern on Wilson's face.

"All the way, please." As she did, Wilson bent so they were eye to eye. "We have a problem, love. What I just gave you wasn't much more than a love tap, and you couldn't stay still. What you did was dangerous and if I hadn't been expecting it, I could have caused damage. If we are to continue, I'm going to have to restrain you. Colour?"

Hildy was no quitter and there would be no mistaking the defiance. "Fucking green."

"Hildy, everyone has different tolerances. If it's too much for you, it's okay. It doesn't make you a wimp."

"I am green, dammit."

"Hildy, I'd adjust that attitude if I were you, or you might find yourself sucking on a soap dildo. A little back-talk when we're playing can add to the fun, but it is absolutely unacceptable during punishment."

Hildy's brain finally found some sense of self-preservation. "I'm sorry."

"Forgiven. Colour?"

"I am green, Wil." And she was.

"Okay. I'm going to secure your wrists and ankles in the straps attached to this bench. Once I've done that, I want you to rotate your hands and feet, and wiggle your fingers and toes. If at any point you feel numbness or tingling you must let me know. Use yellow if you really don't want to call the scene, but I need you to understand how very important this is."

While Hildy didn't want to be taken for a wimp, she knew the difference between taking some pain and risking real damage. "I understand. I promise. Tingling or numbness, I'll call yellow."

Wilson stroked her cheek. "Good girl. I'll also be strapping down your upper back and just below your waist. Once you're secure, I'm going to give you the remaining four stripes fast so it's all done."

Hildy nodded. "Okay." She lay quietly as Wilson set about fastening her to the spanking bench.

"How's that? Any numbness or tingling?"

Hildy rotated her hands and feet, then wiggled her fingers and toes. "I'm good."

"I'll take care of these last two straps and we'll get this over with."

As soon as she felt the strap tighten over her back, Hildy relaxed as calm washed over her.

WILSON NOTED Hildy's reaction with interest when he buckled the final strap in place over her back. There would be time enough to consider it later. Right now, he had to fulfil his responsibility.

As promised, he finished quickly. He drew his forearm back and flicked his wrist. His belt struck its target, right on her sit-spot. He paused a moment, surprised by Hildy's slow, steady breathing. He glanced around the room. With no apparent concern, he pulled back and repeated the action without further pause until he reached four. He flung his belt to the floor and set about releasing Hildy. He freed her wrists and ankles first. The moment he released the final strap, the one over her back, he covered her with a blanket and pulled her into a tight embrace. "Such a good girl, Hildy."

She looked up at Wilson and smiled. "Wil? I'm really sorry."

"I know. It's done and you're forgiven. Now, let's get you a drink of water and some chocolate."

Wilson lifted Hildy into his arms and carried her to the after-care area and sat down, carefully settling her on his lap. Mac sat next to them with a bottle of water in one hand and some of her special chocolate in the other.

"Here, she deserves the really good stuff."

"Thanks, Mac. I agree."

Hɪʟᴅʏ's ʜᴀɴᴅ shook as she held out her house key to Wilson. "I don't think I can do it."

"You had a pretty intense experience, and we're going to have to talk about it."

"I don't know about this whole kinky thing. It seems to be way more talk than sex."

"Communication is key. Yeah, there's lots and lots of talking in the beginning, but as a couple spends more time together, they develop other methods to communicate. Misunderstanding can lead to disaster. It is way better to talk something to death until there is clear understanding, than glossing over it and assuming all parties are on the same channel."

"Kind of like you did with using a safeword if I felt tingling or numbness?"

"Exactly. If I hadn't beat you over the head with how important that was and you had something start tingling, you would've kept quiet, wouldn't you?"

Hildy's face flamed. "Yeah, I probably would."

"Good girl. Thank you for your honesty." Wilson wrapped his arms around her and she felt peace. "And that's something else I want to talk to you about."

Hildy snuggled deeper. "What?"

"You totally relax when you're wrapped up tight. Whether it's in my arms, in a blanket or strapped down to the spanking bench. When you were unrestrained, you found the light smack of my belt unbearable, yet when I had you strapped tight to the bench, you didn't flinch, no matter how hard I hit you. And each strike was harder than the last. You might have a mark from the last one for a day or two, and I think the ride home gave you a taste of what sitting will be like for a while. If being wrapped is what makes you feel secure, don't worry. I have lots of ideas."

Hildy was embarrassed, but relieved. Wilson had picked up on her need to feel squeezed and didn't judge her.

"One more thing, Hildy. How was your sleep last night?"

Hildy had almost forgotten about the deal she'd made the previous night. The truth was her only option, but she'd promised he could do anything he wanted. She swallowed hard and confessed. "I had a really good sleep."

"Good girl. Your honesty is about to earn you a big reward."

"What are you going to do?"

"Anything I want."

"That's what I was afraid of."

"There's nothing to be afraid of, love. I promise. Only good things tonight."

"Will there be fucking?"

"No more questions, or I might become one of those Doms who demands complete silence from his sub. It's time for bed. I'll lock up and take care of things down here. Go brush your teeth and be waiting on the bed for me. Naked and on your tummy."

As she waited for Wilson to join her, Hildy let her mind wander, ramping up her nervous excitement over what the rest of the evening held for her. She heard him come up the stairs, and her heart sped up as he entered the room.

"Good girls get rewards, and you have been a very good girl."

Hildy found she loved it when Wilson called her a good girl, and realised she would do almost anything to hear him say it.

"What do I have to do to be a good girl, Wil?" She really hoped that didn't sound needy and pathetic.

"Hildy, you're always a good girl. Always. Sometimes you might do naughty things that require punishment, but you are always good."

"But what makes you tell me I'm a good girl?"

"Ah. Usually, I do it as positive reinforcement. Like when I ask you to do something and you do it, or when you tell me the truth, even if you think it's going to get you in trouble. You really like it when I call you good girl, huh?"

Hildy nodded as she buried her face in her quilt. "Good girl. We're going to have to work on using your words to answer questions, though. Part of avoiding miscommunication. I think it's time you got your reward, don't you?"

Hildy nodded with enthusiasm as she let out a muffled, "Yes."

"Such a good girl. Stay just like that. Would my good girl like a nice massage?"

She'd never had one before, but Wilson promised her a reward, so she figured it ought to be something she'd like. She turned her face to the side. "Yes, please."

"Such nice manners deserve to be rewarded, too. Would you like to come, baby girl?"

Baby girl? Hildy was shocked at how the endearment sent her already spasming pussy into overdrive. "Yes, please."

Wilson straddled Hildy, sitting on her thighs, just below the rise of her sore buttocks. "Let's start with a massage."

She heard the pop of a bottle, then felt Wilson's warm, slippery hands gliding along her upper back and working their way over her neck and shoulders. Heaven. He worked his way down her lower back and she groaned in complaint when took his hands away.

"Just need more lube, baby girl."

"Lube? You never said anything about shoving stuff up my ass." Hildy tried to rise, but was stopped by Wilson's hand between her shoulder blades.

"Relax, baby girl. The lube is for your massage. There will be plenty of time in our future to shove stuff up your ass, and I am looking forward to it. In the meantime, all I have planned is a nice massage and an orgasm. Maybe if you're a really good girl, I'll give you two."

Hildy let her upper body go loose, but squeezed her thighs together at the thought of an orgasm. Or two. It had been quite a long time, and she had no interest in masturbation.

"There you go. Would you like more massage, or would you like your orgasm now?"

"The massage was lovely, but I think I would really like my orgasm."

"If you're not absolutely sure, then I don't think you are ready for your orgasm. Maybe I should just rub your back some more."

"I'm sure, I'm sure. Please, Wil. I want my orgasm."

Wilson chuckled a little. "Well, if you're really sure."

"Please."

"Such lovely manners, baby girl. You just earned yourself that second orgasm." Wilson lifted himself off Hildy. "Turn over, love. Relax your legs and leave them where I put them."

Hildy closed her eyes and gave Wilson control of her body. He spread her legs and bent them so her knees were up and her feet were flat on the mattress. She wanted to come so badly, she didn't dare move.

"It looks like my good girl has a very leaky pussy. I'll mop the mess up in a minute, and I do look forward to plugging that leak very soon. But first, I have two very luscious tits to work over."

Hildy's eyes shot open when her nipples caught fire, and the hiss she tried to hold back quickly became a moan. Her pussy throbbed, and she could feel moisture dribbling towards her asshole. Wilson was grinning at her as he had a nipple trapped between the thumb and forefinger of each hand. He held tight and pulled them up as far as they would go. "That's my very good girl. I had a feeling you'd like this." He pinched and pulled harder. "Would you like to feel my mouth on your nipple, love?"

"Yes please."

"Such pretty manners." Wilson released one nipple before leaning in to tease it with the tip of his tongue. Hildy whined in frustration.

A white flash of pain shot through Hildy as Wil pinched her nipple harder. He lifted his head, his eyes flashing. "Unless you want to learn a lesson in patience, you may want to stop whining and lose the pout. You'll get your orgasms, but only when and how I want to give them." He lowered his head and caught her free nipple hard between his teeth. Her pussy pulsed, and with her nipple dragging through his teeth as he lifted his head, she was close to coming. She frantically tightened her inner muscles, but before they could have any effect, he let go of her nipples.

"Not yet, love. I've already told you, they're mine to give how and when I want, and stealing my pleasure is not a risk you want to take. You'll do well to take my warnings to heart, because you'll only ever get one before an offence becomes punishable." Wilson leaned down and touched his forehead to Hildy's. "For the most part, you've been good, so I won't make you wait too much longer."

Hildy trembled in anticipation as Wilson kissed his way down her body.

"I'm learning all kinds of interesting things about

you tonight. Some of them I suspected, but some have been rather pleasant surprises."

Finally. Hildy felt Wilson's fingers spread her outer lips. She used all her willpower to remain still when he dipped his tongue inside her, and she was almost to the breaking point when he kept dragging it upwards in long, slow licks, mercilessly teasing her clit. She thought she might die when he latched on, sucking long and hard, pulling and releasing with a rhythm so intense, when his fingers stroked her g-spot, her world spiralled out of control. When Wilson had wrung out the last whimper of her orgasm and she lay panting with her head floating somewhere near the ceiling, he started the whole process over again.

ONCE HE WAS sure he'd exhausted Hildy's second orgasm, Wilson lifted his head from between her thighs and studied her face. Peace and contentment were written all over it, and his heart squeezed. He slid his way up the bed and settled beside her. Hildy turned to face him, her eyes, glassy. "Thank you."

"It was my pleasure, love."

"How? I'm the only one who came."

"There is more to pleasure than orgasms, love. There are a lot of things that give me sexual pleasure that are not orgasms."

"Like what?"

"The puddle you left on the bed when I did mean things to your nipples, for one."

"You liked that?"

"Honey, I loved that."

"Did you like hitting me with your belt?"

"Yes, and no. I didn't like the reason why I hit you with my belt. I want to be clear, I don't enjoy punishing you. What I did enjoy was having you tied down at my mercy and how drenched your panties were by the time I was done."

"I liked being tied down."

"I know, and I have some ideas about that. In the meantime, I think my good girl is very tired and needs to sleep. Would you like me to wrap you up in your blanket?"

Hildy averted her eyes. "No, it's okay."

"Hildy, look at me." She slowly met his gaze, and he continued, "Either I do it, or you do it. Those are your only options."

Hildy thought for a moment, then whispered. "Would you do it, please?"

Wilson touched his lips to hers. "Of course I will." He gathered up the blanket and wrapped it tightly around her body until only her head poked out. Hildy let out a contented sigh and he was convinced she'd love rope as much as he did. Add the sight of his girl completely immobile, and Wilson's cock ready to burst. He gathered her in his arms and held her tight, as he kissed her with a passion he hadn't felt in years.

Hildy fought to stay asleep but the light and persistent tickling on her neck made it impossible. She opened her eyes to Wilson watching her. She glanced at the clock and groaned. "It's the middle of the night. What are you doing?"

"Waking my present up to see if she would like to suck my cock before I unwrap and fuck her."

Hildy's heart fluttered, her arousal, instant. "She would, thank you."

Wilson stroked his knuckles along her jawline. "Oh, there are those pretty manners again."

In an instant, Hildy was on her back with her head hanging off the edge of the bed and Wilson's cock tapping her lips.

"What a gorgeous sight. Open."

In this position, Hildy knew what Wilson wanted, so she parted her lips and relaxed her throat, her tongue extended in invitation. Self-preservation had perfected her ability to swallow cock. She'd had more than her fair share of men grab her hair and plant their balls on her chin in a single thrust. She'd learned quickly to anticipate and plan accordingly.

Wilson settled his bent knees either side of Hildy's head and slid his cock along her tongue, pulling back before he got anywhere near her throat. He slid in again and held still. "Close your mouth and suck like the good girl you are."

Good girl. Hildy didn't think she would ever tire of hearing those words. She closed her mouth and tried to shift her head to accept more of him. "Don't. Move." Hildy continued to suck, but held her head still. "You'll take what I give you. Nothing more."

Hildy was confused. Here she was in the perfect position to take a whole cock down her throat, and the man had given her barely more than the head. She did the best she could with what she had to work with, and almost sighed with relief when Wilson started pumping his hips. Each thrust, a little deeper until he finally reached the entrance to her throat. She wanted all of him, and she opened her throat as wide as she could, hoping he'd take the hint.

"That's very generous of you sweetheart, but not this time. As much as I'd love to feel my cock deep in your throat, it will never happen when biting is the only meaningful way you could tell me to stop. Suck just a little more, then I think I'll be ready to unwrap you."

Hildy continued to suck, alternating between strong and gentle, savouring his taste, but wanting more. She wanted to tease him, lap up the drops of pre-cum with the tip of her tongue, but his movements made it impossible. He was right, she would take what he gave her.

So caught up in what she was doing, Wilson's cock was almost clear of her lips by the time Hildy realised he wasn't going to give her anymore. She fought the urge to whine. She'd been warned. Wilson's hand slipped behind her head, gently lifting it as he resettled her on the bed. He dropped a kiss on her forehead, then retrieved a condom from his trousers.

Wilson peppered her face and neck with feather-light kisses as he suited up. "Mmm, that was lovely, and I look forward to more very soon, but I have another warm, wet place in mind to bury my cock." Wilson's words had Hildy feeling more than warm and wet. Her muscles were clenching rhythmically as she struggled to control her errant mouth.

Wilson chuckled while he slowly loosened the blanket. "Your lips may not be telling me to just fucking get on with it, but your eyes sure are. In my family, we always unwrap gifts slowly and carefully so we can reuse the wrapping."

"I don't think you need to worry too much about this tearing."

"True, but it's a good habit, so I think I'll stick with it."

Hildy fought hard to hold in her frustration, but based on her experience so far, patience did seem to have its rewards.

"Ah, I do believe you've figured it out. Good girl."

Hildy felt the cool air hit her hot skin as Wilson finally removed the last layer of blanket. She reached up and stroked his face. He smiled, then took her hands in his and settled them above her head. "Leave them there, love." Hildy nodded, not trusting her voice. She wanted this so badly, she didn't want to do or say anything to fuck it up. "Good girl. Now spread your legs wide. I need to taste you before I fuck you."

His words had Hildy on edge. Then his tongue started lapping at her pussy, and just when she thought she might go over the edge, he stopped. "Not yet, love. You don't get to come until I decide it's time." He gave her pussy one long lick then lifted and closed her legs before resting them on his left shoulder.

On his knees, with his cock firmly in hand, Wilson guided it into Hildy's weeping pussy, savouring each delicious inch. When his flesh was finally flush with hers, he hugged her legs to him with both arms, using them as an anchor while he savagely pistoned his cock in and out of her body. He watched her face the whole time, waiting until he knew she was almost of out of patience before leaning forward, trapping her legs between them. "Good girl. You can come when you like. I'll be right behind you."

He was almost at the tipping point, but her long, deep moan was all it took for him to put his impending orgasm on hold and slam his hips into over-drive, rolling and pounding, doing everything he could to keep her coming. When she was in the final spasms, he buried his head in the crook of her neck and moaned as he filled her with everything he had.

He lifted his head and beamed with pride at her determined obedience. "Such a good girl, Hildy. Your hands are precisely where they should be. Good girls get rewards." He carefully withdrew from her body, lowering her legs in the process. "I'm going to go take care of the condom, then come back to take care of you. Don't move a muscle."

WILSON'S VOICE sounded far away, but she heard him clearly calling her a good girl for not moving her arms. It took everything she had to keep them still during the longest, most intense orgasm of her life, but she did it, and now there would be a reward.

What kind of reward? Orgasm? She might need days to recover from the one she just had. Was it just one? There had been a point where she worried Wilson might make it go on forever.

"Are you ready for your reward?" Wilson flashed her that wicked grin of his and she was reduced to a puddle on the bed.

"I think it depends on what it is."

"It's not an orgasm this time."

Hildy was surprised at herself. She never thought she'd see the day where she would even consider turning down an orgasm, let alone one of the mind-blowing kind Wilson was clearly capable of providing. "What then?"

"Close your eyes, baby girl."

Hildy let her eyelids fall. Her sudden exhaustion overpowered her temptation to peek. "Good girl."

The next thing she knew, she was being cocooned. The fabric was much, much softer than her quilt, and she moaned as Wilson wrapped it snugly around her bare flesh.

"You can open them, now."

Hildy forced her eyes open and looked down at the fluffy purple blanket enveloping her body and grinned. "For me?"

"Yes, for you, love."

"To keep?"

"Yes, to keep."

Hildy fought back the tears. Nobody but Sully and her uncle ever gave her gifts. "Thank you."

Wilson reached over to turn off the light. "You are most welcome, love. Sleep now." She nuzzled against his chest and let out a contented sigh as he wrapped himself around her.

SEVEN

Wilson picked up the phone for what must have been the tenth time in as many minutes. This time, he pressed the final digit and let the call connect.

"Hey Wil, what's up?"

"I wanted to know if you would like to come to Finn and Mac's with me tonight?"

"I don't know. Things didn't go so well last time I went."

"Remember what Mac and I told you? All is forgiven, clean slate, and no bringing up past transgressions."

"Easier said than done, you know."

"I know, but the fear will just keep getting bigger if you don't deal with it now."

"Who's going to be there?"

"I can tell you Sloan won't be there. Does that help?"

"Not really."

"We don't have to go, but if we do and you can't deal, just safeword, okay."

"I'm too embarrassed."

"I can understand that, and I'm sure as hell not going to try to tell you how to feel, but I would really like it if you would give it a try. You know that's all I'll ever ask of you."

"But what if someone brings up what happened last time?"

"Won't happen."

"How can you be sure?"

"Trust."

"It's not that simple."

"For me, it is. You need to decide whether you trust me enough to keep you safe or not. I'm still earning your trust, and it's okay if you're not there yet, baby girl."

"I do trust you to keep me safe, it's the unknowns that I can't trust."

"I get that, but trusting me to keep you safe is trusting me to take care of the unknowns."

"It's too scary."

"You have safewords for that. If it's really that much too scary, you should call red right now. Are you calling red?"

"No, dammit."

"Brave girl. How about we go early and have supper with Finn and Mac, then we can see if you can relax enough to stay. If not, we can leave before anyone else arrives?"

"We can't just invite ourselves to supper."

"We didn't. They offered it up as an option if we'd like to join them. They're ordering in, so no need for advanced notice. So, what do you say?"

"And we can leave before people arrive if I'm not up for it?"

"Red, and we're out of there, I promise."

"Okay."

"I'm proud of you, baby girl. I'll be there at five. Bring your blanket and whatever you need for overnight. We're sleeping at my place."

"But we always sleep at my house."

"So far, we've always slept at your house. Tonight, that changes. I'll see you soon."

"Fine." Click.

Grumpy girl. He could work with that.

"You're really not mad at me?"

Wilson gathered Hildy into his arms. "I'm proud of you."

"I don't get it. How can you be proud of me for safewording out of staying for the play party?"

"It's another layer of trust between us. You trust me enough to respect your safeword and I trust you enough to use it appropriately."

"How do you know I didn't use it as an excuse to leave?"

"Back to your face showing everything, baby girl. I knew we weren't staying long before you called red. Would you like the ten cent tour?"

"Yes please."

Wilson took Hildy's hand and led her through each room of his house, leaving his bedroom for last.

"It's still early, are you willing to try a bit of rope-play before we head to bed?"

"What kind of rope-play?"

"Nothing too complicated, but a little more intricate than the gauntlets I did on Mac at the last play-party."

"I don't know."

"How about I show you some pictures and video of what I want to do so you have a better idea of what to expect?"

"Okay."

"Good, I'll be right back." Wilson shot out of the room and returned with his laptop a minute or so later. He sat on the bed next to Hildy and clicked through the file directory until he opened a folder called 'Body Harness Tutorial' and set up a slow slideshow. "I use these photos when I teach a class. This first one is of the end result. The next bunch show the steps to get there, and the last bunch are of the more elaborate rigging that can be done once the basics are mastered. If you have any questions, concerns, or want a longer look at a photo, tap my arm. Shall we begin?"

Hildy nodded. "Okay."

Wilson started the slide show and watched Hildy's face carefully as each picture slid across the screen.

HILDY COULDN'T BELIEVE what she was seeing. It was a wearable hug and oh, how she wanted one. "This is what you want to do tonight?"

"If you're game, I do."

Hildy could barely contain her excitement. "Oh, I'm game. What happens next?"

"You watch the demo video while I go grab my gear. After that, we begin. Normally, you'd be naked, but I don't want to overwhelm you, so you'll remain clothed."

Hildy nodded, returning her attention to the laptop. She barely registered Wil's exit as she sat captivated by the activity on the screen.

By the time Wilson returned, Hildy had played the video four times. Well, not the whole thing. She just repeated the part where Wilson does the actual binding and mentally inserted herself as the model.

Wilson brushed a finger down Hildy's arm. "So, are you ready to make that fantasy a reality?"

Hildy's earlier bravado was instantly replaced with

mortification as she felt like a nun caught in the condom aisle. She buried her chin in her chest and felt the burn rise to the tops of her ears. "Um..."

Wilson slipped a finger beneath Hildy's chin and tilted her face up. "Hey now, there's nothing to be embarrassed about, love. We all have fantasies, and I couldn't wish for better than a woman who fantasises about receiving what I like to dish out."

Hildy tried to turn her head, but Wilson latched onto her chin and held it in place while he brushed his lips over hers. "Change of plans, love. You're not ready for this just yet. Be naked by the time I get back."

Hildy stared at the floor and silently berated herself for being so utterly ridiculous. She had the perfect opportunity to try something she could wear anytime, anywhere, that could potentially provide the safe feeling she got from being wrapped in a blanket and she blew it.

"Were my instructions somehow not clear?"

Hildy startled and lifted her gaze to Wilson's. His eyes lacked their usual sparkle. "Huh?"

"Your manners have slipped considerably. That's not a particularly polite response. Would you like to try again?"

Wilson may have worded it as a request, but from the tone of his voice, it was an order, and she'd best comply before she landed herself in an even bigger pile of shit. No matter how badly she wanted to return her gaze to the floor, she toughed it out and maintained eye-contact. "Um, pardon?"

"Marginally better. When I left, I told you to be naked by the time I returned. You are still dressed, and I would like to understand why. Perhaps you'd care to explain?"

Hildy already had hold of a chunk of hair at the base of her skull before she caught herself and snatched her hand away, slipping it, along with her other hand beneath her thighs.

"Stop. What was that about?"

Hildy looked up and glared at Wilson. Fuck! She was an emotional teeter-totter and the urge to run away was overwhelming. This was why she didn't do relationships. Why hadn't she just stuck to her usual routine of bang and bounce where there were no expectations beyond getting off?

Wilson crouched in front of Hildy and laid his hands on her knees. "I'm going to help you get undressed and wrap you in your blanket; then we'll talk."

"I can undress myself."

Wilson stood and stepped to the side. "Okay. I'll give you ten seconds to get on it."

Hildy grabbed the hem of her top and whipped it over her head, firing it across the room when she let go. She'd pick it up later. She didn't want to give him any reason to undress her, that would be too intimate. She stole a quick glance at Wilson as she unhooked her bra, but his face gave nothing away. She returned her focus to removing her clothing. She needed the calm and safety of her blanket, and the sooner she got naked, the sooner she would get it. Except, would she? Wil said they were going to talk.

EIGHT

"Dammit, Mac, I don't know how to deal with this." Hildy paced up and down the length of her living room as she tried to adequately articulate her dilemma over the phone. "I'm so fucking mixed up." She let go of the hank of hair before she tugged hard enough to pull it out. She needed to pay closer attention to what she was doing before it became a problem again.

"Sweetie, we're all mixed up to varying degrees. Life is messy. It's how we deal with that mess that counts. So let's figure out how we can work with your mess, shall we?"

"I don't know. Things get scary, and I'm ready to walk away, then something wonderful happens, and I'm not so sure."

"Oh, honey, I know that feeling. I get the urge to flee back to my place regularly. I've come really close a few times, but Finn has managed to talk me down. Tell me what happened."

"The short version is, Wil was going to do a rope harness on me, and I was totally on board, until I wasn't."

"Short version? That's barely a tweet. Can you give me a little more to work with?"

"I don't know what went wrong. Wilson tried to talk to me about it afterwards, but I couldn't explain something I don't understand myself. I still can't"

"That's fair enough. Do you want to try the rope harness?"

"I'm cool with the idea of it. The reality of it is what I'm not so sure about."

"Is it possible you freaked because you were alone with Wilson?"

Hildy thought for a moment. "I don't know. Maybe."

"I know you aren't ready to play at a party yet, but what if you had some moral support? Finn and I would be happy to help out, but if you're not comfortable with us, I'm sure Sully would—"

"No! Not Sully. I don't think I could be naked around him just yet."

"You wouldn't have to be naked, you could—"

"Look, it's one thing for Sully and me to have in-depth conversations about our sexual escapades, but actually being present for them is something I'm going to have to work my way up to."

"Yeah, I get that. What about having Finn and me being there for you?"

Hildy noticed the small clump of hair and bloody skin in her hand a split second before she felt the pain in her scalp. Maybe she didn't have this as under control as she thought.

"Hildy? Are you there?"

"Shit. Yeah, sorry." Hildy frowned as she continued to stare at the hair in her hand. "Um, you and Finn being there..."

"Hildy, what's going on? Are you okay?"

"Yeah, yeah, I'm fine. Just a bit distracted."

"How about this? You come over for supper. I'll call Wil and invite him to come with his gear and we'll just let the evening unfold. No pressure."

"Okay, I think I can do that. Thanks, Mac."

"You are most welcome. We'll eat at six, so how about you swing by around five-thirty?"

"Sure, sounds good. I'll see you then."

"See ya."

Hildy dropped the phone and let the tears fall. She thought she was done with this shit. She couldn't remember the last time she'd resorted to hair pulling. She checked her watch. Less than half an hour until the next student and she needed to get her shit together.

"Hey, Mac, I was thinking about calling you."

"About what happened with Hildy last night?"

"Yeah, but I'm glad she's already talked to you. She had me pretty worried."

"She didn't really give me any details. All I know for sure is she's feeling pretty messed up. Something happened while we were talking and she became really distracted."

"Maybe I should call Sully."

"I think you should hold off on that. For now, anyway. Her relationship with Sully is changing, and she needs to process it in her own way. She's coming over for supper tonight. I told her I would invite you and your gear along and we'd see how things work out. Just the four of us and no pressure. Are you up for that?"

"Sure. What kind of gear did you have in mind?"

"Whatever you like, but you might want to make sure there's rope in your arsenal."

Wilson chuckled. "Honey, there's *always* rope in my arsenal."

"I know, but I figured I'd mention it anyway, just to be sure."

"And I appreciate that. Is there anything else I can bring tonight?"

"Nope, just your lovely self and your gear. Supper's at six. I told Hildy to be a half hour early, but I think you should already be here when she arrives."

"Will do. Is Finn around?"

"Yeah, he's right here."

Hildy was self-conscious about the wound on her scalp and had struggled all evening to keep her hands away from her head, desperate to avoid drawing any attention to it. Something she was finding harder to do once she and Mac and retired to the living room after supper. At least while they were eating, she'd had something to keep her hands occupied. Now her nerves were getting the better of her, and to fight the urge to pull more hair out, she squeezed her hands into fists so tight, her neatly trimmed nails dug into her palms.

"Hildy, are you okay?"

Mac's question broke her concentration, and her hand shot to the sore spot on her head. "What? Yeah, fine. Just a bit nervous."

"I can understand that, especially since I think those two are up to something."

"What do you mean?"

"After I invited Wil for supper, he and Finn had a long, private conversation. When Finn threatened a week without orgasms if I got within earshot one more time, I figured it was time to give up trying to find out what they were up to."

"Maybe it's time I should go."

Mac made a sad puppy-dog face. "And leave me to face the unknown by myself?"

Hildy snorted. "Oh, come on, Mac. This shit is nothing new to you."

"Yeah, this shit, as you call it, is nowhere near as new to me as it is to you, but there is still an awful lot of unknown and scary out there for me. I do think they're up to something, and knowing Finn, it's going to push my boundaries. I understand if you need to leave, and I can respect that, but if you can bring yourself to stay, even if you red-light out of whatever Wil has up his sleeve, I would really appreciate the moral support."

And that was it, there was no way Hildy could leave now. Mac had been so wonderful and supportive, right from that first phone call. "Okay, I'll stay."

Mac got up and sat next to Hildy on the sofa and pulled her in for a big hug. "Thanks, sweetie."

"So that's why we got relegated to kitchen-elves, Wil, Mac wanted a little alone time with Hildy."

Hildy stiffened as she tried to pull away, but Mac hugged her tighter before gently releasing her. "Relax, he's teasing. Although, I'm sure he'd be all for me participating in a little girl on girl action, it would never happen without his permission."

Hildy looked up in time to see Finn wink at Wil. "Damn straight, love. But not tonight. We've got other plans."

Mac smiled and patted Hildy's knee. "See, I told you

they were up to something." Then she turned to Wil, her voice tinged with steel. "I think it would be a really good idea for you two to tell us what your intentions are now."

Hildy held her breath and fisted her hands again, worried Mac was heading for punishment.

"Calm down, Mac. Wil and I were hoping you and Hildy might be willing to let us rig you up in chest harnesses. Nothing elaborate, and nothing you haven't done before. We thought maybe it might work better for Hildy if she had some company. Wil and I are going to go to the music room and deal with some administrative stuff while you two discuss this. Come get us when you're done." Without another word, he and Wil left the room.

Mac turned back to face Hildy. "So, are you feeling brave?"

"No."

"What are you scared of?"

"Failure."

"Remember that conversation we had before that play party you came to? The one where I said all anyone should ask of you is to try?"

"Yeah."

"Then, if you try, how can you fail?"

"By not actually doing whatever it is I've been asked to try."

"Really? If you agree to try something, you give it a go, but don't finish because it's not for you for whatever reason, is that failing?"

"Of course it is."

"Okay, let me ask you this, if Finn asked me to try play piercing and I did, but safe-worded because it was more than I could stand, have I failed?"

"Of course not."

"Why?"

"Because you tried, just like he asked."

"Now, what makes you any different from me?"

"It doesn't matter."

Mac looked at Hildy's fisted hands. "Honey, you're going to do some damage like that. Let me have a look."

"No, they're fine"

"Either you let me look, or I'm going to yell for those men, and I can assure you, if I yell, Finn will come through here like the devil is on his ass. Now, do you want to deal with me, or a couple of over-protective Domly-types?"

Hildy eased open her hands as she squeezed her eyes shut.

"Oh, sweetie, you've almost broken the skin. We need to find you another way to cope"

"This is my other way to cope." Hildy really needed to regain control of her mouth from her subconscious.

Mac gathered Hildy in her arms before shouting, "Wil!"

Hildy tried to pull away, but Mac was strong even as she soothed. "I'm sorry, sweetie, but I like you too much to let you hurt yourself."

Finn and Wil burst into the room and Wil immediately dropped to the floor in front of Mac and Hildy. "What happened?"

"She's been self-harming. Look at her palms."

Hildy was mortified. Trapped as she was, she buried her face in Mac's neck and tried to hide her hands.

Wil stroked her leg. "Love, I need to see your hands."

"Red."

And with that one little word, Mac released her and she was free. She jumped up, ready to race for the door when she caught sight of the tears rolling down Mac's cheeks. Fuck! The last thing she wanted to do was hurt her friend. Damn Uncle Erich for dying. Ever since that fucking funeral, her life just kept getting more and more complicated. She cast one more wistful look at the door, then heaving a big sigh, she dropped her chin, and held her hands out to Wil.

Wil took her hands in his and kissed each palm gently before pulling her in for a hug. "Oh, sweetie. What could be so bad that you'd hurt yourself?"

Hildy burrowed her face into Wil's chest and struggled not to clench her fists or reach up for a hank of hair.

Mac spoke for her. "She's worried about failing you, Wil."

Wil hugged Hildy tighter to him and kissed the top

of her head. "Even if you did fail me, what's the very worst thing that could happen?"

Hildy squeezed her eyes shut and tried to block out how failure had been dealt with in her family. The everyday careless indifference was bad enough, but it was the wilful neglect she endured for failure that spawned the hair pulling. The worst that could happen for failing Wil? He could walk away.

NINE

Early morning light filtered through the gap in the curtains in Finn and Mac's spare room, and Wil stroked Hildy's hair as she slept in his arms. To say the evening had been emotionally charged was understatement. He was oblivious to so much about Hildy and her past, and he was powerless to help her until he had a better handle on what she was dealing with. He suspected even Sully didn't understand the full extent of the damage.

The plan for the night before had been to keep the subject matter light and transition into some simple rope bondage. He'd known at supper things weren't going to go as planned. As hard as Hildy tried to hide it, her face was broadcasting her struggle in HD and they'd spent enough time together over the past weeks for him to know this self-harm thing probably wasn't new.

What the fuck was he doing wrong? There was no question she liked the idea of bondage. He wrapped her up like a mummy every fucking night before they went to sleep, and she was more than good with it. The squirming she so desperately tried to hide when she saw others all roped up was further evidence of her interest. So why was it whenever he brought the rope out, she lost it? Blanket bondage was all well and good for blow-jobs, but it didn't lend itself well to much of anything else he enjoyed.

Perhaps he could come up with a gradual transition from blanket to rope. He continued to stroke Hildy's hair as he considered his options. It didn't take him long to come up with an action plan with options dependent on Hildy's reactions. He kissed the top of her head and gave her a gentle squeeze. "Wake up, sleepyhead, it's time to get up, and I smell coffee."

"Five more minutes." Hildy whined and snuggled deeper into Wilson's embrace.

After one more squeeze, Wilson pulled away and unwrapped Hildy's blanket. "Nope, it's time to get up. We've got a busy day ahead."

"How's that? We didn't make any plans for today." Hildy stretched her arms above her head, then rubbed her eyes. "What if I already have plans?"

"Do you?"

"Well, no. But I could have."

"No more talking. You're too grumpy before you've had coffee." Wilson climbed out of bed and got dressed. He grabbed Hildy's clothes and laid them on the bed for her. "Here, put these on. We'll have coffee here, then go back to your place to get showered and clean clothes. I'll have your coffee ready for you by the time you get to the kitchen." He turned and left, not waiting for a response. He considered Hildy's pre-coffee grumpiness. Yes, it could be frustrating, but it's part of who she was, so he would work around it.

DAMN HE WAS BOSSY. Why the hell did she put up with it? Life had been so much easier when she didn't have a man in it. What right did he have to make plans for her day without discussing them first, anyway?

Hildy got up and made the bed before slipping into her clothes. She picked up her blanket and held it to her face a moment before shaking it out to fold it. She reconsidered and hurled it on the bed. She was getting too attached. One stupid present and she was ready to change the way she lived her life?

She needed to get the fuck out, now. She gathered her belongings and took one last, wistful look at the blanket, then slipped out of the bedroom. For once luck was on her side, she could hear Wil, Mac, and Finn in the kitchen. She tip-toed her way to the front door, pausing only long enough to slide into her shoes and snag her coat off the hook.

The deadbolt was well-oiled and opened without a

sound. As soon as she was outside, Hildy twisted the doorknob to keep the latch from snapping as she eased the door closed. So far, so good. She raced to her car, thankful she'd parked on the street. She wouldn't have to waste valuable time backing out of the driveway.

Once she was safely away, coffee was her first priority. She considered going to Sully's, but solitude was more appealing. She'd had enough of bossy men for a while. Her phone rang and at the next stop light, she turned it off without bothering to check who had called. She didn't care. Dammit, chances were good someone, probably Wil, would show up at her house before too long, and she wasn't up for that yet. She spotted a coffee shop and pulled into the parking lot.

Yeah, this would do for a few hours. She could happily spend a lazy morning loading up on caffeine while reading magazines. Anything to take her mind of her fucked up life for a while.

Hours later, Hildy had exhausted the magazine selection and moved on to the newspapers. As she idly flipped the page, she almost spilled her coffee. There, in the middle of the entertainment section, was a two-page spread on her uncle. Blinking back tears, she closed the paper, and abandoned her coffee. She thought she had her grief under control, but seeing the photographs brought it flooding back.

She managed to hold herself together long enough to drive home, but by the time she got there, she was too distraught to notice her parents until she was out of her car and it was too late.

———

Wil rang the doorbell and knocked again. "Hildy, love, I'm worried. Please open the door." He tried to stay calm. He'd alternated between angry and worried sick all day. Between Sully's call about her bat-shit crazy parents being on the rampage and Hildy not responding, he was firmly entrenched in worried sick. Fuck. He knew he should have listened to his gut and headed straight to Hildy's the moment he discovered her gone instead of listening to Mac's advice to give her some space.

The silence on the other side of the door was making him crazy. "Hildy, please, just let me know you're okay." More silence. He looked at his watch and said, "That's it, if you don't open this door and show me you're okay within the next sixty seconds, I am going to call 911 and have the police come to do a welfare check."

He heard the locks click and sighed with relief as the door creaked. Hildy's eye appeared in the narrow opening. "I'm fine, now go away."

Wilson stuck out his foot to keep her from closing the door. "Honey, what little I can see of you doesn't look fine. Can I please come in and see for myself?"

"No, I'm fine. I just want to be alone."

"Fair enough. When I see that you are fine, I'll go away. I'm not the only one who's worried about you, though. Sully is frantic, and there is no way I am going to face Mac without being able to tell her I saw you with my own two eyes."

Hildy huffed, and when she opened the door, Wilson had to stomp on his rage. She'd made a valiant effort with the make-up, but there was no mistaking the black eye and split lip.

Fuck, when Sully had asked him to come over to check on her, he'd only said things might get ugly and she would likely be upset. Either Sully's idea of upset was a far cry from his own, or Sully had seriously underestimated the situation. Both options sucked.

God, there were so many things running though his head at that moment, and most of them involved extreme violence, but his number one priority had to be Hildy, and she was hurt.

"There, now you can go report back to the others that I'm fine and want to be left alone."

"Baby girl, what I see does not even come close to qualifying as fine." Wilson stepped through the door, and fought his urge to take Hildy into his arms. She'd just been assaulted, and she needed to be able to trust him. "Honey, let's get some ice on your poor face."

"It shows?" Hildy asked, the disappointment clear in her tone.

Wilson nodded and headed to the kitchen to get something to help with the swelling. He needed some time to get himself together. He needed to be strong for her, and he didn't trust his voice just yet.

It took a minute of rooting around the freezer before he found a small, unopened bag of frozen peas. Perfect. He turned to see Hildy in the doorway, looking so lost and fragile. He held out the package. "Go get comfy in the living room and put this on your face. I'll be there soon."

As soon as Hildy was out of sight, Wilson pulled out his phone and called Mac. "Hey, it's Wil."

"It's about fucking time you called, you inconsiderate jerk."

"Take it easy, she only just let me in, and that was after threatening to call the cops. Look, it got uglier than Sully led me to believe. I haven't had a chance to fully check her over, but she tried to cover up facial injuries with make-up and I need some advice on how to clean her up as painlessly as possible."

"If she has make-up, then she's probably got wipes to remove it. Go have a look in her bathroom. How bad is it?"

"From what I can tell, time and TLC should take care of it. I'll know better once I get that make-up off. I'll let you know right away if I think she needs medical attention, otherwise, assume no news is good news."

"Okay. I'll let everyone else know you're with her and not to worry. You take care of her and let her know we're here if she needs us."

"Will do. Thanks, Mac." Wil disconnected. It

didn't take him long to locate the wipes and when he saw the bottle of Tylenol, he took that too. She had to be hurting. As he passed through Hildy's bedroom, he grabbed her quilt.

He entered the living room and Hildy looked up, the left side of her face obliterated by the bag of peas. "Hey, baby girl, we can talk later, but right now, let's get you fixed up." Wil laid the quilt across the arm of the sofa, pulled a wipe out of the packet, and crouched in front of Hildy. "We need to get that make-up off your face, but it's probably going to hurt. Have you taken anything for the pain?"

"I'm fine."

"That's not what I asked, love."

"No, I don't need anything."

"In case you change your mind." Wilson set the bottle on the table and held up the wipe. "I need to assess your injuries, so let's start with your face. Can you move the bag of peas so we can get you cleaned up and I can have a good look?"

Hildy brought her knees to her chest. "It's nothing that a little time can't heal."

"You're probably right, but I want to make sure."

Hildy lowered the bag from her face and Wilson carefully schooled his expression. Hildy was upset enough without his anger making it worse. "Close your eyes and hold still. I'll be as quick as I can." He reached up and started at her brow, surprised and relieved at how effectively the wipe worked. He worked his way around her eye, tamping his anger harder every time she winced. "Okay, love, almost done. I just need to do your eyelid." He pulled a fresh wipe from the packet and carefully slid it across her bruised flesh.

"It's pretty swollen, but I think you're right, time will take care of it. Where else are you hurt?"

"Just my face."

"Truth?"

"Really, Wil. It's just my face. I'm fine, so you can go now."

"Not a chance, love. You seem a little shocky to me. Let's get you all bundled up, then I'll make you some broth."

"Just go. I don't want you to bundle me up, and I'll get my own food when I feel like it." Hildy put the peas back to her face and turned her head away.

"Hildy, look at me." Seconds ticked by. Finally, Hildy turned back to face him and he smiled. "There you are. Honey, I'm not going anywhere. I'm not walking away. We've had this discussion before about the difference between want and need."

Wilson rose, picked up the blanket, and unfolded it. "Up you get." Hildy stood and laid the packet of peas on the coffee table. He held the blanket open and gently wrapped it around her as she stepped into it. Once she was swaddled, he carefully lifted her into his arms, and laid her on the sofa. He tucked a cushion beneath her head and settled the peas back on her battered face. "There you go, love. I'll be back in a few minutes."

As the broth heated in the microwave, failure and guilt tangled with helplessness and weighed heavy in Wilson's gut. It was all his fault his sweet, sweet Hildy was hurt. He'd pushed too hard, and when she'd left, he didn't go after her. He should have been here, protected her. God, his heart hurt. The microwave beeped. Time to go fight for his woman.

"Here you go, love." Wilson set the cup on the coffee table. He reached down and removed the bag of peas, then helped Hildy sit up. "Comfy?"

"I can't feed myself like this."

Wilson picked up the cup and held the straw to Hildy's lips. "You don't need to. You just need to be comfy. Open." Hildy sighed, opened her mouth, sucked in a mouthful, and swallowed. "Good girl. I'm going to go pop those peas back in the freezer, then you can have the rest."

When Wilson returned, Hildy's head was resting against the back of the sofa, her eyes closed. He wanted to bundle her into his arms and never let her go. He eased down next to her and waited for her to open her eyes. "Ready for more?" She nodded, and he replaced the straw at her lips, holding it steady for her to sip at her leisure.

The straw gurgled as Hildy sucked the final drops of broth through it. She pulled her head back and gave him a half smile. "Thank you."

Her first smile since he'd arrived. "You're welcome, love." A glimmer of hope squeezed past fear and now he had to risk its retreat. "We have to talk about what happened today, and sooner is better than later." Hildy lowered her chin to her chest. "How about, for now, I talk, you listen?" Hildy nodded.

"I want to start with this morning. I need you to understand that I am not angry with you. I pushed you too hard, to the point where you felt the need to quietly disappear. I'm sorry. I'm even sorrier that I didn't come after you. I wanted to, but Mac said you probably needed some space, and I should give it to you. I shouldn't have listened to her."

Hildy looked up. "No, she was right. I spent the morning and part of the afternoon in a coffee shop avoiding you. I'd probably still be there but..." She trailed off and dropped her chin again.

Wilson forced himself to back off. Pushing her was what had got him into this fucking mess in the first place. "Alright, love. It's been a rough day, and you need some rest. We'll leave the rest for now and I'll take you to bed."

"No, just get me out of this quilt and leave."

Fuck, he was losing it. Losing her. "Hildy," Wilson's voice broke, "God, Hildy, I can't. I know it's selfish of me, but I can't leave you by yourself. Going all day not knowing where you were or if you were safe was bad enough, but seeing you hurt ripped my fucking heart out. I need to know you're safe. If you really need me to go, I'll get Sully to —"

"No, I definitely can't deal with Sully right now."

Wil took a long shuddering breath and pulled himself together. "Sweetheart, it's been a shitty day and we both need sleep. I'll sleep out here on the sofa, but I want to get you settled in your bed first. I'll unwrap you so you can get yourself ready, then I'll bundle you back up before you go to sleep, okay?"

"I don't have any choice, do I?"

"Not when it comes to being here by yourself, no."

"Fine. Can you unwrap me please?"

Wilson helped Hildy to her feet and carefully removed the quilt. He was dying to kiss her, but didn't dare. Even if she were open to it, he'd be too scared of hurting her. As soon as she was free, she took off towards her bedroom, not even glancing back. He sank onto the sofa and buried his face in his hands.

How DID her life get so complicated? Hildy stared at her bruised face in the mirror as she tried to find the most painless way to brush her damn teeth. What a mess. Why the hell hadn't this perfectly nice guy, who cooks and could fuck for bloody England, given up on her already? She was fucking neurotic, wouldn't let him tie her up, even though they both fucking well wanted it. What was wrong with her? He should be out finding himself a bloody normal woman, not some stupid—

"What have I told you about that?"

Shit. She caught his reflection in the mirror. God, he looked awful. Had she done that? She'd been so self-absorbed, she didn't notice him arrive. She spit out the toothpaste and carefully rinsed her mouth. "What?"

"You know exactly what, baby girl."

Yeah, he was going to make her ass pay dearly for putting herself down. "You wouldn't, would you?"

"While you're injured? Of course not. Save them up for when you're better? Without a doubt. Are you ready to go to bed now?"

Hildy turned, avoiding Wil's sad eyes as she nodded. Bed and sleep, that's what she needed. Fuck. It had been weeks since she'd slept by herself, weeks in which she'd woken feeling well-rested, where she'd felt safe and loved. What kind of idiot would give that up?

"Hildy, enough. Now, scoot."

Eyes firmly fixed on the floor, Hildy trudged to the bed. She was angry with herself for the hasty choices she'd made. A fit of pique, and if she were totally honest with herself, fear, had led her down the path to misery. Was Wil really here because he cared about her, or was it because he felt responsible? Shit. She didn't want to sleep alone, but she didn't want him to sleep with her out of some misguided sense of obligation.

By the time she reached the bed, Wilson was

sitting on it. He patted his lap and opened his arms wide. "Come sit down, love."

She hesitated for a moment, but it had been a lifetime since he'd held her and the need to be in his arms overwhelmed her doubt and fear. She eased down and leaned into Wilson's chest, sighing when he held her close. She let the silence settle for a few minutes before she gave in to her need to know. "Why are you here?"

Wilson tipped her chin up and gazed into her eyes before placing a gentle kiss on the corner of her mouth. "Because I love you." He kissed her again.

Hildy furrowed her eyebrows in confusion. "How do you know?"

"Sweetheart, when I walked into that bedroom and saw you'd left with everything except the blanket I gave you, my whole world exploded. The thought of not having you in my life sucked the air out of my lungs. Now you're back in my arms, I can finally breathe. When you walked away from me all those years ago, you took a small piece of my heart with you. When you walked away from me this morning, you took the rest."

Guilt burned deep in her belly as she pondered his words. In her desperation to protect her own heart, it didn't occur to her she could be damaging Wil's. Hildy thought back through her day, finally understanding that constant ache in her chest was from leaving her heart behind with her blanket. Now the ache was gone, and he sure as fuck didn't want it to come back.

Was that love? Maybe. "I don't want to sleep alone tonight."

He hadn't blown it, thank fuck. It was so hard to lay his heart on the line after she'd walked away. But he got it, she was scared, confused, and convinced he was going to leave her. After a lifetime of protecting herself, it was going to take time and a lot of testing before she was going to believe he was in it for the long haul. "I don't either."

"Can we sleep the way we did that first night, no blanket around me, just you?"

"If that's what you want."

"It's what I need."

"Okay, baby girl, you get yourself into bed. I'll join you as soon as I check the locks and brush my teeth." Wilson waited until Hildy was settled under the covers before he left the room.

With the house locked up tight and his teeth brushed, Wilson returned to the bedroom. Hildy had the covers pulled up to her ears and she was doing a laughable job of pretending to be asleep. She looked so adorable. He wanted to pounce on her and make her squirm. That would have to go on hold along with the ass-paddling she'd earned earlier. "Faker." Hildy's mouth twitched and Wilson chuckled. Damn, that felt good. He stripped to his boxers and slipped into bed beside Hildy. "Oh, you're naked."

Hildy giggled and placed her hand on Wil's bare belly before sliding it south. "Yeah, I am. The question is, why aren't you?"

He caught Hildy's wrist and pulled it away before she got near his erection. "No sex."

"But—"

"I need you to understand, really understand, I'm not here because I'm a selfish horny bastard and you're a great lay. I am here because I love you. All of you, exactly how you are. And until you trust me, there is no sex."

"I do trust you."

"No, you don't. But you will."

"What makes you think you know better than me whether I trust you?"

"Rope bondage. You want it as much as I do, but without absolute trust, it isn't going to happen."

"Seriously, I don't get sex until you get to tie me up?"

"Pretty much. Your trust is important to me. I can wait."

"What if I can't."

"Honey, nobody ever died from not having sex." Wilson slipped his arms around Hildy and shifted her until her back was pulled tight against his chest. She wiggled her ass into his groin and he almost reconsidered his no sex edict. "I love that you're feeling playful, baby, but you need to stop or I'm going to add to the punishment you've already earned tonight."

"Spoil sport."

Hildy finally stopped moving, and Wil concentrated on deflating his cock. He stroked her head and brushed his lips over her shoulder. "Hildy, what happened with your parents today?"

WHAT THE HELL, she may as well tell him. He was still here, and it wasn't like it could get any worse. "They had discovered Uncle Erich left everything to me, and came to persuade me to rectify his error. When I said no, my mother resorted to more forceful methods."

"Baby, I'm so sorry I didn't protect you."

"Wil, I made my own choices and didn't give you any opportunity, so there's nothing to be sorry about."

"Okay, we'll agree to disagree. Your mother was the one who assaulted you?"

"Yeah. She was just getting started when my neighbour pulled into his driveway. I had enough of my wits about me to not let them come inside, so the minute a potential witness appeared, they legged it. I am fine, Wil. Honestly."

"I came over as soon as Sully called. He'd called to warn you, but it kept going straight to voice-mail. I assume you didn't check your messages."

"No, my phone is still off."

"New rule, baby girl, your phone stays on and you answer when a friend calls. No excuses."

"There you go, being all bossy again."

"Your safety is non-negotiable. You had a lot of people worried today."

He was right. She'd been inconsiderate. Guilt started to eat at her again.

"Stop beating yourself up, love."

Fuck, how did he always know?

"You give it away every time, and that's a good thing. For both of us. I would like to know one more thing. How come you snuck out instead of coming to me and using your safeword? You've used it before and it's been okay."

She'd asked herself the same question countless times already, and the answer was always the same. "I don't know."

"Okay. But don't be surprised if it has something to do with trust."

TEN

THE ROPE WAS rough in her hand. She felt guilty for going into Wil's toy bag, but she wanted to surprise him. She didn't think he really meant it when he said no sex, he was a man, after all. But as with everything else, he was true to his word.

Her face had been healed for almost two weeks and Wil hadn't so much as hinted at rope or bondage. He did occasionally pull out his Dom-voice which made her knees melt. She wondered if he realised she did stuff on purpose just to get him to use it. Probably.

She looked at the rope again. Not so scary. She thought about the photos Wil had of other women he'd tied up, and jealously reared its ugly green head. She didn't want him tying up anyone up but her.

She checked the clock. Time to get moving, he'd be walking through the back door in a few minutes.

Naked, Hildy knelt at the door, her head bowed,

Wil's rope in her outstretched arms. She was terrified this was going to backfire, but her patience had run out. She fought the urge to raise her head when the door opened, and she had a horrifying thought. What if Wil wasn't alone? Maybe she should have given this a little more careful thought.

"A naked woman bearing rope. What a beautiful sight to come home to. Up you get, sweetheart, it looks like we need to have a chat." Dom-voice.

Hildy lifted her head, relieved that Wil was alone and sporting a wide grin. He took the rope from her with one hand, and helped her up with the other. He pulled her into his arms and kissed her, teasing her lips open and plundering. Want surged through her like lightning through copper.

Wil took her hand and led her to the sofa in the living room. He laid the rope down, then pulled Hildy into his lap as he sat. "So, what's this all about?" He asked as he patted the rope beside him.

"Trust."

Wil hugged Hildy tight and kissed the top of her head. "Okay. First, show me your palms."

Yeah, that was fair. She held out her hands. Wil nodded, then lifted Hildy's hair and slowly worked his way around her hairline at the nape of her neck. He wouldn't find anything. She'd been so good. She hadn't ripped out any hair since that awful day.

"Such a good girl. Okay, we'll try something very basic, no knots. Stand up, lift your arms, and lace your fingers behind your head." Wil picked up the rope and folded it in half. "All I'm going to do is wrap this around you, just below your breasts and slip the two loose ends through the middle, or bight. Okay?"

Hildy looked at the rope Wil held out and nodded. He stood behind her and reached around in front, lifting her boobs with his thumbs as placed the rope right where her boobs and chest met. It felt a bit scratchy against her skin, but she liked it. How weird was that? The rope tightened briefly, then was gone.

"Good girl. That's enough for today."

"But—"

"Enough."

She spun around and put her hands on his chest. "Wil."

"Let's end this on a positive note. We can do more another time."

"Please?"

He took her face in his hands and touched his forehead to hers. "Baby, I'm so scared I'm going to fuck this up again, and I can't bear the thought of losing you."

Hildy clutched at his shirt, "Wil, I want this. I need this." He wrapped her in his arms and hugged her tight. She rested her head against his chest and she could hear his heart racing as she felt it pound against her cheek. Gradually it slowed and she felt him relax a little.

"Okay, we can try a rope harness, but I need you to promise me you'll safeword if you have a problem."

"I promise."

Wil released her and spun her around so her back was to him again. "Okay, we're going to start a little differently this time. Hands behind your head again, like you did before." Wil reached in front of her and placed the rope above her breasts and she felt a bit of friction at her back and some tugging as he tightened the rope "Give me a colour, love."

"Green."

"Good girl. Here comes the next one." He brought the rope around the front, this time beneath her breasts before she felt more friction and tugging. "Still green?"

God, she loved it. She didn't think she could get any greener. Each tug brought her a little more peace.

"I need an answer, love."

"Oh, yeah, I'm good."

"On we go, then." Another pass above her breasts, more tugging at the back, then he brought the rope over her shoulder and moved to stand in front of her. He grinned at her and she grinned back. He passed the rope between her breasts, slipping it beneath all the ropes that around her chest. A little more fussing and tugging, then he placed the rope over her other shoulder. "Still good?"

"Mmm."

"I need a colour, love."

"Yeah, I'm green."

"Excellent. A knot at the back, and we're done."

He stepped behind her and a few tugs later, he was done. "Still green, my good girl?"

"Hell, yeah."

"You look beautiful. Now go wait for me on the bed. On all fours, I think."

Hildy raced off. She didn't need to be told twice.

THE JANGLE of Wilson's belt buckle had Hildy wet and ready to beg. She'd waited weeks for this and she didn't want to wait another moment. She felt the bed shift behind her as Wil climbed on.

"I thought I wanted to fuck you like this, but I don't. I want to gaze into those beautiful eyes of yours while I love you. On your back, sweetheart."

Hildy turned over and her heart flipped in her chest. Wil's eyes smouldered as he stroked her cheek. He leaned down and touched his lips to hers before he kissed his way to her earlobe and nibbled. "I love you, Hildy Klein."

She wanted to say those words back so badly, but she was still trying to figure out what they meant. She needed to give him something, but it had to be something that meant the same to both of them. Then it came to her. "Wil?"

He pulled back and looked into her eyes, "Yes, love?"

"I...I trust you."

"Thank you, baby girl. That means everything to me." Wil crushed his lips to hers before trapping her bottom lip between his teeth and tugging gently. He caught hold of her wrists and held them over her head in one hand as he kneed her legs apart. He let go of her lip and kissed a trail south until he reached her nipple. He sucked and licked it as he slid one finger, then two into her eager pussy.

"Please."

He released her nipple with a pop. "Please what, love?"

"Please don't tease me."

"Okay. You've been such a good girl." He let go of her wrists and kneeled up. "Leave them there." He leaned over and grabbed a condom packet from the bedside table and opened it. He paused a moment. "On second thoughts, you do it."

Hildy grinned as she sat up and took the condom from him. Normally, she'd tease him for a bit, but she was done waiting. She deftly rolled the condom over his erection and flopped back on the bed throwing her arms back above her head

Wil positioned his cock at her entrance, holding it there as he leaned forward. He reached up and laced his fingers with hers, then rested his weight on his elbows. He lowered his mouth to hers as he slowly entered her body.

Fuck, she didn't want slow and gentle. She was horny as hell and wanted hard and fast. He eased out of her, and as he slid back, in she thrust her hips up to meet his. "That wasn't quite what I had in mind, but we can go there." He let go of her hands and rolled them over until she was on top.

Hildy knew Wil wasn't likely to give her control very often, so she'd have to make every opportunity count. She laced her fingers with his, like he'd done earlier and lifted up so just the head of his cock was inside. She kissed him as she slid down hard, taking him deep. She rocked back and forth for a few strokes before rising up and plunging down again. She varied her depth and speed until she felt the tell-tale flutter. She plunged deep one more time and ground her clit into Wil's pubic bone. She let go of his hands and guided them to her hips. He pushed up into her as he held her tight against his body, the friction doing delicious things until she finally let go with a long, low moan.

Wilson held her hips tighter and thrust up and ground into her, sending her over once more before she felt his cock pulsate as he came. Spent, she lowered herself onto his chest and his voice rumbled. "A quick cuddle now, then it's off with the condom and the harness." She nodded and drifted off, only vaguely aware of Wil untying her.

ELEVEN

Hᴵʟᴅʏ ᴊᴏɪɴᴇᴅ Mac in the kitchen where she was busy loading the dishwasher. "So, you're really going to give up your place and move in here with Finn?"

"Yup. It's still months away, but it's only a formality."

"Still a pretty serious formality."

"It's not marriage."

"Close enough."

"Brat."

"You love me anyway."

"I do. So, are you really up for this?"

"Yeah, I am."

Mac closed the dishwasher and turned to Hildy. "Safeword if you need to."

"I know, but I'm relaxed." Hildy held out her palms. "See, no nail marks and here," She lifted her hair, "no pulling."

"In that case, let's go. Finn's been vibrating with anticipation all day."

"Ha, so has Wil."

Hildy and Mac sauntered down to the play room where Finn and Wilson sat on chairs side by side.

Finn grinned. "Glad to see you both finally made it. We are beginning to think you weren't coming. Mac, strip and bend over, please."

Mac walked over to Finn, slipped out of her clothes and folded them, then bent forward resting her palms flat on the floor.

"Good girl" Finn picked up a butt plug off the table next to him and loaded it with lube. Mac moaned as the plug slid home.

"Oh, you like that, do you, baby girl?"

Hildy swivelled her head toward Wil. She'd been so absorbed in what she was watching, the soft whisper caught her off guard. "What?"

"You tend to pay very close attention whenever Finn plugs Mac's ass and that little smile that plays over your lips gives you away. Mac's getting a fun spanking tonight, but your ass still has to pay for putting yourself down while you were injured, so we'll be doing a bit of a variation on Mac and Finn's scene."

Shivers shot down Hildy's spine, and oh boy, they were the good kind. She smiled up at Wilson and he couldn't quite keep his lips from tipping up at the corners. "Okay."

"Strip, fold your clothes, and lay over my lap exactly like Mac."

As she removed and folded her clothes, Hildy studied Mac's position over Finn's lap. Her hips were against Finn's left thigh, her own legs extended back and trapped beneath Finn's right leg. Her toes supported her, bent almost like she was wearing high heel shoes, and her palms were flat on the floor. Okay, it looked precarious, but she could do that.

Hildy laid herself over Wil's lap, emulating Mac as best she could. Once she'd settled, Wil clamped his leg over hers. He stroked her back and she relaxed.

"Good girl. You earned ten with the leather strap for putting yourself down. I know you thought I wouldn't follow through, so I decided to give you a little added intensity to make sure you get the message loud and clear."

He parted her buttocks and she felt a little thrill. He was finally going to use a butt plug. She liked anal, but Wil was taking everything so damned carefully, they'd barely got past missionary since they'd started having sex again.

The probing at her anus didn't feel like much more than a cold wet finger. Okay, maybe a bit bigger than a finger, but not by much. It felt pretty good, though. Hildy moaned a little, then Wil wiggled the plug a bit before pulling it most of the way out and pushing it back in. Then the burning started. "Ow, take it out, my asshole is on fire."

"Excellent, now you're ready for your spanking. I'm feeling generous, so I'll make it quick."

Hildy looked over at Mac who smiled and winked while Finn smacked and rubbed her ass. That didn't look so— Holy shit! The burn in her asshole was barely a glow compared to the hell Wil rained on her ass. By the time she had her breath back, the blows stopped, the plug was out, and Wil was stroking her back.

"All done, love, clean slate."

Hildy panted through the waves pain "That hurt."

"It was meant to. I warned you not to say or think bad things about yourself, and I shouldn't have let you get away with it as much as I did. No more. From now on, I have a zero tolerance policy for that shit, and I'll be increasing the consequences with each infraction."

"I didn't think you'd be that mean about it."

"Now you know." Wil opened his legs and caught Hildy under the arms to help her up. "There you go. Are you ready for some fun, feel good stuff now?"

They'd talked in detail about the plans for the evening. She'd been letting Wil tie her up for weeks now and she loved it. She'd even got to the point where she could ask Wil to tie her in a rope harness when she needed to feel snug. Tonight, Wil and Finn were going to tie her and Mac together and play. She couldn't wait.

She cupped his face and kissed him. "I trust you. I'm ready for anything."

ACKNOWLEDGMENTS

Élianne Adams, Elizabeth Varlet, and Zoe York for their unwavering support and encouragement. The wonderful gang of Divas who are generous in so many ways. And of course, my wonderful, supportive husband, who says yes to almost everything...except another dog.

ONE GOLD TRIQUETRA

ABOUT THE BOOK

A decade ago, a bad play-date turned composer Ella Hudson off BDSM.

Now she's been offered a performance opportunity too good to pass up, but it means working closely with Jackson and Griffin--world class musicians, lovers, and Doms intent on adding her to their relationship.

While Ella struggles to deny her true desires, maintaining her vanilla facade becomes increasingly difficult as the men re-introduce her to a world she'd written off.

For my dear friend A.
Thank you for always being there.

JACK SET his toy bag down with far more care than his temper demanded. "Dammit, Griff, I thought this one had promise."

"I know, babe." Griff leaned in and touched his forehead to Jack's. "Look, do you really think we need a beard? Sully knows the score and he's cool with it. Do you honestly think Wil and Finn will care? I'm fucking tired of sneaking around. You like to fuck me, I like to fuck you. So what? It's nobody's business but ours, and I don't like constantly having to produce a third to camouflage our relationship. Don't get me wrong, I'm always happy to have some subbie pussy around to torture and fuck, but not to keep up appearances. It makes me feel like I'm not good enough."

Jack brushed a gentle kiss over Griff's lips. "Idiot. You know it's more than just fucking. I love you. You're way beyond good enough; you're everything to me.

However, the reality is, neither of us subs, so even if we outed ourselves, we would still need a submissive if we wanted to play at Finn's parties."

"You're right, but I'm fed up with playing musical subbies. This one seemed like she might work out, you know? I don't understand how I could have been so blind."

"Don't go taking all the credit. I was just as blind. She took everything we dished out and begged for more. Maybe I was more wilfully ignorant than blind. Can you imagine how deeply we could have got involved with her if that business with Hildy hadn't happened tonight? All the trouble she could have caused for us? I feel queasy just thinking about it."

"We sure dodged a bullet with that one. Speaking of Hildy, what's the deal? Wil is notorious for going out of his way to avoid newbies, yet he shows up to a play party with one?"

"Not our business."

"I know, but I don't think we've ever had a newbie at a party before. Even Mac had some previous experience."

"Again, not our business."

"You're no fun."

Jack grabbed the hem of Griff's shirt and lifted. "Oh baby, I'm lots of fun."

ONE

GRIFF SMILED WIDE as he followed Jack into Finn's music room. "Sully, you old slacker, it's about fucking time you got back to work."

"I figured if I didn't show soon, I'd be looking for a new gig."

"Does this mean you're back in full swing?"

"I don't know about full swing, but I've been swizzling the hitty-sticks a little. Fucking busted ribs completely crimped my style."

Griff just about swallowed his tongue when Mac walked in wearing nothing but clover clamps on her nipples and leather cuffs on her wrists. His head was full of questions, but when Jack caught his eye, he nodded and kept them to himself. Not his business.

Sully, who considered everything his business, was not so polite. "Nice outfit, sweetie. Special occasion?" Mac glared at Sully and slowly flipped him the finger.

Griff held back a chuckle when he spotted Finn leaning against the door jamb. Oh, for a bowl of popcorn.

"Oh dear. What an unfortunate turn of events, my love." Finn walked across the room, sat in his chair, and patted his hands on his thighs. Mac stalked over to him and laid herself across his lap.

He reached down and grabbed the thin wooden cleaning rod for his flute. "Before we begin, why are you being punished?"

"I was disrespectful."

"Yes, you were. I accept that you and Sully have a special understanding, but when I have your submission, you must be respectful to everyone, regardless of your normal dynamic. It's not like you don't know any better. We've had this same conversation before. What was your punishment last time?"

"Ten strokes with your hand."

"And what happens with repeat offences?"

"Double the last with whatever implement you choose."

"That means it'll be twenty with the cleaning rod. Colour, Mac?"

"I'm green."

"Good enough. I'll keep count. Do not move." Finn placed his left hand on the small of Mac's back before taking the first stroke. He laid stripe after stripe across her ass, never striking the same spot twice. Mac's facial contortions and tears were the only sign of her struggle to accept her punishment. By the time Finn was done, her ass was striped like a candy cane. "All done, love. Now go apologise to Sully, and once your slate is clean, we will continue with what you were supposed to be doing before this little interlude."

Mac rose from Finn's lap and accepted the tissue he held out. She took a moment to wipe her tears and blow her nose. Then she went over to Sully, knelt at his feet, and rested her forehead on his knees. "I'm sorry."

"All is forgiven, sweetie. I'm sorry too. I shouldn't have teased you." Sully leaned forward and kissed her head. Mac looked up and smiled, then rose to her feet and returned to Finn.

"Good girl. Hands behind your back and turn around." As soon as her back was turned, Finn clipped her cuffs together and kissed her shoulder. "Off you go, sweetheart."

Griff caught Sully's eye and raised an eyebrow as Mac sat on the piano bench. Sully shrugged and shook his head slightly. How the hell were they supposed to have a productive rehearsal with a naked, decorated Mac in the room? More to the point, how was Finn going to concentrate on the music when most of his focus would be on his sub who would be teetering on the edge of her limits?

"Holy shit, if I'd known it was bring your sub to work day, I would have brought Hildy. She and Mac would look so cute sitting on the piano bench with their tits clamped togeth—"

The colour drained from Mac's face, and Finn flew to her side as he snapped at Wilson. "Enough." He unclipped Mac's cuffs and gathered her into his arms. "Sweetie, I fucked up. I'm so sorry." As he left the room with Mac, Finn turned to the rest of the group and said, "You guys go ahead without me."

Wilson stepped towards them. "Mac, Finn, I'm—"

"Not right now, Wil. I need to take care of her. Maybe before you leave..."

Wilson ran his hand through his hair. "Yeah, sure."

As soon as Finn and Mac were gone, Sully pounced. "Dammit, Wil. What were you thinking?"

"I wasn't. It just slipped out. What was going on, anyway?"

"My best guess is Finn was pushing at Mac's issue with the piano bench and figured doing it during rehearsal with a room full of Doms was the best way to do it. He probably would have been right if he'd thought to give us a heads up. He's usually more on the ball about this kind of thing."

Taking pity on Wil, Griff spoke up. "Don't beat yourself up about it, Sully was rather indelicate himself and Mac's reaction earned her a candy-striped ass."

Sully had the decency to look a little sheepish. "Yeah, I think Griff and Jack are the only ones who haven't caused Mac pain of one kind or another today. Right, I guess we should get on with it. What are we playing first?"

TWO

As soon as the front door snicked shut, Jack was up against the wall, and Griff was kissing him like his life depended on it.

Jack grabbed Griff's shoulders and pushed him away. "Whoa, what's this all about, babe?"

Griff leaned back in and thrust his hips forward, grinding them into Jack's groin. "I'm horny."

"That's obvious, but why?"

"What do you mean, why? Since when do I have to have a reason to be horny?"

"We've been together for almost as long as we've been members of Dominant Cord, and not once have you ever tried to jump me the minute we got home from a rehearsal. So, I ask again, why?"

"I guess it was watching Mac submit to Finn—at least before it all went to shit in a handbag—it was beautiful and sizzling hot. It was love. I want that for us. It made me horny."

"You don't think we have love that makes you horny?"

"Are you being purposely obtuse? Our love makes me all kinds of horny. Sharing a sub with you makes me all kinds of horny, too. But I think having a mutually loving relationship with a sub would make us complete. And before you get all pouty, you know as well as I do that we'd probably end up killing each other if we didn't have a sub to torture, and you love pussy just as much as I do."

Jack had no idea what to make the whole situation. He trusted Griff absolutely, but he had a tiny, nagging doubt he could not shake. Sudden changes in behaviour didn't happen without a reason, and Griff got that horny from witnessing a monogamous, heterosexual, Dominant/submissive interaction—not the homosexual interaction waiting for him at home.

It wasn't that long ago he'd wanted to out their relationship to the world, and lately, he'd stopped banging on about it. Did he really want a bi-sexual, poly relationship or was he looking to go straight? He knew Griff's comment about killing each other if they didn't have a sub was meant to ease his concern, but it only did the opposite.

Despite his fear for his relationship, he decided to smooth things over. "Okay, I get it, but I think we might be asking a bit too much of the universe. How many people are lucky enough to find one perfect love, let alone two who also have to love each other? It's a tall, tall order."

"Doesn't make it impossible, though."

Jack stroked a finger along Griff's cheek and brushed a gentle kiss on his lips. "No, you're right. It doesn't make it impossible." He leaned in for another kiss as he took hold of Griff's hand and guided it to his erection. "But see what you do to me? That's all because of you."

"Aw, fuck! Just because I haven't jumped on you after rehearsal before doesn't mean you don't get me all hot and bothered. Rehearsals take it out of me, and after blowing my horn for hours, I'm not in much of a mood to blow anything else, not even your perfectly delectable trouser trumpet."

If only Griff would shut the fuck up. Every time he opened his mouth, he made it worse, and Jack had to wonder if Griff's subconscious had taken control of his mouth. He wasn't usually this insensitive. They say to fake 'til you make it, so Jack decided to brazen it out and not let his hurt show. Instead, he dropped to his knees. "How about I blow *your* perfectly delectable trouser trumpet instead."

By the time he'd made the offer, Griff had his jeans at half-mast and his cock on parade. "Now you're talking."

Jack held Griff's cock at the base as he swirled his tongue around the head, occasionally darting to the centre to lap up the pre-cum. He continued to tease until he felt hands at the back of his head—Griff's way of telling him it was time to get serious.

He opened his mouth and sucked on the knob, alternating between strong and gentle. Jack fought the increasing pressure at the back of his head that was forcing him farther down Griff's cock.

"Fucking goddammit, Jack. I'm in no mood for being teased."

Jack pinched the inside of Griff's thigh and pulled away from his cock. "And I'm not a fucking sub you can order around. Blow your own fucking horn. I'm going to bed.

STANDING with his jeans around his knees and his rapidly deflating cock swinging in the wind, Griff wondered what the fuck just happened. One minute, he's well on his way to blowing his load down his lover's throat, the next, he's left hanging without a clue. Past experience, while rare, had taught him to leave Jack alone and wait until he was asleep before joining him in bed.

Griff pulled up his jeans and refastened them. He took a quick trip to the kitchen to grab a beer, then he retreated to the living room and flopped on the sofa.

No matter how he looked at it, he couldn't figure out what had set Jack off. Yeah, watching Finn push

Mac to the edge of her limits and how beautifully she submitted totally got his motor running, but did it really matter what got him all charged up as long as he spent the energy at home? Surely there had to be times when Jack came at him with all cylinders firing because he had been turned on by something external to their relationship. It couldn't be the idea of adding a female sub to their mix. Jack had been pushing for that for years.

Griff switched on the television and zoned out. He was done trying to figure out what the issue was. Jack was both a grown up and a Dom, and as such, he had a responsibility to communicate.

An explosion on the TV startled Griff awake. He checked his watch and figured Jack would be asleep. He hated it when Jack fucked off to bed in a huff. It didn't happen often, but when it did, life tended to really suck for a while. At least he'd be able to get some sleep before he'd have to deal with Jack's next wave of anger.

He crept into the bedroom with his arms outstretched to help him feel his way to the bed. He'd already stripped and taken care of all his needs in guest bathroom to reduce the risk of waking Jack.

He was momentarily blinded by the sudden glare of the bedside lamp. "Quit your fucking creeping around, Griff, and get into bed. I'm tired."

Shit. "I didn't want to wake you."

"Bullshit. You waited until you thought I was

asleep so you could avoid any more conflict. It's what you always do. This time I didn't bother pretending to be asleep so you could avoid me."

"What the fuck is that supposed to mean?"

"Did you honestly think I would be able to go to sleep before I knew you were safely in bed with me?"

"I thought you were over that."

"Well, I'm not. Getting called in the middle of the night to come to the hospital because you were injured in a car accident *after* I'd gone to sleep knowing you were safe here at home is not easily gotten over, dammit."

"Look, I've apologised for it time and again. I don't know how many times I've promised to never leave the house when we've had a fight, but you still keep throwing it in my face. It needs to stop. I get it. I made a promise. At some point, you're going to have to trust me to keep it."

"And at some point, maybe I will. But I'm not there yet. Now come to fucking bed, I'm tired."

Griff climbed in and Jack shifted away from him.

"Oh for fuck's sake, seriously? You would rather risk falling out of bed than touching me? Grow the fuck up."

Jack moved farther away and Griff was done fucking around. He slid in behind Jack and slipped his arms around him, dragging him tight to his own body, then shifted them both towards the middle of the bed. "Please stop. We're both tired and running off at the mouth. We can fight in the morning if that's what you want, but please stop for tonight."

Jack's muscles relaxed and he let out a long sigh. "Fine. Goodnight."

"I love you, Jack. Only you. You're my heart." The cold silence he got in return launched a steady stream of tears that continued long into the night.

JACK LAY AWAKE, waiting for Griff to stop his fucking crying and fall asleep so he could get away from him. He knew Griff was upset that he hadn't reciprocated his declaration of undying love, but the truth was, he was really struggling to trust Griff. While he *had* kept his promise not to leave the house after a fight, he thought about the stuff Griff had said earlier, and it had him feeling less and less confident about the security of their relationship.

After what seemed like hours, Jack couldn't stay put any longer. As he tried to gently extricate himself, Griff hugged him tighter. It finally got to the point where he didn't care whether he woke Griff up and hurt his feelings. "For fuck's sake, let me go. You're smothering me."

Griff sprung away. "God forbid I should fucking smother you. I'm going to sleep in the guest room. I'm not leaving the house, so sleep or don't sleep. I really couldn't give a flying fuck." He shot out of bed and slammed the door on his way out.

Jack lay there wondering how they could possibly consider bringing a third into their home when their own relationship was on such shaky ground.

He flicked the lamp on and grabbed his book. Sleep would be impossible without Griff in bed with him, and it was either read or stare into space all night. He'd barely started his second page when he heard the door creak. He looked up to see Griff's sheepish grin. He returned it and flipped the duvet back. "Come to bed?"

Griff bounded across the room and slipped in next to Jack. "I'm sorry."

"Me too. Let's go to sleep. We can talk in the morning, okay?"

"Yeah, okay."

Jack was just drifting off to sleep when Griff insinuated himself between Jack's legs. Normally, he would be thrilled to have a warm, wet tongue traversing the length and breadth of his cock, but this was not hot make-up sex. This felt more like suck-up sex—an attempt to wash away the anger and upset from earlier. It made him want to puke. He reached down and pushed Griff's head away. "Stop. Just stop. I'm exhausted, and we agreed to go to sleep."

Griff pulled away and settled in next to Jack. Close, but not touching. As he finally drifted off to sleep, Jack wondered how they were going to fix this, and more importantly, did he want to?

Griff reached for Jack as he did every morning upon waking, and for the first time in all their years together, Jack wasn't there. They'd had fights before. Long, drawn out, vicious fights, but even if they went to sleep without resolving the issue and a rousing bout of make-up sex, Jack was always there when he woke up. Something was seriously wrong.

He climbed out of bed and slipped on his robe. He didn't normally worry about wandering around naked, but if he and Jack were going to hash this out, he wanted some kind of armour. He sniffed for signs of coffee. There were none. Not good at all. His nagging bladder was over-ruled by his sudden, urgent need to find Jack.

He raced through the house, his panic increasing with each empty room he encountered. He finally found Jack in the guest bathroom, sitting in the tub. His knees were pulled tight to his chest and his face was buried in his arms.

The sight shredded Griff's heart. "Hey."

Jack raised his head, revealing his blotchy, tear-stained face. "Is there nowhere in this fucking house I can be alone?"

"Give me thirty minutes to get some shit together and you'll have *everywhere* in this fucking house to be alone." Griff turned on his heel and stomped out.

He headed straight to the en-suite to finally empty

his bladder and gather his toiletries as he frantically tried to figure out where he could go. Those who had space didn't know about his relationship with Jack, and Sully— the only person who did know—barely had enough space for himself, let alone a house-guest.

Who was he kidding? He wasn't the type to impose. He'd be better off in a hotel. He'd get his ass out of the house first, then worry about accommodations. He considered leaving Jack a note, but decided to text him once he was settled. He'd let Jack worry for a bit before easing his mind.

He took a final look over his shoulder as he headed out the door. He'd hoped Jack would stop him before he could leave. With a heavy sigh, he pulled the door closed, the soft snick of the latch, his only goodbye.

THREE

The fucker probably wanted something. That was usually why he called. The phone continued to ring in her hand and Ella was seriously tempted to let it go to voice-mail. If she didn't answer, she couldn't say yes to whatever favour he'd ask. In the end, curiosity won out. "Well, hey there, Sully, it's been an awfully long time. What's up?"

"Ella, my darling, I have the perfect venue for that piece of yours."

"And which piece would that be? I'm not exactly a one hit wonder, you know."

"While that is true, I only know of one piece you've written that couldn't be scored in a Disney film."

"Oh, that one. Really? You've got a venue for it?"

"Yeah. Friends of mine are having a kinky commitment ceremony of sorts on August 16, and I immediately thought of your piece. So, are you interested?"

For once, Ella didn't have to lie. "Of course I'm interested." It was the one piece she'd written and never heard played. "Give me a second while I check my calendar." She reached across her desk and flipped the pages of her appointment book. "You're in luck, it's one of the few dates I do have free this summer. Hold up—venue is one thing, but it won't play itself."

"How many parts are there, and do they all need to be played by percussionists?"

"I suppose we could get by with one percussionist if we had three reasonably coordinated musicians with a decent sense of rhythm."

"I've got a quintet full of Doms to draw from, so I guess we just need the percussionist."

"If you don't have someone in mind, I know one who'd be perfect. I just need to confirm availability."

"It's your piece, so you would know best. That said, I think it would be a good idea for you and the percussionist to meet with Mac and Finn ahead of time. It's their celebration, and it's crucial that they are completely comfortable with all the attendees—for obvious reasons."

"No problem, but I tend to have weekdays more open than evenings and weekends. Do you think we can work something out to fit with that?"

"Absolutely. Just get back to me with a few times

and dates that will work for both you and your percussionist, and I'll set it up."

"Will do. Thanks for this, Sully. You've just made my day."

"Always happy to help, my sweet. Now we have business out of the way, let's get caught up. You're right, it has been far too long and I have been a bad and neglectful friend."

They'd talked for more than an hour by the time Ella punched the end button on her phone. She'd tried to ignore the stab of guilt when he told her about his busted ribs. It *had* been forever since they'd been in touch, and even with her crazy schedule, she should've made some time for her friend.

She thought back to the reason for his call and let herself get a bit excited. She'd been sitting on that piece for years, and quite frankly, she had expected to be sitting on it until she died.

She needed to call Teagan to double check her availability, but first, she wanted to reacquaint herself intimately with the piece before she discussed it with anyone. She didn't have any difficulty locating the file. Even if she hadn't kept meticulous records, it was the one piece she'd never lose.

Her journey through the piece brought the memories, both good and bad, flooding back.

FOUR

Sully answered the door and swept Ella into his arms. "You look gorgeous, my sweet." He laid a loud smacking kiss on the top of her head and gave her another squeeze.

Fortunately, Ella was prepared for the moment Sully noticed Teagan, because he dropped her like a hot brick. She tried not to let the laughter bubble out when she saw him practically drooling at the sight of Teagan's perfectly pedicured bare feet as she slipped them out of her ballet flats. He was so easy. Teagan was already his type, but with that raging foot fetish of his, Ella, knew he'd be a sucker for some bright red toenails. No, she wasn't above a little manipulation.

"Sully, I would like introduce you to Teagan Fitzpatrick. She's the percussionist I told you about."

From the way Sully's gaze kept bouncing between Teagan's offered hand and her bare feet, Ella was a little worried he might skip the niceties and drop to the floor to kiss her feet instead. Thankfully, his professionalism won out. "Pleased to meet you, Teagan," he said as he shook her hand. "If you will follow me to the living room..." Sully shot Ella a wide grin and turned to lead the way.

The room full of people took Ella by surprise. She had only been expecting to meet with Mac and Finn. She shot Sully her best annoyed look. He just shrugged in typical Sully fashion and led them towards the group. She'd almost forgotten that Sully was more of an ask forgiveness than permission kind of guy.

He pointed to each person as he made introductions. "Ella and Teagan, I would like to introduce you to Finn and Mac, the happy couple. Wil, Griff, and Jack will be the other percussionists, and Hildy, Lucy, Karen, and Jenn will provide the playing surfaces. Everyone, this is Ella Hudson, our composer, and Teagan Fitzpatrick, our percussionist."

Mac stood and took Ella's hand in hers. "Welcome. Sully's told us about your piece, and I have to say, I'm thrilled that the world première is happening at my little shindig."

"I'm glad it's finally getting to see the light of day. Did that miserable reprobate tell you it's been rotting in my bottom drawer for a good ten years?"

"He did. He was like a kid at Christmas who couldn't wait to play with a new toy. I shit you not, his eyes sparkled and he rubbed his hands with glee at the prospect."

Ella laughed. She had no problem conjuring up that image. She had seen it enough times in person.

Ella continued to chat with Mac, occasionally glancing at Teagan to make sure she was okay. She needn't have worried. Sully was being the perfect host, and things looked promising. She turned her full attention back to Mac, and was startled to see they'd been joined by Jack and Griff. She looked back and forth between the two. "Uh, hi." Oh, she was fucked. Actually, she wasn't, and not likely to be, but her panties were soaked. They were both far too tempting.

By the time they'd each flashed her a saucy grin, her panties were in such a state, sitting was no longer an option, and she still hadn't decided which of them posed the greater risk to her self-control.

Griff offered his hand, and the rich timbre of his voice made her want to drop to her knees. "Hi, I'm Griff. I'm looking forward to playing this piece of yours."

"Ella, hi." Oh, how she hated these kinds of things. The awkward meetings and uncomfortable silences. She got more than enough of those when she attended performances of her work. Ella disengaged her hand and was immediately offered another to shake.

"I'm Jack. Pleased to meet you, Ella." Aw hell, Jack's voice would be every bit as effective at getting Ella to submit to anything as Griff's.

"Likewise." What the fuck was that? Who, in this century, says fucking likewise? She tried to ignore the resulting blush that burned to the tips of her ears. She just smiled and waited until she could politely reclaim her hand.

"Oh, pack it in, you two," Mac warned. "Come on Ella, let's get something to drink."

Ella nodded and followed her host. Once they were in the kitchen, she said, "Thanks. I have no idea what the hell just happened there."

"*That* was two Doms trying to claim the same territory." Mac grinned and opened the fridge. "Help yourself."

Ella grabbed a can of Coke and leaned against the counter. "I'm *so* not Dom territory. I will admit to experimenting back in the day, but it wasn't for me." The lie tasted bitter on her tongue.

"Oh dear. Considering your piece is called *Rhapsody in Black and Blue for Instruments of Ass Destruction* and involves hitty-sticks and naked flesh, I got the distinct impression you wouldn't have a problem attending our celebration"

"Crap. I'm sorry, I should have been more clear. While I'm not interested in participating, I don't judge, and I'm perfectly fine with others participating around me. Besides, this will probably be its only performance, and I won't do anything to jeopardise that."

"Fair enough." Mac patted Ella's hand. "If you're comfortable, I'm comfortable. I'm assuming Teagan knows what to expect from the piece and the performance?"

"Yeah, you have nothing worry about there. There are a bunch of reasons why I recommended her."

"Not the least of which, faith she and Sully would hit it off?"

"Busted. I was hoping I'd been subtle."

"I've been trying to get Sully settled for years. One look and it was obvious to me he's his match. "

Ella grinned at Mac. "So far, so good."

"You do realise, I'm going to do everything I can to help this along."

"I'll take all the help I can get."

"Help with what?"

Fuck. Like her panties weren't soaked enough already.

Mac turned. "Nothing that concerns you, Griff. Don't you have somewhere else to be?"

"Nope." Griff flashed another cheeky grin at Ella.

"Look, Ella and I were having a private conversation, so if you do not mind..."

"I can take a hint. Just let me grab a beer, and I'll be out of your hair."

Mac rolled her eyes and smiled at Ella as they waited for Griff to leave.

He grabbed a beer from the fridge and shrugged. "I'll see you both later, then."

As soon as he was out of sight, Mac giggled. "You like him."

Ella groaned. "No."

"Oh, come on, tell me you didn't just cream in your panties."

"I can't tell you that, but I've already told you, he's not for me." The pang of disappointment was hard for Ella to ignore.

"If you don't sub, then you're right, he's definitely not for you. He plays hard."

"Who plays hard?"

"Oh for fuck's sake, Jack. If we wanted to include you and Griff in our conversation, we wouldn't have escaped to the kitchen."

Ella needed to get the fuck out really soon. She was having enough trouble coping with her ridiculous attraction to Griff and Jack, but conflict, no matter how trivial, was something she couldn't cope with. "It's okay, Mac. I need to get going anyway." She drank the last of her Coke and placed the can on the counter with the other empties. "Is there anything else we need to go over?"

"But you just got here," Mac protested.

"I know, but I'm on a deadline." Ella knew it was a flimsy excuse at best, but it wasn't really a lie, more of an exaggeration, and she needed to get out of there before the panic set in.

"I understand. I'll walk you out" Mac placed a hand on Ella's shoulder and gave Jack the stink-eye as they walked past.

Ella scanned the room for Teagan as she entered,

and was not surprised to see Sully had her backed into a quiet corner on the far side of the room. She and Mac exchanged knowing smiles.

As Ella and Mac approached, Teagan raised her eyebrows. Sully turned around and said, "There you are. Teagan and I have been getting better acquainted."

"Look, I need to head out, I have a lot of work to do." Ella paused a moment. "Teagan, I'm sure someone can give you a lift home if you would like to stay longer."

"I'd be more than happy to drive you home," Sully blurted out.

Ella had to stomp hard on her mirth and didn't dare look at Mac as an image of Sully bouncing up and down with his hand in the air, screaming, "Ooh, ooh, pick me, pick me!" popped into her head.

"I appreciate the offer, Sully, but I think I will head back with Ella." Ella knew Sully didn't have much experience with rejection, and Teagan turning down his offer pretty much guaranteed he'd keep trying.

Jack lay awake in his bed. Alone. Again. Still.

What a completely shit week it had been. He had gone from blissfully attached to miserably single in the space of a few painful hours. He hadn't believed Griff would really leave until he heard the roar of the engine. His heart shattered with Griff's broken promise.

When the realisation hit, he'd immediately climbed out of the tub and pulled the plug. He'd tried not to panic as his mind catapulted him back to the last time Griff left home angry.

He'd been asleep in bed when the call came and launched him into a nightmare. He'd had to shake the cobwebs from his brain and process the horrifying news before he could function, wasting precious minutes he could have spent with Griff in the hospital.

The hours he'd spent waiting for the phone to ring since Griff's departure, were unbearable. The longer it was silent, the more frantic he became. The fear and anger had his gut churning so much, he'd spent most of that time dry-heaving in the toilet.

A measly two word text: *Not dead*, finally arrived more than four hours after Griff had left. If the situation hadn't been so fucked up, he'd have probably laughed. Instead he sobbed with relief.

They hadn't talked since. Sure, they'd spoken when necessary to keep up appearances, but they hadn't actually *talked*.

Rehearsals were the worst. It was like some twisted comedy. Guys who were together but pretending they weren't, are now no longer together and pretending nothing's wrong while they're not together.

The house was no longer his safe refuge. Was it ever? With Griff gone, it no longer felt warm and inviting. He missed Griff's laughter. The silence was suffocating.

The one small bright spot in his week disappeared as quickly as she'd arrived. If they'd met Ella before that epic fight, they'd be lying here together, plotting the best way to make her theirs. Considering how fast Griff had moved in on Ella this afternoon, he was probably busy plotting the best way to make her his alone.

The horn solo from Bach's B Minor Mass blared through the silence. Think of the devil, he's sure to appear. He flicked the light on and grabbed his phone to read the text. *Call me?* His heart banged and his fingers fumbled as he stabbed at the buttons.

Griff answered on the first ring, but didn't speak. Jack waited. By his reckoning, it was Griff's turn to do something, and the mere act of answering the phone didn't rate. He glanced at the screen. One minute and forty-three seconds. If Griff didn't say something by the time it hit two minutes, he was hanging up.

"You still there?"

Jack took a deep breath as he willed himself to be civil and not voice all the snark bouncing around inside his skull. "I'm here. What's up?"

There was a heartbeat of silence before Griff cleared his throat. A sure sign he had been crying. "I miss you."

Jack didn't know how to react to Griff's admission. Wants and needs bombarded him at warp-speed, but acting on any of them would make him more vulnerable. He was barely holding it together as it was. He didn't know if his heart could survive another stomping. As tears streamed down his face, he scrambled for the right thing to say—for both of them.

Another deep breath. "I miss you, too." The truth. More silence.

They had been together long enough for Jack to know when Griff was working his way up to something difficult. Griff had made the first move, so he could be patient.

"Can I please come home?"

Fuck. What they wanted and what they needed were not even close to the same thing right then, and

Jack hated being the bad guy. He took a moment to gather his thoughts.

"I understand how hard it was for you to ask, and I want to say yes. I really want to, but we've got to work through how we got into this mess so we can find a way out of it. If you come home before we do that, I'm concerned we'll fall into bed, fuck like bunnies, and be so disgustingly happy in the moment, we'll shove this mess into a closet and forget all about it until one of us trips the latch and it all spews out and buries us.

"To be perfectly clear," Jack continued, "I would love nothing more than to do exactly that, but I think we need to sort through our issues first. My heart can't bear a repeat performance of the last week."

"Not even if I sleep in the guest room?"

"It has nothing do with where you sleep. You know as well as I do, we'd end up fucking the minute you walked through the door."

"Then how are we supposed to work this out?"

"We meet in a public place."

"Can we do it soon?"

"Ten o'clock tomorrow morning for coffee at Brewster's soon enough?"

"Can we make it eight?"

Jack looked at the clock. It was already three. "You want to do this on five hours sleep?"

"I'll be lucky if I manage two. I can do ten if that's what you need."

"No, I'll be there at eight. Goodnight."

"G'night."

Jack wondered about Griff's motivation as he slipped his phone back on the bedside table and switched off the light.

Would Griff have contacted him tonight and asked to come home if they hadn't met Ella? It bothered him that he would probably never know the answer. It bothered him more that it mattered.

GRIFF SAT at the table in the far back corner of Brewster's. He hadn't been able to sleep and had arrived shortly after they opened at six. He checked his watch for what must have been the thousandth time since he first sat down. It was still half an hour before they were supposed to meet, but knowing Jack, he could turn up any minute. He went to the counter and ordered two coffees so he could have one waiting for Jack as soon as he arrived.

He had no idea how they were going to find a way to fix the problem, when he didn't have a clue what the problem was.

This past week had been unbearable and he was exhausted. Sleep had been elusive, and when it did finally come—it was short-lived and disturbed.

He'd let his temper get the better of him, and he was paying for it. Instead of spending the week sleeping in Jack's arms, he'd spent it in an empty bed with nothing but his right hand for company.

The pettiness of making Jack wait hours before letting him know he was okay was among the shittier things he had done in his life, but he felt most awful for breaking his promise and leaving angry. He'd completely blown Jack's trust in him and he'd do anything to earn it back.

The door opened, and Griff thought his heart might fall from his ass. Jack looked as bad as he felt. Worse, maybe. He half stood and raised his hand to get Jack's attention. Their eyes met, and Jack returned Griff's shy smile as he made his way to the table.

Nerves took control of Griff's mouth "It's fresh and hot. I just sat down with it a minute ago. It's exactly how you like—"

Jack placed his hand on Griff's shoulder as he sat. "Hush, you're babbling. Thank you for the coffee. Is all that shaking because you've been here drinking coffee since opening, nerves, or both?"

"What do you think?"

Jack smiled. "Definitely both."

They sat in awkward silence for the longest time before Griff finally mustered up the courage to speak. "I've gotta level with you, Jack. I have thought of nothing else, but I'm feeling pretty clueless about what the hell happened."

Leaning forward, Jack held Griff's gaze. "I've to ask

you something, and I want you to think about it for a bit before you answer. Okay?"

Griff didn't like the sound of this at all. "Okay?"

Jack closed his eyes for a minute, then took a long sip of coffee. Griff's gaze drifted to Jack's throat muscles as he swallowed and he wished his cock could be right there. Jack lowered the mug to the table and Griff returned to reality.

"This is important, Griff, so please give it serious thought before you answer. I'll understand if it's something you'll need more time to think about than we'll spend here."

"Just spit it out, you're making me even more nervous."

"Are you looking to go straight?"

That was the last question Griff expected. "What. The. Actual. Fuck? Where would you get that idea?"

"After that rehearsal—"

Well, shit—he was back to that again? "I got horny after witnessing a beautiful act of submission between a straight couple, and somehow my love life magically becomes no boys allowed? I don't need any time to think about this at all. While I thought I'd made all this clear that night, I guess I didn't, so let me spell it out for you.

"I love you. It is *that* simple. We both have appetites that can't be sated within our relationship. I thought we'd agreed to indulge them as needed, and if the opportunity presented itself, open up our relationship in a way that would permanently fulfil these needs. In other words, my understanding of our relationship was you and me first, and we'd add a third only if the right female sub came along. Replacing you with a woman is never, ever going to happen.

"If you want to remove the option of a third, then let's do that. If I can only have one person in my life until the day I die, I want that person to be you."

"But you got horny after—"

"And I came home to fuck you. Except, as I recall, that didn't happen. There will be times where something outside our relationship will get me horny. If you're honest, the same goes for you. Regardless of what popped my pecker, you're the only place I park it."

Jack chuckled and Griff breathed a little easier. He still had an apology to give, and with the ice broken a little, now was probably the best time. "Jack, I'm really sorry about leaving angry and making you wait to know I was safe. I broke the only promise you've ever asked of me, and I know earning back your trust will not be quick or easy, but I need to know it's possible and that someday you will forgive me."

Jack pushed his mug towards the centre of the table and rose from his chair. "Go get your stuff, I'll be waiting for you at home."

As much as Jack wanted to drop to his knees when Griff walked through the door, Griff would need to assuage his guilt, and bottoming to Jack tended to work best for both of them.

He spent the ride home in the car choreographing their first encounter. While there would be lots of make-up sex where they would take turns being bottom and top, that wouldn't happen before Griff was free of his guilt. God only knew what it would take for that to happen. Griff had never broken a promise before.

He considered and dismissed scenario after scenario. He was almost home by the time he had settled on a plan of action. He didn't anticipate having much time to prepare before Griff arrived. Chances were good that he had already checked out of the hotel, taking a gamble on Jack inviting him back home.

Jack parked the car and hurried indoors. He'd barely finished getting organised before the doorbell rang. What the fuck was that about? He'd expected Griff to walk in and had planned accordingly. Oh well, he could be flexible.

He closed his eyes for a moment and composed himself, then opened the door. "Inside. Leave your stuff by the door, strip, then kneel in front of my chair. Safeword is red."

Griff cocked his head to the side like he always did when he thought Jack had said something outrageous.

"I'm not playing around, boy. If you want my trust and forgiveness, you'll have to earn it. If a sub broke a promise and risked her life like you did, you know she would be severely punished until she'd learned her lesson. What makes you think you deserve less?"

Griff lowered his eyes and shifted from foot to foot, but remained silent.

"I gave you instructions, I won't tell you again." Jack walked to his chair and sat. He hoped his relief didn't show when Griff finally entered the house and closed the door. He'd spent those awful seconds of waiting, frantically trying to figure out what to do if this plan went to shit in a handbag.

Jack's cock grew harder with each garment Griff removed. The cheeky fuck was doing a slow strip-tease. Fair enough, he'd only told Griff to strip, not how to do it. A week without coming was sure taking its toll on Jack now. If he'd known what was in store, he might have taken the edge off. Then again, he would much rather get off down Griff's throat than in his own hand.

Finally Griff was down to nothing but a sultry smile. He sauntered across the room and sank to his knees in front of Jack.

"Good boy." Griff growled, and Jack grabbed him by the chin. "Silence. I don't want to hear a sound from you unless it's your safeword or to answer a direct question. I don't anticipate giving you any reason to do either. You can nod for yes and shake for no. Understand?"

Griff nodded. Jack let go of his chin and stood before undoing his jeans and releasing his angry cock.

"Good boy. Leave your hands by your sides and open your mouth. You'll take it all. Tap my leg three times if you need to safeword." Jack placed one hand behind Griff's head and fed him his cock in one long, slow glide. Once he'd reached the back of Griff's throat, he held his breath and waited a moment to allow Griff to prepare before continuing deep into his throat. Once Jack had his balls resting on Griff's chin, he put his other hand behind Griff's head held it tight to his groin. He had absolute control and Griff was going to have to trust him. That would be the first step to rebuilding their trust in each other.

Jack held Griff's head in place until he was starting to feel a bit uncomfortable, but nowhere close to his limit. Griff had an enviable lung capacity and it was always him or Sully who won breath holding contests. Jack let go and pulled his cock from Griff's mouth before he released his own breath. Breath play was tricky. He rarely indulged, but when he did, he never took uncalculated risks.

Jack stroked the top of Griff's head. "For being such a good boy, you may use only your mouth on me any way you like provided you make me come within the next two minutes and swallow every drop I give you."

Griff took the head of Jack's cock in his mouth, and sucked hard as he swirled and flicked his tongue. Occasionally he took Jack's entire length and swallowed a few times before backing off. Finally, he bobbed up and down in short fast bursts until Jack couldn't hold back any longer. Along with his semen, he pumped a week's worth of anger and hurt down Griff's throat. When Jack was spent, Griff released his cock and laid a gentle kiss on the tip. He looked up and flashed Jack that irresistible grin of his.

"You cut that pretty close, boy." Jack chuckled. "It's a good thing you succeeded, because you wouldn't have liked the consequences of failure. I'm going to need a little time to recover for the next round. So how about you go put your things away and you can join me for a nap when you're done." Griff nodded and Jack left for the bedroom.

Jack opened one eye and spotted Griff standing in the doorway. "Stop walking on eggshells, boy. You rang the bell, and now you wait to be asked into the bedroom? Firstly, as long as you have a key to this house, you have no reason to ring the bell. Secondly, I had already told you to join me when you were done. The invitation had been extended, there was no need to wait for another." Griff crossed the room, and Jack opened his arms wide. "Come and snuggle."

As soon as Griff was close enough, Jack wrapped his arms around him and pulled him close. He hoped he'd pushed Griff hard enough to erase his guilt so they could move on to the make-up sex. "I forgive you, babe. Trust is going to take some time, and until I'm there, I want you to give me the keys to your car—no driving. Can you do that?" Griff nodded. "Are you out of guilt yet?" Griff nodded more vigorously. "In that case, let's get things back to normal."

"Honestly, I'm forgiven?"

"Honestly."

"Thank you." Griff cocked his head and raised his eyebrow. "You know, I'm happy to give up driving, but you do realise you'll have to be my chauffeur until you give me back my keys."

"If it means I know you are not dead or mangled in a ditch somewhere, I'm good with that."

"I do love you, Jack. I need you to know you really are my heart. I let my temper get in the way, and I hurt you, and I'd do anything to take it back. I don't ever want to do anything that will make you feel like you aren't the most important person in my life."

"I'm getting there. I want it to be true, and when the trust is there, I'll know it to be true. Until then, I can't promise not to hold back a little."

"I don't like it, but it's my own fault and I understand."

Jack leaned in and touched his lips to Griff's. "I love you. You are my heart." He leaned back in and with the next kiss, he bared his soul.

GRIFF WOKE and grinned as he realised he was in his own bed and all snuggled close to Jack. He still couldn't believe Jack had gone all Dom on his ass and made him submit. Thinking back on it, though, Jack was right, he carried guilt long and hard, and this fuck-up was by far the worst of his life, and he'd had some doozies. Last time he had self-imposed a guilt-trip, all he had done was accidentally bleach Jack's favourite black t-shirt, and it was three days of grovelling before he felt like he had made amends. Of course, it was all his own baggage. In the grand scheme of things, Jack couldn't have cared less about the shirt, and as hard as he tried, he failed to convince Griff he was blowing the whole thing out of proportion. He turned to look at Jack and was surprised to see his eyes open.

Jack leaned over and kissed him. "Good morning, babe. You were thinking awfully hard. What's up?"

"Oh, I was thinking about how you handled me when I came home yesterday."

"And?"

"It surprised me, but after some thought, it made sense that it worked so well. And before you go there, this is only to be used for extreme situations, and to be clear, I plan to avoid those situations like your life depended on it."

"Good, because I hated every minute of it."

"Not every minute, coming is always enjoyable."

"It was a relief, but for me, enjoying an orgasm involves more than the physical release. "Now, those orgasms that came after," Jack smiled and traced Griff's lips with his finger, "those were most enjoyable." Jack shimmied down the bed and gave Griff's erection a long, slow lick from root to tip.

As much as Griff wanted to come, this morning he needed a connection he couldn't get from a blow job. "Babe, I don't care who's on top, but I want to see your face, to kiss you, to gaze into your eyes and show you just how deep my love is for you."

Jack popped up to the head of the bed and rummaged in the top drawer of the bedside table before straddling Griff's thighs. He opened the condom and deftly slid it over Griff's straining cock. "Here," he said as he handed Griff the bottle of lube, "you drive."

Griff laughed and bucked his hips, knocking Jack off balance enough to gain the advantage and reverse their positions. He slathered plenty of lube over his cock, then he positioned the tip at Jack's anus and applied steady pressure until he was fully seated. He lowered himself until they were nipple to nipple, then he gave Jack a long, languorous kiss. "In that case, it is time to blow out your carbon. You've been driven far too gently, lately."

Jack's eyes lit up. "Floor it."

Griff withdrew and held the head of his cock against Jack's entrance. "Vroom, vroom." He gave a couple shallow thrusts, then snapped his hips forward and pistoned in and out of Jack's body at an unfor-giving pace. He stared into his lover's eyes while he covered his face with gentle kisses.

"Griff, I can't hold back."

Griff brought his mouth to Jack's for a soul-searing kiss as he increased the speed and force of his thrusts. Jack's long moans of ecstasy as he fell over the edge were all Griff needed to send him hurtling off his own cliff. He collapsed over Jack's body, breathless, his heart pounding. "I need a minute."

Jack chuckled. "No hurry, I could stay like this all day."

"Be careful what you wish for because my cock is already on board with that idea. I need to turf the condom and we need to clean up. What do you say to a shower?"

"Yes please."

SIX

Ella laughed when she saw the name on her phone. Of course it was Sully. She was just surprised he had waited two whole days before calling. "You're looking for the skinny on Teagan, aren't you?"

"Perhaps."

"You may have her number, but only because she told me you could."

"Seriously, that's all I'm going to get?"

"Since when have I ever been one to divulge information about others?"

"Since never, but there's a first time for everything."

"Not when it comes to other people's business."

"And to think I have interesting stuff to share with you about Griff and Jack."

"I'm sure you do."

"Hey, sweetie, what's wrong?"

"Nothing, it is fine. I've gotta run. I'll text you Teagan's number as soon as I hang up, okay?"

"Yeah...thanks. I will talk to you soon."

"See ya."

Ella focused on the wind-chimes tinkling outside her window. She let their happy music soothe away the rising panic. The only time she was ever able to stand up to anyone was in defence of others, but doing so always took a big toll.

Trust Sully to pick up on her interest in Griff and Jack. Yes, she was curious, but she couldn't afford to risk her safety because they made her heart go pitter-patter. Besides, how could she possibly choose between them? They were both tall and beautiful, with killer grins and voices so deep and gravelly, she'd obey without a second thought. Of course, looks weren't everything. Her limited experience told her the prettier the face, the bigger the asshole, and life was too short to spend it choosing between the lesser of two assholes. If only her pussy were as sensible as her brain.

She thought back to that awful, terrifying night and the last pretty boy she'd played with and strengthened her resolve. No romantic entanglements of any sort. She had enough scars—emotional and physical.

SEVEN

Jack set the two mugs of coffee on the kitchen table and settled onto the chair next to Griff. Even though their reconciliation was new, he felt better about their relationship than he had in a very long time. It would probably be better for both of them if he brought up the subject, and morning coffee was as good a time as any. "So, uh...Ella?"

Griff had just taken a swig from his mug and fought not to choke. "What about Ella?"

"What do you think?"

"I think you're going to need to be more clear about what you are asking."

Jack took a long sip of his own coffee. "Would you be interested in playing with her?"

Griff looked incredulous. "Seriously?"

"Yes, seriously. I told you I was still open to a third,

and if the wood you sprung when we met her was any indication, you're just as interested in her as I am."

Griff reached over and cupped Jack's cheek. "Are you positive? I need you to be more than sure about this because, like you, I couldn't deal with a repeat of the last week."

Jack smiled and leaned into Griff's hand. "I'm sure."

"Then, yes, I would very much like to play with her."

"Excellent. The question is, how do we go about it?"

"Normally, I'd say Sully was our best bet, but he seems kind of preoccupied with Teagan. Considering the way Ella and Mac hit it off, maybe we should see if Mac is willing to help. We can keep Sully as a back-up plan."

Jack nodded and took another mouthful of coffee as he glanced at the clock. "Mac should be up by now." He reached for his phone and punched in the number.

A breathless Mac finally answered just as Jack was organising his thoughts to leave a message.

"Hey Jack, what's up?"

"Um, sorry, is this a bad time?"

"No, not at all. My phone was half-way across the house is all."

"You can call me back when it is more convenient-"

"Spill it, Jackson Riley."

"Are you sure you're a sub?"

"Quit stalling and spit it out."

Damn, she was bossy when Finn didn't have her at his feet. "Griff and I were wondering whether you know if Ella is spoken for."

"She's not your type."

"What's that supposed to mean?"

"According to her, she experimented a little back in the day, and found it wasn't for her."

"Bullshit. You know as well as I do, that piece of hers is a love song, not some ditty about a failed experiment."

"I know no such thing. Look, you and Griff go through subs faster than Wilson goes through clarinet reeds, so even if she *is* subbie material, I don't think she's *your* kind of subbie material. I think she deserves something more substantial than a few hours as the filling in your sub-sandwich."

"Geez, Mac, you make us sound pretty callous."

"Aren't you? I rarely see you with the same sub more than once or twice. It's like the pair of you are trying to blow your way through the city's entire supply."

"I get how it looks, Mac, but if you understood the situation, you might see it differently"

"Then explain it to me."

Jack shot a pleading look to Griff. "I wish I could, but it is complicated."

Griff nodded and whispered, "Tell her."

"Mac, can you hang on just a sec?"

"Yeah, sure."

Jack hit the mute button and set the phone on the table as he looked at Griff. "You'd better be sure, because there's no unringing this bell."

"I'm sure. It's time, and we could probably use some outside help because we're not doing so well on our own. Besides, I think I trust Mac's judgement over Sully's. Especially now he's tripping all over himself sucking up to that percussionist friend of Ella's."

Mac's voice rose up from the table. "Um, fellas, you just rang that bell loud and long on speaker."

Griff picked up Jack's phone and laughed as he looked at the screen. "You tit."

Jack smacked his head and let out a nervous chuckle before he spoke. "Okay, so you heard all that, then."

"Yeah, but it was still kind of vague. If you want my help, you're going to have to make me sympathetic to your cause, so give it your best shot."

Mac ended the call and joined Finn in the kitchen. "You are never going to believe what that was all about."

"Try me."

"Well, for starters, Griff and Jack finally outed themselves to me. I suppose I could have made it easier on them by admitting I already knew and it's the worst kept secret in the history of secrets, but they've worked so hard to keep their relationship on the down-low, I didn't want to spoil the surprise."

"It's about time." Finn lifted an eyebrow. "Please tell me you didn't leave them under the misconception that I would still be oblivious."

Mac chuckled. "No. In the end, I took pity on them and confessed that everyone knows and it's no big deal. But that's not even the best part. they're actively looking for a third. A female sub to be exact. They haven't been man-slutting, they've been auditioning potential life-partners."

"No. Way."

"I know, right? But it gets even more outrageous. They both zeroed in on Ella and they want me to help smooth the way for them."

"Bad idea, love. Meddling in people's lives can destroy friendships. Besides, meddling in matters of love is entirely Sully's purview."

"Normally I'd agree with you, but they said themselves that they trust my judgement over Sully's, especially now that he's been showing so much interest in Teagan."

"Things could have gone very badly when you interfered between Hildy and Wilson."

"I don't think it's fair to call it interfering. I was asked for help. And as far as the situation between

Hildy and Wilson, I think it's a prime example of why Griff and Jack called me."

Finn tapped his chin with his finger. "Okay, I'll concede the point, but I'm still not comfortable with this."

"It may well be all for naught, you know. Even though Griff and Jack had her totally creaming her panties—and yes, I asked—their Domliness was a show-stopper. Apparently, whatever experience she had when she was younger was not worthy of repeating."

"Just so I'm clear on this, you're going to help a pair of bi-sexual Doms double-team a woman who has no interest in BDSM?" Finn looked skyward. "Sweet, sweaty Jesus, have you lost your fucking mind, woman?"

"Yes, and maybe."

Finn picked up his mug and took a long swig of coffee. "Baby, please be careful, that's all I ask."

"I'm only going to provide a low-key venue for the three of them to get to know each other better. Every-thing else is entirely up to them."

Mac huffed and stalked off when Finn started laughing.

EIGHT

Ella picked up her mug of tea and took a long sip as she tried to process the crazy day she'd had. One minute she was putting the finishing touches on her latest composition, the next she found herself at Mac and Finn's front door, and by the time she'd returned home, she'd spilled her deepest, darkest secret. Enough of it, anyway. One tiny two-letter word and she'd have spent the evening sitting in the comfort of her own home instead of attending a small dinner party at the home of kinky people she barely knew.

When Mac had answered the door, Ella held out the bottle of wine she'd brought and held back a huge sigh of relief. Finn made her nervous. "I hope you like red."

"Oh, I most certainly do like red. How about we get it opened right away so it will be ready for drinking in time for supper."

Ella toed off her shoes and followed Mac to the kitchen, thankful it was empty. "Where are the others?"

"They're all in Finn's man-cave, but I'm almost ready to serve, so they'll show up any second. I don't know what it is about men and their uncanny ability to show up for food as soon as it's ready, but not one moment before all the work is done. Ha! The joke's on them. They're on clean-up duty, and as you can see, I'm not the clean as you go kind of cook—I'm more of a use every pot, pan, and utensil you can find kind of cook. Truth is, I'm just learning. Before Finn and I got together, my cooking skills were limited to opening a packet and heating it in the microwave."

With the sound of distant footsteps, Mac caught Ella's eye and they both erupted into fits of laughter.

"What's so funny?" Finn asked. "We could hear you cackling at the other end of the house."

Ella and Mac exchanged looks and laughed even harder as Griff and Jack followed Finn into the kitchen. Mac, laughing too hard to speak, pointed to the empty plates and waved her hand at the pots on the stove.

Finn kissed the top of her head. "I think my gorgeous, sexy woman, who cooks the most delicious food, is trying to tell us we should go ahead and serve ourselves."

Mac nodded. She and Ella were just getting themselves under control when Ella caught Mac's eye and the tears and laughter gushed anew.

Finn chuckled. "We'll be in the dining room when you two are capable of making it to the table."

Dinner was an uneventful affair filled with meaningless small talk which didn't do anything to suppress the growing puddle in Ella's panties. Knowing the men were Doms should have squelched her arousal, but it only seemed to make matters worse. Every time she managed to get her lust under control, one of the two would speak to her. Griff had the sexiest way of saying her name and Jack made her heart flutter when he called her sweetness.

At the end of the meal, Ella suppressed a giggle and didn't dare make eye-contact when Mac informed the men, in no uncertain terms, who was in charge of cleaning up and serving tea.

"Grab your wine, Ella, we'll finish it in the comfort of the living room."

Ella picked up her glass and followed Mac. She settled herself on the big leather sofa while Mac sat on the matching arm chair.

"So, what do you think of them?"

Ella knew this was coming. Non-committal indifference. That was the key. "They seem very nice."

"You've gotta give me more than that, Ella."

"Really, they seem very nice."

"Come on, I know they've got you hot. You have been doing the wet-panty-shimmy all evening."

It was time to shut this down. Mac was far too shrewd. "Even if I could decide on one, they are Doms, and as you know, that makes them off-limits."

"What if you didn't have to choose? What if you could have them both?"

Ella struggled against the spit-take before safely swallowing her mouthful of wine and setting her glass on the side-table. "Both? How is that an option? I can't even be with one Dom, two would be impossible."

"Okay, but there's something I'm not getting. How could you write that piece without having any interest in BDSM? Can you explain it to me?"

Ella looked nervously towards the kitchen and took a sip of her wine. "Perhaps another time?"

"Do you mean that, or are you deflecting?"

Ella thought for a moment. "Probably a little of both. I think I could probably explain it to you some-time, but it would have to be in private with no risk of being interrupted."

"I can understand that, but trust me, they're going to be busy with the kitchen for quite some time—I have rather exacting standards and you saw the disaster I left for them. I get the feeling it's a lengthy tale, but we've got time for the abridged version. Besides, it'll make it easier for me to run interference if I know the story."

Mac was right. It was pretty weird to write a piece like that and profess to have no interest in BDSM. She stole another look towards the kitchen before fortifying herself with the last of her wine.

"I did experiment when I was younger, and I loved it until the night I met the wrong Dom. In case you haven't noticed, I don't do well with conflict, and I can't say no. Back then, Sully vetted potential Doms and monitored my scenes. One night, I went to the club on my own because he was busy and I didn't want to wait until he had a night free. I was over-confident and had developed a raging case of sub-frenzy." Ella pulled and twisted the hem of her shirt.

"I met a very pretty man who made me weak just looking at him. We played at the club and it was amazing. I went home with him because I wanted the night to go on forever. Within minutes of arriving at his house, I would have given anything for it to end. It did, but not until almost dawn. He loaded me into his car and dumped me, naked and bleeding just inside my front door. Truth is, I probably would have gone home with him anyway because he asked, and I wouldn't have been able to say no."

Mac joined Ella on the sofa pulled her in for a hug. "I'm so sorry. What did Sully do about it?"

"He didn't know—still doesn't. He doesn't even know I went to the club that night. It was my own fault. I got what I deserved."

"Oh, sweetie, I don't need details to know it wasn't your fault, and you definitely didn't deserve what that bastard did to you."

Ella wouldn't argue the point, so she nodded and pulled herself together.

———

Jack spent the whole evening keeping a lid on his anger, but the moment Ella's car left the driveway, he exploded. "Abused? Some self-serving prick claiming to be a Dom abused her?"

Griff laid his hand on Jack's shoulder. "Calm down. What are you talking about?"

"I overheard her telling Mac why she's not into BDSM. She met a guy at a club who showed her a good time until he got her to his place."

"What else did you hear?" Mac asked.

"Nothing. Guilt from eavesdropping got the better of me, and I returned to the kitchen."

Mac frowned. "She believes what happened is her own fault and she deserved it."

Finn wrapped his arms around Mac. "And you set her straight?"

"You bet your favourite cane, I did. Not that it did any good," Mac smiled at Griff and Jack, "but I think I know a couple of Domly fellows who'd be more than willing to do the necessary convincing."

After a nod from Griff, Jack said, "We're in."

"She was sparse with the details, so my under-standing is based on what she's said and the way she acts. She's unable to say no to anyone, and it seems she'll say and do anything to avoid conflict, including outright lie."

Griff took Jack's hand and gave it a squeeze as he spoke. "Toxic behaviour in a D/s relationship, but not unmanageable."

Jack smiled at him and squeezed back. "Griff's right, and regardless of whether she turns out to be the third we're looking for or not, we'll do what we can to help build her self-esteem and find more functional ways to handle conflict. I do have a couple of concerns we need to address. The first is Sully. From what you've said, he's completely oblivious to the situation. When he finds out, he's going suffer guilt of Catholic proportions and we'll need to find a way to mitigate it. He'll be the next best thing to useless if he's busy beating himself up over something he had no control over."

"Secondly, she's terrified of us. Completely understandable, but we're going to have to come up with a way to help her feel more comfortable."

Finn spoke up. "One thing that should help is her presence at rehearsals. She'll see the care with which you treat the subs you're playing in her piece. That said, you'll need to treat them exactly as you would any other sub. I think it's important for you both to come across as the genuinely caring guys you are, not as a pair of pretty boys looking to impress."

Mac picked up from Finn. "Exactly. From what she described, her abuser was on his best behaviour and pulled out all the stops to impress her. If she gets a whiff of anything like that from either of you, it's game over.

"I think Finn is on the right track with Ella being present at rehearsals, but there won't be all that many between now and the performance, so I think we should also invite her to most of our group activities. As evil as it sounds, we can take advantage of her inability to say no. She'll get used to being around the two of you in a safe, nurturing environment. If we invite Teagan along as well, I think she'll feel less like saying no, because she'll be able to help nudge Sully and Teagan together."

Jack chuckled. "Ms. Wallis, you have a rather wide manipulative streak, of which, until this evening, I was blissfully unaware."

"Mac's manipulative streak is admittedly large, but she usually exercises it judiciously. I think, in this case, it's well warranted." Finn pulled Mac in for a squeeze and laid a loud, smoochy kiss on her lips. "Given all dealings with Ella are likely to fall on Mac for the next little while, maybe you two can handle things with Sully?"

Jack and Griff exchanged nods and stood. "Not a problem. Now we have the beginnings of an action plan, I think it is time Griff and I head off."

GRIFF FLIPPED down the quilt as Jack's erection preceded him into the bedroom. "Is all that for me?"

Jack smiled and grabbed the base of his cock. "For now, but if things go our way, you're going to have to share."

"Mmm, I'm looking forward to sharing, can you imagine having it buried deep inside Ella's pussy while I lick and suck on your balls?"

"I can. But right now, I would prefer reality over imagination."

Griff climbed out of bed and knelt in front of Jack with his hands at his sides and his mouth open wide in anticipation. He looked up into Jack's eyes and saw the love. As Jack slid in, Griff relaxed his throat and moaned, prepared to take every inch Jack had to offer. He loved the way Jack's fingers tangled in his hair and held him in place as Jack tilted his hips forward and slowly buried his cock deep before easing back to the entrance of his throat.

"Baby, I'm going to come in your mouth, then I'll do anything you want."

It wasn't often Jack gave him Carte blanche, and he only ever asked for one thing. This time Jack was in for big surprise, and Griff could not wait.

Jack increased the pace and force of his thrusts until he finally clutched Griff's head to his groin and emptied his balls down Griff's throat. He untangled his fingers from Griff's hair and gently stroked his cheek as he withdrew. He grabbed Griff's hand and helped him to his feet.

Griff leaned in and brushed a kiss over Jack's lips. "You know what I want, don't you?"

"Of course I do, it is what you always want when I offer to do anything."

"What if I didn't ask for it this time?"

"Why?"

"Because maybe I love that you are willing to do something you hate more than I love you doing what you hate. Does that make sense? Coming so close to losing you put a lot of things in perspective."

"I don't hate it. I just don't love it."

"Don't start lying to me now, Jack."

"Okay, you're right, I do hate it."

"I know. However, just because I'm not asking for a rim job this time, doesn't mean I won't ask the next time you offer me anything I want."

"I know. If you're not going to ask me for a rim job, what would you like?"

"I want to make love with you." Griff put Jack's hand on his own erection. "I can't wait to be inside you. Go lay on your back on the bed, I'll be right behind you."

After Jack settled on the bed, Griff gathered what he needed from the drawer in the bedside table. He rolled on the condom and popped the lid of the lube before squeezing a generous dollop in his palm and slathering it over his cock. He grinned at Jack and settled into position. "Are you ready, love?"

"Please."

Griff leaned in, letting his weight and gravity provide the slow steady pressure. As he felt the head of his cock breach Jack's ass, he stopped and backed out a bit before leaning forward and resuming his tortuous slide into his lover's body. When he was finally all the way in, he hooked Jack's legs over his arms, and settled into a slow, steady rhythm, every so often, leaning his head in for a kiss, but never taking his eyes off Jack's. "I could do you all night like this, babe. Would you like that, or would you like me to go at you like a jackhammer?"

"Ever the romantic."

Griff slid his cock all the way in and held still. "Just say the word, and I'll bring you flowers and chocolates."

"Damn it, Griff, I don't want flowers and chocolates, I want you to fuck me. Please."

Griff drew back and thrust his hips forward, slamming his body into Jack's. "Like that?"

"Oh God, yeah, just like that."

Griff unleashed, pumping hard and deep. Just as he was ready to come, he released Jack's legs and slid his hand between their bodies and grabbed tight to Jack's cock. He buried his face in the crook of Jack's neck and bit down. Jack's tortured moan and warm spurts of come on his belly set off his own brain-searing orgasm.

Exhausted, Griff barely had the presence of mind to pull out. Jack stroked his cheek before he removed the condom from Griff's cock and headed to the bathroom. Guilt washed over him like the warm, damp cloth Jack slid over his body. "I'm sorry, babe. I was topping—I should be taking care of you."

"Not this time, my love. Sleep. We have lots of plans to make tomorrow."

Griff smiled as his eyes fluttered and closed.

NINE

Jack ran his hand through his hair, as he waited for Sully to answer the door. He and Griff had spent the last two days discussing the best way to bring Sully up to speed regarding Ella's abuse. He was not convinced they'd come up with the best strategy, but they'd run out of time, and needed to work with what they had. He still didn't know how Griff had managed to manoeuvre him into being the one to talk to Sully. His thoughts were interrupted when Sully finally appeared in the doorway, wearing only a pair of boxer shorts.

"Hey, Jack, what's up?

"Hi. Sorry for dropping by unannounced—"

"Not to mention boorishly early. Fuck, man, if you had to wake me up, couldn't you have at least brought coffee and muffins?"

Jack held up a bakery bag and brushed past his friend. "I'll make the coffee."

"This sounds serious."

"Just go get showered and dressed. I'll have coffee ready by the time you're done."

When Sully walked into the kitchen, the coffee and muffins were sitting on the table. Jack drank from his mug and set it down in front of him. "Have a seat, Dave."

"Oh God, this is serious. I swear, only you and my mother use my first name, and then only when I'm in big shit or something bad has happened." Sully sat and took a long sip of the hot coffee.

"It was years ago, but you are right, something bad did happen." Sully looked stunned, and Jack took advantage of the silence and told him everything he knew of Ella's assault.

Sully slumped in his chair, devastated. "Fuck! That's what happened? I didn't see her for about two weeks after that. Every time I invited her to join me at the club, she had other plans. I didn't think much of it. I'd become kind of blind to her deflection tactics and just thought maybe she had met someone. In a warped kind of way, I guess she did. She was relatively new to the scene and prone to sub-frenzy, which was why I was vetting her Doms, and monitoring her scenes so closely. It didn't occur to me she would go to the club on her own. I should have known better."

"Look, it's in the past and you wallowing in guilt is not going to help matters. Here's the thing. Griff and I really like her, but until she develops some trust, we're not going to get anywhere with her. Regardless of what does or doesn't happen between us, Griff and I want to do whatever we can to help her believe she's not at fault and she didn't do anything wrong."

"I was supposed to protect her."

"You did. You couldn't be with her every minute of every day. Nobody could. Like I said, It's all in the past. We need to deal with the here and now."

"What do you need me to do?"

"Talk to her."

"I'm going to need some time to process this first."

"You have got until the next rehearsal."

TEN

ELLA TRIED NOT to let her irritation come through as she answered the phone. Mac's interference was becoming a problem. That weird, uncomfortable conversation with Sully was just the start. Now she's been orchestrating social event after social event that she just *had* to attend. "Where have you decided I should be, and when?"

Mac giggled. "Am I that bad? It is easier to get Sully and Teagan together if they know you're going to be there too, you know."

"No, you're not quite that bad, and you're right, I do want to do whatever I can to nurture their budding relationship." What a joke—that relationship was doing better than fine and didn't need any help. She wondered how much longer Mac would continue trying to set her up with Jack and Griff before finally admitting defeat.

"Good, then you'll join us for a barbecue at our house around four this afternoon."

"Mac, with all your social gatherings, I'm sure I've been spending more time at your house than my own."

"I know, isn't it great? After spending so many years in solitude, it's so nice to finally enjoy a social life and have girlfriends."

Ella was surprised. "What do you mean, solitude?"

"You haven't heard the story? Hell, I thought everyone had heard my sad, pathetic tale of woe by now. My final recital at the end of my first year of university won me a scholarship. One of the oboists from my studio thought that scholarship should have been his, so he decided to punish me. He tied me to the piano bench in a practice room and raped me. Sully saved me and was the only person I trusted enough to let near me as I withdrew further and further from the world. It wasn't until he introduced me to Finn that I started to take my life back."

"I'm so sorry, Mac. I had no idea."

"Different circumstances, but I think it's fair to say we both had good reasons to shy away from BDSM for a while."

"Was the guy a Dom?"

"No, but before the rape, I'd been dabbling in BDSM and I quite enjoyed a side of bondage with my sex. He ruined that for me for a long, long time. I still struggle with stuff, but it's getting better. While I don't know the details of what that asshole did to you, and I don't need to, I want you to understand that I do know what it's like to be terrified to trust another person with your physical and emotional safety. And I'm going to tell you something Sully told me not long after I met Finn. *There are men who are good, and kind, and trust-worthy. Men who will treat you like you deserve to be treated. There are men out there who you can be alone with and be safe.* As much as I hate to admit it, he's right."

Ella considered Mac's words. For the first time since that awful night, she didn't feel quite so alone. Sure, unlike Mac, she was responsible for her assault, but if she looked past the difference in circumstances, she could accept that there was someone else in the world who had some idea of what her life was like. "But at least for you, it wasn't your fault."

Mac snorted. "You're right, it wasn't my fault, just like what that fucker did to you wasn't yours. That didn't stop me from blaming myself and trying to figure out what I did wrong, though. Turns out, I didn't do anything wrong—and neither did you. Now, back to more pressing matters. Finn is doing burgers, so are you able to bring a salad? No need to go to any fuss, bagged from the store is fine, as long as we have some leafy greenery."

"I can make a salad, no problem. Is there anything else you would like me to bring?"

"Nope, just your lovely self. We'll see you at four."

"I'll see you then."

Ella disconnected the call and flopped into her chair. She considered Mac's disclosure. If she hadn't said anything, Ella wouldn't have had a clue they'd both been so similarly violated. Mac seemed so comfortable with the men in her life, and she certainly had no qualms about laying into them, even Finn, if the mood struck. Ella wondered what it must feel like to give someone shit without wanting to pass out. She dismissed the thought for the ridiculous notion it was and went to raid the fridge for salad fixings.

GRIFF SPOTTED Ella sitting on the deck stairs, balancing her plate on her lap as she took a big bite of her fully-loaded burger. He caught Jack's eye before joining her. "Do you mind if I sit here?"

With her mouth stuffed with burger, she shook her head and shrugged. He reached over and stole a tomato wedge from her plate as he parked himself next to her. "You sure know how to build a burger. "

Jack arrived and sat next to Griff. They'd agreed ahead of time for one of them to push a little, but leave Ella with a graceful out. "Hey Ella, is he bugging you?"

She took another big bite of her burger and shrugged again.

Griff reached over to steal a piece of cucumber, but Jack gave his hand a gentle smack. "Dammit Griff, it's bad enough when you raid my plate, but now you're being downright rude."

"Oh, I'm sure Ella would say something if she didn't want to share her food with me."

"I'd hope she would."

Ella swallowed her mouthful. "Oh, it is okay, really."

Ella's response revealed how much she would endure to avoid conflict. He caught Jack's eye and he knew they were both on the same page. They needed a new game plan.

Griff turned to Jack and winked as he stole a potato chip from his plate. Jack grabbed Griff's wrist and squeezed until he dropped the chip. "Griff, that's enough. You're being a bully."

"Sorry. I was just messing around."

Ella's eyes went wide as she prepared to stand up "I should go see how Teagan is doing."

Jack loosened his grip, but kept hold of Griff's wrist as he looked at Ella. "No, you shouldn't. Teagan is getting along just fine with Sully. In fact, I think maybe they could use a break from you and Mac using the flimsiest of excuses to thrust them together."

"I should go help Mac—"

"Ella, it's okay. Not all conflict is unhealthy, and it probably wouldn't hurt you to see it resolved. I didn't like what Griff was doing and I called him on it. We sorted it out, and that's the end of it. Nothing bad is going to happen."

"No, really, I should—"

Griff unleashed his Dom-voice. "Enough. There's nothing you should be doing beyond enjoying your burger and a nice spring evening. If you're really that uncomfortable, say the word, and we'll leave you be."

Jack gave Griff's wrist a gentle squeeze and released it. "Ella, it's entirely up to you. It's okay to ask us to leave. Really."

Ella stared at her plate in silence.

"Griff slowly reached out and gently touched Ella's arm. She flinched, but he didn't back off. "I know this is really hard for you, so how about the three of us sit quietly and eat? Nod if you are good with that."

Eyes still on her plate, Ella nodded and took a bite of her burger.

ELEVEN

Ella couldn't believe she'd agreed to attend Mac and Finn's play party. Well, she could. If only she'd had the back-bone to say no. Of course, truth be known, she was more than a little curious. She'd seen how Griff and Jack handled the subs during those few rehearsals, and found herself wondering if they were putting on a show for her benefit or whether they were behaving normally. The consistency with which they treated the subs almost had her believing their careful attention was standard operating procedure.

She looked at the clock, relieved she hadn't disappeared so long into the void of self-reflection she'd have to rush to get ready. She didn't even know what she was going to wear. Mac told her the dress-code was Dom-defined and because she had no Dom, she could wear whatever she felt comfortable in.

She went to her closet and sifted through

garments, dismissing each in turn for being too frumpy. Why had she left this until the last minute? If she'd checked her closet even yesterday, she could have gone shopping for something appropriate. That was the point she admitted to herself she wanted to dress to impress.

Her phone announced an incoming text. She was so frustrated with her quest to find the perfect outfit for the evening, she was tempted to ignore it. She looked back in her closet, then sighed and reached for her phone. The message was from Mac.

Stop fussing over what to wear. Jeans are fine. Come a little early, and we'll raid my wardrobe for just the right top.

How the fuck could she know this? Ella's eyes darted around the room, almost sure she'd find a hidden camera. She looked back at the phone and responded the only way she could.

Ok, thanks.

She'd grill Mac later. Her only worry now was filling the tub full of hot water and bubbles.

Jack nudged Griff as he spotted Ella and Mac descending the stairs into the playroom. "Check out our girl. She's even more sexy than I thought she'd be."

Griff looked over and grinned. "Want."

"Down boy. This is going to take some finesse."

"I know, but give me a minute to drool first, will ya?"

Jack held Griff's hand, as much to show affection as to keep him in place. "Let's give her a little time to settle in. Mac said she's not here to play, just to get her bearings a little so she'll be able to cope with all the action at their official cohabitation party."

"I wasn't going anywhere, I just need to make a few physical adjustments. Things are getting a little hot and uncomfortable in my trousers."

Jack shifted to partially block Griff from view so he could discretely rearrange his equipment. He took the opportunity to seductively run his tongue over his lip as he winked.

"Not helping, you fucker."

Jack grinned. "I just want to make sure you are all primed and ready to go the minute we get home."

"I was fucking primed about five minutes after I blew my load down your throat this afternoon."

As soon as Griff was done, Jack turned around and scanned the room for Ella. "Are you ready to go say hello?"

Griff nodded, and they sauntered across the floor.

Mac called out to them as they approached. "Hey fellas, where's your sub du jour?"

Before Jack or Griff had a chance to respond, Finn sidled up to the group. "Careful, love, or I might get the idea you like repeating the no rudeness lesson." Mac looked like she had more to say, but clearly had the wisdom to close her mouth before it got her into real trouble. Finn stroked Mac's cheek and nodded his approval before turning to Jack. "Sully is going to be late, so I was wondering if you and Griff would sit with Ella while Mac and I play?"

Jack smiled at Ella as he answered. "We'd be happy to."

Finn turned to Ella, "Sweetie, I know Mac already discussed this with you, but, I want to make it clear to everyone—anything to do with you, comes through Mac or me. We have no problem saying no, and we both want you to feel safe and comfortable in our home. Griff and Jack are going to sit with you, and if they think you're uncomfortable with what's going on, they're going to escort you upstairs and away from the action. Safeword here is always red to stop. It works for everything, conversations, situations, and playtime. If you get uncomfortable and call red before these two galoots notice a problem, there's a reward in it for you." He turned back to Griff and Jack. "Do not let her down."

"We won't. Now go play while we help Ella find a spot to get settled." Jack looked at Ella and smiled. "Okay, honey, I'm going to give you some choices. First choice, would you prefer juice or pop?"

"Juice, please."

"There ya go. Nice, easy questions. Griff can you please grab Ella some juice?"

"On it," Griff said as he left for the refreshment table.

"Would you prefer to sit where you can see the whole room or a part of the room?"

"Part of the room."

Jack considered this promising. He would continue to keep conversation low-key and avoid yes or no questions. "Perfect. Would you prefer to watch the side of the room where Mac and Finn are playing, or the side where Wilson and Hildy are?"

"Where will Sully be playing?"

Jack chuckled at the wholly unexpected answer. "I don't know, but we can move for a change of scenery any time you like."

Griff returned with Ella's juice and Cokes for himself and Jack. "So, where are we sitting?"

"Ella? Finn and Mac, or Wil an Hildy?"

Ella ducked her head a little and avoided his gaze, but spoke up. "Finn and Mac, please."

"Perfect." Jack led the way to a sofa in the aftercare area that had a good view of the space where Finn and Mac were playing. He gestured to the centre of the sofa. "After you."

Once Ella was seated, Jack took the glass of juice from Griff's hand and passed it to her before sitting to her left. Griff handed Jack a Coke and then took the seat to Ella's right.

The three sipped their drinks in a relatively comfortable silence, and Jack kept one eye on Ella as they watched Finn visit all manner of torture on Mac. If her subtle squirming was any indication, leather slapping red ass was a very real turn on for the lovely Ms. Ella. Of course, given the piece she had written, he wasn't overly surprised. He stole a look at Griff and their gazes locked for a moment as they exchanged knowing smiles. Oh, how he wanted to ask her a metric shit-tonne of questions on the subject of leather and bright red asses. Well, really all he wanted to know was how she'd feel about the leather seat-strap from his bassoon on her bright red ass.

ELLA SIPPED her juice and fought not to squirm. She failed miserably, as she felt her panties grow wetter with each stroke of the leather belt Finn laid on Mac's bare ass. Having the two sexiest men on the planet book-ending her only made the situation worse. She thought back to Finn ordering Griff and Jack to take her elsewhere if they thought she was getting too uncomfortable, and she started to worry. What if they mistook her rampant horniness as emotional discomfort and dragged her away? She needed to get herself under control. Ever since she'd resurrected that damned piece, she had been jonesing for some good kink and she desperately wanted to accumulate some decent wank-fodder. Something she had no chance of doing if these guys thought they needed to evacuate her.

She kept waffling between feeling sexy and self-conscious. She was enjoying their hungry looks, but was terrified they would see what she was hiding.

It had been difficult finding something in Mac's wardrobe she thought would adequately cover her scars without being frumpy. She finally settled on a cream stretch lace top. It was sheer enough to give a sense of showing skin, but appeared to have enough pattern to mask the tangle of scars that littered her entire torso. Mac had changed in front of her and when she saw no visible scars on Mac's body, Ella was even more determined to keep her ugliness and shame to herself. On the very rare occasions people had seen her scars, they'd either turned away in disgust or smothered her with pity. She couldn't deal with either reaction from Mac. She'd needed to pee anyway, so she used that as an excuse to get changed in the bathroom. If Mac thought she was weird or a prude, she didn't comment, and for that, Ella was grateful.

She'd been so nervous when she and Mac came down the stairs into the playroom, she'd been frantically trying to think of excuses to leave. Then she saw Jack and Griff. There was no mistaking their hungry expressions for anything less than pure lust. For her. It had been a very long time since she'd felt desirable, let alone lust-worthy. She didn't expect that feeling to last long, so she'd been determined to enjoy it for as long as she could.

"Ella?"

Ella startled from her thoughts and turned to Griff. "Yeah?"

"Can I get you more juice?"

Ella looked down at the empty glass in her hand. "I can get it."

"No doubt, but I asked if I can get you more juice. So, can I?"

Oh shit, there was no question that was his Dom-voice. "Yes, please, that would be lovely, thank you."

"Jack, more Coke?"

"If you don't mind."

"Of course I don't mind. Anything for you, Jack. You know that."

Jack winked and shot Griff a sexy lop-sided grin. "In that case, I have a few ideas for later."

And damn, if that exchange didn't make Ella's scalp tingle and her panties flood. She struggled against her growing need for an orgasm and tried to figure out whether or not she needed to stop for batteries on her way home.

As Griff wandered off, Jack leaned in close and whispered, "Would you like to come, sweetheart?"

And how the fuck was she supposed to answer that? Oh yeah, she wanted to come in the worst way. She kept mentally pinching herself with memories of that disastrous night in order to keep her need in check. What if she said yes? She had no doubt they would make her come, but it was how they'd do it that made her feel anxious. What if she said no? Then she'd have to wait until she got home. A trip that got longer the moment she realised she would have to make a battery stop. She was buggered no matter which answer she chose. Fucking Doms.

"It's a yes or no question, Ella. Do you really need to think that hard about the answer?"

Griff returned with their drinks and sat down. This time, close enough for his thigh to touch hers. "What did I miss?"

Ella felt the heat rise to her hairline, but in a determined effort to pretend the question hadn't been asked, she fixed her gaze on Mac's scarlet ass as Finn continued to wallop it with his leather belt.

"Sweetness, pretending I didn't ask doesn't mean it didn't happen. If you really don't want to answer, you can call red. Finn wasn't bullshitting when he told you red works for everything. I asked the question because you've been getting pretty squirmy, and I'd pretty much bet my Dom-card it's because you're horny and itching for an orgasm.

Ella shrugged, hoping that would be enough to make Jack stop.

"Not good enough, Ella. Clear words are the only thing that work, and in case you have forgotten, your three word choices are, yes, no, and red. Communication is non-negotiable in Finn's playroom, so if you insist upon silence, we'll err on the side of caution and interpret it as a safeword and take you away from the play area. Oh, and one other thing—honesty is always,

always rewarded. So, sweet Ella, would you like to come?"

Ella squeezed her hands into fists and curled her toes. God, how she wanted to come, and she sure as shit, knew she didn't want to go upstairs and miss all the action. Even if he hadn't sweetened the pot for an honest answer, lying wasn't an option—that would mean saying no. "What kind of reward?"

Jack smiled at her. "It usually depends on the situation. In this case, I don't think I can fairly answer that question until I know what your truthful answer is. How about this? You give me a hypothetical answer, and I can give you an example. Would that work?"

As hard as she tried, Ella couldn't really find a problem with it. She could tell the truth and find out what it would get her without having to admit the truth first. "Okay. I think I can work with that."

"Excellent. So, *hypothetically*, would you like to come?"

Ella squirmed a bit more. Damn, that voice was deadly on her won't power. If she wasn't careful, he could get her to do all kinds of things she'd normally baulk at. "*Hypothetically*, yes."

"Then, *hypothetically*, if you were feeling brave enough to let Griff and me give you an orgasm, your honest answer would earn you a second, and just to make it interesting, no toys, and you'd get to keep your clothes on."

It was all Ella could do not to burst out laughing.

Two orgasms? She figured she had hit the jackpot if a man could find her clit without a sat-nav and a flood-light, let alone make her come. As for doing it while she was fully clothed and without toys? In what universe? They seemed so cocky, it was almost tempting to let them try just to see their egos crash and burn. Sully would be arriving soon, and he'd make sure she was safe. Besides, by her calculations, the worst that could happen was no joy, and she'd have to wait and take care of her own happy ending when she got home. At best? Double the pleasure with a fraction of the wait. "That's a pretty *hypothetically* tempting reward."

"How about a real answer to the question, love?"

Ella picked at her cuticles and chewed at the inside of her cheek. Was she really going to do this? She cast her thoughts back through the weeks since she'd met these men. She considered their behaviour, then weighed it against what she had been told by Mac. Taking all that into account, they *seemed* genuine and trustworthy enough.

She thought about the last pretty boy she'd trusted. He'd seemed genuine and trustworthy too. That was when she learned her judgement was defective. It was an expensive lesson, paid for with the tangle of silvery lines that marred her skin. A permanent reminder of unbearable pain and terror.

Then she considered the differences between the situations. That awful night, she was on her own. She hadn't had any outside input about the pretty boy.

She'd never seen, let alone played with him before that night. He'd exhibited impeccable behaviour the whole time at the club, but she hadn't listened to that little voice in the back of her head reminding her never to go home with a stranger, especially without taking any safety-precautions like arranging a check-in call or texting his address to a friend when she arrived at his house. No, sub-frenzy had done a spectacular job of ignoring that little voice.

On the other hand, she'd seen these guys in action at rehearsals, and their care of the subs they played was always safe and consistent. In addition, Mac vouched for their character. That had its pluses and minuses, though. Yes, Mac had been through a similar experience which impaired her ability to trust, but as far as she knew, Mac had never played with Griff and Jack, and even if she had, it was pretty obvious Finn would be paying close attention, not willing to put Mac at even the slightest risk.

Of course, she was ignoring the obvious. Regardless of what they might be like with a sub in private, she was surrounded by people who would keep her safe. Hell, she'd have to be a complete idiot to give up the potential for two orgasms, neither of which, would be self-induced.

She looked from Jack to Griff and considered their patient, but hopeful expressions. Dammit, she was going to do it, she was going to let her pussy do all the talking. Again. "Yes."

GRIFF GRINNED at Jack and stood. "You two talk, I'll go get things organised."

Jack reached over and gently took Ella's hand. "I appreciate that you told the truth, sweetheart, but I can see you're terrified. I want you to understand, Griff and I would never do anything to harm you, and we'll do everything in our power not to scare you. I know you and Mac talked about past experiences, but I want you to know, all she told us was that you have good reason not to trust. She never told us what it was. She said you'd tell us if and when you felt the time was right. I also understand that it's going to take way more than words for you to believe this to be true. Griff and I are more than keen to do whatever it takes to prove it to you, but we can be patient for as long as you need.

"We want to give you those orgasms, but it's pretty clear to all involved you're not going to stick up for yourself, so we're going bring in a referee once our options have finished playing for the night. You can clarify your limits and any concerns with Mac. More anticipation on your part will do you good. So, the question is, should we ask Finn or Sully to officiate. Jack's attention shifted as Ella began picking at her cuticles again. He studied her fingers, the skin around her nails was ragged where she had chewed them. This was a destructive habit they would need to work on, but it could wait. There were so many more important things to tackle first.

"I'd like it to be Finn. I don't think Sully is up for it."

"Good enough, love. Now, while we've got some time to kill, and the opportunity to chat, I'd like to know more about that delightful piece we're rehearsing. What inspired it? If I'm to do it justice in performance, I think I should know its background."

Ella took a deep breath. "I'd have thought Sully would have given you the full story long before now. The man has a mouth like a leaky bucket, big and incapable of holding anything back."

Jack chuckled. "You've got that right. He's an odd duck. Capable of taking secrets to the grave, but if he gets it into his head that telling a secret is in someone's best interest, he won't hesitate to spill it. I guess in his unfathomable wisdom, he must have thought this story was entirely yours to tell."

"Odd duck, indeed. As for why he didn't give you the low-down, I couldn't begin to guess. It's not like it's even an exciting story. Maybe we should wait for Griff to come back."

"I don't think the motivation behind that suggestion is as altruistic as it sounds. I think you'd best quit stalling, and spill."

ELLA LOOKED up as Griff returned, relieved at the opportunity to redirect the conversation. What was she thinking? How could she have admitted to Jack how much she used to love being caned, especially when she knew it would never be any kind of option, even if she were to wade back into the kinky pool. She sure didn't miss how his eyes lit up when she said it used to be her absolute favourite thing. She didn't think he could look any more excited. Then she mentioned her love of leather belts. She could almost hear the *ding ding ding, we have a winner* going off in his head. She also didn't miss the quick flash disappointment he'd tried to hide when she took canes off the table. Obviously, they were a bit of a favourite for at least one of the pair.

Damn it, she should've kept her bloody mouth shut. Even worse, she just kept getting hornier and hornier. As terrifying as the thought of playing was for her, she kept fixating on what it might be like to play with both of these sexy men. She'd never had a threesome before, but that didn't stop her from daydreaming about it and she had no shortage of reading material featuring it. She could feast on the *idea* of being the filling in a Griff and Jack sandwich for months, the reality of it would probably provide her with a life-time supply of wank-fodder. She mentally smacked herself. *And exactly how did that going home with a Domly stranger thing work out for you?* Yeah, she knew better than most how the disaster of reality can be inversely proportional to the ecstasy of fantasy.

She was so deep in her own head, she startled at Griff's voice. "We're all set. Do we have a referee picked out?"

Jack patted her knee. "Ella would like Finn to ref, and she'll talk to Mac about limits and such first." He looked over to the spot where Mac and Finn had been playing and then back at Griff. "It looks like they're done. Would you like to go talk to Finn about it, or would you like to stay here with Ella while I go?"

"I'll go. You two look comfortable and I'm already up. Ella, I'll ask Mac to come and chat with you once she is back to normal, okay? It might take some time, I think she was pretty deep in sub-space there for a while."

"That would be great. Thank you." Ella lifted her hand toward her mouth, but Jack stopped it before it reached its destination.

"I know you need to think about what you'll want to talk to Mac about, but it would please me greatly if you could do it without damaging your body in the process."

Ella looked down at her hand. Embarrassed and ashamed, she tried to pull it from Jack's grip to hide it.

"Stop for a moment, love. I wasn't trying to embarrass you. It's a nervous habit, and one you probably wouldn't notice if someone didn't point it out to you. You're not the only person on the planet to do this, and you won't be the only one to overcome it. Don't worry, Griff and I will help you. I love to reward positive behaviour, so if you can get through the next thirty minutes without chewing on yourself, Griff and I will give you a third orgasm."

Ella did laugh then. She kept it quiet so she wouldn't disturb Wil and Hildy's scene, but the idea of a third orgasm, especially with the limits they had set, was ludicrous.

"Ah, a sceptic. I like that. Things are so much more fun when we have something to prove. Let me guess, most of the men you've been with were all talk and no orgasm."

Yeah, he had it in one. She didn't really want to admit it, but she thought confirming his suspicions would at least make them try harder, and maybe she would have a chance for at least one orgasm before she went home.

TWELVE
Ella had honestly thought Griff and Jack were blowing the same smoke regarding their sexual prowess as every other stud-wannabe she'd ever encountered. Of course, she was already wound up pretty tight by the time they were ready to start, but she still didn't think they'd be able to pull off a hat-trick with her fully clothed and no power tools.

They didn't touch her at all until they'd reached the spanking bench. Mac had promised her she wouldn't be restrained and her limits would be respected, but she was still apprehensive.

Jack took her by the hand and slowly pulled her towards him. He peppered the left side of her neck with tiny kisses as he wrapped his arms around her and his erection brushed against her belly. Oh boy, that was certainly worth bragging about.

Then Griff pressed behind her and nipped at her

right earlobe. Wow, he wasn't lacking, either. Her tummy went all fluttery and her pussy felt like it was on fire. Her attempt to squeeze her legs together to give herself a little relief was thwarted when each man slipped a leg between hers.

Griff whispered in her ear, "Don't worry, honey, we'll take care of that for you, just like Jack promised. You just need to be patient."

Jack lifted his head and placed a soft kiss to her lips, then increased the pressure as he slid his tongue along the seam of her mouth.

"Let him in, baby." Griff's hot breath against her ear sent a new trickle of moisture into her already drenched panties.

She parted her lips and Jack traced them with the tip of his tongue before he caught her bottom lip between his teeth. He tugged gently and that flutter in her belly intensified. Jack cupped her cheek and kissed her once more before he pulled away. "Such a good girl. Now, up you get and lay on your back, sweetheart." Griff nipped her earlobe one more time, then helped her get settled on the bench.

They began stroking their hands all over her body, but never where she most desperately needed to feel their touch. Her breasts ached and her pussy spasmed with every heartbeat. Their fingers were barely a whisper, and for a moment, she found herself wishing her clothes away so she could feel those fingers on her skin. Then she remembered the level of disfigurement and was grateful for the fabric barrier.

She mentally gave her head a shake. Now wasn't the time to wallow in self-pity. She had two gorgeous men itching to do whatever it took to get her off three times without her having to remove one stitch of clothing. Even though she figured they had no chance of success, she missed being touched, and for now, she was perfectly happy to let them waste their time on her. Besides, if they did manage to deliver on their promise, so much the better. But damn, she wished they would just get on with it.

She was almost at her breaking point when heat engulfed both her nipples and sparks shot straight to her clit. Holy hell, she was already horny and now all she wanted was her pussy full of cock. She needed to keep her head in the game. These guys were dangerous. They were making her feel things she hadn't felt in a decade.

As Griff and Jack sucked on her nipples through the fabric of Mac's top, it occurred to Ella she'd need to get it cleaned before she could return it. A sharp nip on her right nipple and a hand slipping between her thighs reined in her wandering mind. Oh shit, she was primed and it wasn't going to take much at all to launch her into space. Fingers pressed hard against her clit and rubbed in all kinds of delicious ways as the suction on her nipples ebbed and flowed. She didn't bother trying to fight the looming orgasm. She wanted it more than her next breath. She was so close she wanted to lift her hips and reach for it, but those clever fingers saved her the trouble. They pressed harder and moved faster until she exploded.

They hadn't given her much time to recover from that first orgasm before they teased out the other two they'd promised and then added one more for the road. Yeah, these guys were dangerous.

GRIFF HAD BEEN silent for the whole drive home, and that had Jack more than a little worried. Working together to make Ella come had been a beautiful experience he was eager to build on, but what if Griff had changed his mind? He still harboured a soul-deep fear that Griff was going to abandon him for a woman, and he didn't know if he could survive it. Jack hated feeling in limbo, and as much as he wanted Griff to hurry up and say what was on his mind, pestering the man would only slow the process down. He left Griff to his own devices while he put his toy bag away and got ready for bed.

Jack was just about asleep when Griff finally slid into bed. He cuddled up behind him and nipped at his earlobe. Fuck, he would swear there was a direct line between his earlobe and his balls. "Hi." Griff continued to nibble and he wanted nothing more than to grind his ass against his lover's hard cock, but until

Griff shared what was on his mind, sex of any kind was off the table. "Griff."

"Hush, I need you."

Dammit. He was screwed six ways from Sunday. It would be easier to go ahead and have sex. After that scene with Ella, he was certainly horny enough, but he needed to be sure this wasn't going to be the last fuck goodbye.

"Griff, stop. I know you've got something on your mind and you know I'm usually content to sit tight and wait until you're ready to talk, but I'm scared and I need to know if you're going to dump me so you can have Ella to yourself."

Griff pulled him in tight and kissed his neck. "Hell no. I was replaying that scene in my head and trying to figure out when we can play with her again, and how long we'll have to wait until we can get her naked and make her ours."

"Really?"

"Really. Jack, I hate that I've given you any reason to doubt my commitment to our relationship and it kills me that you still feel insecure. I meant what I said. If I can only have one person in my life, I choose you. I. Choose. You. Always. Do I want to see where things could go with Ella? Of course. But I'm not willing to risk what *is* for what *might be*. My heart belongs to you and it's yours to share or not. I love you."

God he felt like a selfish heel. "I'm sorry, babe."

"Don't. You can't help your feelings, and I don't ever want you to be sorry for them. Clear?"

"I'll try." And he would.

"Good enough. Now, speaking of selfish, I'm feeling pretty damned horny after that scene with Ella..."

Jack grinned and shimmied down the bed and took his lover's cock deep into his mouth.

THIRTEEN

Ella ignored her phone again as she tried to read her smutty book. She wished they would all just stop pushing. She had successfully avoided sexual entanglements for the last ten years. It wasn't that difficult. She had three rules. Only date men she didn't find attractive; make it clear she wasn't a first date fuck; and make damn sure there was never a second date.

Now she was faced with not one, but two men who she wouldn't hesitate to break the rules for, and for her own safety, she needed to limit her time with them to final rehearsals only. No more letting Mac lure her to social functions where Griff and Jack would be.

She was smart enough to know Mac was manipulating her to attend, and she went along with it because they were a fun bunch of people to be around and she'd mistakenly thought she was strong enough to keep her libido out of the equation.

The knocking on the door was much more difficult to ignore. Damn, she was relentless. Ella finally gave in when it became clear Mac wasn't leaving. She yanked the door open and stood there, saying nothing. She was angry and feeling more than a little regret for agreeing to pull that fucking piece out of mothballs. She wasn't going to make it easy for Mac to worm further into her life.

"Ella, are you okay? We haven't seen you in days and you haven't been answering your phone. I've been worried."

Fuck. The guilt card. "I'm fine, thanks. Just really busy."

"You don't look very fine."

"I'm just tired. I've got deadlines to meet and I've spent way too much time socialising." Not entirely a lie. She did have deadlines to meet, just not anytime soon. And she *had* been doing too much socialising.

"I don't buy that you're too busy to answer the fucking phone or return a fucking message for days on end."

Oh shit, Mac was getting mad. She needed to diffuse this fast. She couldn't handle Mac being angry at her. Time to figuratively roll over and bear the belly. "I'm sorry. I promise I'll return calls by the end of the day if I'm too busy to pick up. Okay?"

Mac gave her an indulgent smile. "Okay."

That wasn't so hard. Now she just had to get Mac to leave. "I'd invite you in for coffee, but I'm right in the middle of a break-through..." She trailed off, hoping Mac would take the hint. Again, not exactly a lie—her book *was* at a crucial point in the story.

"Sure thing. I'll let you get back to it." Mac's expression did nothing to hide her disappointment before she turned and headed down the steps.

Ella quietly shut the door before she let the first tears fall. She swiped at them with the back of her hand and headed for her bed. She was too upset to do anything, even read. She should have just continued to ignore the fucking door. She should have gone out for the day and left her phone at home.

She'd cried herself to sleep, and was a little disoriented when she woke up to a dark room and a persistent banging. All she wanted was her peaceful life back. As much she wanted to bury her head beneath her pillow and ignore the ruckus outside, it would be over much faster if she just sucked it up and answered the door.

She looked through the peephole and forced herself not to groan. She pasted on a bright smile and opened the door. "Mac, what can I do for you?"

Mac stood there with big pizza box, a loaded shopping bag, and a soft-sided cooler. "Girl's night."

Fuck. How the hell was she supposed to get out of this? The only way she knew how, lie. "Look, I've got a headache and I need to go back to bed."

"Too fucking bad, Ella. If you really do have a headache, go take something for it. Now move." Mac was wearing her dictator hat, and Ella had been around her enough to know the only option was to go with it, so she stepped back and let the woman in.

The moment she walked through the door, Mac set down her load and wrapped her arms around Ella, holding her tight. She tried to pull away, but Mac gave her another squeeze before letting her go. Mac picked up the pizza box and held it out. "Here, take this into the living room while I go grab the necessaries from the kitchen."

Ella set the box on the coffee table and lifted the lid. Hawaiian. Of course Mac would bring her favourite pizza—that was how she rolled. She closed the box and curled up in her favourite armchair while she wondered what other goodies Mac had up her sleeve. Girl's night, she'd said. Oh, how long it had been since she'd had one of those. Maybe it wouldn't be so bad.

Mac walked into the room carrying plates, a couple bottles of beer, and the shopping bag. She set everything on the table and rooted around in the bag for a moment before pulling out a handful of DVDs. "Chick-flicks. No girl's night is complete without them. Which one do you want to watch first?" She fanned the cases out so Ella could see the titles.

For the first time in what seemed like for ever, Ella smiled. Mac had brought musicals. "Let's go with *Some Like it Hot*, I could use the laughs."

"Excellent choice." Mac laid the rest of the cases

on the table and inserted the film into the DVD player. She loaded a plate with pizza and sat on the sofa. She looked at Ella and flashed her irresistible grin as she patted the cushion beside her. "Come sit next to me. It'll be more fun. You'll have a better view of the TV and more importantly," she waggled her eyebrows, "you'll be closer to the pizza."

Why did the woman have to make it impossible to stay grumpy? Ella grabbed a plate and a couple pieces of pizza before she parked herself on the sofa next to her friend. Yes, her friend. After so many weeks of fighting it, she finally accepted Mac's friendship. It was just easier. No, that wasn't entirely true. I *was* easier, but more than that, it felt so much better. She really did like Mac, and the idea of losing touch after the performance didn't sit well.

By the time they'd finished their third film, they'd also consumed most of the pizza, all the beer, and couple bags of potato chips. As the closing credits rolled, Mac grabbed a remote control in each hand and simultaneously hit the power button for the TV and the eject button for the DVD player.

"Hey, I was reading those," Ella complained.

Mac retrieved the DVD and popped it into its case before powering down the machine. "Tough titties, sunshine." She tossed the movie on top of the others sitting on the coffee table and returned to her spot on the sofa. "Okay, it's time to talk about your sub-drop."

Was the woman on crack? How could anyone

possibly get sub-drop from a few little orgasms? "I was tired, is all."

"Sweetie, pizza, beer, and a few movies with a girl-friend does not magically make you un-tired. I was there, and you definitely hit a little subspace, and there's no doubt in my mind you've been suffering from sub-drop. And maybe a side of panic?"

"It was just post-orgasm buzz, not subspace, but I'll admit there may have been a little panic to go with the tired."

"Okay, we can call it tired, if that's what works for you, but whenever I think you're *tired*, I'm going to show up at your door with a pick-me-up. Deal?"

Ella sighed and gave in. "Deal." The sigh was more for show than how she really felt, but maybe Mac was on to something with this sub-drop business, because she definitely felt better now than she had in a couple of days. A trip to Google might be in order.

"Excellent. Now that you seem to be in better spir-its, it's time for me to call Finn to come pick me up." Mac grabbed her phone off the coffee table and dialled.

"A DATE."

Jack stopped scraping the reed he was making and looked up. "What are you on about?"

"I think we need to take Ella on a date," Griff said.

"Have you lost your mind? She doesn't even trust us in a group setting, what makes you think she'll agree to a date?"

Griff shrugged. "The worst that can happen is she'll make up some bullshit to avoid saying no, so what have we got to lose?"

"Babe, if we push her too hard, we're going to blow it and she's going to dive back into that hole of hers and never come out."

"Oh for fuck's sake, we've already messed up. We've been too hands-off with her. It should have been us helping her through her sub-drop. It was our responsibility, not Mac's."

"Okay, you make a good point," Jack conceded. "What do you have in mind?"

"Nothing specific. It's more along the lines of what I don't have in mind. Whatever it is, it can't set up the expectation of a post-date fuck or playtime. I think that's the most important thing."

"All right," Jack returned to scraping his reed as he continued, "what I'm hearing is, traditional date activities like dinner or a movie are out. Correct?" Griff nodded. "In that case, I think silly and fun might be in order. How about button pushing at the toy store."

"That definitely qualifies as silly and fun. Maybe go for ice cream after?"

"Yeah, I think ice cream is a great idea." Jack stopped scraping and held the reed up to the bright light on his work table. He flipped it back and forth a few times before placing it on the reed rack to dry.

"Just one thing..." Griff waited until Jack looked at him. "I think it's really important that this is a date—nothing more. No slipping in a little D/s, and for now, if we're alone with Ella, none of the good Dom, bad Dom shit. Getting her to trust us needs to be our first priority."

"Fair enough. However, I think we might have a better chance at success if we ask her in person at tomorrow's game night than we will if we phone her."

"Manipulative—but not unreasonably so. We should make our date on a weekday—there should be fewer kids in the store," Griff flashed a big grin, "and less competition for the buttons. I vote for Monday. I swear, that's the most un-date-like day of the week."

"Of course, it has nothing to do with it being the first available weekday after tomorrow." Jack raised an eyebrow and Griff grinned back. "I wonder if there's any chance of her coming to the play party on Sunday."

"I'll call Mac and ask while you get your shit packed up. Then we can head to bed."

"Sounds like a plan."

Griff grabbed his phone and dialled. When Mac answered, he said, "Hang on, I'm going to put you on speaker." He hit the button and held the phone between himself and Jack. "There, now I won't have to repeat the whole conversation." Jack raised that damned eyebrow again, so Griff winked and suggestively licked his top lip before lowering his gaze to the rapidly growing bulge in Jack's jeans. Someone was getting lucky tonight.

"What's up, you two? I'm assuming you didn't hit mute by mistake."

"You're a cheeky wench. We were wondering whether Ella's going to be at your play party on Sunday."

Mac giggled. "And if she's not going to be there, you'd like me to do everything in my power to change her mind. Am I right?"

"Well..."

"Good grief. There are days when I wonder how

any of you lot got your Dom cards. Yes, she's coming. You'll be happy to know, it didn't take any arm-twisting. Sub-drop aside, her experience with you two was positive enough for her to want to come again—in more ways than one, I'd imagine. We'll take that as a big win and move on."

"Thanks. Any advice for us?"

"Yeah, don't fucking let her suffer from sub-drop like that again."

"We won't."

"You'd better not, because rest assured, I will make it seriously suck to be you."

"Understood. We'll see you tomorrow."

"Goodnight."

Griff pushed the button to end the call and looked over at Jack. "Bedtime?"

"Yup. Last one there, bottoms." Jack jumped up and raced out of the room before Griff even had a chance to stand up.

"You're a dirty, rotten cheater, Jackson Riley," he yelled as he raced after his lover. Ah fuck it—it didn't matter whether he was bottom or top, he'd still get to come a time or two before they fell asleep.

JACK LAZILY STROKED his hand up and down his condom-clad erection, slathering it in lube as he waited impatiently for Griff to arrive. Yeah, he'd cheated, but all's fair in love and fucking. Besides, they tended to bottom and top in fairly equal measure. He let his mind wander to Ella and how beautiful she'd looked when she came. He hoped they'd get to play with her on Sunday. He knew they were a long way from sex of any kind, let alone double-teaming her, but maybe fortune would smile on them and they would get to do a bit more than make her come fully clothed. His mouth watered at the idea of her naked and spread before him, her clit shyly peeking out ready to be sucked, tortured, and teased into submission.

"Care to share what's on your mind?"

Startled out of his daydream, Jack grinned and thrust his pelvis upward. "Later. Right now I'm more than ready to share what's in my fist. Hands on the wall, spread your legs, and brace yourself. I'm not feeling particularly gentle tonight."

As he stood behind Griff, Jack exposed his lover's asshole. Once he had his cock positioned at the entrance, he slipped his arms under Griff's and grabbed hold of his shoulders. "Relax. Deep breath, then let it out, babe." On the exhale, Jack pushed his hips forward with steady pressure as he pulled down on Griff's shoulders and bit into crook of his neck. The head of Jack's cock squeezed through the tight ring of muscle, and he savoured that fleeting moment of near pain before Griff's asshole relaxed and welcomed him in.

He didn't wait for Griff to adjust to him. As soon as

he'd buried his entire length inside, he pulled out and slammed home. Griff moaned and rocked his hips, driving Jack to pump harder and faster. "Don't come," he growled in Griff's ear before he gave the lobe a sharp nip. A few more thrusts and he was there. He bit down hard on the crook of Griff's neck and groaned as he filled the condom.

He kissed the bite mark, then carefully pulled out. "Go sit on the bed, babe. As soon as I deal with this condom, I'm going to suck you dry.

FIFTEEN

ELLA TRIED to keep her jaw off the floor while her traitorous pussy soaked her panties as it throbbed and clenched with every beat of her racing heart. Wilson and Finn were spit-roasting Hildy while Mac teased her mercilessly with a vibrator. Ella felt a little sorry for poor Hildy having her mouth held open with a spider gag. Then again, considering the number, and apparent intensity of the orgasms she was having, chances were good its sole purpose was to prevent Finn's cock from being bitten off. Between sweat, tears, and drool, Hildy was soaked and looked like she'd had just about enough, but unless she dropped one of the balls she held in her hands or someone else called the scene, they'd all keep going. Wil gave Finn a discreet nod and they both increased the speed of their thrusts until Finn came in Hildy's mouth, followed by Wil in her pussy. The men quickly removed her restraints and

Mac wrapped Hildy in a blanket before Wilson scooped her up and carried her to one of the sofas in the aftercare area.

Reading about it and watching videos on the internet could get her a little hot and bothered, but having a front row seat to live action had her downright horny. She wondered where Jack and Griff were. Although she hadn't outright asked Mac if they were coming, it was her understanding they never missed a party. She was a little surprised to find herself disappointed at their absence. Fuck. She needed to get her head on straight and her mind off Griff and Jack. They were dangerous. She should be relieved they hadn't come, not disappointed. She needed to focus her attention elsewhere.

She knew it would be a struggle to hide her envy, so she consciously avoided paying any attention to the sofa next to her where Wilson was taking care of Hildy. Instead, she turned her focus back to the play space where Mac was kneeling in front of Finn while he instructed her on the finer points of deep throating.

"Relax your throat and swallow. You can do it, love. Take it all for me just once, then we can move on to things that make you feel good."

Mac pulled back and dry heaved a couple of times before snapping at Finn. "Why don't *you* fucking relax and swallow while someone shoves something the size of a baseball bat down your fucking throat."

"Mac, that's enough. You're awfully close to crossing the line. Either take it for me or safeword."

"Fuck you."

"That didn't sound like your safeword. Wait there and do not move." Finn went to the back of the room and grabbed some sort of slapper from the wall, then sat on a straight-backed chair in the middle of the room. He crooked his finger at Mac and spoke in a quiet voice that sent a shiver down Ella's back. "Come here, my love." Mac stalked across the room and stopped just beyond Finn's reach. He patted his knees. "Mac, " he warned, "over my knee or use your safeword."

She let out a big sigh. "You're being mean to me," she said as she settled over Finn's lap.

"Sweetheart, I know you meant that as an insult, and I'll try to take it as one, but as a sadist, it's kind of hard to take it as anything but flattery. Now, why are you being punished?"

"Because I was disrespectful."

"And what was your punishment last time?"

"Twenty strokes with your flute cleaning rod."

"Yes, and what is the punishment for repeat offences?"

"Double the last with whatever hitty-thing you choose."

"Indeed. This will be the last time we go with that particular punishment. It doesn't seem to be all that effective, and at this rate, I'm going to end up with a repetitive stress injury before the month is out. You'll have your forty with the viper slapper." He stroked the tip of it all over Mac's ass as he spoke. "This little baby is like a tawse except it's made of rubber instead of leather. No need to count, love. Colour?"

"I'm fucking green."

Finn immediately laid into her ass with rapid swats, but she didn't start screaming until the fourth strike. He stopped at the tenth, and when she was quiet, he checked in. "Colour, love?"

"Just fucking get it done. I'm green, you miserable fuck."

"Fair warning. I'm going to give you the next set of ten, then check in. If you're rude to me again, I'll do the remaining twenty without a break, but I'll drag them out to maximise your pain and discomfort."

Mac screamed, but remained stock still while Finn gave her ass another ten shots with that evil piece of rubber. Ella was fascinated. Mac wasn't tied down, she could use her safeword, yet she stayed put while Finn hurt her. When Mac mouthed off at Finn again during his next check in, Ella wanted to gag her or do something make her shut up before she got herself into shit so deep, she'd suffocate.

Two sets of feet appeared on the stairs and Ella's heart gave a little skip as Jack and Griff descended into the room. They caught her eye and grinned before silently crossing the room to join her. Griff sat to her left, his thigh tight against hers as he stretched his arm across the back of the couch. Jack sandwiched her in from the right. His arm joined Griff's behind her and he leaned in and whispered, "Sorry we're late, sweetie. A truck dumped its load half a block in front of us and we were stuck until they could clear a lane for alternating traffic. We did try calling Mac and Finn, but their phones kept going to voice-mail."

Damn, they made her want so badly and they hadn't done anything except sit next to her and explain their delay. She realised how much less concerned she was over Mac's well being now that her men had shown up. Fuck. They weren't her men. They'd never be her men. She needed to think of them only as friends. Should be easy enough. Their plan to goof off together at the toy store tomorrow totally qualified as a friend activity. Besides, who on earth did date things on a Monday afternoon? She tried to ignore the warm bodies pressed against her as she turned her attention back to Mac and Finn.

"I guess you didn't plan on sitting comfortably for the next few days, love." Finn went back to work on Mac's ass, leaving a short pause between each strike. He maintained a steady rhythm and Mac continued to spout obscenities at him.

Then she screamed, "Red," and everything stopped. Finn immediately dropped the slapper to the floor and pulled her into his arms. He stroked her hair and murmured something into her ear. She nodded, and he carried her to the aftercare area, settling on the sofa next to Wilson and Hildy. Wilson covered Mac with her blanket and handed Finn a bottle of water.

Ella didn't know how to process Mac safewording. Part of her was relieved that it worked as intended and everything stopped, but part of her was freaked out that Finn would push so far she needed to safeword. Jack stroked her cheek and she turned to look at him, her eyes filled with unshed tears.

"It's okay, love. They have a healthy, loving relationship. Truth is, he's usually the one to call a scene, but occasionally, he'll push her to safeword. Look on it as reaffirming their trust in each other. He trusts her to use her safeword appropriately, and she trusts him to stop when she does. I know you had a bad experience, so I get that us saying the right words doesn't mean shit to you right now, but maybe there will come a time when you'll be able to reconcile our words with our actions and even feel safe enough to explore a relationship with us."

Ella shook her head. A relationship meant at some point, they'd expect to hear the whole sordid tale of what happened that night. She had enough trouble with that shit popping into her head unannounced, there was no way she was going to send it an engraved invitation. However, she did think Jack had a valid point on the words versus actions thing. After all the time she'd spent with the group in general, and Griff and Jack in particular, their behaviour had always been consistent with their words. Besides, deep in her soul, she knew Sully would never spend any of his precious time with people who weren't genuine. Sadly, that knowledge did nothing to alleviate her nagging doubt. She made a show of checking her watch. "I should get going."

"Really?" Griff asked. She turned to face him and he continued. "Do you really mean you should be going, or do you mean you're scared and you should be avoiding any possibility of conflict?"

She pressed her lips together as she tried to formulate a believable answer.

Jack gave her thigh a gentle squeeze. "The only right answer is the truth, Ella. Try it. The world won't explode if you say something you think we won't like."

Her heart hammered in her chest and her head felt wonky. She couldn't do this.

"Get her a glass of water, would you, Griff?"

"Sure thing."

She felt the sofa shift as Griff stood, and Jack pulled her in close, stroking her hair and peppering the top of her head with tiny kisses. "It's going to be fine, sweetheart. I promise. Like I told you before, the truth always gets rewards."

It was their fucking rewards that had got her into this mess. Four fucking orgasms and she was ready to throw away her rules and risk the safety they afforded. She weighed her options. Her usual tactics failed miserably with this pair. Most people weren't inclined to call bullshit when she pulled even the flimsiest excuse out of her ass, but these two didn't hesitate. Complete avoidance got her girl's night with Mac and a lecture on sub-drop. Unfortunately, she was down to one last, drastic option. She gave it a pretty good chance of succeeding, but she'd have to make herself vulnerable.

GRIFF SNUGGLED tight against Jack's side with his ear right over Jack's heart, but still felt like he couldn't get close enough. Jack stroked his face and kissed the top of his head. He'd managed to stay tough all night, but now he was safe in his lover's arms, and he couldn't control his tears. While the scene did end in multiple orgasms for Ella, it had been an emotional cluster-fuck of epic proportions for Jack and him.

"It'll be fine, babe. You'll see."

"How can you say that? You saw what that psycho-fuck did to her," Griff said through his sniffles.

"Yes, I did. I also saw how she used it to get us to give up on her. Think about that for a minute. Do you think she would have exposed herself like that if she weren't running out of ways to push us away?"

"Well, I guess not, but—"

"But nothing. The only thing that went totally wrong with that scene was Ella thinking we were shallow enough to walk out on her once we saw what that wasted sperm did to her. How about we talk about all the right from that scene? And I've gotta tell ya, naked Ella eclipsed pretty much everything for me. Yeah, she's marked up some, but damn, she's got a gorgeous shape and she sure does taste good."

Griff smiled as he remembered how much he enjoyed licking and sucking at her juicy pussy. "Mmm. True. You're falling for her pretty hard, aren't you?"

"Not any harder than you are, babe."

"I guess that means we'll have to step up our game."

"Maybe. But I'm not sure she has anything left in her arsenal to fight us with. I suspect her putting her scars on display like that was her big gun. She figured we would take one look and run away screaming. She was wrong. All we need to do is make her understand we think she's beautiful and it has nothing to do with her skin."

"Is that all?" Griff snorted.

"Yup, and we get another chance to do exactly that tomorrow. In the meantime, I have other business to attend to."

Jack wiggled his way down the bed and Griff moaned as he felt the warm, wet tongue swirl around the head of his cock. He lifted his hips to get more, but Jack pinned them to the bed before swallowing him down in a long, slow slide. Oh boy, it looked like it was going to be one of those nights where Jack would tease him mercilessly for hours before making him come. He loved it when Jack was in that mood.

SIXTEEN

Ella paced up and down the length of her living room. Her entire week had gone to shit in a handbag and she couldn't believe how badly she'd fucked everything up. Jack and Griff should have either fucked off without a backward glance, or given her the pity stare. She would have been fine with either option. Then it would have been easy for her to write them off and she could get back to the life she was comfortable with.

Now she was fresh out of options and she didn't know what to do. They'd held her to her commitment on Monday afternoon, and as much as she didn't want to have fun, she'd had a fucking blast.

They'd wandered up and down the aisles of the big chain toy store and pushed buttons on every electronic toy they encountered. Then they'd gone to the video game department and tried out all the consoles. She'd never considered owning one before, but another game or two and she might be convinced to buy herself one of those bad boys.

She smiled as she remembered their trip to the gelato shop afterwards. It was the first time she'd ever been there, and holy shit, she'd never seen so many different flavours of ice cream in her life. They ranged from regular old vanilla and chocolate to the outrageously bizarre, and her men—fuck, there she went with that *her men* business again—convinced her to sample at least three strange flavours of their choosing. They started her off with garlic. It wasn't bad, but she wouldn't want a whole cone of it. She even tried the curry flavour, but when Jack held out the spoon with wasabi on it, she baulked. She just couldn't do it. She started to panic when she couldn't come up with a way to avoid it.

Then Griff leaned down and whispered in her ear. "If you really can't do it, just call red, sweetheart. No harm, no foul."

She'd looked at the ice cream and thought about why she always ordered her sushi with no wasabi. She took a deep breath, and then another before she rose up on her toes and whispered, "Red," into Griff's ear.

The world hadn't exploded.

"Such a good girl," Griff said as he pulled her into his arms. "That wasn't so bad, was it?"

She shook her head. He cupped her chin, tipped her face up, and placed a gentle kiss on her lips. "There you go then. Red is the new no."

Jack shot her a big grin and licked the offending wasabi ice cream off the spoon with a dramatic flourish. Then they'd bought her a homemade waffle-cone filled with three scoops of the most amazing chocolate ice cream she'd ever tasted.

She looked at the clock, they'd be here any minute. She cursed herself for what must have been the hundredth time since agreeing to this. She had to be nuts. A date? An honest to goodness, dinner and a movie date? Then it hit her. This was her out. They'd kept her so off balance lately, she hadn't connected the dots. This was a first date. She only did first dates. Okay, she'd messed up on the rule about only dating unfortunate looking men, but as long as she kept rules two and three, she should be able to send them packing at the end of the evening.

JACK STRUGGLED to hold back the laugh, and he carefully avoided catching Griff's eye for fear they'd both lose it as Ella stood at her front door and politely explained her two unbreakable rules for dating. His sadistic side was looking forward to her reaction when he pointed out she was actually down to one unbreakable rule. His softer side... well, his softer side had a front row seat and a big bag of popcorn.

"Sweetie, what do you consider a date?"

"What we just did. Dinner and a movie." She

paused and added, "I guess you could include going to a café or a pub."

"So, would it be fair to say your interpretation of a date is any outing involving food or drink?"

"I suppose..." She trailed off.

Nope, there was no mistaking her light bulb moment and she made the cutest little frown when it hit.

He reached out and gently stroked her cheek. "It's okay, sweetie. We've reached a fork in the road, and now it's time for you to decide which route you're going to take. I need you to understand, we're here for you and we'll keep you safe, whichever route you take. As much as we'd love to explore an intimate, kinky relationship with you, we're your friends first and always.

"You've got a lot to think about. To help you with your decision, Griff and I will send you our check-lists. Before you read them, fill one out of your own, then compare them. Maybe that will help you with your decision." Jack leaned down and pressed a gentle kiss on Ella's lips. "We're going to head home. We'll give you all the time you need to do your thinking, but that doesn't mean we're going to leave you alone."

Jack stepped aside, making room for Griff, who cupped Ella's chin and gave her a long, lingering kiss. Mildly irritated, he tapped Griff's shoulder. "Enough, studly. It's time for us to go home."

After breaking the kiss, Griff stared into Ella's eyes as he brushed his thumbs over her cheekbones. "Have a good sleep, sweetheart. Jack and I will be in touch. Now go inside and lock the door. We won't leave until you do."

She turned and entered the house, giving the men a small wave before closing the door. Once they heard the deadbolt slide home, they headed down the steps. Jack pointed the remote and pressed the unlock button.

They climbed into the car, and as he fastened his seat belt, Griff said, "Well, that went better than I feared."

Jack turned the key in the ignition, then pulled out into the street. "It did. There's still a lot of work ahead of us, though. I'm glad we filled out new check-lists yesterday. I'm hoping Ella will look on it as more proof of our sincerity than us trying to convince her we're being what we think she wants."

"Regardless of the Ella factor, I noticed we both had a few changes from when we last did them."

Jack chuckled. "Yeah. I'm still trying to figure out if that's a good thing, or a bad thing."

"If everyone involved is on board, does it matter?"

"Well, no."

"There you are then. As with many things in life, our tastes evolve, and as long as we're having a good time, I'm not going to sweat it. Speaking of a good time..." Griff unfastened Jack's trousers and extracted his cock.

Jack had been hard pretty much since they'd picked Ella up for their date. "If you're not planning to blow me, you'd best put that right back where you found it. I'm on a hair trigger, and if I end up spraying the interior of my car with spunk, you'll be the one cleaning it up."

"I was going to, but it's probably safer if I hold off until we get home. I will, however, leave your cock out where I can enjoy it. Besides, if you are that close, I don't want to be stuck cleaning your car just because I tried to cram your dick back in your trousers."

"You are such a fucking tease. I'm tempted to pull over and take care of business myself, and still make you clean up, because if you hadn't pulled my cock out in the first place, I wouldn't be in this predicament."

"You won't. I know you'd much rather come down my throat than redecorate the interior of your car."

"You're right, I would," Jack admitted. "In fact, I'm going to fuck your throat raw tonight, babe."

Griff unzipped his own trousers and pulled out his raging hard-on. "Fair enough, but that means I get your ass, and *gentle* sure as fuck isn't in my vocabulary right now."

"Sounds good to me." Jack checked the speedometer and backed off the accelerator a little. He did not need to get pulled over by the cops for speeding while he and Griff both had their dicks out, ready for action. He tried to focus on the road instead of the cock being stroked in his peripheral vision. Thank fuck they were only a few blocks from home, because, damn, that man knew how to torment.

They arrived home a few minutes later, and they raced into the house, cocks bobbing in the breeze. Once they were safely inside, Griff dropped to his knees and tugged Jack's trousers down to his thighs. He looked up and smiled before sliding his mouth all the way down on Jack's cock.

ELLA LEANED against the door and let herself slide down it. This was not going according to plan at all. They were supposed to run the other way, not try harder to get close. Maybe the check-lists were the answer. If they were totally incompatible, then they'd leave her alone. But what if they weren't?

Somewhere between the tell-tale beep of the car remote and the roar of the engine, the loneliness set in. It was an odd thing, that soul-sucking loneliness. It was like a black hole opened in her chest whenever Griff and Jack left, devouring all the peace and contentment she felt when she was with them. They'd flipped her world on its side these past weeks, and worse, she wasn't sure she hated it.

She picked herself up off the floor and debated whether she wanted tea or something stronger before she went in search of a check-list to fill out. She was awfully tempted to hold off until she'd had a chance to go over Griff and Jack's lists, but it felt disrespectful—

too much like cheating. Besides, deep down, she wanted a real sense of their compatibility.

Tea lost, and she sat on the sofa with her laptop and a beer. She did a search for check-lists and was boggled by the sheer number of results that came back. How the fuck was she supposed pick from these. What if she picked the wrong one? She didn't want to compare beer to wine.

A quick phone call to Mac and her problem was solved. She disconnected the call and started obsessively clicking the refresh button as she waited for the arrival of the email with the promised check-list attached. She took a swig of beer from the bottle, hoping that would speed things up. It didn't. She checked her watch and felt silly. It hadn't even been five minutes since she and Mac had spoken. Staring at the screen wasn't going to make things happen any faster. It would be better to do this business while all comfy, so she picked up her laptop and beer and headed to the bedroom.

By the time she'd changed into her pyjamas and settled into bed with her laptop, Mac's email had arrived. Why was her heart trying to beat its way out of her chest? She closed her eyes for a moment, then she clicked on the attachment and waited for it to load and open.

Holy shit. She didn't remember check-lists being this long and involved back in the day. As she scanned through the document, she had to keep reminding herself that not everyone had the same taste in food, clothes, or kink, and it was not her place to judge. With such a wide-ranging assortment, she figured chances were pretty good that there would be stuff Griff and Jack were into that she'd totally red-light on and she found that thought disappointing.

She clicked to print the document, chugged the rest of her beer, and popped off to the bathroom to pee and brush her teeth. She grabbed the pages off the printer on her way back to bed. She had a drawer full of pens and pencils in a cup on her nightstand and after silently weighing the decisiveness of pen against the versatility of pencil, she settled on her favourite green pen—she was being bold. Why not? It wasn't like she couldn't print off another copy and change her answers.

As she made her way through the list, she hadn't expected to have such strong feelings. Not just about things she felt positive and negative about for herself, but how much she wanted Griff and Jack to feel the same way about these things as she did. She wondered how long they would make her wait before they sent her their check-lists.

It took far longer for her to get through the document than she'd anticipated, and when she was finally done, she knew she should turn out the light and go right to sleep, but curiosity and impatience won out and she checked her email one last time. Nothing. Just as well. She was wound up enough with possibilities without having probabilities swimming around in her head, too.

She already knew they could play her body like a Mozart concerto and heaven help her, she adored it. They'd pulled her so far out of her head, for a short time she'd even felt beautiful. She had forgotten how that felt and she had immediately wanted to bury it away. It was too unfamiliar and scary. Now she'd had some time to let it all percolate, she wanted more.

She lay in the dark, remembering the feel of their hands on her bare skin. How they'd eagerly sought it out. How there had been no hesitation after she'd stripped. They'd both grinned like they'd hit the jackpot instead of the booby-prize. Hell, it was days later and they still looked at her like she was the only woman in the world. She'd stopped playing the *what if* game years ago, but the way things had been going, especially this past week, she was tempted to let herself dream. Just a little.

SEVENTEEN

Ella sat across the table from Jack and Griff and concentrated on not throwing up. How had she gone from a life of vanilla sex for one to negotiating kinky sex for three? She studied the papers she held in her hands while her pussy developed a slow-leak in her panties. Griff and Jack had collated the check-list data for all three of them into an easy to read spread-sheet. Just one more thing to add to the compatibility column.

When she'd received their check-lists, she'd done exactly the same thing, apparently with the same results. It had to be a trick of some kind—there was no way their likes and dislikes could be so closely aligned. Except, completing that list was the first time she'd let her kinky self free in years and if *she* didn't know what she was into anymore, how could anyone else?

The sounds floating up from Finn and Mac's play-room were strangely comforting. As scary as it was to have *the talk* with Griff and Jack, doing it where others were around felt that little bit safer. They'd told her to come prepared to spend the night. She probably shouldn't have, but it didn't hurt to have options. Between the flirty emails and suggestive comments over the phone, those sneaky fuckers had kept her simmering for days.

"Ella?"

She turned her attention to Griff. His brow was slightly furrowed, but he had a twinkle in his eye. "Yes?"

"Any questions?"

"No, I don't think so." Shit, she was really going to do this. She was going to get down and kinky with two men. At the same time. Yeah, she'd been naked while they'd both made her come until she thought her clit might expire from exhaustion, but she'd only been on the receiving end, and didn't consider it to be even in the same universe as the three of them being naked and participating equally. Well, not exactly equally given any threesome between them would always consist of two Doms and a sub.

Griff reached across the table and stroked her hand. "Fair enough. We'd like to start by setting the ground-rules. We'll both be keeping a close eye on you, as will the others, I suspect, and anyone one of us can, and will stop the action if it looks like you're struggling. However, if at any point you don't feel a bright and cheery green, you need to safeword. Yellow will do if you don't want to call a complete halt to the action, but if you feel so much as pink, you'd best call red. Understood?"

"Understood." More than understood. Fuck, she would swear these guys had a direct line of communication to her clit because that little display of domliness sure turned on the tap, and that leak was no longer slow.

"Good girl. We've got a very easy scene planned for tonight. We're going to take things slow, and for now, we'll tell you up front what to expect. We won't give you the details—we don't want to spoil all the surprises—but we will give you a fair idea what's in store. If you think you're going to have any issues, let us know, and we'll talk it through and figure it out. Okay?"

"Okay."

"Excellent. All we're planning to do in the playroom tonight is get half-naked and do some touching. Is that something you're willing to try?"

Touching? She could do touching. Damn, she'd been wanting to touch for ages. Taste, too. "Yeah."

"Remember, we're only asking you to try, sweetheart. If you're ready, then let's get moving."

They all stood, and Griff joined her on the other side of the table. He took her hand in his and brought it to his lips. "Come with me. Jack will join us shortly."

Griff led her down the stairs and she stopped abruptly at the bottom. Hildy was trussed up in neongreen rope and suspended from an overhead beam in the middle of the room. Griff wrapped his arms around Ella from behind and pulled her in tight as he kissed her neck.

She startled, and before she had a chance to move, Griff whispered in her ear. "We're in no hurry. We can watch from here for a bit."

Ella was still getting used to seeing the sexcapades Wil and Hildy got up to with Mac and Finn, and this time was no different. Mac was fucking Hildy's cunt with a strap-on, and every time Mac withdrew, Finn smacked her ass with his belt. Meanwhile, Wilson was at Hildy's head, plumbing the depths of Hildy's throat with his cock.

The more she watched, the more impatient she became for her own playtime to start. A second pair of arms surrounded her waist and hugged her closer. Jack. For him to have that kind of hold on her, he had to be pressed hard against Griff's back and judging from increased twitching, the erection crushed against her back wasn't all for her. Her belly fluttered and she squeezed her thighs together. This was the first time she'd actually encountered Jack and Griff interacting intimately with each other and it shot her straight from a little horny to do-me-now. The reality of the these two men together touched a side of her sexuality she hadn't been aware of. Until that moment, she hadn't really connected with the hot factor of man-on-man love. Sure, she was part of the mix, but up until that moment, they'd both focused all their attention on her and none on each other.

"Time to move, sweetness," Griff whispered in her ear. He gave her another kiss on her neck, then all the hands around her waist were gone. Griff took hold of her hips and gently pushed her towards the aftercare area. She stole a backwards look and saw Jack had a similar hold on Griff. Damn, she was a fucking puddle. They stopped in front of the fainting couch and Griff turned her around.

She looked up into those two gorgeous faces—all smiles and twinkling eyes—and her heart stalled. Love? She gave her head a mental shake. Maybe, but it wasn't for her. It couldn't be. It had to be for each other and she was just misreading their expressions. A little wishing couldn't hurt, though.

Jack reached out and stroked her cheek. "Time to get started. Colour?"

It took Ella a few seconds to get her head back in the game, but she was definitely in. "Green."

"Good girl. Take Griff's shirt off, please."

She didn't bother hiding the grin. She'd been dying to see what these guys were packing under their clothes for far too long. She grabbed the hem of Griff's t-shirt and pulled it up. He leaned forward and she whipped the shirt the rest of the way off.

"Slow down, sweetness, we've got all the time in the world." Griff kissed the tip of her nose and stepped in behind her. She loved the feel of a man's body against her back and his cock nestled in the crack of her ass. "Jack's shirt next. I think I'll give you a hand. You seem a little too eager." He clasped her wrists and guided her hands to the top button of Jack's shirt. She unfastened it and Griff used her hands to reveal the first glimpse of Jack's chest. She tried to touch the naked skin, but Griff moved her hands to the next button.

"Do only as you're told, love. I never said anything about touching." Griff nibbled at her ear as she continued to undo the buttons. By the time she'd got to the last two, she was fresh out of patience. She leaned forward, intending to lick Jack's nipple, but Griff gave her ear a sharp nip and his grip on her tightened before she could get close enough.

"Licking counts as touching. Don't worry, sweetness, you'll get your chance. I promise." He loosened his hold on her as he shifted her hands, and together they finished with the buttons. Griff released her wrists. "Slide it off slowly, then you can lick *one* nipple."

She reached up and grasped the edges of the shirt and eased them over Jack's shoulders. As the fabric skimmed down his arms, Ella leaned in and brushed the tip of her tongue over Jack's left nipple. His small groan made her pussy throb.

She pulled off his shirt and let it fall to the floor, but before she could get her hands on his chest, Jack grasped them and lifted them above her head. "Don't move." He released her hands and leaned in and kissed her. His tongue found its way between her lips and she immediately began to tease and suckle it. Her belly flip-flopped as she thought about doing exactly this to his cock.

Griff slipped his hands under her shirt and slid it up her body. She shivered. His fingers trailed along her skin leaving goosebumps in their wake. She was so turned on, she wanted to reach down between her legs and fix the problem. After so many years of being entirely responsible for her own orgasms, it felt strange not to give in to her urges whenever they arose. Jack broke the kiss and Griff tugged the garment free.

Jack scooped her into his arms. "You are such a good girl." He carried her to the fainting couch and sat, settling her into his lap. She rested her cheek on his shoulder and closed her eyes. His bare skin against hers made her want. Not just the orgasms her men—yes, they were definitely her men—were guaranteed to deliver. No, she wanted so much more than physical pleasure. She wanted to be connected—to *feel*. She wanted love.

A few minutes later, she felt the couch shift with Griff's weight as he sat next to them. Jack leaned in, taking Ella with him. Griff's arms closed around them, and being safely tucked in the middle, Ella felt at peace.

"Not done yet, sweetness." Griff kissed Ella and Jack, then released them from his embrace. "We're going to play a guessing game. Every correctly guessed item is an orgasm for you. Every time you incorrectly guess an item, you lose an orgasm."

"What happens if I end up getting more wrong than I get right?"

"I'm so glad you asked. If you're behind by the time we get to the last item, your answer will determine whether you get an orgasm tonight or not. When I tell you to, you are going to turn around so you're facing Jack. Knees either side of his legs, arms around his neck, and eyes on him. Once you're in position, you are not to move. You may only speak to guess what the object is or to safeword. Understood?"

"Yes."

"Good girl. Time to play."

She wasn't normally a cheat, but she was feeling off balance, so she thought she'd sneak a peek at the things she would need to identify while she re-positioned herself. Jack thwarted that plan. First he guided her in the wrong direction, then he shifted until he was reclining. She wanted to rub up and down the erection nestled hard against her clit, and if he hadn't held her hips so tightly, she might have given in to temptation.

"Soon, baby," Jack whispered in her ear. "We'll get there, I promise, but we've got some games to play first. Green if you're ready, yellow if you're not."

"I'm green."

"Good girl. Let's get started, Griff."

The soft tickle at the base of her neck was easy. "Feather?"

"Well done. The girl wins an orgasm." Ella giggled at the silliness in Griff's voice. "Ready for the next one, sweetie? A quick reminder, green for yes, Yellow for no."

"Mmm, green."

With so many soft tails trailing down her back, the next one was just as easy. "Flogger."

"Excellent. You're up to two orgasms. Shall we continue?"

Ella nodded and Jack nipped her earlobe. "We need a colour, love."

"Still green."

"On we go, then."

The next thing to touch her was trickier. It was wide, smooth, and its coolness made her shiver as travelled down her back. It was hard rather than flexible, so she took a wild guess. "Some kind of paddle?"

"Clever girl. The score is Ella three, Jack and Griff, nil. We're down to the last two, so even if you guess wrong on both, you're still guaranteed to get one orgasm. Ready?"

"Green."

"I love how obedient you are. I think we might have to speed things up a bit, though, because Jack looks like he's just about at his limit."

"Shut up and get on with it," Jack growled. His cock flexed against Ella's clit and she was aching to pull it out of his jeans, slide her panties aside, and impale herself.

Griff chuckled. "Patience, you two. Almost done."

The final two items were impossible for Ella to recognise. She hadn't expected kitchen utensils so it was little wonder she got the miniature silicon spatula wrong. The last one, however, was a complete shock. She recognised the rhythm from *Rhapsody in Black and Blue* as the instruments bounced gently up and down her back, loosening the tight muscles. After all the agony she'd experienced from canes that horrible night, she would never have imagined they could bring pleasure. Even more unimaginable? She wanted more.

"Another day, sweetheart." Griff leaned in and kissed her cheek. "You've earned yourself one orgasm, and we're going to give you a chance to earn a second."

"How do I do that?"

"You need to put the toys away. I'll come with you to show you where they all live, but you'll have to do the work. Are you up to that?"

She turned her head to see the toys Griff had used lined up behind her on Jack's legs.

The canes kept drawing her attention. Could she touch them?

She frantically shook her head and Jack pulled in and hugged her tight and asked, "Can you give me a colour?"

Her mind screamed the childhood tongue-twister, red leather, yellow leather, over and over.

"Okay, baby, I'm going to give you yes or no questions, and you can nod or shake your head. Okay?" Ella nodded. "Good girl. Can you do the job if it doesn't include the canes?"

No canes? No problem. She nodded again and Jack kissed the top of her head.

"All right, then. Griff will take care of the canes, and you can do the rest. When you're done, you'll come back here for your aftercare. Are you green?"

"Green."

"You're our good girl. Off you go, then."

By the time Ella had climbed off Jack, Griff had already removed the canes. She gathered up the remaining toys and followed Griff.

The others had finished playing, and Hildy and Mac were snuggled up in Wil and Finn's laps. Mac gave an exaggerated wink and a big grin as Ella walked past. Bugger, if that woman didn't keep finding ways to make her feel at ease.

When she and Griff reached the other side of the room, he pointed to where she should put the paddle. By the time she'd turned back to face him for directions on where to put the flogger, his hands were empty. He shot her that cheeky grin of his, and she smiled back. It was that moment she realised just how well they understood her. They knew just how hard to push, and when to back off.

Yeah, canes were a hard limit under impact play and she should probably be pissed because technically, they'd violated that limit. But she had marked massage as something she really loves, and damned if those men hadn't used that as a loophole. And she was oddly okay with that.

"Come on, sweetness." Griff took her by the hand and led her back to Jack, who wrapped her in the blanket he was holding.

He pulled her back into his lap as he sat down and Griff handed her some chocolate as he seated himself next to them.

"We're going to spend the night here. So are Wilson and Hildy, although, I suspect they won't be using a guest room, and I highly doubt there will be much sleeping going on. Jack and I would love it if you would spend the night with us. No pressure. You can participate as much or as little as you like. You get your orgasms regardless. If you choose to spend the night, we'll take care of you once we go to bed. If you choose not to stay, then we'll make you come here before we take you home."

The breeding ball of snakes currently residing in the pit of her stomach screamed at her to *go home* before she gets herself killed this time! But Mr. Spock logic kept comparing situations and pointing out these men were nothing like the pretty boy, and if she stayed, it would be nothing like the horrible night. She wanted to go to Mac for reassurance, but it was time to stand on her own feet.

"Yes, I'll stay."

Griff reached around and hugged her and Jack tight. "Now's as good a bedtime as any, I think."

Ella Lay naked on top of the bed while she watched Jack and Griff finish stripping each other. It was scorching-hot having the two of them remove what was left of her clothing, but watching them take care of each other was off the charts. She was dying to play with herself, but once they'd got her completely stripped, they'd positioned her arms above her head and her legs spread wide, then ordered her not to move.

Holy shit, mental bondage did it for her in a way that physical bondage never had. Back before the horrible night, she'd been into being tied up, big-time. But the depth of submission she felt from maintaining a position simply because she was told to, was so much deeper and more satisfying than anything she'd felt from being physically restrained.

"Look at our good girl, Griff. Her clit is pulsing. She's so horny, I bet she's dying to slide a finger or two inside that sweet pussy of hers. What do you think, should we let her play with herself?"

"Maybe later. I see that glistening pussy and all I want to do is feast on it. It's been too long since I've tasted our girl. I think she should have some choices, though." Griff sat on the edge of the bed and teased her nipple with his finger. "So, sweetness, would you rather suck Jack's cock or have him suck mine while I'm dining on you?"

Or? What did he mean, or? "I'd like all of the above."

A look passed between Griff and Jack, then they both smiled wide. "All of the above it is, then. On your side, love."

Ella didn't waste any time getting herself into position. Her mouth was watering and she was anxious for her first taste of Jack. She didn't have long to wait before Jack's cock bumped against her lips. She opened and swiped at the drop of liquid at the tip.

Griff re-positioned her legs before he slid his tongue deep inside her. That man had skills—and a tongue rivalling that of Gene Simmons probably didn't hurt, either.

She focused on the cock in front of her as best she could. She was so out of practice, but if his moans and gyrating pelvis were any indication, Jack didn't seem too concerned. She swirled her tongue around the head before sliding it into her mouth. She thought back to Hildy swallowing Wil's cock to the root earlier. Nope, she was definitely too out of practice for that, but she did take him as deep as she dared without risking her gag reflex. She pulled back and gently suckled at the tip, hoping she might get a glimpse Griff's cock in Jack's mouth before she slid down on him again. There were too many body parts blocking her view, so she returned her attention to the cock in her mouth.

She'd missed this so much. She cupped Jack's balls and squeezed gently with one hand while she worked the lower part of his shaft with the other. She kept taking him as deep as she dared, moving a little faster each time. She could feel him getting close, and in a split second, she knew she'd happily swallow whatever he gave her. She was just about to go to town when Jack withdrew completely.

She only had a moment to care before Jack's mouth engulfed her nipple. He sucked long and hard while Griff sucked her clit with the same rhythm and intensity. Two fingers slid inside, then a third. She was almost there.

Jack released her nipple with a pop and pushed her onto her back. He kissed her hard, sliding his tongue in and tangling it with hers. He cupped her her breasts in his hands and gently squeezed her nipples with his thumbs and forefingers.

She tried to contain her frustration as Griff reduced the suction on her clit. He gave her only enough to keep her on edge, but not enough to go over. She tilted her pelvis up, trying to get more pressure on her clit, but Griff pulled away and lifted his head.

The sharp nip Jack gave her earlobe made her flinch and stop mid-protest. "No whining. You only get what we give you. If you try to take more, we'll give you less." She wasn't quite sure if that nipping thing he kept doing was punishment or not. He always seemed to get it to a point where it hurt, but still managed to make her tingle in all the right places.

"Time for more choices, sweetie," Griff said. "The first decision you need to make is how you get your first orgasm. Tongue or cock?"

It had been so long since she'd had a cock inside her, and as wonderful as Jack and Griff's tongues and fingers felt, she wanted to feel full. "Cock, please."

"Since I got the first taste of you with my tongue, it's only fair for Jack to get first taste of you with his cock. Are you ready for your next choice?"

"Yes." But she wasn't really. She didn't want to make any more choices, she just wanted to get fucked, and she was tired of waiting.

"Good girl. This is the last decision you'll have to make tonight, Do you want to suck my cock while Jack fucks you, or do you want me to fuck Jack while he fucks you?"

Holy shit. Did he really just ask that? Fuck it. This might be her only opportunity to go big before going home and she was not going to miss out. Her heart pounded and her vision started to darken from the edges, but she refused to let the tendrils of panic take over. "I want you to fuck Jack."

Both men smiled wide and Jack said, "You get the supplies, I want to have a taste of our girl first."

Griff rose from his spot between Ella's legs and Jack took his place. His tongue wasn't as long as Griff's, but it was every bit as talented. Seriously, flutter-tonguing had to be the number one reason to date a wind or brass musician. Then Jack provided the reason why one should never discount the thumb dexterity of a bassoonist.

Just as she was getting close to coming, Jack backed off. "Soon, baby. Remember, you're the one who chose orgasm by cock. You stay put while Griff and I suit up."

"Can't I help?" Damn, she wanted to touch.

"Not this time, love. You just stay put and watch."

Okay, watching was *almost* as good as touching. And he'd said not *this* time, she took that to mean a next time was possible and let herself dream a little more.

She tried not to squirm as she watched Griff lay a bottle of lube on the bed and hand Jack a condom. This was really happening. After he unfurled a condom over Griff's erection, Jack squirted a big dollop of lube in his palm and slathered it all over Griff's cock. Ella wished it was her hand gliding up and down the slippery shaft.

Griff moaned and grabbed Jack's wrist. "Enough."

"Oh no," Ella interrupted, "carry on, that's hotter than hell"

"Don't you worry, Ms. Ella," Griff said as he unrolled a condom over Jack's cock, "you're going to get plenty of opportunities to indulge your voyeuristic urges, but right now, we've got other plans for you."

Jack held her gaze as he knelt between her legs and slid one, then two fingers inside her. She wanted to rock against them, but she would be a good girl. He gently pumped his fingers in and out before adding a third. He held his fingers still while his thumb worked its magic on her clit.

He continued to tease her, and when she was on the verge of coming, he withdrew his hand. Just as she was beginning to re-think her position on being a good girl, she felt the tip of Jack's cock at her entrance.

He leaned forward so their chests touched, resting his weight on his forearms. "We're going slow and easy this time, sweetie, but fair warning, hard and fast is definitely in our future."

Ella closed her eyes and clung to his words. *This time*, and *our future*. Maybe there was a chance for her happy ever after. She re-opened her eyes and gave her men a shy smile. Jack gently pushed his way into her body, stretching her. He pulled out a little before working his way back in, farther this time. He repeated this a few times before he'd completely filled her.

He stroked her cheek kissed her. "Be patient a little longer. We'll make it good, I promise."

He kept saying that, but they'd given her enough mind-blowing orgasms since they'd met, she had no trouble believing him. Hang on. Was that trust? Hell, who was she trying to kid? There was no way she'd be right here, right now, even with others in the house, if she didn't trust them.

"Jack, we'd best get this show on the road before our girl gets too bored and starts making a grocery list"

Griff moved in behind Jack and winked. "Our girl might be getting slow and easy, but you aren't."

Griff's quick thrust pushed Jack's cock a little deeper and his groin pressed hard against Ella's clit. Griff pulled back as fast as he'd advanced, and the pressure against Ella's cervix and clit immediately eased.

Jack withdrew completely before starting another slow slide in. The moment he'd bottomed out, Griff slammed his hips home, and the pressure was back.

Fuck—it wasn't going to take too many more moves like this before they had her coming hard enough to see stars.

They only did it once more. This time, Jack didn't withdraw. Instead, he held still while Griff slammed into his ass, each thrust harder and faster than the last.

She could feel Jack's heart pounding against her chest as his breathing got faster. "Come when you're ready, love. Neither of us is going to be able to hold on much longer." He leaned in and claimed her mouth and it only took two more thrusts from Griff for her to come so hard she thought she might pass out. She had no idea how long she'd been making those ridiculous squealing pig noises before she clued in and snapped her mouth shut.

"How about that," Griff said as he flopped onto the bed, "our girl is a screamer."

Embarrassed, Ella looked away, but Jack caught her chin and turned her back to face him. "Don't hide from us, sweetheart." He grinned and gently pumped his hips a couple times. "You puffed our egos up by about three sizes. There's no shame in that. Okay?"

"Okay." She hoped she sounded more confident that she felt.

He kissed the tip of her nose, then reached between them and slowly withdrew his still half-hard cock. "I have some cleaning up to do," he said as rolled to the side.

"No," Griff said, "you stay there with our girl, I'll take care of the clean up."

Jack removed the condom, tied it in a knot, and placed it in Griff's outstretched hand.

As Griff headed to the bathroom, Jack took Ella's hand in his and kissed it. "How are you doing, sweetness?"

"Wonderful." Holy hell, that was better than wonderful, it was amazing.

Then the doubt and insecurity started seeping in. She didn't remember them actually coming. Did they come? Was she so disgusting, they'd lost their erections? What if this was just some kind of twisted game? Maybe she should leave now. Dump them before they have the chance to dump her. Yeah, that was the best thing to do.

"Ella—stop" Jack wrapped her in his arms and held her close. "It's okay, sweetness. We're not going anywhere and you're safe."

"But you didn't come."

Jack gave a little chuckle. "Sweetie, there is no

mistaking a well-used condom—and those were defi-nitely well-used."

"Really?"

"We're going to have to work harder at convincing you that we're serious about you."

"We can start right now," Griff climbed on the bed and stroked the inside of her thigh. "Lift your leg, sweetheart."

After a ten year cock-hiatus, even that fairly gentle sex had left her a little sore and achy, and she appreci-ated Griff soothing her tender flesh with a warm, damp cloth. Maybe that second orgasm should wait. She smiled and got the warm-fuzzies when she noticed he was cleaning Jack as well. So sweet.

When he was done, Griff flung the cloth across the room. "Score." He declared when it landed on the floor of the en-suite bathroom.

"You are such a child sometimes," Jack said.

"Sometimes," Griff agreed as he curled himself around Ella and Jack.

Ella snuggled in, absorbing the warmth and safety she felt being cocooned between these two sweet, sexy men.

As she drifted off to sleep, she considered how special they always made her feel and how gentle they were with her, and her final conscious thought was how much she wanted *this* every night.

EPILOGUE

Finn and Mac's house, two weeks before their commitment celebration

Griff patted his pocket for what must have been the hundredth time since he'd left home. The hand-crafted gold rings and necklace, all bearing the same triangular Celtic knot—a triquetra—hadn't disappeared since he'd last checked. *Was it really only five minutes ago?*

He thought back over the last few months. It had been one hell of an emotional roller-coaster, but the ups far outnumbered the downs.

Ella still had black moments of insecurity and self-doubt, but they worked through them as a family. He and Jack fully understood that the trauma Ella experienced followed by ten years of avoiding intimacy was not something she would fully move past quickly or easily—if ever. And that was okay. They loved and accepted her for who she was.

He was relieved Sully had finally managed to pull his head out of his ass and sort things out with Ella, because it wouldn't have been right to do this without him.

His phone buzzed on the table. The text message was from Sully. *They're here.*

Show time.

ELLA TRIED to control her nerves as she and Jack waited for Griff to appear. Dammit, the way she was carrying on, you'd think she was getting married. Well, it wasn't *that* far off, when she thought about it. The only real difference was the legal stuff.

"Hey, it'll be fine. Nothing will change except we'll all have shiny new jewellery."

She looked up and smiled. Damn, he cleaned up well. "You two sneaky buggers wouldn't let me see—for all I know, it's something from a Christmas cracker."

"You know better." Jack put his arm around her shoulder and pulled her close. She wrapped her arms around his waist and squeezed him tight.

It was amazing what a few months with a couple of guys who really cared could do for a girl. It wasn't that long ago, she wondered what it would be like to be snarky like Mac. Well, not quite like Mac, that was living too close to the edge, but she liked the feeling of power it gave her.

They still kept their BDSM pretty light, and she worried about that sometimes. She knew Griff and Jack had played hard before she came along, and while she still harboured the odd doubt that she was giving them what they needed, deep down, she did believe they accepted her as she was.

She looked over at Sully, thankful they'd managed to salvage their friendship. Ridiculous man—so in touch when it came to the needs of others, yet oblivious when it came to his own. She hoped he got his shit together and sorted things out with Teagan before it was too late.

A figure appeared in the doorway, and Ella looked over to see Griff walk in wearing a new suit and a big grin. Relief quieted her jangling nerves. Somewhere along the way, she'd had a small crisis of faith—terrified this was nothing more than an elaborate prank—and Griff's arrival made all that doubt vanish in an instant. Apparently, it was fear of rejection, not commitment that had twisted her up in knots.

Griff crossed the room and pulled Jack and Ella into a hug and asked, "Are we ready?"

They both nodded and they all turned to face their guests. Jack took Ella's left hand, Griff took her right, and in front of her, they held each other's. They were really going to do this.

JACK LOOKED at the two most important people in his life as he held their hands, and figured he had to be the luckiest bastard to roam the earth. The universe had come through on that seemingly impossible request and he was grateful. That morning, they'd drawn straws to decide who spoke first. Griff had drawn the short straw, and Jack was kind of glad Ella would speak last.

Griff cleared his voice and the room fell silent. "Jack, there was a time when I thought we weren't going to pull through. Those were dark, dark days for me. I was terrified of losing the one person I needed most in my life, but I was even more terrified to fight for him. What if he didn't want me? Then we met Ella, and in that moment, I knew I had to find my balls and fight for you." Griff cleared his throat as he bent his head and shrugged his shoulder to wipe away the tear running down his cheek. He gave Jack's hand a small squeeze and continued. "Ella, the first thing you ever gave me was hope. Since then, you've given me trust and love—precious gifts I hold close to my heart."

Jack took a deep breath and hoped he could keep his emotions in check until he'd said his piece. "Griff, my life with you has been incredible, and I didn't think it was possible to love you more. Then Ella came into our lives, and I discovered how wrong I was. Ella, you brighten my life in so many ways, but it's your trust and love that makes our family complete."

"Jack, Griff," Ella began, "your love and patience has been the lifeline I didn't realise I needed. I was drowning in a sea of loneliness until you came along and reminded me of what I was missing. More than that, you make me feel beautiful, safe, and loved. Three things I'd dismissed as unattainable." She looked first to Jack, then to Griff and said, "I'm yours."

Jack gave Ella a gentle kiss while he lifted her hair out of the way for Griff to fasten the delicate chain around her neck. When Griff was done, he turned Ella to face him. He stroked her cheek, then brushed his lips over hers. Jack almost regretted having a formal commitment ceremony because he wanted nothing more than to drag Griff and Ella to bed and fuck them into oblivion. Instead, they still had to exchange rings and stay until it was socially acceptable to leave.

Ella took the first ring from Griff's outstretched hand. She rose up on her toes and kissed him as she placed it on his finger. Jack took the second and slipped it onto Ella's finger, then he gave her a deep, lingering kiss, a promise of all the good things to come. Jack was unprepared for the feeling of complete peace when Griff slid the remaining ring into place. They pulled

Ella into a hug, then exchanged a passionate kiss of their own.

Jack held on tight to his family and wondered if it would be too greedy to ask the universe for more. Kids that looked like Griff and Ella, maybe. Someday.

Tainted Pearl: A Rock Star Prequel

Lust at first sight has never been a problem for Doug Fraser before, but something about Biddy O'Mara screams "hands off". Except the private, mysterious musician is also the sexiest, most captivating woman he's ever crammed into close quarters with.

Biddy can't afford any distractions while on a month long eco-activism island adventure. The rock star is incognito for a very good cause, but the irresistible camera operator quickly proves a big, bad complication.

A fling is inevitable. But Doug's not relationship material, and the more he gets to know Biddy, the more he realizes she's the type of girl you take home to meet your mother—even if you don't know all her secrets.

Tainted Shadow (Tainted Pearl, Book 1)

Tainted Pearl's lead singer has a stalker problem and bodyguard Brody Clarke doesn't think twice about cutting his vacation short when he's asked to protect her.

Sparks fly—and not the good kind—when he rubs the rabidly independent rock star the wrong way. Now he needs to convince her that letting him be in control might just save her life.

And if it has the side benefit of turning those sparks into a completely different kind of heat? Brody's up for that kind of dominance as well.

Prime Minster (Frisky Beavers #1)

Gavin:

Ellie Montague is smart, sensitive, and so gorgeous it hurts to look at her. She's also an intern in my office. The office of the Prime Minister of Canada.*

That's me. The PM.

She calls me that because when she calls me Sir, I get hard and she gets flustered, and as long as she's my intern, I can't twist my hands in her strawberry-blonde hair and show her what else I'd like her to do with that pretty pink mouth.**

Ellie:

How much I like the PM varies on a daily basis. He's intense, controlling, and a perfectionist in every way—and he demands the same of his staff.

How much I want him never wavers.

There's something about him that tugs at me deep inside, and makes me wish that just once he'd cross the line in a late night work session. I'd take that secret to the grave if it meant I got a taste of the barely restrained beast inside him.***

FOOTNOTES:

* This is a fictional erotic romance. No prime ministers or interns were harmed in the making of this book.

** Except it's a BDSM romance, so they were hurt a little.

*** Spoiler alert: she gets more than a taste. And she likes it.

ACKNOWLEDGMENTS

Élianne Adams, Elizabeth Varlet, and Zoe York for their unwavering support and encouragement. Sidney Bristol for helping me find my way. Gia Alden for the last minute eagle-eye. The wonderful gang of Divas who are generous in so many ways. And of course, my wonderful, supportive husband, who still says yes to almost everything...except another dog.

ABOUT THE AUTHOR

Surrounded by mist-covered mountains, Sadie Haller lives a quiet life with her husband and fur-babies.

Where to find Sadie

sadiehaller.com
sadie@sadiehaller.com

ISBN-13: 978-0995981102

ISBN-10: 0995981108